13 DAYS
TO
DIE

13 DAYS TO DIE

A NOVEL

MATT MIKSA

CROOKED
LANE

NEW YORK

Published in the United States by Crooked Lane Books, an imprint of The Quick Brown Fox & Company LLC.

Crooked Lane Books and its logo are trademarks of The Quick Brown Fox & Company LLC.

Library of Congress Catalog-in-Publication data available upon request.

ISBN (hardcover): 978-1-64385-655-1
ISBN (ebook): 978-1-64385-656-8

Cover design by Michael Rehder

Printed in the United States.

www.crookedlanebooks.com

Crooked Lane Books
34 West 27th St., 10th Floor
New York, NY 10001

First Edition: March 2021

10 9 8 7 6 5 4 3 2 1

For Kelly, Naya, and Ameya

Viruses are bad things, but they sometimes perform a useful function.

—Mao Zedong, Founder of the People's Republic of China

DAY 13

1

Washington, DC, USA

PRESIDENT JAMES BARLOW plunged headlong into the Potomac, heavy stones tied around both wrists. The biting current pinched his sixty-five-year-old heart. Each beat thumped inside his skull as his brain fought to detach from its stem, squeeze through an ear canal, and float to the surface. Barlow's bulging eyes watched the last bubble of oxygen burble from his throat. A final jerking gasp filled his lungs with freezing water, and the world went black.

Hypothermic suffocation. That's what it felt like, apparently, in the moments before ordering a nuclear strike.

Instead of stone and sediment, mahogany paneling and ornate paintings of dead icons lined Barlow's nightmare riverbed. Washington, Adams, and Jefferson—their judgmental glowers immortalized in oily brushstrokes—had presided over more than one presidential drowning in the White House Situation Room. Their austere expressions dripped with disapproval.

Important-looking people surrounded the conference table. Nathan Sullivan, Barlow's national security adviser, sat motionless except for the placid rise and fall of his barrel chest. It took a lot to rattle the old Cold Warrior; this wasn't his first glimpse of the brink. Barlow remembered Sullivan's blunt estimation: *Powerful men take powerful action.* Georgetown gentleman–speak for *Bomb the bejesus out of 'em.*

Allyson Cameron, director of VECTOR and Barlow's long-time confidante, played the dove. She stressed nuance over audacity—the delicate prescription of a consummate spy. Only there was nothing delicate about Cameron. She was a pantsuited lioness, as bloodthirsty as the rest.

An hour of raucous debate had failed to produce a consensus. *Probably because the intel is piss,* Barlow thought. There were only two doors he could open. Behind one was a Noble Peace Prize. Behind the other, a horned beast, grinning through pointed teeth. The Joint Chiefs, State, the CIA, everyone had made their positions clear—the Situation Room was no place for fence-sitters—but it didn't matter what *they* thought. This was a presidential decision, *his* decision. Barlow's next utterance would change the course of history. Would future generations remember him for his courage and resolve? Would they say he stopped a madman from slaughtering millions of innocent civilians? Or would they mark today, this moment, as the beginning of the horror? Barlow's head screamed. He could feel his eyes swelling in their sockets, pulsing against nerve and bone.

The United Nations had refused to act, true to its legacy of impotence. There would be no international coalition, no NATO operation. If Barlow chose to intervene, the United States would go it alone. Again. He'd studied this possibility for weeks now, but it had always seemed unimaginable. A last-resort doomsday scenario.

The president squared his shoulders and reached for a boxy leather briefcase on the table. The case hadn't left his side since Inauguration Day, but he'd never seen it unzipped before. No president had. Inside was a clunky keyboard. Barlow began typing a long, alphanumeric string of characters from memory. Somewhere in the rocky badlands of Montana, a U.S. Air Force general was about to receive an unthinkable command.

A digital timer mounted on the wall beside James Monroe flashed bright-red numbers. The countdown had begun. CERBERUS, the intercontinental ballistic missile launch system, would come online in exactly ten minutes. The preprogrammed delay was designed to prevent accidents. *Or is it to give presidents a chance to back out?* Soon enough, Barlow could give the final order to launch a battery of ICBMs powerful enough to obliterate an area the size of Virginia.

Barlow surveyed his team. The important-looking people, so animated with conviction just moments before, waited in silence, fixated on their leader. A few stared at the countdown clock. It was hard not to. But there were no trembling hands or glistening foreheads, only steely eyes and stoic jawlines—masks designed to obscure any number of political motives. Most were decades-old friends, yet Barlow didn't trust any of them completely. On some level, they were all liars—this was Washington, after all—but what if one of them was something worse?

A traitor.

Barlow had his suspicions, his theories, but it was impossible to think clearly with the pressure building behind his forehead. He'd take another pill, calm the storm, work it out in his mind. He couldn't allow paranoia to cloud his judgment. Not with so many lives hanging in the balance.

DAY 1

CHAPTER

2

*Dzongsar Village, Tibetan Autonomous Region,
People's Republic of China*

HE SCRATCHED MADLY at the soil with purple-tipped fingers curled into claws. A fiery sting punctuated each desperate scrape. His hands hurt like hell. Two of his fingernails had fallen off, and bits of rock dug into the raw nail beds. Still, he didn't let up.

The overnight downpour had turned Tibet's Yarlung Tsangpo rain forest into a mucky bog, which had made it difficult for the man to find the right spot to dig. He'd rambled through the maze of spruce trees since sunrise. As he searched, the nearby river, surging with runoff from the storm, had whispered an evil incantation.

Now, crouched on all fours, he burrowed like a marmot. Scoopfuls of sodden earth piled up next to the growing divot. Finally, the man's bloodied knuckles knocked against something hard and hollow. He pushed into the wet soil, searching for the object's edges. Surging adrenaline gave him a burst of energy. A few sharp tugs freed the object from the pit with a sucking sound.

It was a metal container with a brown leather handle bolted to its lid and a nickel-plated lock on the front, like a banker's strongbox. The man pawed at a key that dangled from a chain around his neck. As expected, it unlocked the box. He lifted the lid, fingers vibrating.

Empty.

Exhausted, the man rested on his knees, head thrown back, eyes bulging. Midmorning sunlight blinked through the dense forest canopy. Branches shuddered in the breeze, and their gentle swirling motion made him dizzy. Fatigue crashed over his body. He barked a lung-busting cough, as he had repeatedly throughout the night. This time he hacked so violently that a piece of his tongue sloughed off. His saliva tasted ferrous—the flavor of fresh blood. Swallowing felt like thumbtacks pricking his esophagus. Medicine wasn't an option. He'd accepted that.

Still, the man sobbed quietly, afraid of what was happening to his body. He couldn't remember when it had started or how he'd gotten sick. He didn't know why purple-black bruises covered his arms and legs. Everything blurred.

Hunched over the pit, he struggled to remember what he was supposed to do next, until a wave of nausea momentarily cleared his foggy brain. He rummaged through the canvas rucksack slung over his shoulder and gripped a small item. Earlier that morning, he'd double-wrapped it in plastic zip bags to keep it dry. He delicately placed the bundle in the strongbox, which he relocked and lowered back into its tiny grave. Sweeping dirt and leaves over the hole, he reburied the metal container with the cursed object now locked inside. It felt good to be rid of it.

Standing was a struggle. The man wanted to lie down, listen to the river's evil whispers, allow his broken body to return to the earth. He knew that would put others at risk—people who counted on him to finish the job. People like HELMSMAN, who didn't accept failure.

So instead, he rose to his feet and staggered toward the forest's edge. A few yards away, there would be a rock formation, and then a clearing, and across the clearing, a small village. He doddered a few more steps, then paused to lean against a tree for balance. He'd almost forgotten; there was something else he was supposed to do.

His bloodshot eyes searched the ground for something sharp. A rock, maybe.

Nothing.

The key swayed from the chain around his neck. Yes, it could work. He lifted the chain over his head, smearing his collar with mud. The key felt too heavy for its size.

The man brushed his fingertips across the rough tree bark, like a blind man reading braille, and landed on a deep vertical gouge—about six inches long—carved into the trunk. The gash oozed sap like a fresh wound. It took his last ounce of energy to press the key's jagged metal teeth into the wood. He carefully etched a horizontal groove to intersect the existing line, making a cross. It felt like marking his own grave.

When he was finished, his cloudy eyes fixed on the strange key in his right hand. The man couldn't remember what it opened. Nothing made sense. He was dehydrated. Drinking something would help. He craved the soothing heat of Grandmother's green tea.

He came upon a stone wall made of large boulders stacked high above his head. *The rock formation. Almost there.* He'd never be able to climb over the wall; his legs scarcely had the power to support his own body weight. A few paces away, sunlight squeezed through a narrow crevice in the stone. He could probably fit. He wedged his body into the cleft, feeling the rough edges of the rock scrape his skin and press on his rib cage. Some of the large pieces wobbled in their settings. He imagined the entire wall would collapse and crush him.

Finally, the man tumbled into the long grass on the other side of the stone barrier. His hands were empty. He'd dropped the key somewhere, but it didn't matter. He didn't need it anymore.

The sun forced the man's pupils into pinheads, his eyelids into slits. He could barely see the image painted on the front of the rock formation. Dazzling golden strokes, iridescent in the bright light, protruded from a luminous spindle rimmed by a yellow circle. It looked like the steering wheel of an old ship—a bizarre image to encounter in the landlocked highlands of Tibet. Then again, maybe it was proof of a greater power at work.

The man smiled weakly. Even now, his mind churning and swirling, his course had been true. He'd made it to Dzongsar Village. HELMSMAN would be pleased.

*   *   *

Investigators crawled over the area days later. They interviewed the locals, but no one reported seeing a hobbling figure emerge from the damp rain forest just after breakfast. No one had noticed him zigzagging across the clearing, stumbling like a horror-movie zombie toward the village.

One woman, however, remembered how she'd gasped when the haggard stranger entered her family's teahouse and flopped into an empty chair. Delirious and filthy, the man had looked more dead than alive. His eyes had inflated like overripe grapes, she said.

Shocked by the man's crumpled body, the teahouse woman had grabbed a girl's small hand and dragged her into the kitchen. She'd returned minutes later holding a steaming cup of tea, which she placed in front of the zombie man. That's when a drop of blood fell from the sick man's nose and landed in his cup. The crimson bead diffused into the hot liquid. It had worried the woman greatly, she told the investigators, but not as much as what happened next.

Zombie Man had begun trembling, which intensified into violent thrashing just before he lurched forward and spewed a torrent of vomit. An acrid mixture of bile and thick black blood covered the table (she showed them the stains), and Zombie Man's cup overflowed with the dark viscous discharge. Bloody spatter stippled the teahouse woman's blouse and neck. She darted to the doorway and shouted into the street, hoping someone would hear her terrified cry.

That day had destroyed her life. A suffering man had come to her doorstep and she had welcomed him. How could she have known? It wasn't her fault, the devastation that came after. That was how she explained it to the investigators, praying they believed her.

DAY 8

3

Vienna, Austria

Dᴿ. Kᴀʀʟ Gᴀssɪɴɢᴇʀ winced when the piping-hot espresso singed his tongue. He checked his leather-banded Aerowatch for the third time in as many minutes. An unseasonably warm breeze danced through Vienna's Brigittenau district, attracting a handful of early birds to the café's calming patio. Unaffected by the laid-back atmosphere, the geneticist hunched over his designer macchiato, shoulders bunched into knots.

Gassinger despised waiting—a rare shortcoming for a laboratory scientist. Gene splicing required extreme patience, but in the lab, it was different. He controlled everything—the exact temperature, set to the tenth of a degree centigrade; the vibration tolerance of every surface; even the decibels emitted by the humming equipment. He worked alone amid an array of marvelously precise instruments, synchronized like a scientific symphony, and Gassinger was maestro.

All around him, the city woke up, beginning its daily routine. Smart-slacked businessmen hurried past the café, weaving through a gaggle of cackling mothers pushing thousand-dollar strollers. A teenager wearing ridiculously oversized headphones leaned against a lamppost, scribbling in a ragtag notebook. One table over, a middle-aged Canadian couple studied a laminated city map. Gassinger had cringed when they'd asked him how to find Mozart's boyhood home. He'd pretended not to understand English.

The geneticist's business contact had insisted they meet at Starbucks—perhaps the greatest insult to any native Austrian. Gassinger could name a dozen remarkable Viennese cafés within a five-minute walk, yet here he sat at an imported megachain, suffering through overroasted espresso that tasted like ash. Moreover, his contact was late. Seven minutes, twenty-eight seconds late, to be precise.

Finally, Dr. Gassinger spotted a plump man crossing the street. More like plodding. Definitely American. The approaching man's sluggish gait made no acknowledgment of his inexcusable tardiness. His pinstriped suit was shamefully wrinkled, as if he'd slept in it, but all the attention went to his absurd, Big Tex cowboy hat. The American's sea-bass mouth released audible puffs with every step. Gassinger could almost hear the man's lard-coated heart hammering away with muffled thumps, like the sound of someone trapped in the trunk of a car, beating on the hood from the inside.

"Balls! It's hotter than a donkey's taint," the American declared through yellowed teeth as he reached Gassinger's table. His sandpaper drawl matched his boorish appearance. He plopped into a painfully small bistro chair.

"How in the name of Baby Jesus can you drink hot coffee? It's ninety-fuck degrees out here." The bloated American lifted his wide brim to blot his brow with a crumpled napkin. "I'm telling you, it's nothing but caramel Frappuccinos for me. And since I've been runnin' all over hell's hot acre since sunup, a cold one would really hit the spot about now. A hardworkin' man is due his guilty pleasures now and again. You know what I mean? 'Course you do, you sick son of a bitch!" The man belched a hearty laugh that quickly devolved into a smoker's wheeze. Gassinger shuddered.

Big Tex wore thick tortoiseshell glasses with a mod 1960s flare—the only style that refused to make a man look smarter. They kept sliding down the bridge of his hooked nose, where a bead of sweat abruptly detached and landed squarely on Gassinger's Italian wing tips. Revolted, the scientist let out a long, slow, contemptuous breath.

"Did you bring the money?" Gassinger asked with Alpine crispness. He was in no mood for banter.

"Well, well. So nice to see you too. Ever heard of small talk, Karl?"

Small talk was for small minds, in Gassinger's view.

"I brought you good news," Big Tex continued. "The boys back in Dallas have agreed to ten million."

"Euro?" Gassinger asked.

"U.S. greenbacks, Karl. This ain't Little League."

Gassinger's cold eyes stared unblinkingly. He wished the offensive creature would stop using his first name. He held a doctorate from Oxford, for Christ's sake. And he'd spent the last six years secretly developing a groundbreaking product. His superiors at Genetix still believed he was tinkering with computer models and spreadsheets. They had no idea what he'd created.

Gassinger leaned in. "You must understand how valuable this is. I am prepared to provide you with a completely stable strain of avian influenza. Engineered for maximum virulence."

"Yes, the birdie flu."

"Genetically *flawless* bird flu," Dr. Gassinger spat. "Twenty million."

Gassinger had no reservations about betraying his corporate masters. Screw the bastards. They had rewarded his thirty years of tireless work with a damp basement laboratory and exactly zero staff. Meanwhile, the top-floor execs fawned over every first-year postdoc chasing the next penis-enlargement pill. Gassinger remembered when Genetix had genuinely sought to make a difference, to pursue scientific breakthroughs that would change history. Those days had ended long ago, along with Gassinger's loyalty.

He stayed for the money; Genetix had a lot of it. Apparently, the world was teeming with impotent men with flush bank accounts. Gassinger had kept his mouth shut and his head down, all the while padding his research budgets to fund his private skunkworks. Those projects belonged to him, not to the Genetix dullards.

The genetically engineered avian flu was Gassinger's masterpiece. He'd named it after his daughter, Lena. If introduced into the general population, Lena would spread throughout Austria and eventually all of Europe, infecting millions in a matter of weeks. About one in twenty-five would die, he estimated. A good scrubbing with simple hand soap could save many, but the masses were too ignorant and dirty for that. Perhaps it was time to cull the herd.

The fat American across the table played coy, but he understood the virus's power. And its value. Gassinger would squeeze the yellow-toothed whale for every cent.

"Fuck a duck, Karl. I thought we were pals," Big Tex replied with melodramatic indignation. "Well, tell you what. You know as well as I do, my client has done pretty well for himself lately. He's been ridin' a gravy train with biscuit wheels ever since crude hit ninety-seven bucks a barrel. But what good are deep pockets when you've got short arms? Ya know what I mean, Karl?"

He didn't.

"So, let's not sit here beating our sticky dickies just to see who blows first," Big Tex continued. "Christ knows that would take an eternity, and my nut sack is beginning to feel like a fried egg." The man's tiny paper napkin was now hopelessly soaked. "Fourteen million, but we make the exchange right here, right now. Put up or shut up, my German friend."

"Austrian," Gassinger corrected.

"For Chrissake, Karl! I don't give a flying fig if you're Finlandian. I've gotta get on a plane in one hour. What's it gonna be?"

The scientist gritted his teeth. "The money?" he snapped impatiently.

Big Tex reached into his pocket and produced a Starbucks gift card. On the front was the word *Congratulations* underneath a cartoon cake. He handed the plastic card to Gassinger like a proud uncle.

Panic swelled in Dr. Gassinger's chest. He'd carefully vetted this buyer, but the whole arrangement was beginning to feel like a setup. Genetix must have discovered he'd removed proprietary research from the company's databases and sent this fool to catch him red-handed. The scientist shot a look over his shoulder, eyes darting from face to face, searching for gray-suited Genetix security thugs.

Don't be a damn fool, he thought. This hunched slob was no corporate puppet—and certainly not the *polizei*. Just a sloppy thief and an amateurish negotiator.

"There must have been a mistake," Gassinger said. "When you contacted me, I believed you were a serious buyer, but now I see you are just another American clod. I am putting everything on the line here."

Big Tex straightened his hat. "Now, just cool your pits, amigo. Nobody lugs around briefcases full of cash anymore. This little do-si-do has to be discreet. So, here's how it's gonna work. Go inside and use this card to buy a cup of joe. The magnetic stripe contains metadata. Most of it's run-of-the-mill stuff—info for the banks and marketing geeks, ya following me?—but this bad boy's got a bit more under the hood." He tapped the card. "When the cashier gives it a swipe, the register connects to a server, and a little extra code sneaks out and triggers a wire transfer to a confidential UBS account in Zurich. *Your* account, Karl." Big Tex leaned in. "Go buy yourself a latte," he growled, before flashing a wide, yellow smile.

Dr. Gassinger stood gruffly and headed into the café.

"I recommend the caramel Frappuccino," Big Tex called after him cheerfully.

*   *   *

Operations Officer Olen Grave removed the cowboy hat to let his scalp breathe. He shifted his weight, eliciting a foreboding groan from the flimsy bistro chair. Through the café's storefront window, he saw the Austrian scientist queue up behind a skinny hipster with a nose ring. Olen whispered under his breath, his lips barely moving, "Looks like he took the bait." His southern drawl evaporated. "After the swap, execute Exfil Beta One."

The hushed command referred to a predetermined exfiltration procedure designed to get Olen off the street as fast as possible while ensuring that he stayed black, free of hostile surveillance. After the swap, Olen would head straight to Handelskai station and take the subway west two stops to Spittelau Bahnhst, where a van would pick him up on the southbound side of Heiligenstädter Strasse. If Olen wasn't there, shuffling along the uneven sidewalk, in under twelve minutes, the cleanup crew would proceed to the next location—a simple leapfrog technique to give him another opportunity to check for shadows.

Olen watched Dr. Gassinger step up to the counter inside the café. The doctor was speaking on his cell phone. Calling his bank, presumably. A moment later, the irascible Austrian emerged looking almost delighted.

"The transfer is confirmed," Gassinger reported. He held two glistening drinks and handed one to Olen. "I suppose this one is on me."

"Well, lookee there. Pals after all," Olen responded gleefully, the phony accent restored.

The geneticist removed his Aerowatch and handed it to Olen. "This is everything," he said. "Start a company, start a war. I do not give a damn."

"This is it, Doc?" Olen asked, pinching the watch face between two stubby fingers.

"There is a chip hidden in the battery compartment. You can download the data via Bluetooth. No one carries around test tubes of live virus anymore," Gassinger retorted, his thin lips spreading into a pained smile. "And you can keep the timepiece. I can afford a replacement."

Olen set the watch on top of his phone. "Well, then let's wrap things up."

Seconds later, a soft voice in Olen's earpiece whispered, "It's good."

Olen extended a plump, sweaty palm, which Gassinger took, looking bewildered. "Pleasure doing business with you, my friend," Olen said, and got up to leave.

"That's it?"

"Like we say in Texas, you can't get lard unless you boil the hog. And I've got a few more hogs that need a-boilin' before sundown." Olen tugged at the brim of his hat. A cowboy's salute.

"I am an artist, you know," Gassinger said. "Not even God could create what I made."

Olen felt a flash of hot rage. This grinning turd had just sold the blueprints of a designer bioweapon to the highest bidder.

"See ya around, Karl," Olen said through a tight jaw. A God complex mixed with a genius IQ was an explosive combination. The Austrian was clearly delusional. Olen imagined putting a bullet in the back of his head. He pictured that brilliant mind splattered all over the patio.

Another day. The Pentagon brass wasn't finished with the good doctor just yet. Gassinger's rare talents made him valuable, and his bruised ego made him easy to manipulate. The United States government would permit Dr. Karl Gassinger to live, so long as the geneticist remained useful.

*   *   *

The gunshot made virtually no noise, only the whisper-spit of compressed air. But when the bullet struck the café's window, the glass shattered with an earsplitting crack. Heads jerked around to see a man in a spotless oxford shirt crumple to the pavement. A teenage girl shrieked when a gooey blend of Frappuccino and bright blood splashed across her linen sundress. Dr. Gassinger's lifeless body lay in a tangle of arms and legs at Olen's feet. A perfectly round hole above the scientist's left eyeball marked the bullet's entry point.

Olen reacted instantly, diving over a small planter and rolling onto the street. The hard impact with the cobblestone might have injured his shoulder if not for the padding stuffed into his clothes.

"Jesus! Who has eyes on the shooter? Talk to me, fellas," Olen shouted. He found his footing and sprinted down the street with no trace of the beleaguered gait.

The voice crackled in his ear again. "Hang on, bud. We're changing position, heading north. Get to the flower shop two blocks south on the corner. We'll exfil you there."

"For *fuck's* sake!" Olen said, exasperated. Gassinger was supposed to have confirmed the deposit and come back out. Who had he called? Not his bank, that was for damn sure.

The fat-man disguise had been Olen's idea—he'd known it would play into Gassinger's sense of superiority—but the bulky suit was unbearably cumbersome. Olen hadn't anticipated dodging sniper fire with forty extra pounds weighing him down. It felt like running underwater.

"Head into the bookshop on your left. No, wait. Hang on. It's on your *right*," the voice instructed. "There's a rear exit leading into an alley. Follow it east for about fifty yards, and you're there."

Olen whipped his body sideways and lunged into the bookshop, vaulting over a bicycle someone had abandoned in the doorway. Dusty volumes with titles in French, Italian, and German lined the walls, stacked to the rafters, giving off a distinctively musty odor. A few reclusive bibliophiles peered over faded hardbacks, visibly appalled at the hefty man charging through the entrance like a wild rhino.

Olen scanned the room, creating a precise mental image of its floor plan. He navigated a gauntlet of puffy armchairs and tables stained with coffee mug rings, weaving his way to the rear exit. Once outside, he could see the flower shop at the mouth of the alleyway. *The exfiltration point.* There he'd find Jason and Dante, two of the best operations support specialists in the business. Total pros. Olen had first learned this after a little misunderstanding with a Hezbollah bomb-maker in downtown Beirut. Vienna should be a cakewalk.

"We're almost there. Ten seconds, my man," Jason said.

Olen forced himself to slow his approach. He wasn't being followed, and no sniper would have a clear shot. The high walls of the narrow alleyway provided excellent cover. Once on the street, he would blend into the throng of forgettable folk going about their mundane morning errands.

A moment later, Olen spotted the red brake lights of Jason and Dante's van, parked beside a basket of white lilies. The van's rear double doors sprang open just as Olen emerged from the alleyway, waddling with urgency. He gripped Jason's hand and hopped inside before the unmarked vehicle pulled away from the curb and melted into traffic.

Jason grinned ear to ear at the sight of Officer Grave's comical disguise. "Welcome aboard, Olen."

" 'Hotter than a donkey's taint'?" Dante teased from behind the wheel. Wheezing, trying to catch his breath, Olen flicked up both middle fingers. Dante coughed up a belly laugh. "You're welcome, you ungrateful bastard."

"We need to get you outa Vienna," Jason said. Olen agreed. Someone had monitored the trade, and whoever it was wanted the virus badly enough to assassinate Dr. Gassinger in broad daylight. They'd come for Olen next.

Dante's phone rattled in the cup holder. He tossed it to Olen. "It's the boss."

"The exchange was compromised," Olen said into the phone, speaking rapidly as he pieced together his next moves. "Someone knew about the trade and they took Gassinger out. I need to get out of Austria *tonight*. I'll cross into Slovakia and regroup at the safe house in Bratislava."

"Olen, relax," said a female voice, smooth and deep. "It's over. The op was a success."

Director Allyson Cameron was famously cool headed, but her indifference under the circumstances was offensive. Olen was a marked man.

"Cam! I'm still wiping brain matter off my boots, and you're calling this a success?"

"You're not in danger," Allyson responded confidently. "It's true, Dr. Gassinger didn't call his banker from inside that café. The NSA was monitoring his cell phone. The man played us. He arranged to make the same trade with a Ukrainian arms dealer later this evening. The Ukrainians will sell to anyone. Iran. Al-Qaeda. You name it. We couldn't let that virus get into the hands of terrorists. Or the Russians, for that matter."

"You're telling me you—" Olen started, but Allyson cut him off.

"Yes, Olen. *Our* sniper put Gassinger down."

"Christ, Cam! A foot to the left and . . ."

"Our guys are the best. You know that."

"You could've just had Interpol pick him up," Olen argued.

"I don't like red tape. Besides, we don't know how many buyers Gassinger had lined up. Letting him leave that café alive was not an option," Allyson said with finality. "Now *we* have his research and no one else does." The line crackled. Allyson puffing cigarette smoke into the phone, no doubt. "Shame about the boots," she said.

Olen understood Allyson's logic, but he resented her decision to order the hit. She'd put the mission before his safety, and not for the first time. "You could've at least warned me," he said.

"It would've caught you off guard. You might have spooked Gassinger."

"I'll contact you from Bratislava," Olen replied, his voice laced with frustration. "The Viennese *polizei* will be searching for me in connection with the shooting. Even if I'm not running from an assassin, I should get out of Austria."

"I agree, but you're not going to Slovakia," Director Cameron responded. "There's been a viral outbreak in the Tibetan Autonomous Region of western China. I need you to report in for a full briefing. I'll meet you at the Hotel Imperial in one hour. It's at the corner of—"

"I know where it is," Olen interrupted.

"Suite five-oh-four. I'm sending you instructions now." The director ended the conversation abruptly, as was her habit.

Olen rested his head against the side of the vibrating van. He took a moment to process the information. Cam was in Vienna?

"Fellas, forget Bratislava," he called out to Jason and Dante. "Drop me at the Hotel Imperial on Kärntner Ring." Olen tugged the wig of thinning blond hair from his scalp and laid it across his padded midsection. "But we need to make a stop first," he added. "I'm not spending another minute in this damn Halloween costume."

CHAPTER

4

Beijing, People's Republic of China

"Patient zero," Dr. Zhou Weilin said, stabbing the air with her laser pointer. "It began with him."

On the screen beside the briefing table was a fuzzy image of a twentysomething Asian man. Dr. Zhou's voice, though raspy from sleep exhaustion, echoed formidably in the Great Hall of the People. The nine men seated behind the elevated dais wriggled uncomfortably. She imagined the sound of amplified female confidence had that effect on them.

It was Dr. Zhou's first time addressing the Politburo Standing Committee—China's most powerful body of political and military leaders. Many of her brownnosing peers would've considered the opportunity a great honor. *More like an epinephrine shot to their languishing careers*, she thought. However, there were innumerable reasons Dr. Zhou would've preferred to spend the afternoon in her lab. Explaining rudimentary epidemiology to a shadowy league of geriatric men—and of course they were men—was torture.

Despite the reams of written briefs and strings of working-group meetings, the top leaders still had questions, and they'd demanded that someone appear before them with answers.

Naturally, the task fell to the woman *Wired* had once called "The Flu Ninja." Last fall, Dr. Zhou had genetically engineered a synthetic antiviral for H5N1 and became an overnight science celebrity, if such a thing existed. She'd argued for sending someone else to brief the Standing Committee so she could focus on doing more "ninja" science, but the suggestion hadn't flown with the bureaucrats in Beijing. They needed a heavy hitter to deliver the odious news.

Turned out, these men didn't care for odious news, especially when delivered in high heels. No surprise there. Dr. Zhou had received an education on the fragile male ego during her emergency medicine rotation after an elderly man wheeled himself into the ER with his own severed foot bobbing in a cooler. Dr. Zhou had promptly removed her sweater and tied it around the man's thigh to stop the blood gushing from his wound. Meanwhile, the male residents had gone banging around in the supply closet, looking for a tourniquet. They raced back, only to discover that the *girl* doctor had already saved grandpa with a cardigan. After that, Dr. Zhou ate most of her lunches alone in the hospital cafeteria.

President Li Bingwen, seated in the center position of the sickle-shaped dais, glowered uneasily. Dr. Zhou kept rolling.

"His name was Chang Yingjie," she continued. "Government health officials stationed in the Tibetan Autonomous Region confirmed Chang as the first known victim of the outbreak. We've worked continuously for a week now, but we don't have all the answers. It's some kind of hemorrhagic fever. That much is obvious from the epistaxis and hematemesis."

More glowers. She searched for politician-friendly language.

"The disease starts with killer headaches, joint pain, vomiting," Dr. Zhou continued. "Then comes all the blood. It oozes from the nose, eyes, ears, even the anus. Essentially, the patient bleeds to death from every orifice."

"So what is it? Ebola?" President Li asked.

"My first guess too. New cases occasionally crop up in West Africa. But no. We ran antibody tests for Ebola, yellow fever, Marburg, and Lassa fever. They all came back negative. This virus is something completely new."

General Huang, a boulder-faced soldier with shoe-polish hair and expertly plucked eyebrows, cut in. "Where is it now, Doctor? We'll have men on the ground by tomorrow morning. Anything you need to sort this out."

Unbelievable. Dr. Zhou had forgone sleep for the last thirty-six hours as she worked to decode the virus's genome, hunting for vulnerabilities at the genetic level. This army man thought he could just pulverize it with tanks. "The epidemic originated in Dzongsar," she answered. "It's a remote village near the Tuotuo River."

"Tuotuo? Never heard of it." The general snorted.

Dr. Zhou displayed a map of Tibet onscreen. "The Tuotuo River cuts through the upper region of Tibet, snaking south along the western border of Sichuan Province."

General Huang looked unfazed. "Looks like the middle of nowhere."

"A fair point. The Tuotuo River isn't widely known, as rivers go," Dr. Zhou said. "Probably because it's less of a river, strictly speaking, and more of a tributary. It's formed by a melting glacier forest in the Tanggula Mountains."

"We didn't call you here for a geography lesson," Huang snapped. "This doesn't sound very relevant, Doctor."

Dr. Zhou paused for a beat, waiting for the man's brain to catch up. "General Huang, sir, the geography is extraordinarily relevant. You can see here"—she traced the river with the beam of her laser pointer—"the Tuotuo is the source of the Yangtze River."

A murmur rumbled across the dais. General Huang rubbed his eyes with the heels of his palms. Dr. Zhou didn't have to explain how a viral outbreak at the headstream of China's most vital waterway would wreak havoc throughout the country. The world's third-largest river, the Yangtze traversed nearly four thousand miles, from Tibet to the East China Sea. It was China's original superhighway, its life force. The Yangtze moved billions of renminbi in commerce and provided potable water to countless farms and villages. One third of the nation's population depended on the river's currents.

Dr. Zhou knew that the virus would use the river to spread to all corners of China if they didn't stop it. She'd actually named the

unknown disease after the Tuotuo—a twisted homage of sorts—
but she preferred the local translation. The villagers called the
tributary something much darker: the Blood River.

"We're referring to it as the Blood River virus," Dr. Zhou said.

"What's that number after the name?" President Li asked,
pointing to the screen.

"Blood River virus's genetic composition is unlike anything
I've studied before. All viruses evolve over time. Some take millennia, picking up bits of new genetic code here and there, but this
virus begins to mutate almost as soon as it binds with its victim's
DNA. We're seeing significant genetic anomalies with every fifteen to twenty transmissions, resulting in an extensive family of
substrains, each one slightly different than the one preceding it. At
first, we assumed we'd need to develop a different vaccine for each
substrain mutation; maybe there would be four or five max, so we
started numbering them. For example, the original virus, the one
that infected Chang, was Blood River virus one, or BRV1. We
began labeling the subsequent mutations BRV2, BRV3, and so
on."

"What are we up to now?" Li asked.

"We stopped counting at BRV45. Number forty-five is the
worst, by far, but the mutations have continued. Essentially, Blood
River virus isn't one virus. It's hundreds of slightly different viruses,
variants with a shared ancestry." The statement struck like a thunderbolt. Dr. Zhou didn't wait for a follow-up question. "If I can
identify the origin, the source of the first strain—an animal or a
plant, maybe—then we can isolate a sample of the primary con-
taminant, and I'll be able to determine—"

"Doctor," President Li interrupted, his deep voice vibrating
authoritatively. "Just tell us, how fast is the problem spreading?"

The problem? *They still don't get it*, Dr. Zhou thought. *This is
a cataclysm.*

"Fast. *Real* fast," Dr. Zhou answered. "Chang Yingjie collapsed inside a teahouse seven days ago. He died within minutes,
and the disease scattered in all directions like marbles on a concrete floor. Within seventy-two hours, the first handful of cases
appeared more than three hundred miles away, in the Tibetan
capital, Lhasa. Within ninety-six hours, my colleagues working in

the Ministry of Health's Lhasa division reported two hundred fifty infected. Local hospitals are completely overwhelmed, and the number of patients grows every hour."

"What exactly are we looking at here?" President Li asked. "How bad could this get?"

The word *apocalypse* came to mind. "Lhasa has a population of half a million people and an airport with direct flights to Beijing and Chengdu," Dr. Zhou explained. "The military closed Lhasa Gonggar Airport two days ago and set up checkpoints to restrict all overland access to the Tibetan Autonomous Region by bus or train. These were standard quarantine procedures, but they may have been implemented too late."

"What do you mean?" Li asked.

"Mr. President," Dr. Zhou continued, "at six o'clock this morning, Beijing University International Hospital admitted a patient with flu-like symptoms. Physicians in the infectious disease department confirmed the diagnosis an hour ago—just minutes before we began this briefing, in fact." The doctor spoke intently, punctuating every word for emphasis. "Blood River virus is already in the capital."

5

Vienna, Austria

RIVULETS ROLLED DOWN Olen's back and curls of steam swirled through his nostrils, loosening the piano-wire tension behind his eyes. The Venetian rain shower—one of the Hotel Imperial's finer delights—rinsed away thoughts of sniper fire and exploding skulls.

Olen had arrived at the iconic hotel sweaty and disheveled. He'd introduced himself as Jeffrey Cunningham to the concierge stationed in the lobby. The wiry Swiss fellow had squeezed out a thin smile and handed him a white envelope with misshapen creases— the way an envelope got when overstuffed with euros. Indeed, not five minutes before, the concierge had swapped a thick stack of bills with a single plastic room key. Following Allyson's instructions, Olen took the key and proceeded directly to the fifth floor.

Suite 504 was palatial but not gaudy. Its furnishings were snow white, in keeping with posh European monochrome. Olen tossed his new suit from Steffl's onto the sofa. The scarlet garment bag looked like a giant tongue licking a scoop of vanilla-bean ice cream. Allyson would be late, Olen knew, so he headed to the bathroom to clean up, leaving behind a trail of plus-sized clothes and a pair of gently used snakeskin boots.

Dewy from the shower, Olen toweled off with a monogramed bath sheet. He smelled like lemongrass. The portly Texan from the Viennese café had vanished, and in his place stood a fit man with a sculpted torso. At thirty-nine, a distinctive ruggedness had displaced the buttery smoothness of youth, but spy work kept his body lean.

Olen enjoyed being naked. It felt honest, liberating. Most of the world knew him as a greasy arms dealer or a dumpy bureaucrat—invented personas designed to conceal and deceive. To pull it off, Olen typically shrouded his hard-packed physique under a closet full of ill-fitting clothes. The habit had strategic value; no one ever felt threatened by a man in a frumpy suit. Olen played the roles well and committed fully, so he sometimes had difficulty shaking the borrowed identities. Stripping off the disguises helped. Sex did too. He still hadn't figured out how to do that in character.

Olen kept his sandy hair—not quite brown, not quite blond—cropped short on the sides and a little shaggy on top, to accommodate subtle style modifications on the fly. Not everything about his appearance was so malleable, though. He felt the ridge of a long mark cutting across his upper thigh, beginning a few inches above the knee and ending at his groin. A wicked battle scar.

Olen dropped the towel and headed to the living room to retrieve his clothes. He found Allyson sitting on the sofa, lips pursed with irritation.

"Feeling fresh?" she asked.

Hands on hips, Olen made no attempt to cover up. Director Cameron was his boss now, but at one time she'd been his partner in the field. They'd tackled tough assignments together and shared a sacred bond. Most importantly, they didn't hide things from each other—at least they hadn't back then. Sadr City, Mosul—out there, she'd had his back. Management had changed her. Power often had that effect, Olen guessed. Still, Allyson's transformation was disappointing. Who was this cold-blooded creature of Washington?

A good boss didn't assassinate your coffee date, midconversation, without warning. It was rude. Ergo, Olen didn't give a flying bugfuck if his lemongrass balls made Allyson a little squeamish. Maybe next time she'd have the courtesy to knock.

"Seems I've lost track of my clothes," Olen said through a boyish smirk.

"Along with your goddamn mind." Allyson huffed and
launched the red Steffl bag at her subordinate. "Get dressed, Officer Grave. We've got a lot more to cover than your wrinkled
dingus."

The points of Allyson's cheekbones sharpened when her tem-
per rose, though they were softened by waves of strawberry-blond
hair cascading to her shoulders. She compulsively tucked the ren-
egade locks behind her ears, revealing freckled temples. Olen liked
to imagine that her emerald eyes had once glinted with hopeful
brightness—maybe back in college, when the world still seemed
salvageable—but years hunting terrorists and war criminals had
burned that out. Allyson was certainly attractive in the classical
sense, but she made little investment in her physical appearance,
instead relying on her instincts and the power of persuasion to
bend the universe to her whims. The woman could coax a wild
turkey into an oven at Thanksgiving.

That was how Allyson had convinced Olen to quit the CIA
and join her at VECTOR—the Pentagon's newest intelligence
agency. In the official record, VECTOR was a division of the U.S.
Army Medical Research Institute of Infectious Diseases, or
USAMRIID—a strictly scientific outfit focused on protecting
America's fighting force from biological threats. Olen had readily
agreed to come on board, figuring the position was simply a cover
for another Agency gig. He still thought that, actually. It wasn't
unusual to nest an ultrasecret CIA operation deep within Washington's bureaucratic leviathan (and outside the reach of nettling
congressional oversight committees).

At first, Olen hadn't understood why a bunch of DoD science
nerds needed to hire Langley spooks. Allyson had explained that
in the age of Islamic terrorists hell-bent on weaponizing biological
agents, the Pentagon required a more aggressive posture. USAM-
RIID was a wellspring of technical knowledge, but the military
brass wanted it to be more proactive. They had modified the lab's
mission and ordered a handful of clandestine intel collectors to
join USAMRIID's microbiologists, virologist, chemists, and stat-
isticians—the science nerds. As the appointed chief, Allyson had

plucked her team of spies from the ranks of the Central Intelligence Agency, and VECTOR was born.

Overnight, the Army's premier medical research lab had sprouted arms and legs, liberated from its airtight laboratory at Fort Detrick. VECTOR agents were scattered around the world, hunting bioterrorists, intercepting the illicit sale of dangerous pathogens, and collecting biological samples for processing back in Maryland.

VECTOR had garnered instant respect within the U.S. intelligence community, thanks to its highly esteemed director. But Allyson Cameron was no doe-eyed administrator. She'd cut her teeth in the field and had earned a reputation as a badass spy. Iraq was proof enough.

Fresh off the Farm, a lifetime ago, Olen had shadowed Allyson on a Baghdad tour. Together they'd scoured the desert for Saddam's infamous mobile bioweapons labs, posing as United Nations inspectors. The Republican Guard gave them hell, but Allyson still ran circles around them. "This is no Camp Peary cotillion," she warned. "Get caught out here, they'll rip out your toenails." Olen believed her. That fall, he learned how to survive on the street from the tradecraft grand master.

The cat-and-mouse game between Saddam and the UN grew tiring, so Olen and Allyson bailed and looked for another opening. Weeks later, two jet propulsion engineers—a man with a boyish grin and a woman with world-weary emerald eyes—took advantage of a thinly staffed Turkish border crossing and slipped back into Iraq. With impeccable Russian accents, they sweet-talked their way into Saddam's inner circle with help from a stack of classified schematics of the fabled Sukhoi PAK FA stealth fighter jet. With much better access the second time around, Allyson recruited a high-level source within the presidential palace. The informant insisted that the Iraqi regime had abandoned its bioweapons program after the first Gulf War. The rumored mobile labs were a sham—high-stakes bluffs meant to bolster Saddam's negotiating position. The dictator wanted the United Nations to lift economic sanctions. The fake biolabs gave him leverage.

The U.S. intelligence community balked at the revelation. Allyson's report contradicted the ironclad Washington Beltway consensus, but at great risk to her career, she pushed the intel up the chain, personally vouching for the veracity of her source.

Then–CIA director James Barlow never forgot Allyson's tenacity, especially after he moved into the White House four years later. As president, Barlow asked Allyson to lead VECTOR, then a promising new intel upstart, and she graciously accepted. Now the intrepid spy was chained to a desk in a basement in Maryland, and Olen knew it was killing her. She'd flown to Vienna to brief him in person to get back into the field. Just like old times.

Sitting straight-backed and stony-faced on the Hotel Imperial's immaculate sofa, Allyson didn't look interested in reminiscing about the good ole days. She launched into her briefing.

"State released a cable this morning via our Beijing embassy reporting an outbreak in China's Tibetan Autonomous Region, the TAR. The disease spreads fast and kills faster. Officially, the Chinese government isn't providing details, but our sources in the PRC's Ministry of Health are feeding us bits here and there. Lhasa already has hundreds of fatalities."

"Damn." Olen's smirk disappeared. He stepped into his new slacks and zipped the fly. "Can we corroborate the reports?"

"Unfortunately, we cannot. The Chinese government restricted access to the TAR after the uprisings back in oh-eight. Since then, Tibetan dissident groups have only grown more assertive. Some of the more extreme voices have threatened to separate from China, and the government has no tolerance for sedition. Beijing is convinced foreign powers—America, basically—want to foment revolt in Tibet. Another flare-up of protests in Lhasa last summer was the final straw, and the government cracked down hard. The army hasn't let foreigners in for months. Not even humanitarian aid workers."

"We must have some kind of network in place, right?" Olen asked, referring to sources on the ground.

"Right now, the TAR's borders are tighter than North Korea's and suspicions are sky-high. It hasn't been easy for us to recruit there. The fact is, we don't know a goddamn thing about what's going on. We're learning details about the outbreak mostly from Chinese state media reports, which are probably downplaying the severity. Nothing is confirmed, but if what we've heard is right, it's worse than

SARS." Allyson fingered the buttons of her blouse—an anxious tic that sometimes manifested when she felt stressed and couldn't smoke.

"Have we ID'd the bug?"

"No. We don't have samples of infected blood, so there's nothing to analyze. We thought President Li was more reformist than his predecessor, but he's just as reticent to engage the global scientific community. It's remarkable, really. The Chinese would let thousands of their citizens die rather than accept a helping hand from the Big Bad West."

"It's a power play. Li doesn't want to look weak," Olen said.

"And it's only hurting him. President Li has blocked the CDC from entering the hot zone or assisting the investigation. From the reported symptoms, it sounds like a flavor of hemorrhagic fever, but if it's Ebola or Marburg, the Chinese aren't talking."

"Balls," Olen said, rubbing the back of his head.

"Yeah," the director scoffed.

"What about Marc? Isn't he still VECTOR's guy in China? How good is his intel?"

Even as he asked, the thought of relying on Marc Chen made Olen cringe. Marc had been his bunkmate during CIA training. From day one, Olen sized him up as a privileged, Ivy League asshole. The Agency's Directorate of Operations was teeming with them. Marc didn't disappoint.

Part math whiz, part man-beast, Marc could break insane codes and then obliterate the Farm's punishing obstacle course, all before breakfast. He was smarter, faster, stronger (and a tad handsomer, to be perfectly honest), and it pissed Olen off. On paper the two recruits had a lot in common, and they might have hit it off, but Marc wasn't interested in friendship with anyone. He only wanted to prove he had the biggest cock on the block. Olen wasn't the type to back down from a competition, but when head-to-head with Marc Chen, he almost always fell an inch short.

The week of graduation, Olen finally turned the tables and beat the snot out of his roommate in a bare-knuckle sparring match. At the field officer's commissioning ceremony, Marc shook the CIA director's hand sporting an ugly black eye. Olen beamed.

The freshly minted spies abandoned their childish rivalry in the forests of Virginia and focused their attention on more pressing matters, like surviving in denied enemy territory. Olen shipped off to the desert, and Marc volunteered for a deep-cover assignment in China. Good thing too, because it had to be Marc. Olen—a corn-fed, blue-eyed Iowan—sure as shit couldn't pass for a Han migrant from Tianjin. However, Marc—the son of a Chinese American neurosurgeon—had a fighting chance. The dude was *still* a privileged Ivy League asshole, but he'd turned out to be a stellar case officer too. Right now, no matter Olen's feelings about the guy, VECTOR needed Marc Chen.

"In his report last week, Chen complained of a severe headache. Then he missed his next check-in. That was three days ago," Allyson said. "He was right there, Olen, in the epicenter of the outbreak."

"You think he's been infected?" Olen asked.

"For Chen's sake, I hope he took some Advil and slept it off. In the meantime, a pandemic is brewing in the TAR and my only field officer within two thousand miles has gone dark.

"After SARS, everyone said it would be different with the Chinese, but it's the same story. Did you know that in the first days of that outbreak, Beijing told everyone SARS was chlamydia? *Chlamydia*, for God's sake! Thousands died because the Chinese government botched the response and then covered it up."

"Beijing knows they can't afford another SARS. Why the silent treatment?" Olen asked.

"Simple. The TAR isn't Guangdong Province. Tibetans already mistrust the government. Politically speaking, the region is a powder keg. Until Beijing feels they have the situation under control, the WHO and the CDC won't get within a hundred miles. The stakes are even higher now. Another public health scandal isn't an option for Zhongnanhai. People would lose confidence in the government's ability to protect them."

"They can't expect to keep everyone in the dark. Plenty of people know how to get around the Great Firewall. Even if they can't get on Facebook over there, you know they're looking at porn."

Allyson frowned. "You're right. China's Communist Party can't maintain a complete information lock-down. So, President Li's administration has agreed to admit one American journalist into the TAR. The reporter will have unprecedented access, embedded within the Ministry of Health's epidemiological team."

"What?" Olen was skeptical. It sounded too easy.

"Li wants the foreign press to document the investigation, but in a manner he can control. It's a brilliant maneuver, actually," Allyson continued. "Li can claim transparency—to both the international community and the Chinese people—without losing face by accepting material aid from foreigners."

"I see where this is going," Olen said.

"You'll penetrate the TAR under media cover as the sole Western journalist with authorized access."

"You sound a little too happy about this, Cam. You're sending me into a hot zone to be devoured by some kind of flesh-eating amoeba."

"This horrific outbreak may have opened a small crack for us to get a peek into one of the most elusive and politically unstable regions of China. We're fortunate to have this opportunity."

"A front-row seat to a—how did you put it?—horrific outbreak. Yep, I'm a lucky ducky."

"You're wheels up first thing tomorrow morning," Allyson ordered. "Langley is sending a pair of analysts to brief you overnight. There's very little time to review the operational plan, so you'll just have to sleep on the plane."

Olen nodded. "But there may be a weensy problem," he said. "You know I don't speak Chinese, right?"

6

Beijing, People's Republic of China

A STIFF SILENCE HUNG over the Great Hall of the People. A disease as dangerous as Blood River virus loose in Beijing was unacceptable. Dr. Zhou knew the outbreak would strain President Li Bingwen's tenuous authority. At the beginning of Li's term, right after the National Congress appointed him to the presidency, Dr. Zhou, like many others, had hoped he could inspire unity and lead China into the future. Childish notions. Over the past year, brutal infighting among the political factions had ripped Zhongnanhai apart. Li lacked the inner strength to rally his people and rebuild consensus, and the members of the Standing Committee were too entrenched in their views. They were vicious, intractable men who had ascended to the country's highest ruling body through a toxic blend of coercion, extortion, and, if the rumors were true, the occasional quiet murder.

Mao Zedong would've crushed them all. Six months breaking up rocks in the northern labor camps would've done the trick. However, Li Bingwen was no Maoist strongman. He was barely in charge. His rivals made sure of that.

China's president was supposed to rule the state, the military, and the Communist Party—the holy trinity of power in the People's Republic. But compared to his predecessors, Li was a maladroit politician, easily outmaneuvered by more ambitious men. The nation's elites—the same hypocrites who had voted him into office—had bailed on Li within months. Like beetles to a lamppost, they'd swarmed to a brighter luminary, General Huang Yipeng of the People's Liberation Army. The final blow had come the previous spring when the Standing Committee blindsided President Li. They stripped him of his authority over the military and anointed General Huang chairman of the nation's armed forces. Huang wielded the PLA as a political weapon, while Li struggled to retain what little control he had over the civilian branches of government.

Dr. Zhou studied the two men, Li and Huang, who were now seated three feet apart behind the mahogany dais. The animus was palpable.

"What do we know about this man, your patient zero?" General Huang interjected. "This Mr. Chun . . ."

"Chang Yingjie," Dr. Zhou corrected, returning to her seat.

The general's question wasn't medical in nature. All eyes focused on a man in a gray suit standing at the opposite end of the briefing table.

Wei Feng spoke with the steely bearing of an officer of the venerated MSS, the Ministry of State Security, China's most elite intelligence agency. "Chang Yingjie worked for the NSB," Wei reported, referring to the Taiwanese National Security Bureau.

"You're telling us patient zero was a Taiwanese spy?" General Huang said. "How the hell did the NSB get into Tibet?"

"He slipped into the country through Hong Kong ten days ago using an alias. Security camera footage at Hong Kong International Airport captured Chang passing through the main terminal at ten-oh-two in the morning." Officer Wei flashed a fuzzy image on the screen. It was Chang, breezing past a crowded duty-free shop. "Our facial recognition software matched Chang with photos taken of him during an operation he ran in Sudan last summer.

"Chang's flight originated in Paris. He'd purchased a round-trip ticket with a return flight departing twelve days later. For a man planning to spend nearly two weeks in our country, he traveled light. The chief of airport security suspected something unusual when guards noticed Chang hadn't checked any baggage."

"Well, if airport security spotted a known intelligence officer of the NSB waltzing through Hong Kong International, why didn't we snatch him up?" Huang asked.

"We considered it, but we decided to follow him instead, to see if he planned to meet with anyone. Chang jumped into a taxi, and MSS surveillance teams tracked him to the Lo Wu train station thirty miles away. Three trains, two buses, and over forty hours later, he arrived in Chengdu, in Sichuan Province." The MSS officer paused to clear his throat. "That's where we lost him."

General Huang grimaced. "How did you *lose him*, Officer Wei?"

Wei Feng looked nervous. As the leader of the MSS surveillance team, Wei had personally tracked Chang to Sichuan Province. That made him responsible for the failure.

Wei went on to explain the details behind the pursuit that had spanned two full days. He'd followed Chang from the Chengdu train station to Tianfu Square in the city center. Chang had wandered aimlessly in the expansive plaza, gawking like a dumb struck tourist. Wei wasn't fooled. He knew Chang was scanning the crowd, searching for someone.

Officer Wei maintained a safe distance, finding a bench in the shadow of a mammoth Mao Zedong statue lording over the plaza. Giggling children scurried across the square, flying colorful kites. A wrinkled man with a gray kitten perched on his shoulder sold bags of *jaozi*, steamed pork dumplings, from a wooden cart. Nothing seemed out of place.

Then Chang lit a cigarette, and Wei knew something was wrong. Chang Yingjie didn't smoke—not according to his dossier, anyway. Officer Wei had memorized every page. The cigarette was a signal. Wei couldn't be sure what it meant, but it confirmed his suspicion: the Taiwanese spy wasn't sightseeing. Officer Chang Yingjie was operational.

The sun sank lower, making it difficult to observe Chang from across the square. Then music blared from speakers hidden in the trees. The plaza's centerpiece, a regal fountain, lit up in radiant red, and the nightly water show began (right on schedule, Wei would later learn). The booming, symphonic score and synchronized flashing lights drew the attention of hundreds of spectators. A swarm descended on the fountain like ants to a popsicle. Wei lost his line of sight. Moving in, he filtered through the throng, attempting to reestablish a visual, but it was no use. Chang had vanished.

"Intelligence Officer Chang Yingjie may have been young, but he was a professional," Wei explained to the Standing Committee. "He never looked over his shoulder. He didn't run an SDR, a surveillance detection run, or make any attempt to shake us, yet his behavior near the fountain was decidedly evasive. Chang pushed into the wide-open plaza to force us to fall back, and then he used the crowd as a smoke screen to slip away. He knew about the water show and timed everything perfectly."

"He obviously spotted the MSS lurking," Huang said derisively.

"Actually, sir, we don't believe Chang detected surveillance. He didn't have to. He bought his airline ticket using a well-worn alias guaranteed to send up red flags. He knew we'd be watching from the moment he stepped off the jet bridge in Hong Kong. He counted on it. In my estimation, Chang deliberately lured us to Chengdu."

"Well, *someone* must have seen him leave Tianfu Square, Officer Wei," Huang said. "The next time Chang was spotted, he was a thousand miles away, sipping tea with Tibetans. Does the MSS have any idea how the man infiltrated one of the most restricted areas of Eastern Tibet unnoticed?"

General Huang's neck pulsed with visible frustration as he continued. "As soon as the MSS learned a Taiwanese spy had arrived on Chinese soil, the ministry should have handed the matter over to military intelligence."

Dr. Zhou wasn't surprised by the general's view. The man had spent his career serving the Second Department of the PLA's General Staff Headquarters—the esteemed 2PLA—and the military intelligence outfit didn't play nice with the civilian branch.

Officer Wei continued his report. "We suspect Chang Yingjie went underground. The nearest subway station is inside the subterranean shopping mall underneath the square. He likely traveled directly to the airport. From there, it would not have been hard to hop a shuttle flight to Lhasa. For that leg, we assume Chang used a different alias, one we don't know about, to book a ticket."

"And why do you believe that, Officer Wei?" Huang asked.

"Because we have no record of his trip," Wei answered.

"To be clear," Huang said, "a Taiwanese intelligence officer infiltrated our borders, evaded our surveillance teams, and *then* unleashed a deadly virus that ravaged our citizens."

Wei nodded. "It appears that way, sir."

General Huang looked down the row of powerful men flanking his sides. "Gentleman, we must recognize this for what it is—nothing less than a direct act of biological warfare. Taiwan has attacked us from within, and our obligation as leaders of this great nation is unambiguous. We must retaliate."

"Let's not jump to conclusions," President Li Bingwen broke in. "If Taiwan intended to cripple us with an outbreak, why attack a cluster of isolated monks and farmers in the hinterland? Why not hit Beijing or Shanghai? There are fifteen million people in Guangzhou alone. Targeting any one of these cities would have done considerably more damage."

"You're thinking like a politician, not a military strategist, Comrade Bingwen." Huang leaned into the table, craning around President Li to address the other members of the Standing Committee. "Taipei has thrown a match into a barrel of gasoline. Those people of Tibet need very little encouragement to provoke this government. When news of the virus spreads, and you can be sure it will, there will be blood in the streets. We will look helpless, impotent, too weak to protect the nation. Dissent will spread faster than the disease! There will be riots. Shops vandalized. Property torched. And therein lies the real attack, you see. Taiwan doesn't want to make people sick—it wants to make them *angry*. Angry with *us*."

"A bit melodramatic, don't you think?" Li replied.

"The Taiwanese know this government's legitimacy rests on thin ice. Zhongnanhai will not survive a major groundswell of opposition. If Tibet rebels, what's next? Xinjiang? Hong Kong?" General Huang's thundering baritone echoed as he paused for breath. "I will mobilize the People's Liberation Army tonight. A show of strength will quash any misconceptions about our capacity to restore order. Taipei will get the message. We'll plaster it across the tips of our Dongfeng-16s."

"We cannot hurl bombs at innocent people because one man got the flu," President Li countered.

"Not just any man. An enemy *spy*," Huang replied. "And the Taiwanese are not innocent, comrade. They're seditious needlers, too feeble and too cowardly to challenge us overtly, like men, so they chip away little by little, weakening us from the inside. Their NSB spies infiltrate our corporations, steal our technology. Who knows how many have already penetrated our intelligence services? When was the last time you took a hard look at your MSS, Mr. President?"

President Li bristled. The general had trespassed on sensitive territory. Official authority over the civilian intelligence service fell to Li as head of state, and the men of the MSS were not bumbling amateurs. They risked their lives for China, and in return for their selfless commitment, some had made the ultimate sacrifice.

The president slammed his fist into the heavy tabletop. "Your insinuations are slanderous. Chairman Mao is long gone, General Huang. There will be no great purge of your imagined enemies."

The general pulled his shoulders back like an osprey lifting its menacing wings before dive-bombing for trout. "You're right. Chairman Mao is dead, and thankfully so, for his own sake. The Great Helmsman would be humiliated by this committee's impotence." Droplets of Huang's spittle dotted the table.

"Your distaste for my administration is well established," Li rasped. "Despite the ever-widening chasm dividing our views on foreign policy, it is now clear that China's future rests not in our ability to achieve political consensus but in our ability to effectively mitigate this rapidly deteriorating public health emergency." Li folded his hands. Huang was a bully, but Li couldn't ignore that the general had raised a legitimate concern.

"Now, I must agree, on its face, we'd be foolish to disregard the connection between this Taiwanese intelligence officer and the outbreak in Tibet," Li conceded. "But a connection alone is not evidence of malevolence." The president refocused his attention on Dr. Zhou. "Doctor, is it your expert opinion that Chang brought this disease to the mainland intentionally? Did his autopsy reveal any indication he'd purposefully infected himself, perhaps as part of an elaborate suicide attack?"

"I didn't perform an autopsy, Mr. President," Dr. Zhou said flatly.

"Well, who did then?" Li asked.

"No one did," she answered. "No body. No autopsy."

"What?" Huang barked. "Where's the body, Doctor?"

"They burned it. The villagers, that is."

"Why would they destroy the body before an autopsy?" Li asked. "Aren't there standard operating procedures for such things?"

"Dzongsar Village is a place frozen in time. There are no modern hospitals or labs. The people are deeply religious and highly superstitious," Dr. Zhou explained. "Their only clinic is a row of spare rooms in a private residence. The community's sole healthcare professional—if you can call him that—is a self-taught doctor whose approach to medicine is based more in mysticism than in science."

"So they burned the man to please the gods? Or is it Buddha?" General Huang quipped.

"I suspect they were terrified of him," Dr. Zhou answered. "After Chang collapsed, subcutaneous edema would have made his body look puffy and deformed, like a half-melted marshmallow. His skin was likely covered with hematomas—dark-purple splotches. The hemorrhaging from his tear ducts would've looked like he was weeping blood. This must have horrified the villagers, so yes, they burned Chang's body immediately. And without it, we cannot determine how, or when, he was exposed to the virus."

"Then it is possible Chang got sick *after* he arrived in Tibet," Li postulated.

"Very possible. Even probable, I'd say. True, there are no previously documented cases of this disease in Eastern Tibet—or in all of China, for that matter—but the subtropical climate of the Yarlung Tsangpo Valley is consistent with other natural environments that have produced similar viruses. And some researchers believe deforestation can stir up otherwise dormant pathogens. For example, one theory presumes that jungle clearing in Zaire, to make room for plantations, unleashed Ebola in the late 1970s. China's logging industry is aggressively encroaching on untouched forests blanketing the area surrounding Dzongsar Village. Blood River virus may have thrived for centuries within a woodland host species that until recently was isolated from human populations. Maybe something bit Chang in Tibet and that's how he got sick."

"And is that your prevailing theory, Doctor?" President Li asked.

Dr. Zhou sighed. "Not at all. Bottom line, whether it was a fruit bat or a foreign spy, the true source of the virus is still unknown. We don't even fully understand how it's transmitted."

"Then we require more information." Li spoke definitively, as if he'd anticipated the virologist's response. "A retaliatory counterattack on Taiwan would be impetuous at this stage. Dr. Zhou, you will lead the investigation in Dzongsar. You are to report any new information directly to my office."

Dr. Zhou could think of a hundred objections to President Li's order. The epidemiological field survey was already complete. That was how they'd determined Chang was the index case. The Ministry of Health had an army of doctors tracking new infections in Lhasa. At this point, the critical work—deciphering the pattern of mutation, determining the virus's genetic vulnerabilities—was in the lab. *Her* lab. In Shanghai, not the Tibetan rain forest.

Dr. Zhou sat frozen in place. An image of Chang's burning body flashed in her mind, flames licking his swollen flesh, flakes of charred skin swirling in the hot updraft, a dark cloud of toxic smoke roaring into the atmosphere. Finally, her mouth began to form words.

"With all due respect, Mr. President, the Ministry of Health can call upon the World Health Organization to assist with—"

President Li raised a palm to silence the doctor's demurral. "We cannot allow the WHO or the Americans at the CDC to intervene. This is a Chinese matter, and we're fully capable of handling it ourselves."

Dr. Zhou knew the president's reluctance to involve the international community stemmed from political expediency. Li's rivals would say the man lacked backbone if he ran to the Americans for help. Dr. Zhou read the conviction in Li's eyes. She firmly believed he was making a mistake—this wasn't just a Chinese problem—but the president had made up his mind. Protesting his decision was pointless.

Like it or not, she was going to Tibet.

CHAPTER

7

Beijing, People's Republic of China

THE FERVENT BELLOW of a hundred men rumbled like thunder. The guttural roar echoed throughout the PLA National Defense University as it did most evenings, especially near Yan's Pit.

Army recruits had affectionately named the gaping mud crater on the far edge of campus after the mythological Chinese god of death. Yan ruled over hell. The demon god passed judgment on the departed, one soul at a time, condemning the wicked and the weak.

Similarly, no academy trainee could avoid the unforgiving evaluation of Yan's Pit. The odious hole tested the mettle of hopeful soldiers. Those who possessed strength of body and character would ultimately ascend to the officer ranks of the honorable Chinese army, the largest standing ground force in the world. Those who did not were rejected, expelled from the university in disgrace.

General Huang Yipeng overlooked the pit, where a throng of exhausted young men executed crisp martial arts maneuvers. They lunged into powerful stances and hurled clenched fists at invisible opponents, their hardwired muscles performing automatically.

Battle-hardened drill instructors paced the elevated pathway along the pit's rim. They shouted under wide-brimmed hats, lobbing orders at the bare-chested recruits, whose PLA uniforms had yet to be earned. A sea of sinewy arms and legs, smeared with dark mud and sweat, pulsed in unison like forlorn souls struggling to escape purgatory. Yan's Pit gurgled beneath their bare feet as the nether-world threatened to swallow them from below.

The platoon released another primal yell, and General Huang shivered with a semierotic charge. The deep, masculine vocalization reminded him that real power exuded from the raw flesh of men, not from missiles and tanks. Men were infinitely more dangerous than anything metal. When properly motivated, that is.

A young lieutenant approached, his pant legs swishing, and invaded the general's concentration. Huang returned the junior officer's obligatory salute. Lieutenant Wang Peng served as the general's aide-de-camp, but Huang thought of him more as a son than as a subordinate. The two men, a generation apart, had discovered their shared philosophy on geopolitics early in Lieutenant Wang's posting. Huang took pride in shaping the junior officer's worldview. China advanced only when its youth carried the banner for revolution; history had proved this. Huang saw great potential in Wang. One day he would become a respected leader.

"Xiao Wang, what do you have for me?" General Huang asked, referring to his aide by the paternalistic sobriquet "Little Wang."

"Lhasa is getting worse, sir, but the army has secured a perimeter. Ground transit throughout the TAR is under tight control."

"You don't seem convinced," Huang said.

"Despite our efforts to confine the disease to Tibet, nine new cases of Blood River virus were reported in Chengdu this afternoon. Three of them are university students from Nanjing on a backpacking trip. They likely contracted the disease somewhere in the Sichuanese countryside. The Ministry of Health is testing the residents and livestock at local farms."

"Where are they now?" Huang asked. "The ill ones?"

"Three men, six women. They've all been quarantined at West China Hospital. It's on the Sichuan University campus. The Ministry is keeping this quiet for now. Nobody wants the city to panic. The public still thinks the contagion is contained in Tibet."

"Word will leak. It only takes one paranoid nurse to start a flood of rumors," Huang said.

The general descended a battery of stairs and began a brisk march toward the academy's eastern quadrant. Lieutenant Wang lengthened his stride to keep pace, yet the general seemed to cover twice the distance with each step.

"Send in a squad of PLA patrolmen to guard the hospital," General Huang instructed. "Full combat uniform."

"Sir, won't that raise suspicion?" Wang asked. "Everyone is talking about the disease. If armed soldiers show up at a hospital in Chengdu, people will know the virus has spread."

"Let them. The people must know the truth, Xiao Wang, and President Li refuses to tell them."

"Surely there must be a more delicate way to—"

"We are under *attack*." The general's voice snapped with electric passion. "Li is a fool. He's a disgrace to the men who rebuilt this nation after a century of abuse at the hands of the imperial dogs. He submits to the West like a whore with an opioid habit. But, Xiao Wang, do you see the great irony?"

"Power never respects weakness. Only strength," Wang answered.

"Precisely. For thousands of years, kings and sultans sent lavish delegations to pay tribute to our emperors. They bowed before our rulers, begged for protection. China was the Middle Kingdom. The nexus of worldly power." General Huang halted and gripped Lieutenant Wang's shoulders. "I believe we can achieve greatness again, Xiao Wang. But we must never ask for deference. Do you understand me? We must *demand* it, through sheer, unrivaled dominance."

* * *

Lieutenant Wang Peng typically found the general's grandiose musings on Chinese supremacy engrossing. Today, however, he worried that the man's deep-seated disdain for President Li, his political nemesis, had clouded Huang's judgment. Challenging the general was never prudent, and especially unwise while the man was so spun up. Better to concede with bobbing head nods and firm *yes, sir*s.

General Huang had a point, after all. President Li believed that committing wholeheartedly to the international order—the same one rigged by the Americans and their Western allies—would protect China's peaceful rise. Li's flowery speeches bloomed with words like *reform* and *liberalism*. It was the immature vision of a hopeless optimist, Wang thought. The Americans' lust for iPhones and cheap T-shirts would feed China's economic engine, but only as long as it remained docile and supplicant. If the sleeping dragon were to awaken and threaten American hegemony, the United States would certainly wrestle China back into submission. For this reason, China's military had to modernize in secret. Not even President Li knew how powerful the PLA had become over the past few years. Huang had built an impressive war machine, and Wang believed the general fully intended to use it.

The two men traversed a large, rectangular courtyard, the junior officer following his boss in lockstep. Enormous cypress trees, their twisted branches extending from thick, gray trunks, cast webbed shadows across the stone pavers. General Huang pivoted forty-five degrees to his left and headed in the direction of the airfield. Wang spun on his heel to keep up.

"Are you familiar with the Mandate of Heaven, Xiao Wang?" General Huang asked. The lecture resumed.

"Yes, sir. Our ancestors believed the emperor ruled by divine blessing. Our leaders were ordained by Heaven as kings on earth," Wang said.

"As long as they governed justly," Huang added. "If the emperor failed, Heaven revoked the mandate and bestowed its blessing upon another—someone worthier of the position. The sitting emperor lost legitimacy and his claim to the throne."

Wang remembered the stories from childhood. He'd dismissed the Mandate of Heaven as a superstitious remnant of a less sophisticated era. Yet he knew some Chinese still believed today's leaders governed with a divine endorsement of sorts—a tenuous privilege that required a careful balance of strength and benevolence.

"I realize it may sound old-fashioned, but the concept has merit," Huang said. "Our people once thought floods and earthquakes were proof the emperor had lost his heavenly mandate to rule. Entire dynasties crumbled because the people believed it was

Heaven's will." General Huang's breakneck march slowed to a shuffle. He paused and squinted into the setting sun. "This disease. This plague. Maybe it's God's judgment. He has unleashed this pestilence to decry President Li and his gang of spineless capitulators."

Lieutenant Wang was puzzled. The outbreak certainly wasn't born from the wrath of a disappointed deity. The idea was absurd, and surely Huang—the consummate realist—agreed. Sure, the government's limp response to the virus revealed its incompetence and frailty, but Lieutenant Wang didn't need God or any other supernatural force to tell him that.

The approaching helicopter's rotor blades whooshed above them. The general and his aide stood beside the landing platform, their eyes drawn skyward as the craft gracefully descended to the helipad. Wang pinched the brim of his olive-green hat to prevent it from flying away in the warm downwash. He shouted over the chopper's throbbing hum. "Li wants to bring in a foreign reporter."

"Yes, I heard," Huang said.

"The man lands in Beijing in the morning. President Li has approved his full access to the research team."

"American?" Huang asked.

"Yes, sir. Seven years with the AP. Two with the *New York Times* before that, where he covered the Middle East. Recently, he's written a few puff pieces about West Nile cases in North America, mostly about prevention. Wash your hands. Wear long sleeves. Nothing overtly political."

"Do we have a photo?" The chopper rested on the pad but didn't power down. Huang made a beeline for its open hatch.

"The Ministry of Foreign Affairs is handling his paperwork and security orientation," Wang said. "All of his information is in their database. Naturally, I've requested a copy."

"Who is on surveillance?"

"MSS," Wang replied.

The general scowled. "We can't trust the Americans. And we certainly can't trust the half-wits at the MSS. Brief the 2PLA on everything we know about the reporter. Tell Foreign Affairs we'll handle all in-country transportation—as a courtesy to President

Li, of course. In fact, the entire investigative team will take my personal plane to Lhasa. It's the least I can offer."

Huang deftly climbed into the helicopter. A member of the flight crew began to close the door, but the general reached out an arm to hold it open.

"And Xiao Wang," he shouted. "Get me that reporter's picture."

Lieutenant Wang backed away from the landing pad, and the chopper climbed into the blackening sky. The trip didn't appear in the general's official schedule, but Wang knew where his boss was headed.

Ngari Prefecture. The rocky badlands of northwestern Tibet were over a thousand miles from the epicenter of the outbreak, but the general didn't plan to survey the quarantine zone. Huang was overseeing the construction of a new air base. Lieutenant Wang had seen the documents—mostly topographical surveys, engineering plans. Sometimes the general asked him to compile briefing books. The entire project was highly classified.

The new air base would give the PLA superior access to trouble spots in the region, like Kashmir and Pakistan. China needed to keep a close eye on its quarrelsome neighbors—so went Huang's pitch to the National Congress. Lieutenant Wang knew his boss cared more about monitoring the internal threats: Tibetan and Uyghur rebel organizations that operated in the area. Huang obsessed over separatists. If the recent outbreak sparked uprisings in the western regions, the general would use the nearly complete Ngari installation to squash the insurgency. As a bonus, Wang knew, the far-flung outpost gave Huang something he enjoyed even more than oppressing seditious minority groups.

Privacy.

DAY 9

8

Beijing, People's Republic of China

AEROFLOT FLIGHT 704 wrestled a patch of rough air, shaking Officer Olen Grave from a shallow sleep. The flight crew had dimmed the cabin lights for the red-eye to Beijing. Dozing passengers draped themselves across their tiny seats, folding into unnatural positions. Called by a familiar urge, Olen unfastened his seat belt, lumbered to the forward lavatory, squeezed inside, and unzipped.

He caught his reflection in the mirror. A scrappy, field-tested journalist stared back. The faded flannel shirt, worn Levi's, and mud-stained Timberland boots spoke of years chasing stories in war-torn Afghanistan. The overgrown hair and perpetual stubble marked him as a true reporter, not some plastic anchorman. This dude kicked over rocks in dark places and didn't give a nut about looking shiny on camera. The cover persona—Kipton Stone—fit comfortably. Kipton was a man who thrived in the wild. A man who owned a mountain bike, went fly-fishing in the Snake River, had friends with beards who called him Kip.

Olen washed up and dried his palms on the front of his jeans. He searched his pocket for his digital recorder, which he tucked into a sock before opening the bathroom door. In the main cabin, now illuminated for landing, passengers twisted their contorted bodies back into shape. Some pulled white surgical masks over their faces. A flight attendant moved down the aisle handing them out.

The U.S. Department of State, along with a handful of European governments, had warned travelers to avoid China, to steer clear of the outbreak. Easier said than done. Like Olen, the other passengers probably had little choice in the matter. In reality, nobody on that plane would come within two thousand miles of an infected person. Nobody except Olen. He was headed directly into the hot zone.

Olen settled into his seat. Outside, the sky slowly brightened to deep cobalt as the first light of morning peeked over the horizon.

Not long after, the wheels of the Boeing 747 touched down with a puff of white smoke. Olen gathered his gear. Field journalists carried everything on their backs, so he'd packed light—a pair of backup jeans, a half dozen boxer briefs, two flannel shirts, laptop, camera, cell phone. Most of it would be confiscated by Chinese customs agents. He could feel the digital recorder still concealed in his sock.

Once the aircraft parked at the gate, Olen joined the line of passengers tottering up the aisle to deplane. In Beijing's international terminal, sunlight flooded through the towering glass walls. Thousands of crisscrossed steel beams reinforced the lofted ceiling as if it were a space-age cathedral. Olen had only seconds to appreciate the terminal's grandeur before an Asian man in a dark suit and absurd *Top Gun* sunglasses approached him.

"Mr. Stone, Beijing welcomes you!" the man said through a toothy smile, arms spread wide.

"Kipton Stone, Associated Press," Olen responded, extending a hand. "You must be Maverick."

"Who?"

"Never mind. Hey, nice shades, man," Olen joked.

"Yes, yes. Please, come with us. We have much to do." Maverick whisked Olen from the gate, his heels click-clacking on the shiny tile.

"I'm here at the invitation of the Ministry of Health," Olen explained. He'd expected some special attention, given the sensitivities surrounding his visit. No other foreigners had visited the quarantine zone. "I assume they've sent you to escort me, but I don't need—"

"Of course, Mr. Stone. But first you must complete your safety briefing. It's compulsory," Maverick said. "Come, come. There isn't much time. We must hurry."

Olen nodded compliantly. The outbreak had everyone a little jumpy. No doubt the Ministry would insist on babysitting him at all times, which would make his mission more challenging.

The two men moved deftly through a sea of tourists and businessmen. The airport's usual frenzy seemed unaffected by the news of a terrifying disease plaguing the hinterland. Olen's host led him through a set of double doors marked RESTRICTED ACCESS in four languages. At the end of a long passageway, they reached another door guarded by a short man in a military uniform. Maverick held up a badge, prompting the guard to punch a code into a keypad. The code had seven digits, Olen noted, listening to the bleeps. The door opened with a buzz, revealing a narrow corridor lined with long windows fitted with two-way glass. Through each window, Olen saw cramped, closet-sized rooms, furnished with identical square tables and aluminum chairs. Interrogation rooms.

"Right this way, Mr. Stone," Maverick said, and ushered Olen into one of the empty rooms. He then grabbed Olen's backpack and camera bag and handed them off to a soldier who had materialized from nowhere. The soldier vanished again, along with Olen's gear.

"Hey, what the hell! That's my stuff, man," Olen objected.

"Inspection. For your safety," Maverick explained. "Lift your arms, please." He vigorously frisked Olen's torso. In one fluid motion, he removed Olen's belt and shoved it into a clear plastic bag. Then Maverick dropped to one knee and roughly patted Olen's pant legs, traveling up his inseam.

"Easy, fella," Olen barked when Maverick cupped his genitals.

"It's compulsory," the man repeated. "Sit down, please." Maverick tugged on Olen's left boot and immediately noticed the unnatural lump in his sock. Olen made a guilty face, as if the school principal had just discovered his weed stash, but actually he was pleased. He'd expected the Chinese to examine him for contraband, so he'd planted something for them to find. A street-smart journalist might've considered it clever to hide a digital recorder in his sock, but no self-respecting intelligence officer would risk such an obvious deception. The amateurish ploy strengthened his cover—audacious American journalist, *not a spy*.

Maverick stuffed the recorder into the plastic bag along with Olen's belt and cursed sharply in Mandarin. No doubt some unlucky technician would waste days scrutinizing every inch of the completely benign device. Olen had filled its hard drive with Taylor Swift tracks just to drive them all batshit.

Maverick took a seat across the interrogation table, still wearing the ridiculous mirrored aviators. "Listen carefully, Mr. Stone. I am going to explain the rules." The Chinese man futzed with his tie, smoothing the silk. "In a few moments, we will escort you to a military aircraft, where you will join a scientific research team bound for the restricted area. You will interact solely with the members of this team. You are not permitted to speak to military personnel unless they engage you first. You are not permitted to conduct interviews of ordinary people while in China. You will be under the direct supervision of the scientific team leader and will obey all instructions without question. Most importantly, Mr. Stone . . ." Maverick leaned back, arms crossed high on his chest, morphing from Asian Tom Cruise to Triad Crime Boss. "No photographs, no recordings, and no phone calls. Is this clear?"

"No interviews? No pics?" Olen feigned outrage. "There must be some misunderstanding, man. That's precisely what I came here to do. I work for a news organization. I don't know what you guys expected, but I have no intention of filing a bunch of Party propaganda."

"Mr. Stone, you have no business—"

"My *business* is the truth, and as long as I'm working this story, that's exactly what I intend to write." Olen played the part well— principled reporter, *still not a spy*.

"You are here at the invitation of the Chinese government. Please understand, your access may be revoked failing your cooperation. We cannot control what you write after you return to the United States, but while you are here, the rules are explicit."

Olen huffed.

"Time is short. We must leave." Maverick stood abruptly. The soldier reentered, clutching a black velvet sack.

"Oh, sh—" Olen started to say before the black hood muffled his words and the room went dark. Someone yanked his arms back, and he felt cold metal cuffs pinch his wrists.

Olen struggled against the restraints—more playacting. He knew the B-movie hostage act was part of the game. Next they'd toss him into the back seat of a sedan and pump up the car radio (so Olen couldn't listen for identifying sounds, like train whistles and construction noise). All unnecessary theatrics, but the power play probably gave Maverick a stiffy.

Quite frankly, Olen welcomed the hood and the handcuffs; they meant it was finally time to get moving. "You fellas aren't gonna gimme my shit back, are you?" he said.

9

Washington, DC, USA

"So, in a nutshell, you're saying we don't know?" President James Barlow asked, his tone more surprised than peeved. The man didn't get peeved. Barlow topped off his Scotch and filled a second glass halfway. He plopped a fistful of ice cubes into the amber liquid.

"You know that's why they give you those little tong things, Jim," Allyson Cameron said. "I hope you at least washed your hands."

"Whatever's in this will kill anything," Barlow said, handing the drink to Director Cameron, ice rattling against the glass. "Including us, Cam. Just more slowly."

Allyson returned what might have passed for a smile in better lighting. "We know it's bad. Could be five hundred, maybe as many as a thousand infected. The Chinese were more open about the outbreak at first, but once it began to snowball, they clamped down."

"The customary Chinese deep freeze." Barlow sat opposite Director Cameron on one of the matching blue- and gold-striped sofas that flanked the presidential seal on the Oval Office rug. "What's Beijing doing about it?"

"Everything's locked down in the big cities. Travel is tricky but not impossible. Communication is hit-or-miss. China Mobile's network keeps crashing, but the Internet is still up—at least the sites the government hasn't blocked. CIA's collectors can't find most of their sources in all the madness. The best intel is coming in from Singapore and Japan, actually, so it's tough to verify the exact scope of the epidemic. We're not completely blind, but—"

"We've got pretty thick cataracts."

Allyson nodded.

"Has it spread outside China?" Barlow asked.

"A guy—pretty young too—checked into a Toronto ER last Tuesday with chills, diarrhea, headache. The whole mess," Allyson reported. "He told the doctors he'd just returned from Malaysia on business. Scared the holy hell out of everyone. Police cleared out the entire hospital. Sealed off his room. Luckily, the guy bounced back. It wasn't Blood River virus." Allyson hadn't touched her Scotch. She just swirled the glass.

"At least the Chinese shut down their airports," Barlow said.

"Well, the commercial flights, at least. The cargo jets still come and go. COSCO's mostly operational at the seaports too. Beijing's not willing to risk precious trade dollars over this. If the disease gets out of China, it'll probably be in the gut of some ship hand unloading Nikes in Long Beach."

The president rose and moved behind his stately oak desk—the same formidable workstation once used by Franklin Delano Roosevelt. He gripped the back of his chair, his fingertips turning pink as they pressed into the leather. "Was this virus a bioweapon?"

Barlow's blunt question hung in the air. The matter was Director Cameron's area of responsibility. The president looked to her for answers, yet she had few to offer. Allyson took her first sip of the Scotch.

"There are some nasty bugs out there," she said. "The more rocks we turn over, the more creepy things we'll find crawling in the mud."

"So, you think Blood River virus is natural? The result of deforestation? Encroachment on the habitat of an undiscovered species?"

"The fact is, we don't have a clue where it came from," Allyson admitted. "I've been working with Geneva to get a WHO team past Beijing's government sentinels for days. Anyone they send just gets 'detained for further processing.' "

Barlow removed a prescription pill bottle from a drawer and popped a yellow capsule into his mouth.

"They're getting worse, aren't they?" Allyson asked.

Barlow took a swig of Scotch to wash down the meds. "It's just a headache, Cam."

Allyson knew not to press. The president had enough on his mind.

"What do we know about the Taiwanese man, the index case?" Barlow asked.

"Chang was a spy with the Taiwanese NSB. An ISI source ID'd the guy from one of Chang's past diplomatic stations in Africa."

"An ISI source? You trust the Pakistanis?" Barlow snorted.

"No one trusts the Pakistanis," Allyson replied. "That's why we corroborated the intel with the Five Eyes. Turns out the Canadians bumped into him in Burkina Faso about four months ago. Overall, there's not much history to go on."

"Maybe he picked this thing up in West Africa," Barlow said.

"Unlikely. Chang flew to China from Charles de Gaulle, so we would have seen some cases in Paris by now. He either brought the bug with him to Tibet in a hermetically sealed biohazard transport container, which would have been extraordinarily difficult to conceal, or something bit him in the rain forest of Eastern Tibet. My money is on the latter."

The president loosened his tie, unbuttoned his collar, and took a seat behind his desk. Leaning back, he folded his hands behind his head and looked up at the ceiling. "You're probably right, but let's game this out anyway. Assuming Taiwan is behind the outbreak, what's the motive?"

"Well, for starters, Taiwan's current leader, President Tang, is obsessed with independence from China—something Beijing has vowed to prevent at any cost. Violently, if necessary. Tang's landslide election last May suggests the Taiwanese people are willing to call the mainland's bluff. So, to get the ball rolling, Tang releases a debilitating virus deep within the PRC's most politically unstable region: Tibet. Overnight, he creates a perfect storm for his enemy—a public health crisis *and* a political crisis—and it only takes two weeks and one foot soldier. Hypothetically speaking."

"Taiwan draws Beijing's attention and resources into the hinterland. Away from the coast," Barlow added. "Is Tang planning an offensive strike on the mainland, perhaps? Maybe take out some of those missiles pointing at him from across the strait?"

"No, he wouldn't have to go that far. Tang doesn't need to degrade China's military capability to neutralize the threat. He only needs to make it too politically hazardous for China to invade his island. If the mainland were falling apart, Beijing would be completely preoccupied with restoring internal stability. Zhongnanhai wouldn't risk adding Taiwan to their problems."

"There's still a major flaw in Tang's plan. Two, actually," Barlow said.

Allyson agreed. She'd already grappled with the obvious contradictions of a Taiwanese bioattack scenario, but she allowed the president to enumerate the tactical defects. She knew he enjoyed the mental gymnastics of intelligence work. It probably conjured nostalgic memories of his days at the helm of the CIA.

"A virus is too damn unpredictable," Barlow said. "You can't just point and shoot. With so much cross-strait commerce and tourism, there's no way Tang could ensure the epidemic wouldn't spread to Taipei. His people could suffer immeasurable casualties. Independence from the PRC would be the least of his worries. No one is that masochistic."

Allyson blinked. Power-hungry men did monstrous things to satiate their appetites. She'd even seen Barlow cross the line once or twice. Besides, an underdog like Taiwan, facing a military powerhouse like the PRC, would see vast advantages to biological warfare. Why fight with a few hundred thousand men when you could strike the enemy with an army of a billion microbes?

Regardless, the president had a point. A lot of warm bodies hopped back and forth across the narrow body of water separating the two foes, and that greatly increased Taiwan's risk of spillover.

The sheer unpredictability was a major problem with the Taiwan theory.

"And the second flaw?" Allyson prompted.

"That's easy. It didn't work!" the president replied, throwing up his hands. "Within twenty-four hours, every intel agency on the planet confirmed Chang as NSB—a Taiwanese spy! President Tang's plan only works if he maintains plausible deniability, but Taipei made no serious attempt to obscure their man's identity. The NSB connection hasn't gone public yet, but surely it will. The Chinese will rally around the government and demand retaliation. Beijing will pulverize Taipei. That's the opposite effect Tang would want."

"Taiwan says Chang isn't one of theirs," Allyson pointed out, playing the devil's advocate.

"Which tells us nothing. That's the standard bullshit response whenever a spy is caught, no matter the circumstances."

"So, Tang's innocent because a professional intelligence service would never be so sloppy?" Allyson could think of a few bungled CIA ops. Bay of Pigs, Mogadishu, Benghazi. Some of her own ops would probably make that list too, but she'd never admit it publicly.

"Not exactly. It's just that they'd use someone new—someone with no footprint—who couldn't be linked to Taiwanese intelligence. Besides, what Chang did, it was a suicide mission. Why sacrifice a trained operative with a growing résumé of foreign postings if you don't have to? I wouldn't."

The two veteran spooks sat in silence. Allyson finished her Scotch. They were having the wrong conversation, and they both knew it. Frankly, it didn't matter if Taipei was responsible for the outbreak or not. Beijing blamed President Tang and was preparing to hit back. What really mattered was how President Barlow would respond if the PRC invaded one of America's allies.

The president spoke first. "What are my options, Cam?"

"Don't you think that's a question for Sullivan?" Allyson asked. Nathan Sullivan, the president's national security adviser, was notoriously hawkish on matters concerning the People's Republic of China. He'd challenged Barlow in a fierce primary battle for the Democratic nomination and lambasted the would-be president for "letting China cheat its way to the top." When Barlow tapped Sullivan for a prestigious cabinet post, it shocked the Beltway, but Allyson wasn't surprised. She knew the president shared some of Sullivan's ideological realism, and the two men had history predating their political rivalry. Barlow would probably even claim they were friends if pressed.

"I've already met with Nate. I want to know what *you* think," Barlow said.

The director paused for a beat, collected her thoughts, and chose her words carefully. "It's difficult to ignore an act of Congress."

"The Taiwan Relations Act doesn't tie our hands completely. What about strategic ambiguity?"

"There's nothing ambiguous about our relationship with Taiwan," Allyson answered. "We've been arming them since seventy-nine. Sure, the TRA doesn't *legally* commit us to defending Taipei, but four decades of foreign policy precedent sends a pretty strong message."

"I could argue we've softened our support of Taiwan in favor of the mainland. We've formally recognized the People's Republic and embraced their 'One China' credo. Carter tore up the Mutual Defense Treaty we made with the Taiwanese. Taipei has no guarantee from us."

Allyson scoffed. "In 1996, it had two guarantees."

"What?"

Allyson counted on her fingers for emphasis. "USS *Nimitz* and USS *Independence*. First, Beijing got fussy and fired test missiles into the Taiwan Strait, conducted amphibious assault exercises, ramped up troops in Fujian. So, Clinton sent not one but two carrier battle groups right up their asshole. The One China idea works for us because the alternative is messy. We'll support the status quo as long as it maintains peace in the Asia-Pacific. If Taipei declares independence, Beijing invades. That's pretty easy to predict, and we don't want that to happen. Then there's Russia. Which side would Moscow support? Hell, even Pyongyang could get in the game—take advantage of the chaos and breach the thirty-eighth parallel. Then the whole region implodes."

"That's all a little sensational, don't you think?"

Allyson smirked. "Probably not half as dramatic as what you got from Nate."

"That's actually true," Barlow said, smiling. "Nate described China as a clean-cut honors student with a pocketful of Rohypnol. You can't turn your back for a second."

"How urbane," Allyson said. She could only imagine Sullivan's advice. The man was probably warming up the nukes already. Modern diplomacy demanded finesse and subtlety, not the reckless bluster of the 1980s.

"I've met President Li," Barlow said. "He wants stability in the region as much as we do. However imprecise, the current arrangement has worked well for everyone for a long time."

Barlow fidgeted with a ballpoint pen. Allyson recognized the old habit. It meant the president wasn't telling her everything. Then again, full disclosure was her responsibility, not his.

"The fact is," Allyson said, "Beijing knows if they lay a finger on that little island, we'll get involved. Period. It's the only reason they didn't invade decades ago, and it's the reason President Li won't invade now. Even as payback for this outbreak."

Barlow set down his pen, which rolled toward the edge of the desk before catching on a row of tangled paper clips. He leaned on his forearms, shoulders hunched. Allyson knew the president was in pain. The migraines had started shortly after Inauguration Day. Barlow hid the condition well, but a handful of his closest advisers knew when it got bad. The president became temperamental, made snap judgments. Mostly still good judgments, thankfully. For now.

The time for sporty intellectual sparring had concluded, and the weight of the office returned. "Who's your guy in China?" Barlow asked, his voice grimmer.

"Officer Marc Chen *was* my guy in China, but he's been missing for over a week," Allyson answered.

"Dead?"

"Probably."

Barlow frowned.

"I'm sending in Olen Grave," Allyson said. "He'll have unprecedented access to the epidemiological investigation."

"Media cover?"

"AP stringer." Allyson waved a hand dismissively. "Li wanted transparency."

"There's more to that," Barlow said.

"Most certainly. But we'll play along, as long as we're getting decent intel."

"You're taking a big risk, Cam. It's probably too dangerous," Barlow warned.

"You want me to pull Grave out?"

"Of course not," Barlow replied. "Grave worked for you at Langley, right? Counterproliferation?"

"He specializes in biochemical. Got a real knack for arms dealing," Allyson explained.

"This op is different. These aren't half-wit desert dwellers. He's got to stay under the radar."

"Relax, Jim. Grave's a natural. He's going to keep a low profile." Allyson paused. "There is a minor complication."

The president rubbed his eyes.

"The intel about Chang Yingjie. It came in less than three hours ago." Allyson set her empty glass on the table. "Grave doesn't know that patient zero was a Taiwanese spy. There's no way to tell him until he initiates contact. Our guy could be walking into a firestorm."

10

Lhasa, Tibetan Autonomous Region, People's Republic of China

SUNLIGHT BEAMED THROUGH the aircraft's oval windows. It nearly blinded Olen, but at least, with the velvet hood removed, he could finally get a clear sense of his surroundings. His neck ached from the stop-and-go car ride that had whipped him around for the last hour, and it felt good to inhale something other than his own hot breath. Moments ago, his captors had frog-marched him across a hard-packed surface—a tarmac, he'd guessed—and then up a steep staircase that clanged with each step. The wind smelled like jet fuel.

Olen studied the plane's cabin. His buddy Maverick wasn't around, just a pouty-faced soldier who removed Olen's handcuffs and motioned him toward the rear of the plane. It was definitely a military aircraft, but a swanky one, like a five-star hotel room with wings.

In the back, a young woman sat behind a shiny wooden desk with deep spirals carved into its legs. Olen doubted it was her plane. Her furrowed brow and steely concentration definitely said *worker bee*. Plus, she wore the sensible, rubber-soled shoes of an ER nurse—someone who spent the day on her feet. The woman alternated between scribbling in a notepad and feverishly typing into her laptop, a jet-black ponytail swishing behind her. Her sleeveless tank top showed off the lean musculature of her arms.

"I'm Kipton Stone with the—" Olen started to say to the busy bee.

The woman popped an index finger to silence Olen's introduction while her other hand clacked away at the laptop.

Olen waited a beat, then tried again, this time in his deep, reporter-man voice. "I'm with the Associated Press, and—"

Her stinger finger sprang up again. Olen sighed. This woman was clearly accustomed to putting noisy boys in their place. He tried not to take it personally. Judging by the three Red Bull cans lined up in a neat row on the desk, labels out, her intensity was borderline compulsive. And then there was the Fitbit on her left wrist, jewelry for the step-counting, five AM CrossFit warrior. Olen knew the type, evidenced by a growing list of hypercompetitive ex-girlfriends.

Olen watched her fluttering fingers and attempted one final thrust. "I'm supposed to meet the team leader. Is this his plane?"

The pitter-patter typing stopped. "What makes you think this isn't *my* plane?" the woman said.

"Oh, I just assumed—"

"This aircraft belongs to General Huang Yipeng," she snapped. "It's on loan."

"I see. Well, I'm looking for the man in charge of the field investigation. Is he onboard?"

"*She's* right here. I'm Dr. Zhou Weilin, the lead investigator. Unless you brought me more caffeine, then scram. I have very little time." She spoke pristine English.

Olen doubted Beijing would assign someone so young to lead an investigation of such significance. Either the woman was a scientific savant or the Chinese were jerking him around. "Jo? That's an unusual name. Is it short for Josephine?" Olen asked.

"Zhou is my family name. We introduce ourselves differently in China," the doctor responded.

"Oh, my apologies, Miss . . . uh, how do you spell it?"

Dr. Zhou grabbed a ballpoint pen, scratched out a few Chinese characters on a yellow legal pad, and slid it across the table without looking up.

Olen squinted at the pad.

The doctor exhaled slowly. "I allow foreigners to call me Jo. Keeps things simple, and at least it's pronounced the same way."

"Well, it's a pleasure to meet you, Jo," Olen said. "And it's an honor to be included on such an important assignment. I promise to stay out of your way, as much as I can help it." Olen flashed his signature smile and settled into a leather chair. He marveled at the pages of handwritten notes sprawled across Jo's desk—mostly tangles of complex equations. An iPad peeked out from the pile. On the screen was a diagram that looked like a bell curve.

"What's this? Is it part of your investigation?" Olen, like most spies, cherished working under media cover. A reporter could ask the most intrusive questions without raising suspicion.

Jo shot him a piss-off look that made his skin tingle.

"Hey, your buddies took all my stuff," he said. "I'd ask Google if I could, I swear." Olen played the American ignoramus quite well. Most likely, President Li's staff had promised to send the doctor a wallflower who could work as a passive observer. Olen had never liked walls. Or flowers.

"It's the epidemic curve—a model of the disease's progression," Jo said. "Well, it's my hypothesis, anyway."

"I'm not sure I follow."

Jo leaned over the desk and traced the graph's smooth line with her finger from left to right. "The line rises gradually with the first few cases. A handful of patients get sick, but at that point, hometown doctors generally don't know they're dealing with something out of the ordinary. Cases mushroom, and the disease feeds on the locals. That's what you see here." She pointed to the sudden rise on the graph. "That's when we know we have an epidemic."

"But then the line drops again," Olen remarked. "Why does the curve decline? Wouldn't the outbreak just continue to spread faster and faster with each newly infected person? What stops the contagion?"

Slow down, cowboy, Olen thought. *Pull her in gently.*

"Not necessarily," Jo answered. "Most of the time, an epidemic will taper off naturally as the virus depletes the pool of easy victims—children, the elderly."

"You said it's just a hypothesis. How—"

"This is complicated science, Mr. Stone. A hypothesis isn't just a wild guess. Our models are based on empirical data," Jo explained.

"How do you get your data?" Olen asked with genuine curiosity. He'd spent most of his career preventing terrorists from weaponizing biological agents *before* they created a public health crisis. He had no experience with outbreaks and epidemic curves.

"Simple. We count the sick. A full epidemiological survey of the region began six days ago," Jo said. "Research teams from the Ministry of Health record every new case. We track the disease's progression and determine how long it takes to overcome the victim."

"Overcome?" Olen questioned.

"To kill them," Jo responded clinically. She recounted her work with such emotional detachment that others would probably call her heartless, but Olen understood. Some jobs required clearheaded objectivity, especially when death was routine. For this woman, it was just another day at the office.

"So, where are we on this curve now? Have the cases peaked?" Olen asked.

"New cases are still emerging rapidly, so we can't yet predict the epidemic's apex."

"Why not?" Olen was pleased by how easily Jo was opening up, but he was quickly getting out of his depth with the science talk.

"I based this hypothetical curve on the assumption of a fixed population—the people living within the Tibetan Autonomous Region. The TAR spans a half million square miles, but it is home to barely three million people—a relatively small population by Chinese standards. That's why quarantine is so crucial. If contained within the TAR, the virus will burn through most victims in a few weeks, and the crisis will be over."

Jo paused her rapid-fire explanation. Olen sensed she was holding something back.

"But this bug won't die out so easily, will it?" he asked.

"If the virus escapes the TAR and gets loose somewhere with a larger population—a major city, for example—it will explode.

The massive pool of new, vulnerable targets would feed the contagion. Twenty million people live in Beijing alone. Complete isolation of a city like that would be impossible. We couldn't contain it. The constant flow of tourists and business travelers would carry the disease to Tokyo, Seoul, even as far as London and New York."

The doctor tapped the iPad, and the epidemic curve shifted. Olen's eyes widened as he studied the adjusted graph. The line rose rapidly, as in the first model, but this time it had no peak. The curve continued off the screen in a perpetual climb. The worst-case scenario.

"In the fourteenth century, the bubonic plague wiped out one in five humans on the planet," Jo said. "Five hundred years later, the Spanish flu claimed another one hundred million. Blood River virus tears through human hosts, and it mutates quickly. It has the potential to be one of the deadliest infectious diseases mankind has ever encountered, worse than the plague and the Spanish flu combined. If we don't figure out how to stop it, the virus could annihilate the human race. This isn't just about Tibet. The entire world is at risk," the virologist warned soberly. "So, you see now why I've got to get back to work."

*   *   *

Jo thought about the new patients in Beijing and Chengdu. They were the only cases of BRV45 outside the TAR so far, but there would be more. The government had slapped a top-secret classification on all of it. If people knew how fast the virus was spreading, panic would erupt around the world. Governments would first point fingers, then missiles. Ultimately, someone would pay for the catastrophe.

True, her epidemiological models were theoretical. A whole host of variables could change the outcome. Unpredictability came with the territory, but her equations gave her a feeling of control. Better yet, her computer models ignored the depth of suffering, allowing her to stay focused on the big picture. Her data tables and graphs made no reference to the pain of watching a bright-eyed teenage son degenerate into a stinking heap of flesh or an infant daughter suck in her last breath. Jo blocked out the dread, choosing to concentrate on the dispassionate science. With a tap, her iPad could calculate the rate of the disease's transmission and the rate of an infected person's recovery as a function of time. Just math, neat and tidy.

Jo wondered if she'd become too callous over the years. Had she completely lost the ability to empathize with the sick and dying? And what about the grieving families? Jo knew the pain of loss. She'd felt it herself as a six-year-old girl. *You remember that feeling, don't you? That pang in your heart muscle when your parents never came home?*

Jo pushed the memory from her mind. To hell with empathy. There was a ticking clock to worry about. Her iPad told her so.

* * *

Throughout the interview, Olen tested the doctor. He asked probing questions about the crisis and the government's response, and Jo answered with remarkable candor. Scientists often struggled with the concept of state secrecy. They were hardwired to believe that knowledge belonged to all humankind and no nation held the exclusive right to scientific discoveries that could advance humanity. Secrecy hindered progress and made research annoyingly cumbersome.

The doctor's enthusiasm was also operationally convenient. Utterly engrossed in her explanation of viral vectors, Jo never noticed Olen attaching a listening device to the surface of her desk. It was easy to miss. The NSA's tech team had built the bug using revolutionary nanotechnology—some real-deal spy shit. While Jo shuffled through stacks of papers, hunting for a specific data report, Olen pressed a small, round sticker about the size of an aspirin into the tabletop. The thin plastic melted into the smooth surface as it bonded with the wood grain on a molecular level. After three or four seconds, the difference in texture and color was indiscernible.

The device picked up vibrations in the wood caused by sound waves. It could separate human speech from ambient noise and then send the data to Maryland via a wireless satellite uplink. The challenge was keeping the bug powered up. A battery would have made it too large, so it ran on light it soaked up with an array of microscopic photovoltaic receivers. A paperweight would shut it down completely, but it was better than nothing. If a hotshot Chinese general usually flew on this plane, U.S. intelligence could learn a lot by eavesdropping on his conversations. The boys at the NSA would probably cream their jeans.

Olen left Jo to her work and went hunting for a puffy chair. Toward the front of the cabin, a trio of soldiers amused themselves with a deck of cards. They razzed the loser after each hand, in the manner of all young men. They obviously hadn't seen Jo's doomsday graphs. The world was about to get a serious wake-up call.

CHAPTER

11

International waters

THE MARINER LET out the mainsail, perpendicular to the wind, and allowed the steady breeze to push the sloop westward. Sailboats would soon become more popular, but not right away. At first, people would flee the cities and head inland, to the country-side. They'd hole themselves up in farmhouses and cottages. The isolation would protect them from contracting the virus, which would ravage the dense, urban areas. The grocery stores would run out of food, gas would become more valuable than gold, kitchen faucets would slow to a drip, and entire skylines would fall into darkness. Then those rural farmhouses, with their natural wells, backyard gardens, and flimsy front doors, would be under siege. The desperate, starving, diseased masses would rip them apart, seeking refuge. Before long, sailboats would be the only safe place left. A sky full of wind, an ocean full of fish, and total seclu-sion from the madness swallowing the world.

The thought was pleasing, seductive. And not without irony. A season surviving in open water would ultimately reground humanity. In the resulting hush, unheard for centuries, human-kind would once again listen to the secret of the sea, receive its wisdom in the melodic whispers of waves and wind. Was it Long-fellow who had written of this?

> *Helmsman! For the love of heaven*
> *Teach me, too, that wondrous song!*

Yes, to be HELMSMAN. To sing and to teach. To steer the course to a new world order. That was the greatest responsibility, thought the mariner. And the greatest privilege.

CHAPTER

12

Outside Dzongsar Village, Tibetan Autonomous Region,
People's Republic of China

THE HUMVEE'S MIGHTY tires crushed through clumps of gravel littering the road. Olen's boots vibrated against the floor. After the epidemiological research team landed in Lhasa, PLA soldiers had divided them into three army transport vehicles. A female private had tried to usher Olen into the rear vehicle—a cozy Land Rover packed with five scientists—but he'd politely resisted and followed Jo into the lead car. The center vehicle was a cargo truck with a spacious flatbed that hauled a grab bag of expensive-looking laboratory equipment.

Olen spread out comfortably, draping his long arms across the back of the seat. It felt good as hell to be back in the field. Nothing like the bounce of a no-shit Humvee to tickle the pickle.

"I need to brief you on quarantine procedure," Jo said, all business.

"Okay, what do I need to know?" Olen asked.

"We don't know much about BRV45, but we *do* know it's not airborne, so we won't need masks, generally speaking. However, it's a different story when engaging the locals directly. The disease causes severe internal hemorrhaging that allows blood to seep into the lungs, so coughing can release contaminated droplets. Even a tiny speck can infect you if it gets into your eyes or mouth. It's highly likely the virus spreads through sweat too."

"Sweat? Really?"

"And semen, of course," Jo added.

"Roger that. Don't touch the semen."

Jo continued. "Surgical masks, goggles, and double-layer latex gloves are required when interacting with patients."

"That's it?" Olen asked.

"There isn't time to train you on the finer techniques of infection control, so just wash your hands as much as possible and don't touch anything I don't touch. Better yet, don't touch anything at all."

The distant shimmer of Dzongsar Village came into view. Olen lurched forward as the Humvee squealed to a halt.

"Why are we stopping?" Jo asked. Her brow wrinkled with concern. The driver shut off the engine and abruptly exited the vehicle. Jo said something in Mandarin, then switched to English. "What's going on? We're almost to the checkpoint. There's no time for a pit stop, gentlemen."

The driver yanked open Jo's door and motioned for her to get out. "This is as far as we go, ma'am. Please step out of the vehicle."

"What are you talking about? The Quarantine Zone is still three miles away. It's getting dark. We've got to keep moving," Jo said.

The soldier avoided eye contact. "You'll have to walk from here, ma'am."

Olen had seen it before—the look in the soldier's eyes. He was terrified. Jo must have noticed too.

"This disease feeds on fear and weakness," Jo said. "Now is not a convenient time to lose your nerve, Sergeant."

The soldier bunched his fists. His face flushed. Jo, a civilian—a *female*—had questioned his valor. When Jo didn't budge, the man roughly extracted the virologist from the back seat. Jo staggered onto the dirt road, recovering her balance.

Olen's door flew open next. He raised his hands, palms out, to signal cooperation. "Okay, buddy. I get it. End of the road."

The soldier pulled Olen from the back seat by his shirt collar. The man's grip was weak. He couldn't have been a day over seventeen. Olen could toss him twenty yards—one-handed, probably—but journalists didn't toss soldiers. Damn shame. So, Olen followed instructions and politely stepped out of the Humvee.

Jo continued to object. "You have orders to take my team to the provisional laboratory *inside* the Q-Zone. It's at least an hour walk to gate one from here. And what about my gear? We've got a truckload of equipment to deliver." Jo tried to sound authoritative, but she failed to penetrate the driver's unflappable bearing.

"Ma'am, the army has ordered level three isolation of the Q-Zone. Entry is highly restricted and no individuals are permitted to leave. If we pass through that gate, we're not coming out," the driver explained firmly. "You still want to go in, fine by me. But you walk."

"Level three!" Jo shouted. "Just this morning my field research team traveled freely across the checkpoint. The Ministry of Health has designated this site level two. Level *three* is completely unreasonable. How could we possibly work effectively if imprisoned inside the gates? Who ordered the escalation?"

The petite virologist stood inches from the driver, assuming her most confrontational posture. Her nose barely reached the man's throat. He didn't appear remotely intimidated.

"This comes straight from Beijing, ma'am. General Huang signed the order this afternoon."

Olen perked up. Did the military have the authority to lock down the Q-Zone? Why was the Ministry of Health completely unaware? Was this some kind of martial law? In any case, nothing Jo could say was going to convince the soldiers to drive them through the gates.

The wind picked up. Olen looked skyward. No stars. Lightning strobed across a thick layer of clouds. They needed to get moving if they expected to beat the storm to Dzongsar.

The doctor pivoted sharply and marched toward the rear vehicle. Olen watched her silhouette, backlit by the Land Rover's powerful headlights. She approached the cluster of bemused scientists congregating on the road. Olen couldn't hear their conversation, but his instincts told him to hang back until the tension diffused.

Within a minute, Jo returned. The five scientists climbed back into the rear vehicle. The Land Rover executed a three-point turn and lumbered away, heading back toward Lhasa.

Jo stood beside Olen, hands on hips. Her rage seemed to have subsided, but not her determination. "Level three isolation is extremely risky, even for professionals. Infection is very difficult to avoid over a protracted period of exposure in an active hot zone. Those men and women are good people, with families who care about them. They're scientists—not soldiers. I won't ask anyone to go on a suicide mission. That goes for you too, Mr. Stone. The Humvee will take you back to the city."

Jo didn't wait for a rebuttal. She turned and headed toward the cargo truck.

"What about you?" Olen called after her. Her grit continued to impress him. "You're not going to walk there, are you? In the dark? Alone?"

"I don't expect to be mugged, if that's what you're concerned about." She jabbed a finger toward the faint glimmer on the horizon. "The answers I need are in there. We don't even know the primary vectors of transmission. The virus could be spread by bats, rodents, maybe even insects. If I don't figure this out soon, it won't matter how many fences the army puts up. This entire region will be overrun by the disease." Jo pounded twice on the back of the cargo truck to signal its driver to unlock the hatch.

"In that case, I'm sticking with you. If we're all facing infection anyway, I might as well have China's best virus hunter by my side to protect me," Olen said.

Jo smiled for the first time that evening. She twisted her ponytail into a tight bun, baring the slender nape of her neck.

"Fine. Then load up. We'll need to take as much gear as we can carry on our backs." Jo lowered the truck's heavy rear hatch, revealing stacks of neatly arranged wooden crates. She began heaving the crates out of the bay. "Most of the light machinery was loaded first, so it's all near the front of the truck bed. The centrifuges will be too heavy to bring with us, but they're only backups. The provisional lab should have a few that are still operational." She crouched and ripped into one of the smaller crates. "There's extra agar, glassware, and syringes in this one. I'll need those to collect and preserve my samples. The box by your left foot has some antiviral medication and sedatives for treating the sick. Here, give me a hand with this one."

Olen rushed to Jo's side to help her pry off the wooden planks stapled across the top of the crate. The soldiers paced restlessly. They wouldn't stick around for much longer. Jo sorted through the carefully packaged crate and expertly triaged the most crucial items. When her rucksack bulged to capacity, she reached for Olen's without bothering to ask for it first. His bag had ample room now that he'd surrendered his camera and laptop to the goons at the airport.

Jo surveyed her work. Shards of splintered wood and foam core packing material lay strewn across the road. The two swelling rucksacks balanced against each other on the ground. "It's the best we can do." She wiped her dusty hands on her pants and brushed aside a rogue strand of hair. Her eyes shone with tenacity. She looked like a woman heading into battle, ready for hand-to-hand combat if necessary. "Let's get moving," Jo ordered.

* * *

Inky darkness dripped from the branches overhead, coating the primitive roadway. The PLA vehicles were long gone. The village flickered in the distance. The occasional flash of lightning revealed the narrow, unpaved path ahead. Walking single file, with Jo in the lead, they trod cautiously to avoid muddy sinkholes.

Leaves rattled around them. The breeze grew colder. On cue, the sky cracked open and the deluge began. Jo wiped rainwater from her face. The steepening uphill slope and the weight of her pack eroded what little energy she had left, but she refused to let it show. Especially since the American journalist seemed unfazed, totally in his element. His soaked flannel shirt clung to his body, revealing the bulges of his arms and shoulders. The man was built like a tank, industrial grade. Good, she thought. That meant he wouldn't slow her down. And she could make him carry heavy things.

Sheets of water flung in all directions. The blurry lights of Dzongsar still looked so far away.

CHAPTER

13

Beijing, People's Republic of China

"COME IN," GENERAL Huang barked at the staccato rapping. It was late, but Lieutenant Wang knew that Huang was restless. The general often said insomnia was the cruelest side effect of an active mind. The man's usual soporific—Dostoyevsky paired with a full-bodied Tempranillo—must've had no effect.

Lieutenant Wang twisted the knob and tentatively opened the door. A summons to the general's personal residence after midnight was not unprecedented but rare enough to raise alarm. He hoped it wasn't about the American reporter. The Ministry of Foreign Affairs had yet to provide the man's full dossier. Cooperation between the MFA and PLA had degraded over the past few months, turning even simple requests into painstaking exercises in intragovernmental diplomacy. Wang had promised a friend at the ministry's home office a ride on a military transport to Hainan Island in exchange for the reporter's visa paperwork and photo. The docs should've arrived in Wang's in-box an hour ago, but they still hadn't come through.

When awoken by the familiar chime of the general's text message, Wang had scrambled into his impeccably pressed uniform, which bore a collection of variegated service ribbons. A brass pin decorated his right lapel—a flaming torch in the center of a crimson sunburst. The badge had been worn by revolutionary Red Guards in the 1960s and was a gift from Wang's late grandfather. The lieutenant affixed the vintage symbol to his jacket every day to remind himself of the importance of upholding one's convictions, especially in turbulent times.

General Huang was dressed considerably more casual. He wore a yellow linen bathrobe, loosely secured at the waist. An overstuffed wing-back chair swallowed his languid form.

"Sir, I came as soon as I could. Has something happened?" Wang asked with concern.

The general snorted. Deep plum laced his lazy grin. "Why Tibet?" He tilted his head back in deep reflection, and Wang sighed. It was too damn late for pontification, but alas, he was in no position to protest.

"You're referring to the outbreak. Why Tibet and not the coast?" Wang played along.

Huang refilled his wineglass. "When I was a boy," he began, "a Tibetan woman from Nyêmo—a nun, in fact—claimed she could summon Buddhist gods into her body at will. It sounded like nonsense to a rational person, but not to those living in the mystical land of Tibet. Supernatural mediums, voluntary possession—these things were not considered peculiar to those people. In short order, the villagers began to revere this woman for her alleged holy correspondence. They believed she had become a goddess." Huang tilted the bottle of Tempranillo toward Wang, who shook his head in polite refusal.

"But this goddess wasn't virtuous. She fed on the absurd credulity that only her specious religion could engender. Her little parlor trick made her respected, powerful. And the nun exercised this potent influence to assert a dark control over the impressionable community."

"Dark control?" Wang asked.

"It wasn't long before the murders began. Her army of warrior heroes, as they called themselves, savagely mutilated thirty-four people, mostly Party officials posted to Nyêmo. Did you know that, Xiao Wang?"

Wang had not.

Huang continued. "She didn't just have them killed. No. She instructed her followers to sever the victims' hands and feet. No one really knows why she did it—why she became consumed with such inhumane rage. The nun later explained that the Dalai Lama had visited her in the form of a bird and ordered her to carry out the violent attacks. Any reasonable medical professional would have diagnosed her as insane, locked her away. But no, not the Tibetans. To them, she was a god."

Huang paused. He swirled his glass. Finally, Wang broke the silence.

"So, why Tibet?" Wang tried not to sound impatient.

"You see, Xiao Wang, the Tibetans claim their religion is under siege. They assume we awaken every morning dreaming of new ways to suppress their way of life. Cultural genocide, they call it. How could this accusation be any further from the truth? Buddhism is one of the five officially recognized religions in China. Perhaps it's their own lack of conviction that threatens their culture."

"What do you mean?" Wang asked.

"Our traditions possess a certain . . . fortitude. A virility. Wouldn't you say?"

"Are you implying that Tibetan culture is too weak?"

"Precisely, Xiao Wang. Perhaps their cultural inadequacy makes them susceptible to more dominant influences. The Tibetan resistance blames the Chinese government for restricting their religious freedoms, but history reveals just how eagerly the Tibetan people have turned against their own faith willingly. During the Cultural Revolution, Tibetans destroyed hundreds of their own Buddhist monasteries. They simply replaced one sacred symbol with another—the Great Helmsman, Chairman Mao.

"We see the same thing happening now. This time it's the Dalai Lama. The man is a fraud. A cult leader. He's obsessed with the separation of Tibet from China at any cost. Even if it means self-destruction. And the Tibetan people lionize this false deity just as they did that murderous nun from Nyêmo. Time and again, Tibet has proven itself to be nothing but a vessel for the powerful to fill with their own agenda. Tibet is not complicated. It's a tool. If used correctly, it can be quite valuable."

"I see. So, given the state of affairs, how do you plan to capitalize on Tibet's . . . infirmity?" Wang asked with genuine interest.

The general's eyes pinched into a squint. He took another sip of wine, letting Wang's question ferment for a moment.

"Hmm," Huang finally vocalized. "I want you to release the identity of patient zero."

Lieutenant Wang was certain he'd misheard the general.

"The Taiwanese intelligence officer, Chang Yingjie," Huang continued. "I want you to leak his name and affiliation to the media. Not just Xinhua; those sycophants are in President Li's back pocket. The *Post* and the *Times*."

"You want me to tell the American press that Chang was a Taiwanese spy?"

"Leak it carefully. Make it nonattributable. Anonymous source. It mustn't be traced back to this office," Huang said.

"Of course. But sir, this will lead to major instability. Ever since the Taiwanese election, our relationship with Taipei has been tenuous, to put it mildly. Maybe we should—"

"Xiao Wang." Huang cut him off. The general's eyes flared intensely. "There is no *we*. Is that understood?"

The lieutenant swallowed his rebuttal and nodded obsequiously. "Yes, sir."

"Taiwan is getting away with the most brazen act of bioterrorism in history. Unchallenged!" Huang sat up and leaned toward his aide. His voice rumbled. "We will not be victims," he declared. "Not anymore."

"Yes, sir." Wang stiffened to attention and waited to be dismissed.

Huang's tense expression faded, and he sank back into the chair. "This wine is piss," he said with a chuckle. "I'm never going to be able to rest."

Huang looked up at Lieutenant Wang, whose posture remained rigid. The general impulsively reached for the fabric of Wang's pant leg, just above the young officer's knee. Wang didn't react, not even as the general's hand moved slowly up his thigh.

"You know, Chairman Mao was an insomniac too," Huang said. "He swallowed sleeping pills by the fistful. I understand why he did it, but drugs aren't for me. They cloud the mind."

The lieutenant could feel his boss's knuckles brushing against his testicles through the thin wool of his trousers.

"You'll help me get to sleep, Xiao Wang," the general rasped, opening his robe.

Lieutenant Wang held his breath, dropped to his knees, and obediently lowered his head into the older man's lap.

14

Dzongsar Village, Tibetan Autonomous Region,
People's Republic of China

O LEN AND Jo trudged through sticky mud and soaking rain
for more than two hours. When the torrent finally let up,
Olen could see the uniformed figures of three PLA soldiers guarding the entrance to the Q-Zone. Their spindly arms and legs swam
inside pine-green camouflage. They looked like children playing
schoolyard war games.

When the sentries spotted two drenched drifters staggering
toward their post, their military training kicked in and they assumed
defensive postures. Olen was well acquainted with the business end
of a firearm. Nevertheless, staring into the barrels of QBZ-95 automatic assault rifles clutched by anxious teenagers would make any
man nervous. One of the soldiers shouted in Mandarin and then
blew a whistle. The high-pitched squeal further agitated the other
riflemen, their hearts pulsating in their bird chests.

"He says to stop walking and kneel on the ground," Jo trans-
lated, her voice strained.

"So much for a warm welcome. Guess we look worse than I
thought," Olen quipped, kneeling beside the doctor. Jo shielded
her eyes from the blinding spotlight bathing the roadway.

The soldier with the whistle barked another command, and Jo raised her hands behind her head. Olen did the same. Even if he couldn't understand the guard, Olen recognized the man's skittish tone. It was the taut desperation of a sleep-deprived combatant. Except this was no war zone. Why were they so high-strung, itching for a reason to shoot?

The riflemen advanced in a crouch-jog. They trained their muzzles on the interlopers. Six black boots splashed through pools of rainwater. The whistle blower shouted again, his voice cracking a little. Olen watched Jo in his peripheral vision. Her gaze looked focused and clear-eyed. She spoke in Mandarin with measured calm. Her reply seemed to confuse one of the sentries, who thrust his weapon in Olen's direction.

Jo continued, but the guard cut her off. His eyes flared and he shouted threateningly, this time in English. "No reporters! Absolutely no reporters in the Quarantine Zone!"

The man-boy moved in, tightening his grip on the QBZ-95. He pressed the muzzle into Jo's cheek. Whatever she'd said, the guards didn't believe her. Why would they? She'd walked up to the gates of the country's most restricted territory, in the middle of the night, with a foreigner. Understandably, it had raised a few red flags.

The young men continued shouting. "Absolutely no foreigners! Stop lying! You are not authorized to be here! Stay down!"

Olen scanned each of the three soldiers. They weren't thinking clearly, and that meant they'd get sloppy. The man hovering above Olen held his weapon too low, which weakened his control. A swift jab to the rib cage and the man would reactively angle his rifle to the side. A reflexive shot would miss Olen completely; disarming the soldier would be a breeze. The sentry guarding Jo leaned too far forward in a narrow stance, resting his weight on his front leg and destabilizing his balance. Olen could tackle him, roll underneath the guard's featherweight body, and use him as a human shield. From that position, he could use the first guard's weapon to take out the whistle blower. *Bam, bam, bam.* Piece of cake. But overtaking the three soldiers would wreck Olen's mission. Journalists didn't go full Rambo on armed Chinese soldiers. His cover would blow sky-high and VECTOR would lose its only opportunity to penetrate the Q-Zone. If Jo couldn't talk them down, though, he'd have no choice.

As Jo opened her mouth to speak, another female voice echoed from behind the barricades. "Dr. Zhou! Thank God you're finally here." A chubby Asian woman in dingy khaki cutoffs and a man's blue dress shirt ran to the waist-high barrier. The woman wore a baseball cap with the Baltimore Orioles logo stitched on the front. She appeared more American than Chinese but spoke English with a heavy accent. "There's been an accident at the lab," she said. "We've got to get back, pronto."

The guards looked puzzled. Their postures relaxed. The whistle blower turned his attention to the woman behind the gate. She seemed to be in charge.

"That's Dr. Zhou Weilin," the woman said. "She heads up this entire investigation. Geez, Jianheng. Let her through these gates."

The soldiers lowered their weapons, but Olen and Jo froze and waited for the whistle blower's response. "What about the man?" he asked.

"He's with me, Amy. He has permission to enter," Jo explained, sounding relieved at the well-timed appearance of her colleague.

"But he's American," the guard protested.

"Aw, heck, Jianheng. So am I," Amy said, coming out from behind the gate and approaching the group. "Well, half American, anyway." Amy bent over to catch her breath, a hand clasped on the guard's shoulder for balance. "Relax, Jianheng. If Dr. Zhou says the big boy is good, he's good." Amy waved Jo over. "Come on. The lab is only ten minutes in the Jeep."

The whistle blower grunted in agreement and motioned for his riflemen to open the gate. The soldiers looked even more juvenile without their weapons drawn.

"You said there'd been an accident. What happened, Amy?" Jo asked with concern as she and Olen crossed into the quarantined region.

"It's Dr. Sun," Amy replied, as she helped Jo and Olen load their gear into the black Jeep. "He's . . . he's infected. I think we're gonna lose him."

"Ru's *here*?" Jo wrinkled her nose in disbelief.

"Whose Dr. Sun?" Olen asked. He noticed Jo's hands tremble a bit before she shoved them into her jacket pockets.

"He's my husband," Jo replied.

15

Beijing, People's Republic of China

WANG DIDN'T BOTHER to flip on the lights. A few stray beams of moonlight bounced around the expansive work space, searching for an escape from the maze of cubicles. The workday had ended more than eight hours ago, but Wang was too agitated to relax. After leaving General Huang's chambers, he'd marched across the National Defense University campus to Building 31, the Office of the Superintendent. The general's office. Huang had assumed the position as head of the military academy shortly after ascending to the PLA chairmanship. All good leaders invested in developing the virile young men who would one day carry the torch of victory, Huang had argued. Wang wondered how many of those virile young men had visited the general's private quarters after hours. How many had sipped the Tempranillo and knelt, cherry lipped, before their emperor?

Wang was just relieved that General Huang hadn't asked about the reporter. He cursed his contact at the Ministry of Foreign Affairs for taking so long to deliver the American's dossier.

After a pair of blundering MSS intelligence officers picked up the reporter at Beijing International, Wang had managed to wrestle away all of their transportation responsibilities. The entire epidemiological investigation team had traveled to the TAR on General Huang's private jet, under the military's close watch. Babysitting the American had already consumed considerable resources and attention. President Li's insistence on media transparency was not only naïve but also unnecessarily risky. The 2PLA didn't have sufficient time to thoroughly vet the foreigner. He could be anyone.

Sitting at his computer, Wang entered a pass code—the first of three needed to access his top-secret email. When his in-box finally loaded, he groaned. Nothing from the MFA. He'd follow up with his friend in the morning.

Alone in the dark office, Wang considered the general's latest order. Huang's hostility toward Taipei seemed excessively nostalgic, he thought. Mao Zedong had chased the Nationalists off the mainland seventy years ago. The rebels had built a thriving society on the little island, thanks to American protection, and it drove Beijing mad. Mao had desperately wanted Taiwan back, and a generation later, men like General Huang kept the fantasy alive, clinging to the wistful ambition of China's founding strongman.

As far as Wang was concerned, Taiwan was a twenty-two-thousand-square-mile floating turd. An unflushable nuisance. A hostile seizure would bring about a crushing international backlash. And yet, dropping the matter would provoke the ire of prideful mainlanders. Zhongnanhai couldn't risk losing face with 1.4 billion citizens. So, for decades, Beijing had walked the high wire, careful not to fall on either side of the issue. Meanwhile, cross-strait trade blossomed, cultural and educational exchanges abounded, and each side prospered under the tacit entente. The delicate balance, for all its deficiencies, preserved the peace.

Or it had until about five months ago.

When the people of democratic Taiwan elected President Tang Chen-wai, they had sent a strong message to Beijing. Tang had run on a platform of independence, and his fiery calls for Taiwanese sovereignty had ignited his people's passions. He won by a landslide. Taiwan was primed for change.

Tang made global headlines with a fervent plea to the United Nations General Assembly: recognize an independent Taiwan, or condemn it to generations of humiliation at the mercy of an oppressive regime. Mere theatrics. China's veto would squash any such motion. Nevertheless, Tang had broadcast his message loud and clear. He'd walked right up to China's proverbial tightrope, swinging a sword.

If Wang leaked Taiwan's involvement in the epidemic, it would light a fuse, and General Huang had to know the consequences of such a strategy. Why take the risk? Wang thought about his visit to Huang's quarters earlier that night. His boss had been drinking, but certainly he hadn't been drunk.

Huang had Mao on his mind, that much was clear. The general had become increasingly obsessed with the departed chairman, which possibly explained Huang's erratic temperament. Mao Zedong had thrived on chaos, intentionally inflaming the masses, even when doing so seemed counterintuitive to the Communist cause. Early in his ascendency to power, Mao had encouraged the people to "bombard the headquarters" of his own Party simply to eliminate his more powerful political rivals. Was this General Huang's strategy too? Did he want to leak patient zero's identity as a Taiwanese spy to incite public outcry? The disclosure could result in a ruinous backlash against President Li's administration.

Whatever the general's reasons, orders were orders. The leak had to appear to have originated from within the Taiwanese government. Otherwise, the Western press would dismiss it as Chinese propaganda.

Wang reached under his desk and pressed a button on a console. The button lit up, indicating covert mode. The console scrambled his keystrokes and randomly rerouted his IP address through dummy servers scattered across the Asia-Pacific. With the simple push of a button, Wang became a ghost.

The lieutenant logged into an anonymous 163.com email account and created a new message. The note would contain a single word, yet its potential impact was immeasurable. Wang attached an image to the email. It was the same photograph of patient zero plastered on the front page of every global newspaper—the unremarkable head shot of a twentysomething Asian man staring blankly into the camera—but Wang's version wasn't cropped tight around the man's face. He attached the full, original image, a photograph of Chang Yingjie's official Taiwanese government ID. The uncropped image revealed the man's true name, birthday, and rank as a consul of the Ministry of Foreign Affairs, Republic of China, Taiwan. The last bit was false. The man actually worked for the National Security Bureau—Taiwan's civilian intelligence arm—but with minimal investigation, the press would discover he'd been stationed throughout Africa under diplomatic cover. The prototypical résumé of a spy.

Wang didn't enter a recipient's email address. He didn't intend to send the message. Following the same hackneyed—yet still surprisingly efficient—method employed by Al-Qaeda terrorists, Wang saved the email as a draft and closed the browser. A well-placed asset within President Tang's administration would log into the same 163.com account the next morning to discover the draft email. The contact would undoubtedly recoil from its bombshell attachment, but the instructions would be unambiguous, as explained by the note's simple message: Meiti.

Media.

CHAPTER

16

Dzongsar Village, Tibetan Autonomous Region,
People's Republic of China

"Ex-husband," Jo clarified as Amy revved the Jeep's muscular V8 engine.

Dr. Sun Ru had first caught Jo's attention at an academic conference on zoonotic viruses—pathogens that jumped from animals to humans. Ru was a third-year resident in the University of Hong Kong virology department and Jo was a fresh-faced virologist just out of medical school. The two doctors snickered in the back row of the world's dullest presentation on bovine tuberculosis and eventually ditched the stuffy auditorium for the hotel bar. Five drinks and two years later, they married at an enchanting lake house near Guilin. Jo was elated. The two things she loved most in life, science and Ru, had merged beautifully.

The wedding bliss faded almost immediately. Long hours in the lab, followed by longer stints in the field, created distance that went beyond the physical. Jo was prepared to make those personal sacrifices for the sake of scientific discovery. Ru was not.

The couple's second anniversary approached, and Jo was fourteen hundred miles away in Guangdong Province investigating an outbreak of avian flu. Ru urged her to return home. He'd made a reservation at their favorite restaurant, right on the lake, in Beijing's Houhai district. Jo refused. She was close to determining the disease's primary vector—probably a sick duck at a swampy street market. Hundreds had died already. Jo couldn't just leave. Didn't Ru understand?

Nevertheless, guilt overcame her. She'd neglected her husband. Again. There would always be another outbreak, but only one Ru. Jo left her team and hopped a late flight to Beijing. Shortly after midnight, her taxi pulled up to her apartment building. The windows were dark. Ru had probably turned in for the night. As expected, she found him in the bedroom, but he wasn't asleep. Neither was the twenty-year-old research assistant clawing at his naked back.

Jo had never loved Ru as much as she loved her job. But he should have confronted her, ended it, moved on. Jo could have forgiven Ru for betraying her trust—everyone had secrets—but she couldn't stay married to a coward. That was worse. The divorce was swift and final.

Separation from Ru had been easier than expected. Jo felt liberated from her nagging guilt and immersed herself in her work. Her career soared. The Ministry of Health promoted her to national director of epidemiology before her thirty-third birthday. She'd never felt more fulfilled.

Ru, meanwhile, remarried quickly. The moaning research assistant had turned out to be more than a fling. Now, Ru and Jo rarely spoke—she simply had nothing to say—but the two doctors crossed paths professionally from time to time. Every virologist in China was searching for answers to the Blood River virus outbreak. Jo had assumed they'd bump into one another eventually, but she hadn't known Ru was working *inside* the Q-Zone. He'd probably wanted it that way.

*   *   *

Amy expertly navigated the Jeep through the waterlogged roadway. The vehicle's rear tires flung bits of mud in its wake. The storm had passed, and the moon's blue light painted the midnight sky. Whitewashed buildings glowed shades of indigo with an apocalyptic iridescence. The village appeared completely deserted except for a stray dog resting in a patch of tall grass. The animal lifted its head curiously as the Jeep approached. Its eyes shone in the headlights.

"Dogs are unaffected by the virus," Amy pointed out, as if obligated to explain the presence of life.

"Thanks back there, by the way," Jo said. "Those guards would've turned us away."

"They would have done worse than that. Believe me," Amy said. "Everyone's had ants in their pants since we went to level three. What were you thinking, bringing an American? At least tell me he's a doctor. We could use the help."

"He's a writer," Jo answered.

"Oh, great. I was just thinking we were short on secretaries in the Q-Zone," Amy quipped.

"I'm a journalist—a reporter for the AP," Olen explained.

"He's been cleared by President Li's office. He's a little nosy but strong as a bull. Really great for hauling gear. Just try to be nice to him," Jo said, eliciting a grin from Olen.

Amy rolled her eyes. "Okeydokey, boss." She tilted her head toward the back seat but kept her eyes fixed on the road. "Hey, man. I'm Amy Chow, field director and hot zone tour guide. So, as long as you're in Dzongsar, that makes me the sheriff of your ass. Stay out of the way and we'll be best buds."

Olen bowed his head. "As you wish, Sheriff."

The windshield fogged up. Olen cranked his window down to let in a blast of cool air. The breeze smelled sulfurous, the way he imagined hell would smell.

After winding up a steep slope, they arrived at the base of an enormous structure. Amy threw the Jeep into park. The building looked ancient. Intricate geometric patterns were carved into the colorful trim of its multitiered roofs. The edifice rose regally from the crest of a hill overlooking Dzongsar Village. Olen was awe-struck by its magnificence. Amy dismounted from the driver's seat and rushed toward a stone staircase leading up to the building's palatial entrance. Olen and Jo scrambled to catch up.

"What is this place?" Olen asked.

"We set up shop here last week," Amy replied. "The lab's in the main building, and the clinic is in the annex along the western side. The monastery's isolation from the village made it a perfect choice. Plus, the dormitory has almost two hundred beds."

"Monastery?" Olen was confused. "You just seized a sacred religious landmark?"

"We didn't *seize* anything. The monastery is the property of the People's Republic of China," Amy answered defensively.

"What about the monks?" Olen pressed as the group reached the apex of the staircase. "Weren't they sleeping in the dormitory? Where did they go?"

Amy didn't immediately answer, so Olen took a moment to survey the area. The view was spectacular. A light fog flowed down forested hillsides and washed over the ancient village nestled within the valley's cozy pocket. From this elevated vantage point, Olen could see flames flickering on the far edge of the Q-Zone.

Amy paused to catch her breath. She pointed to the distant bonfire. "We had to burn the monks' bodies." A column of black smoke rose from the fire.

"How many have died from the infection?" Olen asked.

"A hundred and eighty-seven," Amy replied. She pounded her fist against the monastery's colossal iron doors. The deep bellow resonated through the metal like a macabre moan. "The virus swept through the monastery in about three days. We considered demolishing the place. Fortunately, decontamination was successful, and we moved in." The entrance creaked open. "We've got to hurry. Dr. Sun is in critical condition."

Inside, Amy led the group down a dark hallway that spilled into a sprawling foyer. Long plastic sheets draped the walls. A single halogen floodlight attached to a metal tripod reflected orange light off the lofted ceiling. Olen heard the soft hum of a diesel generator. The entire place smelled like bleach.

Two oblong pods, each about ten feet tall, stood side by side next to a steel table. They looked like alien spacecraft. Each egg-shaped capsule opened in the front by way of a bowed doorway that molded to the container's curved shape.

"Decontamination chambers," Amy explained. "The pods use focused ultraviolet light to eradicate any viral remnants or infected biological material clinging to skin or clothes. No one leaves the provisional laboratory without going through a decon cycle. You'll see these outside the clinic too. They're super cozy. Like being in the womb."

A stack of powder-blue hospital gowns, individually packaged in milky plastic, lay on the metal table. Next to the gowns were three cardboard boxes containing surgical masks, latex gloves, and goggles. Jo and Amy tore into the packages.

"This is the best protection we can get without full-body condoms," Amy remarked.

"Body condoms?" Olen echoed.

"That's what Dr. Chow calls the positive-pressure suits," Jo explained, with noticeable irritation. She turned back to business. "Remember to double up on gloves. Keep your mask and goggles on at all times once we're inside the clinic."

Amy swiftly tied her shoulder-length hair into a stubby plume on top of her head. "And try not to freak out, okay?"

The threesome dashed through an open courtyard carved into the heart of the monastery. A handful of laboratory staff whisked across the enclosure, each clad in identical powder-blue gowns, their faces obscured by the same white masks. No one made eye contact, as if even superficial human interaction could transmit the disease.

Amy led them down a narrow corridor lined with smooth limestone. Thick curtains made of plastic strips partitioned the passageway about every ten feet, creating pockets of musty air. The strips slapped together as the group pushed through. Each section of the hallway felt slightly warmer than the last.

"The main building connects to the annex through here," Amy informed. "We have to conserve power, so the generators only feed electricity to the lab, clinic, and staff quarters. It should warm up in a sec."

They emerged from the hallway into the clinic's makeshift lobby. Olen squinted under the bright lights. An assortment of medical equipment emitted a chorus of mechanical beeping. In the center of the space was a simple nurses' station composed of two tables, an array of plastic bins, and a laptop. Olen had expected the clinic to be buzzing with activity, but the room was eerily calm.

Then three masked nurses almost tackled Olen to the ground when they burst through a wooden door directly behind him. The

women sprinted across the lobby, pushing a gurney carrying a grotesque pulp of black-and-blue flesh. The sick man's face swelled
with purple veins that bulged like spider webs across his cheeks.
Black foam collected at the corners of his mouth. Olen had never
seen anything so hideous.

The patient looked like a three-day-old corpse pulled from the
Hudson River. Yet somehow the man was alive. His bloodshot
eyes, sunken deep into his skull, darted chaotically around the
room. He jerked and thrashed while the nurses struggled to
restrain him. His violent coughs spattered thick, bloody mucus
across the white sheet hanging loosely across his bare torso.

"He can't breathe," one nurse yelled to Amy in English. "His
air passages are completely blocked. We tried to intubate, but his
throat is too swollen. We're taking him to the OR for an emergency tracheotomy."

"Copy that," Amy said. "We'll need to sedate him or else we'll
slice his carotid. Prepare fifty milliliters of ketamine and meet us
in OR three," Amy ordered the nurse.

Olen and Jo followed closely as the nurses expertly guided the
gurney into an intensely lit operating room.

"This man must be at least four, five days in from initial infection," Jo observed.

"No. He was strong as an ox just twenty-four hours ago," Amy
said.

The blood drained from Jo's face. "The virus is mutating
faster."

Amy nodded.

"He's medical staff. Who is he?" Jo asked.

"You don't recognize him? Dr. Zhou, it's Ru."

17

Beijing, People's Republic of China

WANG SWITCHED OFF covert mode, and the screen flashed back to his in-box. He'd just received a new message. The subject line read, **Begin countdown to Haikou heavenly massage.** Wang grinned. His MFA contact had a terrible weakness for paid companionship.

The email had two attachments. The first was a PDF named **Ministry of Foreign Affairs, Information Sheet—STONE, KIPTON.** The second was a JPEG image file. Wang opened the PDF first and scanned the text.

Stone was a veteran field reporter, about the same age as Wang. Degree in journalism and media communications from American University. Spoke English, French, and passable German. Parents deceased. Only known family an older sister in Alexandria, Virginia. Recent stints in Egypt, Poland, Sudan, Turkey. Never China. *Strange choice*, Wang thought. Though no red flags. The journalist seemed fairly mundane. On paper, the man was clean.

Wang moved on to the JPEG. He opened the image file, and his heart leapt into his throat. "No," he mumbled to himself in disbelief. He slammed the heel of his palm into his desk with a loud smack. *Shit!* Wang tried to concentrate, but his stomach churned, his face flushed.

The lieutenant fumbled with the computer mouse. He closed the JPEG and promptly deleted the email. Before his computer finished logging off, Lieutenant Wang was already racing out of the office.

18

Dzongsar Village, Tibetan Autonomous Region,
People's Republic of China

PERFORMING SURGERY ON a patient infected with Blood River virus was perilous. The disease's hemorrhagic nature made the potential blood loss from shaving nicks dangerous, let alone deep surgical incisions.

Amy and Jo had completed the tracheotomy on Dr. Sun with the help of two Tibetan nurses, a powerful sedative, and an iron focus forged over years of stressful fieldwork. The patient now drew breath through a tube inserted directly into his esophagus just under his Adam's apple. He'd remain sedated until morning, but no one realistically expected Dr. Sun to survive the night. The man was a swollen, oozing pile of flesh, and there was no bouncing back from that. At least now he wouldn't drown in his own blood.

During the surgery, Jo had untied the patient's hospital gown. She'd needed to clear his neck, but she had another reason for doing so. She suspected Amy had been wrong about the man's identity. Ru, her ex-husband, had a crescent-shaped scar with a line through the middle under his left collarbone. Jo used to tease him that it looked like a hammer and sickle, the mark of a true communist. When Jo pulled down the front of the patient's gown, his shoulder was completely clear. The man lying on the operating table, writhing in pain, swimming with virus, was not her ex-husband. He was Ru's brother.

* * *

Amy led Jo and Olen to the monastery's kitchen, which the clinical staff had converted into a break room. They sat around a cheap folding table drinking day-old coffee. Olen observed Jo carefully. Why wasn't she more distraught? Blood River virus had ravaged that man's body—a man she'd once loved. Something felt off.

Jo broke the silence. "We still don't know where this thing came from. Do we?"

"The reservoir is a complete mystery," Amy answered. "We're no closer to figuring it out."

"Reservoir?" Olen asked.

"The reservoir host," Amy clarified. She refilled Olen's chipped coffee mug and got up to make herself a peanut-butter-and-jelly sandwich. "No virus intends to kill its victims. It's the microbial equivalent to suicide. Viruses crave one thing—to replicate. And they need the healthy, living cells of another creature to do it. That creature dies, it's game over. That's why every virus survives within a natural host—something it can infect without causing major harm. This animal or insect serves as a reservoir for the little bug. Viruses can sometimes live for millennia, safely replicating within the population of their reservoir host."

"So, find the reservoir host and you can stop it from infecting more people," Olen interpreted.

"Well, it's certainly a good place to start," Amy agreed. "Unfortunately, it's not always so easy. About sixty percent of diseases that infect humans are zoonotic, meaning they jump from animals to people. We've tested more than a hundred and fifty species living around Dzongsar Village. Bats, pigs, birds, mosquitoes, even bedbugs. They all came back negative for BRV45. We may be running out of places to look. It's like Ebola all over again."

"What happened with Ebola?" Olen asked.

Amy's mouth was stuck with thick peanut butter. She yielded to Jo with a quick nod.

"Ebola virus appeared out of thin air in Central Africa forty-five years ago," Jo explained. "The disease went on a murderous rampage. Only rabies is deadlier, as viruses go. Hundreds died. And then it just vanished.

"A couple of years later, a variation of the virus flared up on the opposite side of the continent, in Sudan. Again, those infected fell quickly, and then Ebola retreated into the jungle, that time for almost fifteen years. No one knows where it comes from or where it goes when the outbreaks fizzle out. We've searched for Ebola's reservoir host for decades. Researchers have tested thousands of species without success. We think it's a mammal, probably forest dwelling. The fact that Ebola can survive in the shadows for such long intervals makes us think the reservoir host rarely comes in contact with people. Quite possibly, it's a species we've yet to discover. The same could be true for Blood River virus. It would help if we knew what specific part of the forest patient zero had spent time in before entering the village. Otherwise, it's like searching for a needle in a thousand haystacks."

Olen was unnerved. In his line of work, he found the bad guy, destroyed his cache of biological or chemical weapons, and then celebrated over beers. His targets had addresses and cell phones. Sure, some of the assholes were pretty clever and could be difficult to track down, but none could make themselves invisible for decades at a time. Jo's enemies sounded far more elusive.

Amy finished her snack, licking her fingers, and picked up where Jo left off. "Finding the reservoir host allows us to do more than just contain the spread of the disease. We need its juju."

"You need what?" Olen asked.

"Antibodies," Jo said. "For some reason, it doesn't get sick. Studying the host's peculiar immunity to the virus is critical to developing a vaccine. If we inoculate everyone, the virus won't stand a chance of reemerging on the same scale. In the field of public health, prevention is still our most powerful weapon."

"Why can't you just extract antibodies from the survivors?" Olen questioned.

"We can, and we do," Amy said. "But even the survivors still got sick. They recovered because they had dynamite immune systems. Their serum helps us understand how to beat the virus, but we still need antibodies from the reservoir host to figure out how to render it inert. Typically, the most important thing we can get from survivors is information about how they contracted the disease in the first place. If they work with animals or ate a bat or something, we can often trace back to the source."

"The problem is that BRV45 kills too fast," Jo added. "The infected are too delirious to remember any useful details, and so far, we haven't identified any survivors."

"Well, that's not entirely true," Amy corrected.

"What do you mean? We found a survivor?"

Amy grinned, a glint in her eye.

DAY 10

CHAPTER

19

Dzongsar Village, Tibetan Autonomous Region,
People's Republic of China

THE POISON QUEEN sat motionless in a hickory rocking chair.
Amy had given Sumati the grisly nickname in homage to
Zhou Zuofeng, a fishmonger from Guangzhou who'd kick-started
the SARS epidemic. Like Zuofeng, Sumati was a superspreader,
Amy explained. The average person infected with BRV45 transmitted the disease to just two or three others. A superspreader
exposed upwards of twenty. Sumati had been the first villager to
come into contact with patient zero; she'd served the man tea.
With cruel irony, Sumati's kindness toward a suffering stranger
had brought about the devastation of her entire community.

Sumati circulated the virus throughout Dzongsar with breathtaking efficiency. According to Amy, the middle-aged Tibetan
woman had infected thirty-three people. Her friends, neighbors,
family members—they all died. Brutally. Perhaps a punishment
worse than death, Sumati recovered, just like Zuofeng, the Poison
King. Whether it was the disease or the hulking guilt that ravaged
Sumati's mind, no one could be certain. Whatever the case, by the
time Jo and Olen met her, the light had vanished from Sumati's
eyes, replaced by something much darker.

Jo approached cautiously. The rocking chair enveloped Sumati's emaciated body. She sat stone-still except for the ping-pong ticking of her glassy eyes, which had locked on the swinging pendulum of an old clock. Blood River virus had ruined her body. Most of her hair had fallen out, leaving behind scrappy patches of gray and black. Her skin sagged in folds and flaps around her neck. To Jo, she looked seventy, but Sumati's medical file said forty-eight.

A teenage girl—a daughter or niece, maybe—spoke slowly, her voice thick with exhaustion. "She is not accepting visitors today," the girl uttered pointlessly. In the Q-Zone, the investigation took top priority. The Ministry of Health required permission from no one, not even to enter this woman's home to ask intrusive questions. Or to take biological samples. Jo noticed the black-and-blue tracks of bruising puncture wounds stippling Sumati's forearms.

"No blood today," the girl whimpered, and began to tidy up the parlor. Jo knew the clinic's medical staff probably came around three, four times a day, demanding Sumati's serum. The woman's antibodies could save others. Jo looked at Sumati's colorless form. Dried drool caked her lips. She'd survived Blood River virus, but if this was surviving, why bother?

The girl placed a vase of purple orchids on the table beside Sumati's chair, rotating it to catch the light. She pruned the dead blooms with a pair of garden shears, trying her best to ignore her unwelcome visitors.

Jo tingled with anticipation. BRV45 destroyed nearly every living creature it touched. It penetrated every cell, feeding on its victim's flesh from the inside out. *Millions of virus particles.* It liquefied vital organs and dissolved muscle tissue until the body collapsed into a shapeless pulp. *Billions of virus particles.* Yet this woman had somehow defeated the onslaught. Her immune system had overcome the invasion. She had not died. Jo needed to know why.

"Sumati, please pardon our intrusion," Jo said. The virologist hunched down to kneel at eye level with the woman. "Tell us, how did you get sick?"

"She can't help you. Her mind is gone," the teenager explained weakly. With a trembling hand, she put down the pruning shears and turned to face Jo. A thin layer of moisture coated the girl's anguished black eyes. "She's a ghost."

Sumati's vacant gaze and acute lethargy reminded Jo of the Ebola patients she'd seen in northern Gabon. The fever had cooked their brains. They babbled incoherently, overwhelmed by delirium. The Gabon strain killed eighty-eight percent of its victims, but the lucky few who survived recovered completely. The dementia and hallucinations simply disappeared. Blood River virus was different. Sumati had expelled the disease but not the unshakable madness it caused. Jo found that fact irresistibly fascinating.

* * *

An hour with Sumati produced no answers, and Jo grew impatient. This ghost-woman had been the first person to encounter patient zero. Had she noticed where he entered the village? If so, maybe Jo could retrace his steps, look for nests or burrows. But Sumati couldn't focus on anything other than that maddening clock.

Jo rose to her feet and moved into Sumati's line of sight, blocking the woman's view of the clock's swinging pendulum. The doctor crossed her arms and pleaded with the feeble creature. "Sumati, you must concentrate!"

Something clicked in the woman's tortured mind. A wave of clarity rippled through her viscid consciousness, clearing narrow channels that allowed a few imprisoned thoughts to slip through. Sumati's eyes squeezed into a razor-blade squint and locked on to Jo's. Her cracked lips formed words—a mishmash of Tibetan and Mandarin. "His blood was *poisoned*," Sumati hissed. Her voice grew louder and more intense. "I should have known! He came from the sun. Why didn't I see it? Now it's too late, too late, too late."

"Yes," Jo answered, her heart racing. "You're talking about the sick man who wandered into Dzongsar. You saw which direction he came from. You must try to remember."

The teenage girl perked up. Sumati hadn't spoken in days.

"The sun! Listen to me. He came from *the sun*. I didn't see it before. He was *poisoned*." Sumati wept. Her face twisted, arms stiffened, fingers spread wide. Her entire body rattled against the chair.

Jo moved closer to the tortured woman. "Who? Who hurt the sick man?"

"Gdon! Gdon! He was possessed. He brought death to our village. I couldn't stop it," Sumati blubbered. Mucus dripped from her nose. She stomped her feet, marching in place. Her mouth opened unnaturally wide, and she gasped for breath in lung-scraping rasps.

Sumati knew something that could help the investigation and save lives. Before she could stop herself, Jo reached for the woman's shaking arm and pinned it to the wooden armrest, attempting to pacify her. "What did you see?" Jo shouted.

Sumati wailed. "*Deeeee-mon*. You want my blood? Take it. Take it all back to hell!"

The old woman snatched the pruning shears, which still rested on the table beside her chair. She swung the weapon violently through the air and then stabbed its sharp point into the crook of her own arm. Dark-red streams spilled from Sumati's abused veins as she hacked at her own flesh, striking her arm over and over. Flaps of skin tore away from the muscle underneath, and the metal blades chipped away at bone. The teenage girl shrieked in horror and tried to wrestle the weapon from Sumati's grasp, her feet slipping in the gathering pool of blood.

Warm, crimson drops splashed across Jo's face and neck. She backed away, frozen in shock. Sumati had recovered from the infection, so the woman's blood was safe. Still, Jo's stomach crawled up her throat. The American journalist rushed past her to help the girl subdue the manic woman. Sumati thrashed ferociously despite having seriously injured herself. Her eyes swelled with tears. "Take it all, demons! Take all of my blood and let me *die*!" she shrieked.

The reporter finally seized the pruning shears and tossed them aside. The flustered teenager grabbed Sumati's shoulders and pleaded for her to be still. The man pushed his flat palms onto the woman's gushing wound to stem her bleeding. Jo heard the metal shears scrape across the hardwood floor, creating a sinister harmony with Sumati's unearthly howl.

20

Singapore, Republic of Singapore

HUDSON REECE WAITED for the screen door to snap shut and then strolled into the Singapore Zoo's manufactured jungle, careful to blend in with the other tourists, who craned their necks and ogled the exotic wildlife. Like Reece, most of the world's creatures were active after dark, emboldened by the veil of night. Tonight visitors were sparse, probably due to the heat. The afternoon humidity had seeped into the evening, offering no reprieve from the island's unrelenting mugginess.

The leaves rustled overhead. A shadow danced across the canopy. Tiny goldenrod eyes watched Reece's every move. The zoo animals could be dangerously unpredictable. Last year a grounds keeper had lost his footing and tumbled into the habitat occupied by the park's two white tigers, Omar and Winnie. They pinned the man to the wet rocks, and Omar's three-inch teeth expertly punctured the grounds keeper's neck, extinguishing his screams with a swift crack.

Reece had entered an enclosure that housed far less menacing residents. He spotted one of the exhibit's red giant flying squirrels resting on a high branch, illuminated by the soft moonlight. The rodent glared suspiciously but posed no danger. Reece blinked, and the skittish animal vanished.

A middle-aged couple gawked, mouths agape, scanning the spindly tree limbs for a peek at the elusive squirrel. The husband fumbled with an expensive, professional-grade Nikon he probably rescued from the basement once a year. Bits of cheese crackers clung stubbornly to his beard. The wife's bulky fanny pack cinched her pudgy waistline. Reece imagined it bursting with spare ketchup packets and sanitizing Wet-Naps.

The exhibit's fourth human occupant, an elegant woman with sultry features sitting alone on a bench, seemed out of place. She wore a turquoise evening gown and clutched a three-thousand-dollar Lady Dior handbag. She was probably Indonesian, but Reece couldn't be sure. He'd met her only twice before and knew her as Kalina. It wasn't her true name, of course. HELMSMAN, their leader, had determined that aliases were safer and had instructed all of them to keep their true identities hidden, even from one another. After a few short minutes, the enchanting woman rose and floated past Reece on her way to the exit. The ethereal fabric of her gown brushed against Reece's trousers.

The cheese-bearded tourist finally located a squirrel among the dewy leaves and snapped a photograph. The camera's flash startled the animal. It leaped from its perch and glided across the habitat. The chubby wife squealed in delight.

Reece turned to the screen door exit. The beguiling woman had evaporated into the humidity, probably headed back to whatever gala or premier she'd slipped away from earlier. Soon she would unfold the scrap of paper he'd dropped into her handbag. His scribbled message would be unambiguous. *Olen Grave is in Dzongsar. Terminate the investigation.* Kalina, a skilled assassin, would know what to do.

He waited ten minutes before departing the zoo and then hailed a taxi to the airport. Hudson Reece would take one final flight before retiring for good. Lieutenant Wang had taken an enormous risk in using the false identity to slip out of China, but he'd had no other option, given the urgency of the situation. If Kalina succeeded, HELMSMAN would be pleased. But first, Wang needed to return to Beijing before someone noticed that one of his old aliases had resurfaced.

21

Dzongsar Village, Tibetan Autonomous Region,
People's Republic of China

O LEN BOUNCED ON his toes, weaving through the mob of giggling children. The littlest ones didn't seem to understand
the rules. A grinning toddler, no older than two or three, clung to
Olen's leg as he dribbled the soccer ball through the thick grass.
Spotting an opening in the gauntlet of tiny feet, Olen swiftly
passed the ball to an older kid. The lanky boy sprinted across the
field and fired a shot between two large branches marking the
makeshift goal. All the children, even those on the opposing team,
threw their arms up and whooped. The boy superstar hurled his
body into a backflip before his teammates tackled him to the
ground in a noisy dog pile. Olen chuckled and walked off the field
toward the bonfire. The kids had brought some levity to an otherwise heavy couple of days.

The sun dipped and the temperature dropped. A handful of
villagers collected around the fire, pulled together by the irrepressible need for human connection despite the health risks. Still, as a
precaution, they spread out in a wide semicircle, even as their children wrestled on the field. Separating the kids seemed too cruel.
The disease could ravage their village, destroy their crops, burn

their homes, but it wouldn't rob their children of their innocent desire to play.

Jo sat opposite the villagers, her back to the field, scribbling in a notepad. In the span of twenty-four hours, she'd performed surgery on her dying ex-husband and watched a victim chop away at her own flesh. Most people would be traumatized. Jo appeared unfazed. Olen recognized this stoic reaction to emotional distress. He'd experienced it too. *Compartmentalize the grief. Ignore the pain. Just keep moving.*

Olen used the front of his T-shirt to wipe the sweat from his forehead. "Those kiddos have major skills," he said, approaching Jo.

"Maybe fifteen against one was a bit unbalanced," Jo suggested.

"I know. They didn't stand a chance." Olen cocked a grin.

Jo flipped the pages of her notebook. He suspected she was pretending not to be amused.

Olen sat and watched the sun retreat behind a natural stone formation lining the western edge of the field, where shaggy grass gave way to dense forest. The boulders, adorned with brightly painted symbols reaching ten feet high, created a stunning mural. From his vantage point, Olen could see the entire panoramic scene, which seemed to tell a story. Lotus flowers with delicate pink petals and scaly goldfish swam around what looked like a sunflower or a ship's wheel, whose eight spokes protruded from an orange hub. Dramatic gray-and-black swirls curled in from the right and left edges, stretching toward the serene pond with menacing tendrils. The darkness prepared to overtake the colorful paradise and strangle the wildlife like an invasive vine. The art was disturbingly prophetic.

"It's incredible how they do it," Olen said, watching the children.

"Do what?" Jo asked.

"Act so . . . normal."

Jo shrugged. The kids began another game. The teams were unclear. Everyone converged on whoever had the ball.

"Where did you get that key?" Jo asked, without looking up.

"What?"

"The one hanging around your neck. You weren't wearing it before."

"Oh, right." Olen looped a thumb under the chain and pulled a small silver key through his collar. Jo must've noticed it when he lifted his shirt. "One of the boys gave it to me."

"Doesn't he need it?" Jo asked.

"Don't think so. He found it lying in the grass over there, beside those painted rocks." Olen pointed to the mural. "Seems like a pretty friendly neighborhood. I don't imagine they have much need for locks around here."

"He spoke English?"

"The boy? Yeah. Pretty good, too. These kids are remarkable. He said he used to live on the coast but his father got a better job out here."

"In Dzongsar?" Jo sounded skeptical. This village was about as rural as it got—not exactly an economic hotbed.

"They're going to build a railroad. Or at least they were." Olen sensed Jo's discomfort and decided to push a bit. "So, what's with the firewall around Tibet? I don't mean now, under quarantine, but in general. Even before the outbreak."

"Because it's dangerous out here." Jo's response came easily, as if she were a schoolgirl faithfully reciting the Party line.

"I've reported from a lot of dicey places, Doc. If you take this organ-melting virus out the equation, Tibet doesn't seem so dangerous."

"Politically, Kipton," she explained, using Olen's cover name. "Despite what you see here, there are people in the TAR who wish to do us great harm."

"Us?"

"The government. Some radical groups don't recognize the Chinese Communist Party as the legitimate governing authority in Tibet. Rebels have formed underground militias, attacked public buildings, coerced people into supporting their misguided cause."

"What cause is that exactly?"

"The Dalai Lama's cause. He foments unrest within the TAR. He inflames the rebels. It's subversion," Jo explained.

"Why would the Dalai Lama provoke the Chinese government? Tibet has no army of its own. Beijing would pulverize any organized resistance. Thousands of his people would be slaughtered."

Jo glared at Olen. "You make us sound draconian. This isn't Mao's China. We don't want conflict with the Tibetans. There's no reason we can't coexist under the harmonious arrangement that's worked so well for decades."

"So, what changed?" Olen asked.

"You tell me." Jo sounded angry. "The Chinese government has spent millions to develop the TAR. We've built roads, hospitals, brought quality education to people who were still living in the Tang dynasty."

"Sounds a bit like colonialism," Olen said.

"It sounds like *progress*. In the last ten years, the Tibetan standard of living has skyrocketed. Life expectancy has doubled. Poverty and starvation are lower than ever and drop more every year. Beijing's investment in Tibet has significantly increased the quality of life here."

Olen kept pushing. "But can they still be Tibetan? Are the people here allowed to believe whatever they want? Speak their own language? Maybe they'd trade the paved roads for a little more . . . freedom."

Jo's porcelain skin burned deep red. The stress of the past few days finally boiled over. She slapped her notebook shut. "You know, it's not just the Dalai Lama instigating the hostilities. It's people like you."

"Me? What did I do?" Olen asked.

"The Western media. Your biased view of Tibet—painting it as a helpless victim of an oppressive regime. It's brainwashed the global community. There are elements within the UN—and your own government, for that matter—who would love nothing more than to see the Party fall. Has America learned nothing from the Arab Spring? You thrust guns into the hands of angry young men and act surprised when they use them to advance their own radical agenda."

Olen waited. Jo didn't seem quite finished.

"And you're hypocrites!" Jo continued. "China lifts millions of Tibetans out of destitution so they can enjoy the same economic benefits as those of us living on the coast. For this, we are vilified. For God's sake, *your* politicians in the United States deride the poor for using food stamps. At least we're doing something to help the less fortunate."

"I guess I never thought of it that way," Olen admitted.

"That's my point—and it's a problem. You're a journalist. People read your articles and think they're reading facts. But you don't consider the other side to the story."

Jo's breathing became more even. She'd released some pent-up steam. Olen regretted upsetting her.

The two sat on the grass in silence. Jo's soft features flashed in the light of the bonfire. Deep shadows painted tortured expressions on her face. She hid her anguish well, but Olen knew she couldn't keep it bottled up forever. The pressure she was under could crush a diamond.

Soft giggles from the children floated in the breeze.

"I've got to get back to the lab," Jo said, rising to her feet.

*   *   *

A few cold raindrops tapped Olen's forearm. Heavy clouds vanquished the last bit of sunlight. Mothers beckoned to their children, their long scarves whipping behind them like broken wings.

Olen had pushed Jo too far, but the conversation had helped him gauge her political loyalty. Something wasn't right. Jo had been ordered to include him on her research team, but beyond that Beijing's intentions were fuzzy. She'd made no attempt to isolate him. She'd allowed Olen to shadow her all day. He'd attended briefings with the clinic staff, met with the epidemiological surveyors, and even visited patients. Jo had explained everything to him, in English, and never refused to answer his questions. Why would Beijing grant an American journalist such unfettered access? Was the Chinese government actually serious about transparency? Not likely.

An alternate scenario nagged at Olen. Maybe Dzongsar was a charade—a carefully orchestrated performance designed to manipulate public opinion in the West. Where were the hazmat teams, the helicopters, the armored cars, the detachments of soldiers patrolling the streets? Where were the swarms of doctors? The Q-Zone's provisional lab barely met biosafety level two standards. Where were the pressurized rooms, the sealed double-door access, the electron microscopes? A soon as the Ministry of Health determined the danger the virus posed, wouldn't it have descended on Dzongsar with the full might of its resources? Olen knew USAMRIID and the CDC wouldn't touch this bug without sealed suits, decontamination showers, and labs with completely segregated air supplies. Was the Q-Zone nothing more than a sideshow? If so, Jo's team would never uncover the truth behind the outbreak here. She had never been meant to. Her entire investigation was a farce.

Olen hoped he was wrong. He needed more time to assess Jo. She might be deceiving him, but Olen didn't think so. Quite possibly Beijing was keeping the good doctor in the dark. Jo seemed genuinely determined to stop BRV45, and she was smart enough to do it. If Olen's theory was right—if Dzongsar was an elaborate deception—what would her government do if she got too close to the truth?

The patch of grass became soggy. The villagers and their children retreated to escape the approaching storm. Olen started walking back toward the monastery, thinking about how to smooth things over with Jo, his shoes squishing in the mud.

DAY 11

22

Beijing, People's Republic of China

"THE OFFICIAL NUMBER published by the Chinese Ministry of Health is now twenty-two thousand, but outside experts with the World Health Organization estimate the actual number of infected to be as high as fifty thousand," veteran correspondent Amanda Hughes reported from the northern edge of Tiananmen Square, directly across from the entrance to the Forbidden City. Her steely expression concealed her uneasiness. The situation in the square was approaching a fever pitch. Even mild protests could escalate into violent riots, she knew, and the protesters were committed. They came to the square in blatant defiance of the government-imposed restrictions—a ballsy move, especially in China.

No one had expected the disease to spread so fast. Within a matter of days, the bug had cut down perfectly healthy adults. A *lot* of them. In just the last forty-eight hours, everything had changed. Parks, schools, shopping malls, movie theaters—any place that drew large crowds—had all been closed indefinitely. Even the subway had stopped running. Hospitals were accessible by official order only. And, of course, there was the curfew. Police threatened to arrest anyone on the street after nine o'clock. It had sounded like an empty threat until people started disappearing.

Not just adults either—kids too. Rumors were spreading of work camps in the Gobi, full of curfew violators who had been bused to the desert wilderness for hard labor.

Gripping the microphone, Amanda stared unblinking into the camera's lens. "China's five largest cities have been hit the hardest. As you can see behind me, the crisis has enraged the people of Beijing. In defiance of the city's stringent curfew, thousands of residents have convened here in Tiananmen Square. Authorities have urged the crowd to disperse, citing the public health emergency, but as the hours pass, the demonstration has only surged. Police in full riot gear line the square, but as yet they have not engaged the protesters. Some citizen groups have set up small campsites, suggesting they have no intention of leaving. At this hour, there is no indication the square will clear by the afternoon. The entire scene is eerily reminiscent of the infamous government crackdown on student protesters that ended so tragically in this very spot thirty years ago. I'm Amanda Hughes for the BBC."

The cameraman cut the feed and lifted the hulking equipment from his shoulder.

"Let's shoot some quick B-roll and get the hell out of here," Amanda suggested. Her voice had shed its confident broadcaster's veneer. The mob, comprising mostly university-aged people, had grown unruly. Surgical masks dampened their passionate shouts, but the sea of flaring black eyes conveyed their visceral rage clearly enough. A group of young men punched the air in unison, chanting, "*Zhonggong shi bingdu.*" The Party is the virus.

Homemade posters depicting a defaced President Li bobbed above the crowd. One, reading FIRST PRESIDENT LI, THEN TAIWAN, featured a crude drawing of missiles. The object of the protesters' fury was unmistakable. They held President Li Bingwen personally responsible for allowing Taiwan's biological attack to go unpunished.

News reports had broken alleging that a Taiwanese intelligence officer had intentionally unleashed the virus in Tibet, and a mostly acquiescent public had transformed into a raging mob, demanding retribution. With their own government refusing to avenge the people's suffering, protests were flaring. President Li had withdrawn. No one had spotted him publicly for days. In all her years reporting on China, Amanda had never seen the Party's grip on power so tenuous.

The cameraman panned across the square. He paused on the gates to the Great Hall of the People—the legislative seat of the government. They'd captured this visual before. It was the same footage they'd shot in Idlib, Sana'a, and Tahrir Square. Images of the seeds of revolution.

Without warning, the pavement shuddered from an earsplitting blast. Amanda instinctively ducked, almost knocking into the cameraman, who swung his lens toward the sound. A brilliant orange fireball rose from the top of the Great Hall of the People. She could feel the heat, even from a hundred meters away.

"Christ! Did you get that?" Amanda yelled over the commotion.

The bomb caught the protesters by surprise, yet only a few ran off, panicked. Someone had attacked the Chinese Communist Party. Flames engulfed the building. Across the square, the mammoth portrait of Chairman Mao, positioned over the entrance to the old Imperial Palace, grinned in the flickering light. A few seconds passed before a deafening cheer, almost as loud as the explosion, thundered into the sky.

23

Fort Detrick, Maryland, USA

DIRECTOR CAMERON RUBBED her eyelids. Back in her Fort Detrick office, she unplugged her computer and detached the Ethernet cable, just as she did every evening. Basic cybersecurity measures, she'd explain if asked. Everyone worried about Russian hackers, but Allyson didn't trust the U.S. Army either. She'd learned to trust people, not bureaucracies.

Allyson buttoned her raincoat and began the long walk to her car. She hadn't bothered to lock her office door. A locked door only stirred up curiosity. She'd left the lights on too. Not that she had a choice. The switch had been disabled. The hidden surveillance cameras didn't see that well in the dark. It seemed the Army didn't trust *her* either.

VECTOR headquarters—a lofty designation for a cluster of five dusty offices—sidled right up to the entrance to USAMRIID's biosafety level four laboratory. Allyson had visited the lab only twice, and she didn't want a reason to make a third trip. Past the locker rooms, the decontamination shower, and a series of airtight chambers, a team of brilliant researchers studied the world's most deadly diseases. The scientists worked all day in a negative-pressure environment, trapped inside space suits. Oxygen fed through narrow yellow tubes that coiled from their backs up to a complex system of piping in the ceiling. Supposedly, people became accustomed to the claustrophobia. Allyson didn't feel compelled to test the hypothesis herself. Her own windowless office was cramped enough.

The night air instantly energized the desk-weary operative. In her past life as an intelligence officer, nightfall had triggered a certain thrill. Nowadays the most danger Allyson faced was falling asleep in the bathtub. She should've turned down the VECTOR job. She was a goddamn spy, not a politician. But Barlow wouldn't have taken no for an answer. Presidents needed allies in the Community. Allyson had always been part of Barlow's inner circle a fact that drew the contempt of her peers. Many of them wanted to see her fail. When Allyson staffed VECTOR with CIA-trained operatives, the Pentagon brass had bellyached. They believed she'd enlisted a ring of Langley spooks to spy on the Army's own intelligence service, the Defense Intelligence Agency. God forbid they actually cooperate with one another.

Before 9/11, the CIA and the Army had stayed out of each other's way. After the towers fell, the Agency had drifted away from human intelligence and transformed into a paramilitary organization. It had started with those damn drones. A consortium of bookish academics now directed the country's most lethal assassination campaign from a basement in Virginia. Elbow-patched philosophy majors with bombs.

The spy organization lacked the discipline and training for such potent combat, the military had contended. Langley chose targets too recklessly, under the protection of ambiguous legal justification.

Allyson tended to agree, but for different reasons. Drones were for unimaginative lunkheads. Anyone could tell a computer to unleash a Hellfire missile on some shit hole. What did it accomplish? There would always be more buttons to push and more shit holes to flatten. The Agency was wasting its best talent. The real work was on the ground. Infiltrating foreign communities that were naturally suspicious of outsiders, slowly earning their trust, building networks of sources willing to assume great risk to provide vital information to the United States—that was *real* intelligence work. The Army could never do that. They could keep their missiles.

The director found her car, one of the last remaining vehicles in the expansive parking lot. She'd purchased the used Ford Focus three years ago after returning from Saudi Arabia. She'd never appreciated the simple act of driving until she spent a summer in a country that prohibited women from such an unremarkable activity.

Typically, Allyson would switch on NPR and cruise down I-270 to her one-bedroom condo in McLean, but tonight she still had work to do. After nightfall. Just like old times.

About an hour later, the veteran spook pulled into a public parking lot along K Street in Washington's posh Georgetown neighborhood. She pulled up her collar to block the wind whipping off the Potomac and made her way to M Street, passing the Thai embassy, blending in with the evening shoppers. Her hand automatically reached for the pack of Marlboros nestled in her coat pocket, but she resisted. Cigarette smoke would provoke the ire of Georgetown's ubiquitous hipsters, who preferred vegan cookies and green juice to clouds of toxic nicotine. Allyson didn't give a fig about their sanctimonious judgment, but she wanted to avoid the attention.

A perky blonde emerged from a store advertising overpriced pants with empowering names like Curator and Executive Producer. Pants for women fed up with the patriarchy. Allyson paused and pretended to inspect the headless mannequins arranged in unnatural poses in the shop's window. *Feminist pants on broken women with no heads*, Allyson thought. *Brilliant marketing.* It was too dark outside to use the reflection in the glass to check for shadows (and that old ploy was for amateurs anyway), but sometimes just waiting a beat did the trick. Two minutes passed. She turned back toward the street and casually scanned the faces. No repeats. So far, so good. Still, she entered the shop to be on the safe side.

She purchased a handbag and scarf, which cost more than she'd have liked, so she paid with her Visa card and was careful to get a receipt. The cashier placed the items inside a shopping bag. The director exited the store, continued to the end of the block, and turned back toward the river. Minutes later she arrived at the

AMC movie theater tucked neatly at the end of Wisconsin Avenue across from Washington Harbour. The lobby bustled with people standing in line to see thick-necked superheroes battle in 3D. Allyson purchased a ticket for a romantic comedy that had already started. The kid running the box office looked concerned.

"You're gonna miss the first ten minutes, ma'am. Don't you want to wait for the nine o'clock?" he asked.

"I'm sure I'll figure it out," Allyson assured him.

The theater was nearly full—mostly gal pals and lovebirds—so she climbed into an empty seat in the back row and watched the door for latecomers. Two seats over, a teenager with greasy hair had his tongue down some poor girl's throat. Allyson groaned when the young lady grabbed his crotch.

No one else had entered the theater. Allyson removed her coat, folded it inside her new purse, and wrapped the scarf around her neck. Onscreen, a tear-soaked misunderstanding involving a handsome man with impossibly perfect hair gripped the audience, allowing Allyson to slip out the emergency exit, leaving her empty shopping bag behind.

The door dumped her out onto Wisconsin Avenue, only a block from the Ritz-Carlton Hotel. She walked briskly. It was just cold enough to be uncomfortable without her coat. She'd put it back on as soon as she was out of sight. A string of taxis had lined up in front of the hotel. Allyson jumped into the first one.

* * *

The ride to the Kennedy Center took less than fifteen minutes. The opera's first act had already begun, so Allyson easily glided along the back of the dimly lit hall without attracting any serious notice. Onstage, the mezzo-soprano's throaty vibrato commanded most everyone's full attention. Allyson found the staircase leading up to the box tier. She casually slipped her hands into her coat pockets and began climbing.

The spy chief quietly entered box 2D without knocking. A petite man, sitting alone in the velveteen room, heard Allyson enter but didn't turn around. He perched on the edge of his seat, craning his neck over the brass railing, peering through bejeweled opera glasses.

"You're late, Cam. You've missed the entire prelude," the man fussed. He removed a green-checked pocket square and delicately wiped the lenses of the glasses.

"I wasn't aware this was a date," Allyson countered.

"Don't flatter yourself." The man turned. His beady eyes surveyed Allyson from head to toe. "Really, Cam? An *actual* trench coat. At bit on the nose, don't you think? You could've at least worn something black."

"Why am I here, Roland?" Allyson sighed. The little British diplomat annoyed her, but he wouldn't have contacted her without good reason. She'd known Roland Birch for more than a decade and had tolerated his subtle ridicule for nearly as long.

"I have information you might find of interest."

Allyson crossed her arms and shrugged, unwilling to be lured into some kind of spy-movie repartee.

Roland huffed. "Very well. Have a look." The man produced an envelope from his left breast pocket and handed it to Allyson.

The director tucked a lock of hair behind her ear and pulled a small photo from the envelope. "You're shitting me."

"Your language!" Roland scolded. "This is Puccini, not some rowdy sport tournament."

"Where did you get this? Is this from Legoland?" Allyson asked, referring to the postmodern ziggurat that housed British intelligence on the bank of the River Thames.

"Don't be silly. I'm just an ordinary cultural attaché for Her Majesty's foreign office." Roland batted his eyes.

"Right. And you weren't ogling the tenor's bulge through those binoculars either," Allyson retorted sarcastically. "I know all your secrets, dear Rolly."

The Brit gasped playfully. "Well, I won't tell you where I got it, but I thought you'd want to know what we saw."

"When was it taken?" Allyson had already slipped the photograph into her handbag.

"Yesterday."

"What? Where?"

"Singapore," Roland answered. "It's a zoo, or something equally dreadful. Surveillance picked him up by mere happenstance. We were following the woman."

"Who is she?" Allyson asked, remembering the elegantly dressed woman in the photo.

"You don't recognize her? We assumed she was one of yours." Roland turned his gaze toward the stage.

"Since when do the British shadow American spies in Southeast Asia?" Allyson didn't mask the irritation in her voice.

"Let's not revive that old row, Cam. I've given you a golden egg. Do what you wish with it. I certainly hope you'll thank—"

Before Roland could finish his thought, Allyson was gone, racing out of the performance hall. She'd have no way to confirm the photograph's authenticity without raising great alarm. If it was real, MI6 had just dropped a bombshell.

She had many questions, and none of them had good answers. One thing Director Cameron knew for certain: no one must ever see this photograph. Especially not President Barlow.

Allyson sneaked back into the Georgetown cinema in the same way she'd left. Thanks to a strip of tape she'd placed over the door's latching mechanism—the classic "Watergate" maneuver—she quietly reentered the theater long before the film ended. Handsome Man with Great Hair had evidently patched things up with his lady friend—*oh, thank heaven*—and moved into a spacious Manhattan apartment he could never realistically afford.

Allyson ambled out of the building with the herd of moviegoers. A short walk later, the director hopped back into her Ford and headed toward the GW Parkway.

*   *   *

The doughy man slouching behind the wheel of a black Audi waited until Director Cameron's car crossed the Key Bridge. He popped a sunflower seed into his mouth—a regrettable habit he'd developed after too many hours sitting in parking lots. When he was younger, he'd actually fought for surveillance shifts. He'd fantasized about chasing drug lords around the Beltway, weaving in and out of traffic at top speed. More often he'd ended up spending an evening outside a roach motel, staring through binoculars and peeing into Gatorade bottles. Nevertheless, this target was a high priority. Some top dogs in Washington were watching Director Cameron's movements very carefully.

The man tugged on the rearview mirror to check his teeth for seeds. He was in no hurry to begin his pursuit of the silver Ford Focus. The GPS transmitter he'd attached to Director Cameron's undercarriage meant he didn't have to follow too closely. In any case, it looked as if she planned to head home. That was a good idea.

CHAPTER

24

THE ACRID SMELL of burning corpse flesh clung to everything, despite the incessant rain. Puddles dotted the courtyards like land mines. They were difficult to see until you were ankle deep in cool water. The monastery's ancient tile roof leaked in a few places, including above Jo's dormitory. Amy had arranged private rooms for her and the reporter. There was plenty of room in the inn when the lodgers kept croaking, she'd explained.

Within days of the initial outbreak, the monastery, once the cultural anchor of the community, had transformed into a house of death. The tight living arrangements had created an ideal incubator for BRV45, and the monks had provided plenty of fresh DNA. The pathogen had likely mutated two or three times within that building alone.

Jo had never stepped foot inside a Buddhist monastery before visiting Dzongsar. She was a woman of science. Ideas like reincarnation and supernatural phenomenon were foolish. Now she must eat, sleep, and do science inside a temple. It was just a building, after all.

Her bedroom, furnished with a rock-hard cot, small writing desk, and wobbly stool, had the ambience of a prison cell. Jo removed her damp leather boots and socks and placed them on the windowsill to dry out. Her toes were stone-cold, but at least they weren't wet. She attempted sleep, but her mind wouldn't settle. The doctor lay still, staring unblinkingly at the droop in the water-logged ceiling directly over the bed. She thought of Ru's brother, of Sumati, of the dead monks. And she thought of Kipton.

She didn't need the American journalist around. He served no purpose. She should sequester him in his dorm, keep him away from the investigation, away from her.

But she didn't want that. Kipton was a pain in the ass, a dumb American, yet impossibly magnetic, even charming. She felt drawn to his roughness. Jo typically spent her days (and occasionally her nights) with nerdy science boys; Kipton was the opposite. She'd never been with an American man. What would it feel like? Urgent, fevered, sweaty? *Treasonous.*

Jo dismissed the ridiculous fantasy. She knew where her loyal-ties lay, and they certainly weren't underneath Kipton Stone. Still, Jo regretted their argument on the soccer field. Tibet was a com-plicated matter for everyone. At least Kipton was making an effort to understand.

She sat up, pushed her arms through the sleeves of her jacket, and slipped into her still-moist boots. If she couldn't sleep, she might as well head back to the lab.

When Jo stepped into the hallway, she noticed that the door to the adjacent room stood ajar. She peeked inside. A gas lantern sat on a writing desk, its wick still glowing. Thousands of leather-bound books lined the walls, creating variegated rows of ruby, olive, and charcoal. The library held a vast collection of texts on topics ranging from history and politics to religion and society. Jo even spotted a tattered copy of the Kama Sutra. The timeworn volumes beckoned the virologist with murmurs of lost knowledge and untold secrets.

A small notebook rested next to the lantern on the table. The distinctive curls of classical Tibetan script danced across the unlined pages. Jo couldn't read the handwriting, but when she leaned in, she noticed that the black ink still glistened.

"Friend, are you lost?" The voice startled Jo. She whirled around to see an old man standing in the doorway. He wore blood-red robes streaked by a goldenrod sash over his left shoulder—the traditional garb of a Buddhist bhikkhu. His close-cropped hair did nothing to conceal the deep wrinkles running across his weathered forehead.

"I'm sorry for intruding," Jo answered with embarrassment. "I didn't realize—"

"Take a chill pill, Doctor," the man squawked gleefully. He toddled toward her and plopped onto the stool, which was much too short. Still grinning, he rested one hand on each knee and smacked his lips. "I'm glad to see *someone* take the time to visit our collection. This is the only room you doctors haven't ravaged, and yet it's probably the most important." The old man snorted to dislodge the phlegm clinging to his windpipe. When satisfied, he resumed speaking. "So, what were you snooping for?"

"I wasn't—"

"I know, I know. Just busting your chops, Doc."

Jo smiled. The old man's waggish charm began to infect her. "You're a monk. I thought they were all . . ."

"Kaput?"

"But you didn't get sick."

"Pretty spry for an old guy," the monk said. "Your doctor friends aren't the only ones who avoid libraries. Usually it's just me and the books. Well, and a few suspiciously erudite spiders."

Jo admired the towering bookshelves. "It is an impressive collection."

"It's a wonder it survived the fire."

"What fire?" Jo asked.

"Most of this monastery burned to the ground when I was a child." The bhikkhu's voice cracked. "Luckily, the books were saved. We can rebuild temples, but we could never replace these texts. Some are from the eighth century."

Jo ran her fingertips along a row of faded leather spines.

"They don't bite, Doctor."

Accustomed to her digital world, Jo found the ancient library irresistibly mysterious. It was a portal to a forgotten history—a time before gene sequencing and artificial intelligence and cloning. "Does the name *Gdon* mean anything to you?" she asked.

The monk squinted. His playful demeanor turned wary. "Where did you hear that?"

"I met a woman in the village. A survivor. The only one, in fact. She also happens to be the only person who witnessed the sick stranger enter the village. We've been trying to determine which direction he came from so we can retrace his steps. The forest is just so thick, we've already wasted days combing through roots and branches, collecting insects, checking nests. Most likely the man contracted the virus somewhere out there, and we need to determine the source. It will take weeks to survey the entire region."

"And the woman you met offered no clues?" the monk asked.

"She kept shouting the name Gdon. She was obviously very disturbed."

The old man stood slowly. His legs wobbled, yet he refused Jo's help. He hobbled across the library, mumbling something so low-pitched it sounded like humming. The Buddhist scholar waved a bony hand over the wall of books as if to summon a specific volume. "Su-ma-ti," he finally said, pronouncing each syllable much too loudly, like a wizard casting a spell. He pulled a large, green tome from the stockpile.

Jo nodded.

The bhikkhu cleared a space on the writing desk and briskly thumbed through the book. "I am not surprised."

"Why is that?" Jo asked.

"Sumati is a member of the Black Sect, more formally known as the Bon. It's an ancient religion of Central Asia."

"Is that like Buddhism?" Jo asked.

"Hmm. You aren't the first to ask that. Scholars disagree on whether Bon or Buddhism spread to Tibet first. Rumor and politics have clouded the facts. In any case, the two schools of thought battled for supremacy for two centuries. Did you know this very monastery was originally founded as a Bon temple?"

The doctor shrugged.

"Gah! Of course, you didn't," the old man scoffed. "In the early days, Buddhist priests attempted to suppress the Bon-po—followers of the Black Sect—to wipe out their beliefs. They did not prevail. Bon's core tenets endured. Tibetan Buddhism simply absorbed much of the Bon faith, along with its worshipers. But a handful of Bon-po clans have kept the original religion alive. They desire to restore the purity of the faith."

"Sumati thinks the sick man was possessed," Jo said.

"And what do you think?" the monk asked.

Jo didn't answer.

"Sumati, like all Bon-po, believe all elements found in nature possess a spirit," the bhikkhu explained. "Some spirits are benevolent and bring good fortune. Others are malicious creatures. The worst of the bunch live in rocks and trees. That's where you'd find Gdon."

Jo perked up. "The forest?"

"In the old times, Bon-po shaman would head off into the wilderness, alone, and spend days wandering the forest without food or water in search of a spiritual experience. They sought peace and joy in nature's benevolent spirits, but most importantly, they hoped to confront the evil ones," he said.

"Why would they go looking for evil?" Jo asked.

"They wished to defeat the malicious spirits so they themselves could remain pure and virtuous. These quests were grueling, and they often ended with violent visions of evil forces brutally attacking the shaman. If he won the battle, his mind received the gift of mystic knowledge.

"Of course, not all emerged triumphantly. These journeys were physically and psychologically punishing. Some shamans lacked the spiritual fortitude to conquer nature's demons. They sank into the dark bowels of the forest, swallowed whole."

Jo flipped the book's dusty pages. The images were graphic, disturbing. She stopped on a sketch of terrifying creatures with long faces and sharp fangs cowering in the light of a brilliant rising sun. The horrific beings hunched over, their spindly limbs raised to shield themselves from the penetrating beams.

"Are these the demons?" she asked.

"No. They are the lost souls of the deceased—the shamans who lost their battles."

"They look evil, possessed. Is that why they shun the sunlight?"

"On the contrary, Doctor. The light is guiding them. According to the Bon faith, that's how these men reach the beyond. Their detached souls must come *from* the sun and walk *toward* the darkness."

The bhikkhu flipped to another section of the book, and Jo caught her breath when she saw the image on the page. The monk's explanation replayed slowly in her mind. "They come *from* the sun," she murmured. Sumati had said the same thing about the sick man. After the interview, a team of scientists had spent the entire afternoon picking through a patch of spruce trees along the eastern edge of the village, the direction of the sunrise, but they'd turned up nothing. Jo had concluded that Sumati's reference to the sun was just delirious babble. But Jo was mistaken. The drawing in the monk's book explained everything.

"We've been looking in the wrong place!" Jo slapped the tattered tome with her palm, releasing a puff of dust. Before the old monk could react, Jo zipped up her jacket and bolted from the library. She'd left a faint handprint on the page, directly on top of an intricately sketched traditional Tibetan symbol for the sun—a wheel, with eight spokes protruding from a goldenrod hub.

25

Dzongsar Village, Tibetan Autonomous Region,
People's Republic of China

KALINA GRIPPED THE limestone wall and climbed silently toward the monastery's pitched roof. Her small fingers slid easily into the narrow grooves in the masonry. She balanced her weight on the pointed tips of her boots, which she'd expertly wedged into deep crevices in the weathered stone. The woman had shed her couture evening gown for a tactical body suit and grappling gear. Truthfully, Kalina felt equally comfortable in either attire. The smooth polyurethane fabric hugged her lissome figure, allowing her to snake up the fifty-foot edifice unencumbered.

Slipping into the Q-Zone had been simple. The young guards, anesthetized by boredom, had failed to notice a shadowy silhouette slinking through the thick brush. Infiltrating the monastery would require more skill and patience, however. Kalina had no idea how many people were inside, or how many were armed. If anyone got in her way, she'd simply cut them down. The most effective way to terminate the investigation would be to terminate the doctors and scientists running it. They'd scurry like field mice until she dropped them, one by one. Then she'd hunt her primary target. He'd be tougher to dispatch. Ideally, Kalina would pad noiselessly into her target's bedroom and eliminate him in his sleep. If she found him awake, it could get messy.

The assassin pulled herself onto the sloped eave of the monastery's roof. Despite the exertion, her breath remained measured. From this elevated vantage point, she could see the entire village. The whitewashed dwellings reflected the moonlight, looking like the crooked molars of a sleeping giant. A few emaciated dogs trotted through the deserted streets, pausing to scavenge rotted fruit from heaps of rubbish. Dzongsar Village might as well have been the end of the earth.

The monastery's roof cascaded in a series of tiers, like layers of a cake that got smaller toward the top. A row of tiny, paneless windows lined the gaps between each tier to ventilate the fortress. Kalina leaned through one of the windows and peered into the cavernous chamber below. Her long, sable braid dangled into the room.

Rows of folding tables crossed the floor. Blocky equipment and clusters of glass containers spread across nearly every available inch of horizontal space. Refrigerators hummed in the corner. The space had a modern atmosphere that contrasted with the historic architecture. It looked like a laboratory.

Kalina removed a five-clawed grappling hook from her belt and fastened it to the end of a long nylon cable wrapped snuggly around her waist. She wedged the hook's sharp flukes into the grooved lip lining the window's frame. Holding the line taut, she leaned backward and silently rappelled into the lab. The search for her target, Officer Olen Grave, began.

26

Beijing, People's Republic of China

PRESIDENT LI BINGWEN watched a perfect crimson bead form on his fingertip. He'd pricked himself tugging stubborn weeds from his rose garden. Li worked an old towel in his soiled hands, leaving muddy streaks on the terry cloth. His manicured hedge of white China roses shimmered in the glow of approaching head-lights. Squinting, the president watched a black sedan roll up the gravel driveway of his private estate.

Only a handful of people could have made it past the security guards. The sedan crunched over loose pebbles and rumbled to a stop about ten meters away. A familiar figure emerged from the vehicle's rear passenger side. Li grimaced and pulled himself up to stand.

"Don't get up on my account," the silhouette said. "Those bushes won't prune themselves. What in God's name are you doing out here so late anyway?"

President Li wobbled on two stiff legs. His aging knees ached from kneeling too long. He rarely spent time in the garden any-more—he employed a crew of capable grounds keepers. Yet tonight the thought of those pernicious weeds growing taller and thicker, sucking the nutrients from his flower bed with impunity, had simply been too unsettling. He'd spent the last hour outside, confronting the vegetative invaders.

Li approached his visitor with a stooped yet confrontational stride. Within seconds, he stood nose to nose with General Huang. "I should ask you the same thing," Li spat. "You shouldn't have come here."

"Then how else would I have had the pleasure of enjoying this breathtaking landscape? It's quite masterful, what you've done with the grounds." The general gestured facetiously toward the expansive natural tapestry of lavender Russian sage, speckled toad lilies, and plum trees blanketing the hillside, running up to the base of President Li's palatial residence. "How do you find the time, comrade?"

"Get to the point, Yipeng. You didn't drive all the way out here to admire my withering peonies."

"Withering, indeed." General Huang's disingenuous grin melted into his customary glower. "Xu Kang is dead," he said bluntly.

The president nodded silently. He'd expected the news. At last count, the bombing of the Great Hall of the People had claimed fifteen victims. As of yet, the public was unaware that a member of China's highest political body was among them. Xu, one of the Politburo Standing Committee's newest members, had stood only a few paces from the blast site. His injuries had been inoperable.

Xu Kang's luck had been bound to run out sooner or later. Three years ago he'd been an unremarkable Party boss in Shanghai. Since then, Xu's career had skyrocketed. He owed his success to General Huang, who had handpicked Xu for ascension into the upper echelon of Beijing politics.

The choice made perfect sense. Xu hailed from a distinguished family of PLA heroes and was staunchly promilitary. Huang had needed friends at the top. Of the committee's seven members, only two could be counted as his allies. Three out of seven votes had relegated him to the minority—not a position Huang enjoyed. So, last October he'd convinced the Politburo to increase the members of its preeminent council from seven to nine. With two new slots up for grabs, the general had stacked the deck with Xu and another of his puppets from Guangzhou. President Li had never determined how Huang pulled it off, but presumably his strategy involved the typical blend of bribery and blackmail. Overnight, the general's power base on the committee had expanded to five voting members, including Huang himself. A majority. The maneuver had allowed Huang to blindside President Li at the next plenum and commandeer China's top military post.

"Your coalition is down a man. Xu's soul has barely left his body, and you're already vying for my vote," Li said, disgusted. If the general hoped to retaliate against Taiwan, he would need to convince Li's faction to change its position.

"We haven't time for grudges, Bingwen. Not since the fall of the Qing dynasty has our country faced an existential crisis of this magnitude. Our enemies are pounding on the gates. The Chinese people see only weakness in their government. We mustn't forget, revolution runs deep in our veins. The bombing was just the beginning."

"You think the attack was a targeted assassination? And we're next?"

"This isn't about you and me, comrade. You must see that. The entire system is crumbling. Men like us are all that hold this government together. We must put our differences aside and act. Tonight."

The president lowered his voice. "If we invade Taiwan, it will mean war with the Americans."

"I refuse to accept that as an inevitability. Washington is completely overextended in the Middle East. The Americans can't afford another unfounded war," Huang countered.

"They would be coming to Taiwan's defense. What makes you think the U.S. would view that as unfounded?"

"Because we were not the aggressors! The People's Republic of China is a sovereign nation defending itself against a vicious biological attack. *Taiwan's* attack. Tell me this, Bingwen, if Iran dropped a dirty bomb on Times Square, fifty thousand American soldiers would swarm Tehran within hours, would they not? Taiwan hit us ten days ago, and we've done nothing but give speeches. How many of our people must die from this virus before we acknowledge the real disease is our own cowardice?"

"You're wrong, Yipeng. Now is the time to be cautious and prudent, not impulsive. We still don't know where Blood River virus came from. Not definitively."

"I suppose an infected NSB officer just happened to wander into the TAR for some sightseeing," Huang quipped.

"It's all circumstantial. Chang was operational—no doubt about that—but we have no evidence that his illness had anything to do with his reason for visiting Tibet. What if he contracted the disease by accident? We mustn't hurl Asia into chaos because some insect bit an NSB officer on his way to having tea with a handful of Tibetan separatists."

"You're not thinking clearly. Asia is *already* in chaos. You can't see the bloodshed from inside this compound, but China is suffering. The war is at your doorstep, comrade."

Li moved in closer to the general until he could smell the man's breath. His footing felt more solid than before. "Unless you can prove Tang's complicity—that Taiwan intentionally unleashed the virus—you'll never convince me to support an invasion. Your stranglehold over the Standing Committee died with Xu. At best you've got four votes, and that's not enough."

General Huang's steely eyes revealed no expression. Li doubted the man had ever believed this late-night entreaty would succeed.

"Do you know the worst part about all this?" Huang asked. "Taipei is counting on us being too divided and too craven to fight back. President Tang is using our weakness against us, and it's working."

Without waiting for a retort, the general returned to his sedan. Before ducking into the back seat, he said, "You may want to wash out that cut, comrade. We'd hate for it to get infected."

Li felt the warm trail of blood dripping from his finger. He hadn't noticed the wound open up again. The rose's thorn must have punctured the skin deeper than he'd thought.

General Huang's car crunched down the path, turned the corner, and drove out of view. A moment later, another set of headlights appeared at the mouth of the driveway, racing toward President Li, kicking up clouds of gray dust. Li recognized the vehicle. It was a police cruiser. The same model used by the army. Huang's army. President Li dropped the mud-stained towel, defeated. They were coming for him.

CHAPTER

27

Dzongsar Village, Tibetan Autonomous Region,
People's Republic of China

OLEN SPRINTED THROUGH thick smoke. Swirls of dust enveloped him. Seconds later he was facedown in the dirt, spit-
ting gravel. He'd tripped over something.

A body.

No, an arm. Its contorted elbow twisted unnaturally from a
bloodied stump. Five crooked fingers snatched his ankle.

Olen scuttled away and pulled himself up briefly, but an explosion forced him back to his knees. A stinging pain ripped through
his side. His shirt felt wet and sticky. He was bleeding out.

*   *   *

The man's heart thumped as he slept. The woman standing over his
unconscious body could see it pulsating in the center of his bare
chest. He had kicked off the blankets, which made it easier for her to
see whether he had anything in his hands. She would work quickly
and slip out of the monastery unnoticed. She raised a pair of needle-
nose wire cutters and inched toward the man's throat.

*   *   *

Olen's lungs filled with blood. His legs seized up. He sucked in shallow, dust-filled breaths, then coughed violently, choking, struggling to the end.

Olen burst awake, disoriented from the nightmarish dream. A woman stood over him, wielding some kind of knife. He rolled onto his side, toward the attacker. Reaching up, Olen grabbed her outstretched arm and pulled her off-balance with a firm grip. Shifting his weight, he hurled the woman onto the mattress and snatched the weapon from her hand. He rolled on top of her, pinning her to the mattress, and pressed the tip of the wire cutters to the soft skin just under her jawbone.

"Kipton! Stop! It's me!" the woman shouted.

Olen sat up, keeping his attacker immobilized under his body. He relaxed when he saw the distress on Jo's face.

"There are easier ways to get me into bed, Doctor," Olen said.

Jo rolled her eyes. "If that were my goal, you'd be the one on bottom."

"Sounds fun. Minus the part when you slice off my balls." Olen tossed the wire cutters on the bed.

Jo's eyes traced down Olen's naked chest, slick with sweat. The key hung from his neck, inches from Jo's face.

He followed her gaze. "Ah, you know what it opens. You could've just asked me for it." Olen pulled the chain over his head and dropped the key into Jo's open hand. "Are you gonna let me in on your little secret?"

* * *

Jo explained the story she'd heard from the monk, about Sumati and the Black Sect. "I think Sumati believed patient zero was the physical embodiment of a lost soul—a dead man, overcome by demonic spirits, searching for the path to heaven, stuck in a kind of earthly purgatory."

"Neat," Olen said. "How does that help us?"

"According to the monk, followers of the Black Sect are deeply religious people. They see things differently. For them, the natural world and the spiritual world are not as distinct as in Western faiths. Sumati said patient zero 'came from the sun.' This makes more sense to me now. The Bon faith explains that the souls of the dead follow the path of the rising sun in search of the afterlife."

"So, patient zero entered the village from the east. We should search there, retrace his path through the brush, search for anything that might explain how he got sick."

"No, we've already checked the east side. We need to search near the *other* sun."

The answer clicked in Olen's mind. "The painted rocks near the field. It's not a flower; it's a sun," Olen said. "Sumati must've seen patient zero emerge from the woods behind those stones."

"Right where you said the boy found this key." Jo raised her fist, clutching the chain.

"Do you think the key belonged to patient zero?"

"Like you said before, people don't lock their doors in Dzongsar. This key was brought here by a visitor, an *outsider*," Jo replied. "Patient zero hid something out there, in the forest, behind those rocks."

Olen pouted. "I'm hurt, Jo."

"Because you thought I was trying to murder you in your sleep with wire cutters?"

"No, because you weren't going to take me with you."

"Do I still have that choice?" Jo asked.

"Not a chance, Doc."

28

Dzongsar Village, Tibetan Autonomous Region,
People's Republic of China

THE EVENING CLOUDBURST had softened the soil into slop. Jo hopped over puddles of rainwater, refusing to allow another storm to soak her newly dried boots. Her leaps and lunges amused Olen, who trudged indifferently through the sopping terrain.

The clearing ended at a thick tree line about a hundred yards ahead. The field looked much larger without the children playing on it, scampering after an underinflated soccer ball. A generous moon offered more than enough light for them to stay on course. The heavy clouds had passed, and countless glimmers dusted the night sky. Underneath the universe, here in Dzongsar Village, Olen felt incredibly isolated. Beijing was a world away. Washington even farther. A man wandering out of these woods—alone and delirious—seemed absurd.

"The key," Olen said. "What exactly do you expect to find out here?"

"A lock," Jo teased.

Olen guided Jo to the precise spot where the kid had found the key. It took only a few minutes to discover the tree—Jo noticed it first—and the small cross etched into its bark. The marking was subtle. If they hadn't been examining the tree line so intently, they might have missed it altogether.

"A crucifix?" Olen asked. He tried to sound naïve, but his gut told him the marking was not a religious symbol. It reminded him of something he'd seen many times before, in Paris, Moscow, Baghdad. A signal site for a dead drop.

To communicate covertly, spies like Olen sometimes rolled messages into tiny tubes and hid them under bridges or rocks, anywhere out of sight, and then signaled to their contacts that they were ready for pickup. Sometimes the signal was a chalk mark on the side of a mailbox or a piece of chewing gum stuck to a street sign. Or a scratch in the bark of a tree.

But there can't be a dead drop hidden in the dark depths of the Tibetan rain forest. Right?

Patient zero was becoming more and more interesting.

"No," Jo finally answered. "It's not a cross. It's the Chinese character for the number ten." She moved closer until her nose nearly touched the bark. She traced the carving with the jagged end of the key. It slid smoothly through the crevice. "In China, ten symbolizes rebirth. It marks the end of one cycle and the beginning of the next. You can count to ten on your hands before you run out of fingers. Then you must start over from the beginning."

"That means—"

"Patient zero had reached the end of his cycle here on earth. He knew he was a dead man."

"But why mark this tree?" Of course, Olen thought he already knew the answer. But did Jo?

"He was communicating with someone," Jo said. She fixated on the marking. Her eyes refused to break contact.

"Maybe he hid something?"

"That was my thought exactly. Look in the trees, on the ground. Whatever he hid, it would have to be big enough to have a locking mechanism."

The pair split up to cover more ground. Olen cleared clumps of fallen leaves with sweeping kicks. A few clung to his muddy boots. Examining the forest for an unknown object—and in the dark—seemed futile. Besides, a dead drop required two people.

Patient zero's contact had probably emptied the drop days ago. They could be searching for something that was long gone. He should come back in the morning when—

"He buried it," Jo announced.

Olen couldn't see her—she'd wandered too far into the thicket—so he headed in the direction of Jo's voice. Gnarled roots grabbed at his feet. When he reached the doctor, she'd already begun scooping handfuls of mud from an unnatural depression in the earth.

"He didn't pack the soil enough," Jo explained. "The rain condensed it. I spotted the sinkhole right away."

Olen crouched and helped the doctor scrape out the backfill. The ground was saturated beneath the surface, and a pool of brown runoff filled their hole. Finally, Olen's knuckles knocked against something hard and flat. Jo heard the thud, too, and stopped scooping. Olen pushed into the earth, feeling around for the edges, grunting from the exertion.

"Move, Kipton. Let me do it," Jo insisted. She pressed against his shoulder and slipped her hands over his forearms.

"Hang on. I can feel the sides."

Olen pushed into the mud to get his hands underneath the object and work it free. Murky water dribbled off the metal box as he lifted it out of the pit. It looked like a steel cashbox. Jo snatched the box and wiped the muck from the top and sides. She found the lock and used her finger to clean out the keyhole.

The instant Jo lifted the lid, everything changed. She revealed an object sealed inside a plastic bag, neatly wrapped in a piece of cheesecloth.

A syringe with a long hypodermic needle.

29

Dzongsar Village, Tibetan Autonomous Region,
People's Republic of China

OLEN AND Jo backtracked through the clearing at a quickened pace. Their discovery of the needle in the cashbox would redirect the entire investigation. Olen could sense Jo's mind churning. The doctor held her arms tightly across her body, gripping the steel box against her chest.

When they returned to the monastery, Olen said he planned to head to his room to organize his notes. It seemed like a logical activity for a journalist who wanted to record the details of the evening while they were fresh. Olen didn't like lying to Jo. He'd grown fond of the doctor, and they worked well as a team. Under different circumstances, they might have made a decent couple. Olen imagined the hot nights, wrestling in sweat-soaked bedsheets (ideally without the wire cutters).

He shook away the thought. Jo was a government official of the People's Republic of China, not some weekend hookup. He needed to contact Fort Detrick, and so far he'd spotted only one working telephone in the entire village.

Before Olen left Vienna for Beijing, analysts across the intelligence community had created a laundry list of hypotheses for what might have caused the outbreak. Bioterrorism seemed too farfetched, too risky. More likely, a sick monkey had ended up on some poor fuck's dinner table. That was how these things normally happened. But a hypodermic needle, hidden in the woods, pointed to something much more nefarious, something premeditated. Dzongsar Village had been purposely attacked. But why? By whom? Who the hell was patient zero?

*   *   *

Olen didn't have to break into Sumati's home. The front door didn't have a lock, and even if it had, the PLA would've already smashed it. The army required unfettered access to Sumati's miracle blood. Olen, however, was more interested in the woman's phone. During his visit to Sumati's home earlier that day, he'd noticed a landline in the kitchen. He planned to use it to send an urgent message to his boss, Allyson.

The house was quiet and dark, its occupants tucked into bed. Olen padded toward the phone, shifting his weight from one foot to the next to minimize creaking from the floorboards. The phone looked ancient. It had a long, curling cord, and part of its plastic base had chipped off. He hoped it still worked.

*   *   *

In the provisional lab, Jo examined the syringe, squeezing the plastic cylinder gently between her double-gloved fingers. The piston wasn't fully pushed in, leaving a small amount of solution pooling at the tip of the nozzle.

Jo depressed the plunger, ejecting a single drop onto a glass microscope slide. She added a fluorescent stain and overlaid a thin cover slip to prevent contamination. The limpid bead spread into a wide circle. She deposited the remainder of the sample into a test tube and placed a rubber cap over the tube's mouth to seal it in. She'd eventually need to examine the fluid with an electron microscope in her state-of-the-art lab in Shanghai. That examination would reveal much more than what she'd see with the field lab's basic optical equipment. Regardless, she had to take a peek.

Jo flicked on the microscope's base light and peered into the ocular lens. She'd left the overhead lights off to enhance the resolution of the specimen through the lens. Working in the dark was a safety violation, but the lab was deserted, so Jo wasn't concerned about protocols.

Jo's pupils contracted at the bright light in the eyepiece. Tiny oblong shapes speckled the field of view, ablaze with vivid color. Cells. They weren't smooth and round like healthy cells. Their edges had collapsed to form grotesque morphologic aberrations. Dark plaque collected in inky splotches, indicating the unmistakable cytopathic effect—the unique fingerprint of a nasty viral infection.

Jo's heart thumped. Her team had tried unsuccessfully for a week to generate a viable culture and isolate the virus. The illusive particle was a hundred times smaller than a typical bacterium, so Jo couldn't visually examine its biological structure using the simple light microscope, and she'd have to run antibody tests to confirm it. But in her gut, Jo already knew the truth. She was staring at Blood River virus.

The image in the eyepiece confirmed the searing fear Jo had felt after first discovering the hypodermic needle. The epidemic wasn't a spontaneous occurrence, not Mother Nature defending herself against the scourge of deforestation. There was no rare primate or bat species harboring BRV45 deep within its tissue. Someone *intended* for this vicious infection to spread. Someone knew the disease would massacre thousands, if not millions. Someone wanted China to suffer. There was no denying it now. BRV45 was a weapon, and patient zero had been its human delivery mechanism. Chang Yingjie: the Taiwanese spy.

Had he acted alone? Not likely. Jo recalled her briefing to the Standing Committee. General Huang's concerns had seemed like paranoid delusions. Could it be true? Was Taiwan responsible?

The doctor twisted the knobs on the compound microscope to sharpen its focus. Staring, sometimes for hours, into a droplet the size of a single tear had strange side effects. Some people felt painfully confined, imprisoned within the small circle of light. Jo felt liberated. The microscopic world was a wondrous terrain. The detail of her specimen absorbed her. She dove into it, climbing towering mountain ranges, sliding down rocky cliffs, washing away in silvery rivers. She lost touch with her physical surroundings, at the desk, in the lab.

Perhaps that was why Jo didn't notice the silhouette materialize in the shadows of the second-floor balcony overlooking the work space.

Leaning into the microscope, Jo studied every facet of the sample's rugged landscape. She blinked to moisten her eyes, and the puzzle pieces snapped into place, one by one.

The truth about Blood River virus was worse than she'd ever imagined.

*   *   *

Sumati's phone was bugged, Olen assumed. A team of MSS linguists, holed up in a dark room thousands of miles away, were probably waiting for someone to lift the handset. The voice of an American, or anyone speaking English for that matter, would light their hair on fire. That's why Olen's prearranged signal didn't require him to speak at all.

He reached for the phone and held his breath so he could tune his ears to the slightest noise. If anyone discovered he'd returned to Sumati's home without his escort, he'd have a difficult time avoiding a PLA prison cell.

The house was dead silent.

*   *   *

Jo jerked back from the microscope. Her lungs tightened. She pulled the surgical mask from her mouth and swallowed gulps of air with her eyes squeezed shut. She opened them just as the microscope burst apart. Flying metal and plastic crashed into a rack of empty test tubes and beakers. A shard of glass clinked against Jo's safety goggles. She yanked them from her face and tossed them aside. Had the rogue fragment come from the virus-tainted slide? Jo dropped to her knees and tucked in her chin, keeping her head low.

Microscopes didn't just spontaneously explode. There was a shooter in the lab.

30

*Dzongsar Village, Tibetan Autonomous Region,
People's Republic of China*

THE BULLET HAD smashed the microscope's LED bulb and extinguished the lab's only light source. Jo's eyes struggled to adjust to the darkness. She crawled across the floor. Glass shards cut her knees, and somewhere buried among the debris was a needle laced with a hellish virus. Even the smallest puncture could expose her to a fatal infection.

Arms outstretched into the abyss, Jo felt her way to the nearest wall. Her pupils soaked up the ambient moonlight seeping in from the narrow windows in the roof. She paused to listen for her attacker's footfalls. The wind moaned outside the monastery's fortified walls. Where was the shooter? Where was Kipton?

Jo crept across the lab toward the animal containment center—the room Amy had called "the Zoo." A curtain of thick plastic strips hung in the doorway. The translucent slats refracted blue beams in a thousand directions, creating a kaleidoscope of geometric shapes. The patterns of color and shadows were disorienting, and Jo couldn't tell if someone was waiting on the other side of the curtain. She reached out and made a gap in the strips. The plastic felt slick. She pushed through and almost slipped on a puddle. Catching her balance, Jo felt all the air rush out of her lungs when she saw the body sitting on the floor, slumped against the wall. *Amy.*

The bullet had entered just above her right eye, ripped through her brain, and blown out the back of her skull. A dark starburst glimmered on the stone wall just above Amy's head. Jo looked down at her own feet. Fresh blood coated the soles of her shoes. Horrified, she tore them off. She didn't want to leave a trail of bloody footprints.

Jo heard the attacker crunching through broken glass in the lab. She stepped over Amy's splayed legs, careful to avoid the pooling gore. She wanted to get out of the building, just start running, but someone could be waiting for her outside. Another gunman. Jo's best option was to hide inside the monastery until the intruder found whatever he'd come for and left.

*   *   *

Olen was preparing to lift the phone's handset from the cradle when it screamed under his fingertips. *It was ringing.* He froze. Any second, Sumati or the girl would emerge from the bedroom to answer the call. The spy leapt behind the sofa and crouched low. Even with the lights off, he could see the bloodstain on the wood floor under Sumati's rocker. Large, circular smears.

The phone rang three more times. Olen's pulse returned to a normal speed. If someone had spotted him, called the phone to knock him off-balance, a team of security guards would've already stormed the house and shoved Olen into a sack. Phones rang. People called sick relatives. It was nothing.

The house fell silent, and Olen rose from his hiding spot. Something wasn't right. Even if Sumati and the girl had decided to ignore the late-night call, the shrill ringer should have stirred them. Olen heard no movement at all coming from the back of the house. No rustling of bedsheets. No footsteps.

Olen considered aborting his plan. Surely there were other landlines in Dzongsar, in other homes. He should leave, make contact with VECTOR some other way. Instead, he fought back his better judgment and headed deeper into the house.

*   *   *

The animals shrieked and rattled their aluminum cages. The gunshot had agitated them, especially the Tibetan macaque, its fiery orange eyes blazing, head whipping side to side. Running on adrenaline, Jo pushed through a swinging door to the decontamination chamber, leaving the Zoo and its unnerving soundtrack behind. The assailant would follow her. Jo had only a few seconds to hide.

The illuminated control panels of the decontamination pods washed the room in an eerie cobalt glow. Jo rushed to the farthest pod and sealed herself inside. If the killer discovered her hiding place, there would be nowhere to run.

*   *   *

The door to the first bedroom was ajar. Olen could see only blackness through the cracked opening. With the light touch of his fingertips, he nudged the door, and its hinges squealed. He paused and listened. Nothing. He'd managed to expand the gap between the door and the jamb about two feet. Enough to squeeze through.

Hugging the wall, Olen examined the room. The bed was a nest of ruffled sheets. A torn pillow leaked tufts of cotton. The bedroom was in complete disarray. Moreover, it was unoccupied.

Possibly the teenager and Sumati were together in the other bedroom. Olen checked it with equal caution. In stark contrast to the first, the second bedroom was barren. A tin chamber pot sat on the floor, and a small cot, like the ones used in shelters after a natural disaster, was pushed up against the wall. The cot was empty.

A draft prickled the skin on Olen's forearm. The night air seeped in from a broken window. Glass glittered on the floor like diamond dust. A line of blood trailed from the cot to the windowsill. Sumati and the girl had been taken, possibly killed. Someone did not want the outbreak's sole survivor talking.

Olen feared his instincts about the Dzongsar investigation were right. He couldn't ignore the mounting evidence: the absence of a full-scale emergency medical response team, the utter lack of biohazard safety equipment, and now, Sumati's abduction.

He rushed back to the phone and dialed a number from memory. In a few seconds, the kitchen phone in a noodle house in

Lhasa's Chengguan District would ring, but only once before Olen promptly hung up. He waited thirty seconds and then dialed a second number, this one belonging to a low-end hotel in Dagzê County. He disconnected after two short rings.

The signal was simple. The guys and gals at NSA kept a close watch on certain predesignated phone lines in Tibet. A multimillion-dollar computer at Fort Meade would intercept and log the two incoming calls. The quick succession of the calls, both with the same origin, created a unique transmission pattern that the system would flag. Any moment, an NSA analyst in Maryland would see a blip on his computer monitor. In less than sixty seconds, Olen had covertly communicated a critical message to his chain of command: *Get me the hell out of here.*

Olen left the house and jogged back to the monastery. An exfiltration from the TAR was a long shot—and it would probably take days for his message to get to Allyson—but he had limited options and it didn't hurt to try. In any case, it would inform Allyson that he'd uncovered critical intelligence and needed to debrief as soon as possible. In the meantime, he needed to find Jo. She'd become a pawn in someone's vicious plot. The thought of her in danger stirred feelings of raw anger. Jo was tough, not a damsel in distress, but Olen flooded with a desire to whisk her away, sweep her into his arms. The brave knight. He hoped he wasn't too late.

CHAPTER

31

Fort Meade, Maryland, USA

SENIOR INTELLIGENCE ANALYST Gabriel Snyder reached for his desk phone the moment he saw the alert flashing on his computer screen. After a single ring, a gruff voice answered.

"Grave just checked in," Snyder explained. "TRIDENT registered two blips. It's a code six. He's requesting exfiltration."

TRIDENT was the NSA system that monitored signal lines all over the world, like the two Lhasa-based landlines Officer Grave had dialed. The billion-dollar surveillance platform functioned as a vital covert communications tool for field officers who needed to preserve cover.

"Location?" the gruff voice asked.

"Tibet. Lhasa." Silence. *Did the connection drop?* "Hello?" Snyder said.

"Has NSA disseminated anything yet?"

"No, I placed all of Grave's lines under restricted access, just as you instructed. I'm the only one who can see the alert."

"I see."

"You asked me to notify you of any activity. I'll need to fire this off to the emergency exfiltration team, get our boy out of there," Snyder explained.

"No," came the sharp reply. "Do not disseminate."

"But—"

"I'll handle it on my end. Deactivate the TRIDENT alert, and don't even think about activating the exfil teams."

The call cut out before Snyder could reply. TRIDENT signals were lifelines for overseas operatives, especially those working in denied enemy territory who needed help getting out of dangerous situations. Snyder should be setting a tactical plan in motion. Every minute counted. Why was he being ordered to stand down?

What was going on at VECTOR? First, an officer had gone missing. Then, another had been hung out to dry. And then there was Director Cameron. That woman was as slippery as a sea otter. Still, it was clear Cameron had no idea Snyder had been watching her for weeks.

Snyder rolled his mouse and deleted the TRIDENT alert—a serious breach of protocol that he regretted almost immediately. *What if no one responds? That man could be in serious danger.* Snyder felt his stomach rumble. He leaned back in his swivel chair and popped a handful of sunflower seeds into his mouth.

*   *   *

HELMSMAN disconnected the call with the NSA analyst and thought through the next move. It seemed Officer Grave had made it to the Tibetan Autonomous Region. Alive. A regrettable outcome, to be sure, but a rectifiable one.

Now the priority concern was Snyder. The man had demonstrated his loyalty, discreetly reporting the TRIDENT alert, but it didn't cost him much to place a phone call. Denying a distress signal from an officer in the field, however, would raise the stakes for Snyder. Eventually, someone would discover that the analyst had ignored Grave's exfiltration request, covered up the signal intercept. Snyder was now complicit. The man had to understand the risks. He wasn't a complete idiot. But how far was he willing to go?

Be a good boy, Snyder. Follow orders and don't ask questions.

CHAPTER

32

Dzongsar Village, Tibetan Autonomous Region,
People's Republic of China

KALINA TOOK GREAT pride in her marksmanship—a skill that had earned her high praise among her peers. She'd missed the shot only because that woman had jerked her head back at the last second.

Locating her primary target was becoming more tedious than she'd expected. Kalina had managed to take out a handful of doctors, but she needed to find Grave and complete her assignment. First, she would eliminate the woman in the lab coat. Now was not the time to get sloppy. There could be no loose ends.

The huntress crouched low and stalked her prey.

* * *

Jo struggled to control her breathing inside the decontamination pod. Hiding in such a tight, enclosed space didn't help to calm her frayed nerves. She focused on the low hum of the generator. She thought of Kipton. He was out there, somewhere. Kip was a good man. She hoped he hadn't ended up like Amy.

Minutes felt like hours. Eventually, the animals in the Zoo stopped screeching. Jo strained her ears, trying to listen for the assailant's footsteps. With any luck, he would breeze past the decon pods and Jo could escape unnoticed.

Then an earsplitting scream tore through the monastery. *The Tibetan macaque.* The shooter had left the lab and was now passing through the Zoo. In seconds, the killer would enter the decontamination chamber.

The idea that someone would break into the Q-Zone laboratory and begin murdering doctors seemed absurd. However, Jo knew what the intruder wanted: the evidence contained within the hypodermic needle. When patient zero buried that syringe in the forest, he certainly hadn't intended for Jo to dig it up. No, he'd hidden the needle for someone else to find, and Jo was almost certain that person was already in Dzongsar.

* * *

Olen sprinted along the narrow, winding road leading up to the monastery. The moon shone brightly, so anyone watching Sumati's residence would have easily spotted him fleeing the house unescorted, but he had bigger concerns now. Once he found Jo, they needed to evacuate the Q-Zone immediately. The teen soldiers guarding the checkpoint would offer no challenge. If Olen's instincts were right, they were already long gone.

* * *

Kalina considered putting the macaque out of its misery, if only to silence its piercing cry. One clean shot through the giant monkey's hairy forehead would do the trick. She held back, knowing the gunshot would alarm the other wild animals. The room smelled like excrement. She was happy to find the exit and leave the fetid beasts behind.

The next room was sterile, nothing like the jungle she'd just passed through. There were neat stacks of medical gowns and a tower of boxes containing latex gloves. Maybe it was some kind of scrub room. There were three egg-shaped pods in the center of the space. What were they used for? Storage? Experiments? Whatever the case, they were big. Big enough to conceal a person.

The assassin studied the control panel on one of the egg pods. It was a touch screen displaying a simple alphanumeric keypad.

The pods required a code to open—a code Kalina didn't have. She considered firing a few rounds through each of the life-sized capsules, but she'd already wasted enough time, and finding Grave took priority. Let the doctor hide. Kalina turned away and scanned the chamber for an exit. An iron door led out to an adjoining courtyard. She'd started for it when one of the egg pods suddenly lit up. The white orb radiated, and the touch keypad changed from deep blue to crimson.

Kalina smiled wickedly. The assassin raised her Sig Sauer and aimed squarely at the glowing pod.

33

McLean, Virginia, USA

ALLYSON TOSSED HER car keys into a mason jar on her kitchen table. She grabbed an apple from an unpacked grocery bag and bit into the skin. She never took the time to wash fruit.

A maroon file rested on the counter. Allyson placed her palm over it, splaying her fingers to keep its secrets from seeping out. What would President Barlow do when Allyson showed him? And she *would* show him—wouldn't she? Of course, she could withhold this too, just like the photo from MI6. Some things Barlow didn't need to know. She'd worked too hard to have him, or anyone, mess this up.

The file had arrived that morning, before dawn, delivered by a private courier. The shipping label didn't identify a sender. Under normal circumstances, a mysterious unmarked package delivered to the home of a senior government official would warrant a call to the FBI. But when the sharply dressed messenger rang her doorbell, Director Cameron hadn't been concerned. The man worked for the world's most exclusive courier service. SwissPax had built its reputation on privacy and discretion. They didn't advertise, and they certainly didn't work with just anyone. The company's stellar reputation came with a considerable price tag. SwissPax wasn't the kind of resource available to your run-of-the-mill anti-government nutjob.

When Allyson tore open the parcel, she'd found the plain maroon folder tucked inside. That flimsy folder guarded a distressing revelation.

Of course, the reliability of this information, like all intelligence, depended on the quality of its source. Unfortunately, the sender's excessively discreet method was designed to preserve anonymity. Allyson knew that if she called SwissPax for details, she'd learn that the package had come not from an individual but from a nondescript company in the Caribbean with a generic PO box. The delivery was truly untraceable.

Except Director Cameron knew exactly who had sent her the file.

34

Dzongsar Village, Tibetan Autonomous Region,
People's Republic of China

JO FLINCHED WHEN the decontamination pod switched on
unexpectedly. The device was designed to activate when the
person inside pressed the START DECON button. Jo was certain she
hadn't accidentally bumped into it.

Then she remembered. The pod automatically began its cycle
precisely two minutes after the hatch closed. This allowed the staff
to sterilize large equipment. Pulsing ultraviolet radiation now
enveloped Jo. The doctor squeezed her eyes shut to shield them
from the brightness. The short bursts of concentrated UV light
were harmless to people but lethal to most microorganisms. At
least the radiation would obliterate any trace of the virus that
might have clung to her body. If she'd been exposed in the lab, the
disinfectant cycle might save her life, as long as the shooter didn't
notice the pod light up like a Christmas tree.

A digital green bar slowly encircled the START DECON button,
indicating the cycle's progress. It reached about halfway around
the button, inching forward. The hatch wouldn't open until the
entire circle filled in and the decontamination sequence was complete. For at least another sixty seconds, Jo was a sitting duck.

A series of chirps cut through the low-pitched whirring of the UV pulses. Someone was accessing the pod's keypad. The shooter had found her. Jo's entire body tensed. Eyes wide open despite the blinding light, she fixated on the green progress bar. In seven seconds, the cycle would end and the hatch would snap open.

Four seconds.

Jo crouched helplessly into the fetal position and held her breath. The bloody image of Amy's limp body flashed into her mind.

Two seconds.

The green bar completed the full circle around the button and began to blink. The blinding lights shut off, and Jo could hear a hissing sound as the hatch seal cracked open.

Jo kicked her feet out forcefully as soon as the pod's door unlocked. Blinded by the UV light, she could barely make out the shadowy outline of a figure standing over her.

"Jesus, Jo. Why is it every time we meet, you're attacking me?" The shadow's voice rumbled with a familiar low pitch.

"What? Kip! Is that *you?*" Jo said, fighting back tears at the sight of the American. "I thought—"

"Later, Doc. We've got to get out of here."

"Kip, be careful," Jo replied breathlessly. "There's a shoot—"

Olen's head snapped back. Hot blood splashed against the white decontamination pod. He staggered backward, pressing his palm into his temple, but it didn't stop the gushing. Slick rivers flowed down his forearm.

CHAPTER

35

Washington, DC, USA

"TOO MUCH IS beginning to add up, Jim. It can't be a coincidence." National security adviser Nathan Sullivan never shied from giving the president tough news, no matter how much the man disliked hearing it.

"Here are the facts," he continued. "Our best-placed VECTOR officer in China supposedly vanished within days of the outbreak. Then Cameron sent a Mideast expert in his stead. The man couldn't order Kung Pao chicken in Chinatown. And, according to Director Cameron, now he's missing too."

"Grave is more capable than you think," Barlow said. "He's worked with Allyson going back to the Saddam days."

"That's my point, Jim. Cameron is CIA. That woman has allies deep within the Agency doing God knows what."

"It's a brotherhood, in a manner of speaking. We learned to trust each other with our lives." Barlow still identified strongly with his Langley brethren. "So, what are you suggesting, Nate? Do you think Allyson is deliberately bottlenecking the intel?"

"I'm not here to make accusations. Quite the contrary. It's time we all took a step back and looked at the situation with fresh eyes. For the first time in a half century, we know less about a major world crisis than goddamn CNN. Your desk should be plastered with intelligence reports, hot off the press by the hour. The best we've got is a watered-down assessment prepared with piss-poor confidence."

"Nate, I trust Allyson. I have no reason not to."

"Maybe now you do," the national security adviser said. He handed the president a report marked TOP SECRET.

Barlow's eyes narrowed as he scanned the document. "This came in this morning?"

"About twenty minutes ago."

"Does Allyson know?"

Sullivan just raised an eyebrow.

"I know how Allyson thinks," the president argued. "She's working an angle. Playing it out a little before coming to me. There's got to be more going on."

"Perhaps you're right, Jim. But it's my responsibility to be intellectually skeptical. We can't ignore the evidence before us." Sullivan gestured to the report. "This morning Officer Grave pinged TRIDENT with a distress signal. He's found something in Tibet, and for some reason, Allyson is keeping us in the dark."

36

Dzongsar Village, Tibetan Autonomous Region,
People's Republic of China

GETTING BLOWN UP sucked. Bomb shrapnel stung every-where—like a thousand stabs from a short knife—but this time the pain was localized behind Olen's ear. He'd been shot. The room spun. He tried to focus on Jo's terrified face, but the image kept contorting. The overwhelming dizziness pushed Olen to his knees. He couldn't control his body's downward momentum, so his forehead slammed into the floor. The pain overcame him. Chunks of vomit gurgled up his esophagus, coating his teeth.

A familiar voice rang inside Olen's mind. It was the same one he'd heard after a firefight in Baghdad. Allyson's voice.

You're not dead. Get up!

He hadn't lost consciousness. That meant the bullet had probably just grazed him. He'd survive.

Olen squinted. The spinning slowed. From his vantage point—his head still glued to the floor—Olen saw a pair of black boots approaching. The attacker, realizing the first shot had missed, was closing in to finish the job. In a moment the shooter would fire a bullet directly through his cerebral cortex. Olen had to strike now.

Marshaling every ounce of energy, Olen threw his weight sideways and rolled onto his back. Using the momentum, he torqued his waist and spun his left leg in a high arc over his body. At the apex of the kick, Olen's shoe connected with the assailant's outstretched arm. Something heavy tumbled across the wooden floorboards.

The gun.

Before the shooter could react, Olen swept his other leg a few inches off the ground and forcefully slammed it into his attacker's Achilles tendon. The second kick threw the shooter off-balance, and his assailant hit the ground with a thud. Olen felt a feathery rope brush his face—a long, black braid.

With the gun out of play, he had a much better chance of neutralizing his opponent, but his stomach was still roiling. The floor underneath his head felt slippery. Olen wondered if his brain was bleeding. He needed to regain control, so he swiftly wrapped his legs around the shooter's back like a human claw and yanked. Olen was now fairly certain his assailant was a woman. She grunted as her nose smashed into his right shoulder.

Olen crossed his thick forearms behind the woman's head, creating a vise. He twisted his wrist clockwise so he could pull down on the back of her neck and apply pressure directly to her windpipe. His legs squeezed the assassin's rib cage to prevent her from breaking free. A classic rear scissor choke hold.

Most amateur opponents would instinctively push up off the ground with their free left arm—their only point of leverage in this frustratingly prostrate position. Wickedly, this countermaneuver only tightened the stranglehold, quickening the victim's inevitable suffocation.

This woman was no amateur. Instead of struggling to pull away, she pressed downward, collapsing her body deeper into the choke. This transfer of weight allowed her to lift her left hand off the floor, which she used to smash a solid fist into the seeping bullet wound on the side of Olen's head.

Stunned by the searing pain, Olen released his grip. He wiped the fresh blood from his eyes in time to see the woman's arm cock back again, preparing to fire another punch.

Raising both knees to his chest, Olen launched a powerful double kick to the woman's stomach, sending her flying. Her body crashed into the tower of latex glove boxes. She howled. Maybe the blow had broken a rib. Olen hoped it had. He coiled in agony, rolling onto his side, hands pinned to his injured temple. He fought through the pain. It was only a scratch, after all.

You're not dead. Get up!

Olen lifted himself onto all fours and attempted to stand. He didn't notice the assassin pull a double-serrated combat knife from a sheath concealed in her right boot. With fire in her eyes, the woman lunged. She swung the blade high above her head, ready to drive the chiseled tip directly into Olen's spine.

*   *   *

A sudden concussive blast shook the walls. Another gunshot. The bullet slammed into the female assassin, hurling her body backward.

Jo wasn't sure where she'd hit the woman, but seeing the attacker's lifeless form crumpled on the floor gave her a sense of relief. The medical doctor was no stranger to death, but the act of intentionally taking a life required a certain numbness. She hadn't had time to wrestle with the morality of her decision. She'd acted on pure instinct to save herself—and Kipton.

Jo hadn't fired a weapon in years, but she was pleased her aim hadn't suffered. Once Kip had disarmed the shooter, Jo had rushed to recover the woman's Sig Sauer. Somehow she'd remembered how to check the safety, slide back the barrel to chamber a round, and cock the hammer. The motions came naturally, as if her muscles knew exactly what to do. Planting her feet in a wide stance, Jo had firmly raised the handgun and carefully squeezed the trigger with the very tip of her index finger—just as she'd practiced hundreds of times, in training, so many years ago.

Jo registered the shock on the American reporter's face. No doubt her proficiency with the semiautomatic pistol, not to mention her willingness to fire directly into the heart of another human being, surprised the man. She hadn't been completely forthright with Kipton. And judging by the man's tiger reflexes and expert grappling skills, it seemed he'd guarded a few secrets of his own. Maybe she should tell him the truth.

Jo tore into a plastic bag from the stack on the table and unwrapped a fresh pair of scrubs. She ripped the thin fabric along the shoulder seam to remove one of the sleeves.

"This will stop the bleeding," Jo said, winding the strip of cloth around Kipton's skull. "Head wounds bleed a lot, so it looks worse than it is. You have a minor contusion beside your left ear, but there's no trauma to the sphenoid or temporal bones."

"I've never seen a virologist shoot like that," Kipton said. "You're incredible."

Jo smiled weakly. "Pathogens aren't the only hazards of fieldwork."

The reporter took a deep breath and tried to stand. Jo grabbed his elbow to help the man to his feet. Already he seemed to be bouncing back from the attack.

"We've got to go, Doc," he said. "Dzongsar is a smoke screen."

"I know," Jo said with disappointment. She'd reached the same conclusion. The Politburo Standing Committee had never expected her to find anything in the Q-Zone. "But first I need to have a talk with the man pretending to be my ex-husband."

"That man you operated on wasn't your ex?" Kipton asked.

Jo shook her head.

"I don't know what's going on here, Jo, but that ninja lady almost shattered my face, so I think I deserve some answers."

"You're right, Kip. I haven't been honest with you."

CHAPTER

37

Dzongsar Village, Tibetan Autonomous Region,
People's Republic of China

THE RATIONAL PARTS of Jo's brain told her not to trust the
foreigner, but she ignored them and decided to go with her
gut. The American journalist had saved her life—and then she'd
saved his—so that bonded them, in a twisted sort of way. She had
no other allies in the Q-Zone. Kipton was it. He sat with a hand
pressed to his wound, smiling stupidly, even as a stripe of blood
trailed down his cheek. There were worse men to bond with. Yes,
it would be better if he knew the truth. At least part of it.

"I work for the Ministry of State Security. The Ministry of
Health is my official cover for this mission," Jo admitted.

"You're MSS?" Olen asked. "Since when do spies know so
much about viruses?"

"I'm a medical officer. My background in microbiology and
infectious diseases allows for special access to an array of sensitive
information. Medical conferences, leading-edge laboratories, pio-
neering university research—the scientific community is generally
prone to academic openness."

"So, you use your medical degree and respected credentials to
steal technology for the Chinese government," Kipton said bluntly.

"Not at all. The MSS's foremost concern is national security, just like the intelligence agencies in your country. We know bio-terrorism is an extraordinary threat. Biological weapons are easy to make, difficult to track, and even harder to contain. My job is to investigate the sudden emergence of new diseases and deter-mine if they were introduced deliberately."

"That sounds reasonable, but why does that have to be secret? Why the MSS?"

"Investigating outbreaks within China is simple. The govern-ment has full authority to access whatever it wants. I primarily collect intelligence on overseas epidemics. Even if China isn't the target of a bioattack, we want to know who has the capability to launch one. We can't take the risk that China could be the next victim. The American CDC and the World Health Organization are not going to let Chinese intelligence officers just waltz onto their teams, but they are reticent to turn away good civilian doc-tors when battling a major health crisis."

"Doesn't that seem a bit deceptive? Like you're taking advan-tage of people when they're most vulnerable?" Kipton asked.

"I don't see it that way. I use my skills and training to help determine the cause of an outbreak. I'm good at what I do, and oftentimes my involvement helps to curb the spread of a disease before it decimates a population. In return, my work allows the Chinese government to keep a close eye on dangerous contagions to better safeguard our own public safety. The intelligence I col-lect saves lives, even if I have to be a little deceptive to get it. There's no victim in what I do."

"If the MSS sent you to Dzongsar, they must have suspected foul play," Kipton said, moving closer. "Do you know where that syringe came from? The one we found in the forest?"

Jo considered telling him about Chang Yingjie. She was now certain patient zero had injected himself with a synthetic virus and buried the evidence in the forest. General Huang had been right. The Taiwanese government had used one if its own spies as a human biological weapon.

Jo nodded in the direction of the assassin's limp body, still coiled on the floor. "I think it's fair to say someone doesn't want us asking that question."

The reporter's furrowed brow suggested that he wasn't satisfied with her vague answers. He could tell she knew more than she was letting on.

"Who's the man in the clinic, Jo? The one pretending to be your ex-husband?" he pressed.

Jo sighed. Someone wanted her dead, and although she hated to admit it, she needed Kipton's help. In fact, she wanted it.

"It's his brother," she said. "Ru has a twin. His mother underwent an illegal in vitro fertilization procedure in the early 1980s. The method was highly experimental at the time, and a little dangerous, but it was the only way they could have two children and stay in China. Or so they thought. Someone reported the family to the local Party boss. Ru's parents fled to Taipei to avoid spending the rest of their lives in a work camp."

"Wait, so Ru is Taiwanese?"

"His mother was six months pregnant when they fled to Taipei. Ru was born in Taiwan, but technically you could call him a political refugee," Jo explained.

"But Amy said he came to the Q-Zone to investigate the virus. Why would the Chinese government let a Taiwanese doctor into Tibet?"

"Things have changed since the eighties. There's more political tension between the mainland and Taiwan, but also more cooperation. Cross-strait trade hit a trillion renminbi last year." Jo paused. Her voice grew softer and more vulnerable. "Besides, this virus is ravaging our country."

"And governments are reticent to turn away good civilian doctors in a crisis," Kipton repeated.

Jo nodded. She knew Ru's brother must've entered the Q-Zone before the MSS identified patient zero as a Taiwanese spy. Otherwise, he wouldn't have gotten past baggage claim at the airport. "A crisis like this can forge unlikely alliances."

"Amen, Doc," Kipton said, touching his bandaged scalp. "So why would Ru's twin show up in Dzongsar, impersonating his brother?"

"I don't know, but we need to find out," Jo replied.

"What if he's dead?"

"Then we may never know . . ." Jo trailed off.

"Know what?" the reporter asked.

"Kip, listen to me," Jo said grimly. "That man in the clinic isn't Ru, but he may be able to help us find him."

"Why is it so important that we track down your ex-husband?"

"Because I think Ru knows where this disease came from. I examined the biological sample from the syringe. It had . . . certain characteristics. I recognized the technique used to develop the culture. The cell line—"

"Okay, I believe you." Kipton cut her off. "How could Ru know where Blood River virus came from when no one else seems to have a clue?"

Jo inhaled deeply. Time to take the plunge. "I believe Ru engineered it," she answered soberly.

"What?" Kipton recoiled. "You think Ru cooked up this bug as a big 'eff you' to the Chinese government? Some kind of twisted revenge for exiling his parents?"

"I don't know why. Ru's an ass, but he wouldn't hurt—"

"What makes you think he'd even have the resources to pull off something this big?" Kipton continued. "He'd need help. A lab, materials, equipment, a staff. Years to conduct research in secret. And a mountain of money, probably."

"Kip," Jo said, "there's something I need to tell you about patient zero."

* * *

Olen digested Jo's sensational story.

"Just so I'm clear, Blood River virus is the result of a Taiwanese plot to destabilize the Chinese government," he said slowly. "Your ex-husband is some kind of evil genius who weaponized a synthetic disease for an NSB spy to unleash behind enemy lines."

"I don't have proof, but the evidence is starting to look that way. I wanted to think patient zero's affiliation with the NSB was coincidental, but when we found the hypodermic needle, it became clear that Chang infected himself intentionally."

"How do you know Ru is involved?"

"The solution in the syringe . . ." Jo paused, as if searching for a simple way to explain what she'd seen. "The solution contained live virus."

"I thought you couldn't see virus particles without an electron microscope."

"I can't. The virus itself is too small to see with the equipment we have out here in the field lab, but I can confirm its presence based on the observable damage to the cells."

"Cells?"

"A virus isn't like bacteria. It can't grow on a door handle or spoiled food. A virus can only survive inside a live cell. That's why growing a viral culture in a laboratory is so difficult. Essentially, we must expose healthy cells to the pathogen and wait for infection to occur. My team in Beijing has tried for days to produce a BRV45 culture in the laboratory with zero success."

"So, how do the cells point to Ru?" Olen asked.

"Virologists utilize a variety of cell lines to culture viruses, but the most efficient cell lines come from humans."

"Not just any humans, right?" Olen had learned a thing or two working for VECTOR.

"That's right. Typically cells from unborn fetuses. Human embryonic stem cells, to be precise."

"The Blood River virus culture we found in the syringe contained human stem cells. So, what?" Olen shrugged. "The practice may be controversial in the United States, but I know it's common elsewhere."

"The stem cells I saw in the syringe weren't actually embryonic, but they were *similar*."

Olen stared, waiting for the punch line. "I've just been shot in the face. Please make this easier to follow."

"In just the last few years, researchers have experimented with ways to artificially generate stem cells," Jo explained. "The process is extremely difficult and requires incredibly precise timing, but a recent scientific breakthrough proved we can actually reprogram adult human cells to *behave* like embryonic stem cells."

"So, the cells you saw in the hypodermic syringe were these—"

"Synthetic stem cells. Yes," Jo said.

"And what makes you think Ru had the ability to replicate these artificial human stem cells?"

"Because he invented them."

Olen shut his eyes. His temple pulsed.

Jo's voice lowered to a whisper. "There's only one man alive with the scientific expertise to produce the biological material in that syringe, and that man is my ex-husband. I don't know how or why, but Ru was undeniably involved in this outbreak."

Olen watched the doctor disintegrate from despair. The revelation had a profound physical effect on her, as if her heart was breaking all over again. She deserved better. How would Jo react if he reached out for her, pulled her in, held her? The idea was ludicrous. He wasn't thinking clearly. Jo had just revealed that she was MSS—a spy from a rival intelligence service. Olen couldn't let himself get too close.

The doctor's moment of vulnerability evaporated, replaced by her usual ironclad resolve. "Ru's brother knows where my ex-husband is," Jo hissed. "We've got to make him to tell us. No matter what it takes."

CHAPTER

38

Dzongsar Village, Tibetan Autonomous Region,
People's Republic of China

THE MASS OF bruised flesh rose and fell with a mechanical cadence. Next to the bed, a ventilator clicked in regular intervals. The machine's rubber hose twitched as it forced each breath through a narrow tube inserted directly to the patient's windpipe.

Purple contusions blotched the man's bare chest. His torso was lopsided and doughy, as if his rib cage had collapsed into his body. Two hollow eyes stared blankly from their swollen sockets. Olen could tell the man wasn't conscious. The putrid stench of urine and decay made him wonder if they'd come too late.

Jo marched across the makeshift clinic toward a medical supply cabinet. She didn't even glance at the gaunt man before returning to his bedside with an uncomfortably long needle. One quick prick and the lifeless jumble jolted awake.

"Epinephrine," Jo explained to Olen. The N95 respirator strapped to the doctor's face muffled her voice. Following the revelation that BRV45 was a genetically engineered killer, Jo had elected for more stringent safety measures. Olen didn't bother. If BRV45 could be contracted by breathing contaminated air, they were already dead.

The patient instantly reacted to the powerful neurotransmitter coursing through his veins. He thrashed like a fish, tearing at his soiled bedsheets. The ventilator screamed.

Within minutes, the initial shock from the injected hormone began to taper and the patient's convulsions subsided. He stared at Jo, who loomed over the man's decrepit form. His glossy eyes now flared with terror.

"Hello, Aiguo," Jo said.

The man gnawed at the air. His tongue curled and flicked, but only guttural grunts escaped from his bandaged throat.

"How is he supposed to tell us anything?" Olen asked. "I don't think he can even talk."

"I don't need him to talk," Jo said. She pulled a small whiteboard off the wall. The doctor shoved a dry-erase marker into the sick man's hand and held the board over his abdomen. "Where's Ru?" she demanded in English.

The man grimaced and turned his face away. Jo squeezed his chin with a gloved hand and yanked his head toward the whiteboard. "I know Ru had something to do with this outbreak. He sent you here. Why?" she asked.

The man's neck muscles flexed like those of a crane swallowing a frog. He spat in Jo's face, sending a glob of black mucus onto the mask of her respirator. Then, in defiance, he hurled the marker to the floor.

Jo twisted the knobs on the ventilator. The clicking and hissing stopped and the machine powered down. The man's face contorted into grotesque expressions of frenzied desperation. Jo had cut off his oxygen supply. She ignored his gasps and retrieved the dry-erase marker.

"Where's Ru?" she asked again, holding up the marker within the man's reach. His face turned blue. The capillaries in his eyelids bulged. He needed air. Suffocation was one of the cruelest forms of torture—something Olen knew from experience.

"What are you doing?" Olen barked, stunned by Jo's ruthlessness. He doubted the man would write anything. Deprived of oxygen, the mind entered a primitive survival mode, shutting down higher-order cognitive abilities to conserve energy. You started to see crazy shit, like purple elephants on surfboards. Jo wouldn't learn anything useful this way.

Jo leaned over the bed until her mask nearly touched the patient's nose.

"You'll be dead in less than a minute," she murmured breathily, a glint of raw pleasure in her eyes.

With a trembling hand, the man reached for the marker and scrawled a big circle on the whiteboard, filling it in with thick, black scribbles.

Satisfied, Jo stepped back from the bed. The diseased man shook his head violently as his blood cells swelled with carbon dioxide. Within seconds he'd black out. Jo seemed prepared to let him die.

A moment later she switched on the ventilator. The plastic tube twitched and the patient's chest heaved with each unnatural breath. Jo turned calmly to Olen. "It's time to go," she said, her voice like ice.

39

Beijing, People's Republic of China

GENERAL HUANG YIPENG's heels clicked against the lobby's marble floor. The commercial high-rise blended into Beijing's glistening Haidian District just outside Third Ring Road. Four guards protected the main entrance. They wore generic blue uniforms with white patches on their sleeves that read PINNACLE PROTECTION, but Lieutenant Wang recognized their QSZ-92 semiautomatic pistols—the standard-issue PLA sidearm.

Lieutenant Wang followed the general, flanked by a pair of smooth-skinned infantrymen armed to the teeth. Even Huang, who rarely carried a weapon, had a handgun holstered tightly to his right hip. After the attack on the Great Hall of the People, everyone was on high alert. The city had become unpredictable, dangerous. Even for generals.

The military retinue waited for the elevator doors to open. General Huang turned to his lieutenant. "The time?"

Wang tugged on his sleeve. "It's eight past eleven, sir."

"Ah, lucky eight! Good fortune. Remember that, Xiao Wang." The general patted his subordinate on the shoulder with fatherly affection.

The lieutenant didn't feel lucky. The general had dragged him from bed for the second night in a row. Wang couldn't imagine what emergency would require them to visit an empty office building on the other side of the city. When the security guards made no attempt to stop the four armed soldiers barging into their lobby, the picture grew clearer. It was a safe house. Huang was meeting a source. If the general planned to make contact personally, the source must be important. Still, the lieutenant couldn't recall a time when his boss had met directly with an informant. It was too risky for a man of the general's stature.

The elevator chimed. The soldiers stepped inside, and they descended to the basement. Seconds later, the doors opened into a wide hallway. It was decidedly less polished than the ultramodern lobby. A cadaverous gray coated the walls. Black scuff marks streaked the linoleum floor. The air tasted thick and stale. The men marched down the corridor behind Huang, who seemed to know where he was going. They passed doors with mundane labels like BUILDING MANAGEMENT and FACILITIES DIRECTOR. The general paused before one marked STORAGE. An electronic key card, like the kind used to enter a hotel room, materialized in his hand. Lieutenant Wang inhaled sharply when the door swung open, revealing a staircase leading down into a subbasement. Ceiling-mounted red lights illuminated the hidden shaft in a hellish glow. The walls were made of reinforced concrete. This was no safe house. It was a bunker.

The men burrowed deeper into the subterranean labyrinth, passing through another series of locked doors. The general's clearance defeated all obstructions, including a keypad code scrambler and fingerprint scan. The final chamber was cold and cramped. The kitchenette, lumpy sofa, and twenty-year-old television set did nothing to soften the bunker's jailhouse charm. Two men in civilian clothes slurped noodles in front of the TV. The watchmen.

When the general and his entourage charged into the room, one of the watchmen started to stand, his mouth bursting with half-chewed ramen. Before the man could speak, General Huang raised his pistol and fired two shots into the watchman's chest. Bloody broth erupted from his mouth, and he fell backward, toppling over his chair.

The second watchman raised his arms in surrender, palms trembling. The general swiveled his outstretched arm and fired again. The bullet tore through the man's windpipe. He collapsed, clawing at his punctured neck, gurgling. His lungs filled rapidly, and within seconds his wriggling stopped.

General Huang turned to face his lieutenant. His eyes flared with a menacing thrill. "It's a new day, Xiao Wang."

Lieutenant Wang's pulse raced, but he knew better than to react. The other PLA soldiers in the general's entourage looked astonishingly calm. One even appeared to smile.

The massacre had begun so unexpectedly, and then it was over. But Huang had more business to conduct. Wang noticed a steel hatch behind the table. It opened by turning a small wheel, like a bank vault. The general rotated the wheel and stepped inside. Wang followed dutifully, stamping red shoe prints onto the floor.

The lieutenant caught up to the general, who stood before a desk situated in the center of the vault. Behind the desk sat President Li Bingwen. He'd been reading by the muted light of a brass lamp. Silver roots now streaked his shoe-polish-black hair. He wore a wrinkled undershirt and clearly wasn't expecting visitors. Most likely, only a handful of people knew the president's location.

Li's voice wobbled. He must have heard the gunshots. "General, our country is suffering. You can't hold me here forever." Li looked so feeble, so decrepit. His eyes glistened.

General Huang lifted his pistol. He pressed the muzzle into the president's eye socket. "I don't intent to," he growled.

The top of President Li's head cracked like an egg.

40

Dzongsar Village, Tibetan Autonomous Region,
People's Republic of China

J O USED HER sleeve to erase the whiteboard. Aiguo had given up
his brother's location more easily than she'd expected, probably
only because he was in extreme pain and not thinking clearly. The
virus had ravaged Aiguo's internal organs. Death would come
within days, if not hours. Aiguo must have known it was only a
matter of time, yet when Jo switched off the ventilator, raw panic
had filled the man's eyes. He wanted to live, and that desire was
powerful enough to force him to divulge even the most guarded
information.

Jo believed Aiguo had come to the Q-Zone to retrieve the
hypodermic needle Chang had buried near the soccer field. Aiguo
had meant to ensure no one would ever uncover the evidence of
Ru's biological weapon. In a twist of ironic justice, Aiguo had
become infected before he could recover the needle.

The thought of her ex-husband and his brother helping the
Taiwanese government develop a weapon of mass destruction
sickened Jo. Ru was an acclaimed virologist. He'd dedicated his
professional life to the eradication of devastating diseases—or so
Jo had thought.

At one time, Jo had believed that science—a field devoted to the advancement of humankind's understanding of the natural world—was supposed to operate above the trivialities of politics. However, over the years she'd learned that ideology was still the most potent contagion, and no one was immune to its noxious effects. That didn't excuse what these men had done. Blood River virus hadn't emerged from the depths of the virgin rain forest. It had burrowed out from the darkest corners of the human soul.

Jo watched Aiguo's shapeless body sink into the hospital bed. She'd increased his morphine drip after reactivating the ventilator. The man drifted into unconsciousness. Jo doubted he would ever wake up.

*　　*　　*

"We've got to get moving, Jo," Olen said. "The military has cleared out. The streets are deserted. I think they're planning to—"

A deep rumble cut him off. The floor beneath them vibrated, and loose bits of plaster rained from the ceiling. The tremors felt like an earthquake, but Olen knew it was something worse.

They were bombing the Q-Zone.

A succession of blasts echoed like fireworks. The explosions were getting closer. Olen heard the whoosh of two PLA H-6K bombers screeching overhead. Seconds later, a thunderous boom knocked him to the ground. Thick black smoke filled the clinic. His throat stung with every shallow breath. A section of the roof lit up in flames.

Olen waved his arm to clear away the smog. He crawled along the floor, searching for Jo. They needed to evacuate the monastery before it collapsed on top of them.

A hand grabbed his elbow and yanked him to his feet. Olen stared into the face of an unworldly creature—part human, part machine. Jo was still wearing the N95 respirator. A layer of soot dusted her face and hair, but she appeared to breathe normally. The doctor pulled a spare mask over Olen's head, and filtered air spilled into his grateful lungs.

"Follow me," Jo yelled over the sounds of crackling fire and crumbling stone.

Olen struggled to keep up with her as she leapt over debris. Instead of heading for the exit, she began climbing a staircase. After vaulting up three flights of stairs, Olen's legs ached. The two reached the monastery's pitched roof, and Olen peered over the edge. The entire village was ablaze. Families ran through the streets, frantic, searching for refuge from the attack, but there was no shelter to be found. Everything burned.

Olen thought he heard the distant whistle of the bomber jets returning for another flyover, but when he looked up, he saw a different aircraft approaching. The helicopter glowed orange from the fire consuming the monastery. It hovered noiselessly about ten feet over a level section of the roof. The bird had advanced composite skin and near-silent rotors, perfect for radar evasion. *A stealth helo.* A CIA exfiltration team wouldn't have arrived so quickly. So who were they?

Jo scrambled over the steep rooftop toward the chopper. The side of the aircraft slid open and a rope ladder tumbled out. Jo reached it first and lifted herself onto the rungs. The doctor had anticipated the attack, and she'd already arranged for a getaway. *Damn impressive*, Olen thought.

Once they were safely inside, the helicopter ascended quickly and banked to the east. The smoke billowing from the burning village would screen their escape, and with any luck, the aircraft's stealth technology would elude the bombers' radar.

Jo pulled off her mask and strapped into a jump seat.

"What did he write on the whiteboard?" Olen asked.

"You saw it," Jo replied.

"Sure, it was a blob."

"Not a blob."

Olen frowned.

"It was an egg. A black egg," Jo clarified.

"Sounds spooky. What does it mean?"

"It refers to an ancient story, a Chinese creation myth about the birth of the universe. In the beginning, all matter swirled within an enormous black egg. When it cracked open, the two halves of the shell became the heaven above and the earth below—two opposing forces held in perfect balance. You've seen the black and white yin-yang symbol? It's come to signify the interconnectedness of everything. Fire and water. Life and death. Peace and war."

"I didn't take Aiguo for a philosopher," Olen said.

"The 'Black Egg' is also the unofficial name of a state-of-the-art military laboratory equipped for biosafety level four research. That's where we'll find Ru. In Shanghai."

"Shanghai? I thought Ru was helping the Taiwanese."

"The situation is complicated, Kipton. Despite the political tension, the Chinese government still recruits plenty of scientists from Taiwan. Ru is one of the foremost experts in our field. The PLA probably showered him with grant money. He must've developed the virus on the mainland, secretly, at the Black Egg. Right under the PLA's nose, and then handed it over to the Taiwanese," Jo explained.

"Then let's go to Shanghai."

"No," Jo said. "First, we must return to Beijing."

"What? Why?" Olen asked.

"Because, Kip. If we're going to break into one of China's most heavily fortified bioweapons labs, we're going to need help."

Darkness settled within Jo's eyes. The woman's soul was wounded. Her ex-lover had deceived her. Again. Her own government had sent her on a wild-goose chase in Dzongsar and then tried to kill her with firebombs. Too many men had treated this remarkable woman as expendable—a pawn in a game with no clear rules or objective. Most people would want to crawl into a hole, tear out their hair, scream into a pillow. But not Jo. She was made of titanium alloy—lightweight, corrosion resistant, high tensile strength. This betrayal would not pierce her armor. Jo would fight back. She'd been transformed. From this moment on, Olen knew Jo would focus intensely on one goal: revenge.

DAY 12

CHAPTER

41

Washington, DC, USA

"COULD EVERYONE JUST shut up for a second?" The president's chief of staff raised his voice over the maddening cacophony in the White House Situation Room.

The National Security Council Principals Committee had convened an emergency meeting after rumors of a Chinese military coup began seeping into their intelligence feeds. The room swelled with the president's top military and foreign policy advisers, each armed with freshly bound briefs hastily pulled together by overcaffeinated staffers. The secretary of state tore a page from hers and waved it in the face of the director of national intelligence. The man pulled his chin into his neck as the secretary pilloried him with the top-secret diplomatic cable. Allyson couldn't discern the woman's specific grievance over all the other shouting. It was something about PLA surveillance of Chinese consulates in Belarus.

As the leader of a fledgling agency, Director Cameron rarely attended NSC meetings. Since the outbreak, President Barlow had extended her an open invitation. Allyson knew her inclusion in the White House's inner circle irritated a few statutory members of the council, most notably national security adviser Nathan Sullivan.

"Seriously. Just sit down. All of you," the chief of staff barked. "The president is on his way."

The fracas subsided, and everyone found his or her assigned seat. Allyson was sandwiched between two crew cuts wearing polished flag pins.

General Thomas Goodyear snapped up when the door to the Situation Room cracked open. Three decades in the Army had made some habits unbreakable. Of course, President Barlow was now the only man for whom the chairman of the Joint Chiefs of Staff rose to his feet.

Secretary of State Darlene Hart wasn't so ceremonious. She'd known James Barlow for longer than most people in the room. The sixty-three-year-old former senator from North Carolina had succeeded in recruiting Barlow to run for office when all others had failed. Hart had argued that the country needed a man of keen intellect and sound judgment to navigate the chop of a changing world. Moreover, America needed someone untainted by the corrupt dysfunction that mired Washington. It needed someone outside the beleaguered Beltway—but not too far outside.

Like Allyson, many agreed that Barlow's celebrated career in intelligence made him an exemplary candidate for the job. He understood the nuances of modern geopolitical affairs—how friends could become enemies in a heartbeat. Besides, as every late-night pundit dutifully observed, the Democratic field was total shit that year. The Party needed a dark horse, and Darlene Hart had delivered.

Nevertheless, no one thought of Hart as a hero. The woman's legendary brusqueness over a twenty-year career in the U.S. Senate had earned her the cherished title "Bitch of the Hill." Some accused Hart of landing the SecState appointment as a reward for securing Barlow's nomination. They called her manipulative, cunning. Gold-digging housewives and beauty queens were "cunning," Allyson thought. If Hart had been a man, they'd have called her a political savant.

Allyson didn't believe any of it anyway. Nepotism wasn't Barlow's style. Besides, Hart had chaired the Senate Committee on Foreign Relations. She was a well-qualified choice for chief diplomat in her own right.

"Motherhumper of a day, Jack," Hart remarked in her enchanting southern drawl.

"It sure looks that way," President Barlow said. "So, does anyone want to tell me what the hell is happening in Asia?"

"It's a kung fu clusterfuck," Hart continued, not waiting for others to speak. "General Huang, the thundercunt running the Chinese military, just took control of the government. A gosh-dang military coup! Good morning, everyone. The People's Liberation Army is now in control of the largest economy in the history of Planet Earth. Please pass the banana pancakes and gooseberry jam."

Allyson spoke up, if only to subdue the secretary's hyperbole. "Our reporting shows General Huang sharply clashed with Chinese President Li Bingwen over the government's response to the Blood River virus epidemic. The men initially kept the infighting behind closed doors, but after word leaked that patient zero was a Taiwanese spy, all bets were off. Huang demanded retaliation, and he took his case to the people. The Chinese were already terrified by the spread of the disease, and rightfully so. Tens of thousands have died in less than two weeks. The idea that Blood River virus may have been a biological attack pushed people over the edge. Nationalism hit fiver pitch, and—"

"And sixty-five years of détente flew straight out the window," Barlow said.

"President Li looked weak," Allyson continued. She didn't appreciate being interrupted, even by the president of the United States. And Barlow should've known better. Good spies knew that people who interrupted others tended to miss things. "No one thought Li was doing enough to stand up to Taiwan. Massive anti-government protests swept through the country. We think General Huang took advantage of the populist backlash to seize power."

"He wouldn't be the first general with that idea," Barlow mused. "What's the word on the street?"

Allyson shrugged. "Huang has the people on his side. They love him."

"So, what happens next?"

"There's only one possible scenario, Jim," Nathan Sullivan cut in. "Huang is going to retaliate. He's preparing to invade Taiwan, pure and simple."

Not so simple, Allyson thought. *Definitely not pure.*

"And we've got to decide if we're going to do something about it," President Barlow reasoned solemnly.

Allyson knew it was the outcome he dreaded most. For decades, the United States had walked a thin line—building diplomatic and economic ties with the PRC while simultaneously shielding Taiwan from Beijing's reunification fantasies. Maintaining the status quo was the key to regional stability, and every president since Richard Nixon had wrestled with the puzzle before them now—what to do when the status quo collapsed. Perhaps Hart had it right. A kung fu clusterfuck, indeed.

"We must respond prudently," Allyson warned. "Chinese trade is critical to our economy. Beijing owns nearly three trillion dollars of U.S. debt. We can't afford to—"

"We can't afford to let a military junta ride roughshod over Asia," Sullivan interjected. "If Huang takes Taiwan uncontested, what's next? Japan? We have no idea how hungry this maniac is."

"And what if Taiwan is, in fact, to blame for the virus?" Barlow questioned.

"I know you don't believe that, Jim." Nate was agitated. No doubt the president had discussed the possibility with his national security adviser at length, just as he had with Allyson. Barlow clearly had serious doubts that President Tang had resorted to biological weapons. They were just too messy, unpredictable.

"It doesn't matter what *I* believe," Barlow contended. "The whole world seems convinced that Tang did it."

" 'Taiwanese Spy Unleashes Plague to Cripple Chinese Superpower.' That's today's headline in the *New York Times*, Nate," Secretary Hart added. "It's a modern-day David and Goliath. Except in the Sunday school version, David didn't pick the fight. Who knows? The international community might actually support a Chinese counterattack."

"We need to make sure we're not taking the wrong side on this," Barlow said.

"Only way to do that is to prove Tang isn't a psychopath," Hart mused.

"Okay." Barlow surveyed the room. "What else do we know?"

Allyson thought of the anonymous parcel that SwissPax had delivered to her home that morning. The edge of the maroon folder peeked out from the stack of papers on her lap. She still hadn't decided whether or not to share the intel with Barlow. The information could be misinterpreted. Or worse, it could be flat-out wrong. Allyson needed time to corroborate the document. Revealing it now would only push the hawks over the edge. Sullivan would probably spontaneously ejaculate when he saw what she had in the folder.

But not Barlow. The president would see the big picture, weigh the possibilities, assess the credibility of the intel. Yes, perhaps the president should know sooner rather than later.

"Mr. President," she began. "I have—"

"Jim, I have reason to believe the Taiwanese government was *not* behind the outbreak," Sullivan interrupted. Allyson blinked and pushed the maroon file back into her stack of briefing materials. It seemed Sullivan had some beans to spill too. Best to give Blurty Boy the honors.

President Barlow furrowed his brow. A row of heads turned to the national security adviser.

"Why ya holdin' back, Nate?" Hart asked.

"Now, I just learned of this a few hours ago," Sullivan said, his tone defensive.

"Well, don't keep us in the dark, Nate. What've you got?" Barlow asked.

"Chang Yingjie, or patient zero," Sullivan began, "was indeed an intelligence officer with Taiwan's National Security Bureau. This isn't news. However, by the time he showed up in Tibet, Chang was no longer working for the NSB."

"So, you're saying he went rogue?" Secretary Hart asked. "A lone-wolf attack?"

"Not exactly. The recent Taiwanese election changed everything. Officer Chang began his career under the previous administration. Not everyone working for the government agreed with President Tang's hard-line position on independence. Some bureaucrats were more outspoken than others. So, shortly after his inauguration, Tang cleaned house."

"Chang was purged," Barlow concluded.

"Precisely. Tang needed to ensure absolute loyalty from his top spy agency. There were already too many operatives playing both sides. Officer Chang didn't support Taiwanese independence. His grandparents were from Chengdu. Chang was proud of his Chinese heritage. He considered himself an exile, banished from his motherland. His family had fled to the island during the civil war in forty-nine, along with thousands of others. Chang wanted to bring them home. He wanted reunification with the mainland.

"Men like Chang joined the NSB hoping they could put pressure on the Chinese Communist Party to reform. He didn't see the PRC as the enemy and he didn't consider himself a separatist. To Chang, Taiwan's new leader—President Tang—was an agitator, a radical revolutionary."

"So," Barlow began, "Officer Chang sees his government moving in a dangerous direction, one he believes may lead to all-out war with Beijing. He launches an outbreak on the mainland—an act that almost guarantees military conflict. Seems counterproductive, no?" Barlow sounded skeptical of Sullivan's theory. "Chang must have known the Chinese would identify his body and retaliate with force."

"Yes, I believe he was counting on it," Sullivan explained. "Chang had been fired from a job he loved. The problem was President Tang—the man who ruined Chang's professional career and his dream of Taiwan's reconciliation with the mainland."

"He had to do something to stop Tang," Hart reasoned, weighing the possibility.

"Time was running out," Sullivan said. "President Tang's position on Taiwanese independence has been gaining popularity in the United Nations. The man might actually succeed in breaking away, officially." Sullivan paused. "Officer Chang couldn't let that happen."

General Goodyear—who had sat quietly, taking in the new intelligence—suddenly broke his silence. "So Chang infected himself with Blood River virus and unleashed a devastating plague on China, hoping Beijing would take revenge and invade Taiwan. It's reunification by force."

"Precisely. If the plan works, Taiwan reunites with the mainland in a matter of days, and President Tang, along with his radical agenda, is out. Probably killed," Sullivan said.

"That explains why we linked patient zero to the NSB so easily. Officer Chang wanted everyone to think his rogue operation was sanctioned by the Taiwanese government," Barlow inferred. "That way, the Chinese invasion would appear justified, and the international community—specifically, the United States—would stay out of it."

"A man's gotta be dang-dumb desperate to pump his veins full of Blood River virus," Hart said. "He may as well have stuffed dynamite down his tighty-whities."

"Chang Yingjie was a terrorist, motivated by his own twisted political agenda," Sullivan explained. "He's no different than an Al-Qaeda suicide bomber."

"Except Chang was the world's first terrorist to successfully acquire and deploy a weapon of mass destruction—a biological weapon," Hart said.

"And we never saw it coming," Sullivan added. His coal-black eyes focused on Director Cameron. The statement was a blatant indictment of her organization. VECTOR's explicit mission was to prevent the proliferation of biological weapons around the world. As its leader, Allyson would take the fall for failing to thwart Chang. There would be congressional hearings, media condemnation, public outcry. They would bury her. Sullivan would love that.

The entire theory was bull, Allyson thought. A disgruntled low-level intelligence officer had somehow marshaled the resources to single-handedly deploy a monstrous bioweapon? And without anyone noticing? Ridiculous. Chang must've had help. Sullivan knew more than he was sharing. Or he was lying.

"All right, Nate," Allyson spoke up. "You have a stunning imagination. Truthfully, you do. A real knack for vivid imagery. Have you considered taking up oil painting?"

"Make your point," Sullivan croaked.

"May I? Oh, how thoughtful of you, Nathan. Let's see, am I supposed to have a talking stick or something?" Allyson fumbled around in her lap. "Ah! That's right, no stick down there. Am I still allowed to speak?"

"Cam, please." Barlow sighed. Secretary Hart snickered to herself.

Allyson nodded, satisfied. "For any country, firing a spy is slippery business. You don't just hand them a pink slip and send them on their way. The NSB would've kept Chang on a short leash. We're supposed to believe he masterminded this magnificently complicated plot and the NSB, the MSS, and the 2PLA all missed it?"

"Not to mention U.S. intelligence. The Five Eyes. We didn't hear a peep about this guy from our allies," Secretary Hart added.

"Chang would've needed advanced lab equipment, a BS level three facility—oh, and probably a doctorate in virology," Allyson explained. "This isn't like figuring out how to build a pipe bomb in Grandma's kitchen from a YouTube video. We're talking hundreds of thousands of dollars, top-flight scientists, and access to restricted biological material. VECTOR has coverage all over East Asia. There's been zero chatter about a disgruntled former NSB officer involved in anything like what you're describing." Allyson paused. "How *did* you come by this intelligence, Nate?"

Allyson knew where to punch. Discredit the source, discredit the intel.

"Director Cameron, you know better than anyone that I can't divulge my sources or methods," Sullivan retorted.

"Sources!" Allyson raised her voice in frustration. "You're the national security adviser. Your *sources* are the seventeen U.S. intelligence agencies—the thousands of people working their asses off to feed you that stack of briefs. You're supposed to be a consumer of intel, not a collector."

Allyson fumed. Never had a United States national security adviser recruited his own sources. The very idea was an insult to the professionals who'd dedicated their careers to the craft of intelligence. Sullivan wasn't even a trained spy. He was a dilettante with a Jason Bourne fetish.

Sullivan bristled. "And what about *your* collectors, Director? Last I heard, your guy in China fell off the grid just hours before the outbreak."

"What about his replacement?" President Barlow asked, looking at Director Cameron. "The officer we sent in under media cover, Olen Grave. What reporting do we have from him?"

Allyson felt exposed. It had been almost two weeks since the outbreak began, and she'd offered very little in the way of meaningful intelligence. She'd have to give them something.

"Unfortunately, Officer Grave hasn't reported in yet," Allyson admitted.

Sullivan scowled. "*Two* missing operatives? So much for your East Asian coverage. With all due respect, Director, it sounds like you're in no position to debate. At least I'm bringing something to the table. *My* source is credible and operationally vetted. This intelligence is fresh and highly reliable."

"Okay, Nate," Barlow interjected, palms raised as if to declare a truce. "For now, it's the best we've got on the Taiwanese side. What about the PRC?" The president turned his attention to the chairman of the Joint Chiefs. "General Goodyear, tell me about their military readiness. Is General Huang preparing to invade Taiwan?"

Goodyear's voice resonated like a deep growl. He spoke incisively with the frankness of a four-star. "It's difficult to discern any meaningful escalation in China's military posture along the Strait of Taiwan because they've been piling up missiles for two decades. Taipei is one of the most threatened cities on earth. That said, Bruce has something you should see."

Goodyear nodded to Bruce Kinsey, the man who oversaw America's seventeen intelligence agencies as director of national intelligence. Like President Barlow, Kinsey had also had a turn at the helm of the CIA.

"For the last eight months," Kinsey began, "our eyes in the sky have been watching the People's Liberation Army build a massive air base in Ngari Prefecture, northwestern Tibet." Kinsey slid a glossy satellite photo across the conference table. "The site is about fifty miles east of the Kashmir border."

Barlow adjusted his reading glasses to get a better look at the photograph. Cranes, cement mixers, steel pipes, and hundreds of trucks dotted a rocky landscape. "No surprise there. That's hotly contested territory," he said. "We know Beijing is concerned about flare-ups along its border. It stands to reason that they would establish an air base there."

"*That* image was taken about ten weeks ago," Kinsey explained. He then produced a second photograph and flicked it, facedown, toward the head of the table. "*This* is the same site."

Barlow slapped his palm down to catch the photo before it sailed off the edge. He thumbed a corner and flipped it over. "When was this taken, Bruce?"

Kinsey paused a beat. "Three hours ago, Mr. President."

A geometric pattern consisting of three immense triangles covered an entire section of the southeastern corner of the construction site. From the bird's-eye view, the smooth shapes stood out among the craggy terrain.

Tarps.

"The PLA is building something under those vinyl sheets that they don't want our satellites and spy planes to see," Kinsey explained.

"Do we have any idea what it is?" Barlow asked.

"Well, I'm betting it isn't Disneyland Ngari," Secretary Hart cut in.

"Prepare an intel-collection plan," Barlow ordered. "We need to know what General Huang is concealing at that air base."

Damn, Allyson thought. There was no avoiding it now. She had to share what she knew—the intel from the SwissPax parcel. She cleared her throat. "I may be able to help with that."

All chairs swiveled in Allyson's direction. Secretary Hart threw up her hands. "Well! Isn't our garden party just bursting with little blond bombshells?"

Allyson fished out the maroon file and handed it to Barlow. Hart and Kinsey huddled over the president to get a closer look. The document inside was an engineering blueprint. The plans matched the satellite image of the PLA's Ngari construction site, minus the tarps. They revealed what the Chinese had planned to build in the southeastern corner of the air base.

"Where did you get this?" Sullivan demanded.

Allyson glared at him. "Oh, Nate, you know I can't divulge my sources and methods."

Barlow smoothed the paper with his palm. Even without translation of the Chinese annotations, the cylindrical structures were unmistakable.

Underground missile silos.

At a secret air base in Ngari Prefecture, General Huang was hiding a launch site for intercontinental ballistic missiles. The kind that could sink an island like Taiwan. Barlow turned to Allyson, his fingertips pressed into his temples. "You still think Huang intends to turn the other cheek?"

42

Washington, DC, USA

THE NATIONAL SECURITY Council disbanded, and its high-ranking members dispersed to their respective bureaucratic fiefdoms. Most of them climbed into bulletproof Cadillacs, ushered by grim bodyguards with coiled wires sprouting from their ears.

Director Allyson Cameron wound her way through the labyrinthine ground floor of the White House to the staff parking garage. It took longer than usual to find her car. The garage was packed, and she was still buzzed from the combative meeting.

In Washington, when things went to hell, everyone pointed fingers. It was an "intelligence failure," the press would report. After a major global disaster, people in her line of work spent more time dodging political blowback than working together to overcome the crisis. They covered their asses and slaughtered scapegoats. Nathan Sullivan had his sights set on VECTOR. He would make sure Allyson took the fall for Chang's bioattack.

Director Cameron had taken no satisfaction in obtaining the engineering plans for the Ngari missile silos. Her source had taken an immense risk to acquire that document, and good intel was good intel, but the implications turned her stomach. If Huang planned to use nukes against Taiwan, he'd launch them from Ngari. That's what Allyson's source had wanted to communicate by sending the document via SwissPax. Barlow might have no choice but to destroy the air base—a preemptive strike to neutralize weapons of mass destruction. America had gone down that path before in Iraq, and it had led to a decade of war.

Allyson found her silver Ford Focus wedged between a concrete pillar and a yellow Jeep Wrangler. She fished her keys from her jacket pocket. She planned to head back to McLean and make a few calls from the privacy of her home. Her Fort Detrick office wasn't clean. Sullivan had tentacles everywhere—especially in the Army.

The keys slipped from Allyson's hands. She stutter-stepped in an attempt to catch them but accidently kicked the jumble of metal farther under her car. "*Shit,*" she hissed to no one.

The stress was getting to her. She hadn't slept in two days. Allyson crouched, trying her best not to snag her pants on the rough concrete. She peered under the vehicle, but it was too dark. She turned on her phone's flashlight, and that's when she saw it.

A small electronic device was affixed to the Ford's undercarriage, just behind the rear tire on the driver's side. It was nearly identical to the one she'd planted on the Mercedes of a Saudi middleman in Riyadh three summers ago. A GPS tracker.

She sighed. "You've got to be kidding me."

43

McLean, Virginia, USA

D IRECTOR CAMERON SPENT the evening glued to her cell phone. First, she called the commander of USAMRIID's biosafety level four laboratory.

"The cursed virus just mutates too rapidly," he explained, his voice thick with defeat. "We're still trying to produce a viable culture, but it's all trial and error. Mostly error, at this point."

Allyson tried to raise the commander's spirits but found herself feeling similarly dejected. Her next two calls, to the CDC and the World Health Organization, went about the same way. *Director Cameron, do we have any idea where this bug came from? If we just had a little more to go on . . . What have we learned from the field?*

The field. Everyone wanted answers from the field, as if at any moment a feverish baboon was going to wander into a Lhasa police station and turn himself in. Tibet constituted nearly one-sixth of China's land mass. It was the size of Texas, California, and New York State combined. Four hundred seventy-five thousand square miles of windswept meadows, sprawling pine forests, winding mountains, frozen glaciers, and arid desert. That meant a lot of habitats for an infected host species to hide. Assuming, of course, that the damn thing hadn't been cooked up in a Taiwanese military lab. Which no one believed—not even General Huang, probably.

The director's phone clattered against the granite counter top. Nine o'clock. Time to jet. She'd set an alarm so she wouldn't leave too late. In the midst of endless phone calls, Allyson had planned a small countersurveillance operation. Someone had planted that GPS tracker on her car, and she intended to find out who.

Allyson had left the device untouched to avoid tipping off her shadow. She pulled out of her condo parking garage and turned right on Westpark Road, heading toward International Drive. The place was deserted. Most of the neighborhood's defense contractors had already punched out and fled to suburbia. Late at night, the only people out on the street were construction workers. Allyson rolled to a stop at a red light.

Even in the dead of night, the traffic lights took forever to change. Allyson's eyes flicked to her rearview mirror. She wouldn't spot surveillance that way—another pair of headlights following that closely would be too conspicuous—but she checked anyway. Old habits and whatnot.

The stoplight flipped to green, and Allyson drove straight through the intersection, crossing Leesburg Pike, even though it meant going out of her way. She wanted to give her pursuer a long leash. He'd likely parked at the multilevel parking garage at the Tysons Galleria mall—close, but hidden from view—waiting for his mark to leave home. That's what Allyson would've done. Her shadow wouldn't start his engine until the Focus was at least a block away.

Allyson planned to head up to Chain Bridge Road and then double back. With any luck, she'd hook her tail and drag him along for a little ride.

*　*　*

Senior intelligence analyst Gabriel Snyder almost missed the blinking red light on the screen mounted to his windshield. He must've dozed off. He reached for his coffee, resting askew in the cup holder, but it was empty. The long hours were killer. He wasn't a young man anymore. The higher-ups had doubled surveillance coverage on Director Cameron. Such high-intensity observation typically involved two teams in alternating shifts, but this case required more discretion, so Snyder had been working solo.

Mole hunting was tricky business, and Snyder had some experience in the matter. He'd served twenty-five years in the FBI, the last four as a supervisor in the Bureau's counterintelligence program. Last fall, after graciously accepting his hard-earned pension, the fifty-six-year-old had traded high-wire spy hunting for a peaceful desk job at the NSA. The respite didn't last. Snyder's distinguished track record in ferreting out traitors within the U.S. government had attracted the attention of a few bigwigs. And those bigwigs suspected Director Cameron, apparently.

Snyder slapped his cheeks to wake himself up and reached out to reposition the digital display. He watched a red dot inch across a map. The device started pinging automatically when the GPS tracker he'd planted on the director's car began moving. Cameron was out for a midnight joyride. She never did that.

Most people stuck to their long-established routines, which made surveillance predictable work. A coffee stop on the way to the office. The gym on Monday and Wednesday evenings. Grocery shopping on Sunday afternoons. When subjects deviated from their pattern, it was time to pay attention. However, Director Cameron was no ordinary subject. She was a spy, and spies buried operationally sensitive activities within the normality of mundane errands. The number of oranges placed in a grocery cart could signal the time of day a brush pass would occur. A forgotten sock left behind in a gym locker room could indicate a loaded dead drop. Espionage was an art of deception and misdirection. Snyder knew that great spies gave meaning to the meaningless as a way to communicate with their compatriots and fool their opponents.

Cameron's conspicuous break in her pattern intrigued the former FBI agent. It could be nothing, but at least he'd have something to write about in his surveillance log. Snyder waited to fire up his car engine until the digital red dot passed through a couple of traffic lights. Slowly, Snyder emerged from the shopping mall's parking garage and began the silent chase.

44

Washington, DC, USA

PRESIDENT JAMES BARLOW heard the pitter-patter of footfalls trailing behind him—an unsettling sound, especially when jogging after dusk. It conjured memories of plebe year at Annapolis. Barlow stored a mental library of fond memories from his four years as a midshipman at the United States Naval Academy. Endless running, in the dark and the cold, wasn't among them. Gunnery Sergeant Carter had taken sick pleasure in leading the boys of the Seventh Company around the town's harbor in subzero wind chill. Yet despite the torturous experience, Barlow still found a brisk evening run invigorating. The steady motion untangled his mind and released some of the pressure building in his skull. The pain from the migraines lessened when he ran, and even with five secret service agents in tow, Barlow could be alone with his thoughts.

"You're slowing down, Jim. Looks like this job's finally wearing on you," a woman called out from a jet-black Escalade rumbling along the president's right flank.

Barlow recognized the sarcastic twang. He turned to see Secretary Hart's round glasses peeking over a half-lowered, heavily tinted window. The president shook his head and picked up his pace.

The Escalade rolled along in tandem. "Now, hold on, Usain, before you blow a gasket," Hart scolded. "Come, take a breather. I promise your ten-K won't suffer."

"Why don't you join me out here?" Barlow asked. "The last time I got into a car with you, I ended up in the Oval Office."

"And I feel truly awful about that. Just look what it's done to your gut. Like a sack of soggy yams. It's an American tragedy, really."

President Barlow laughed for the first time that day.

"Enough foreplay, Jim." Hart's tone flattened. "We may have a problem. You need to see this."

Barlow came to a halt. His breath created puffs of condensation around his face. The president threw a sharp nod to his security detail and climbed into Hart's SUV.

The secretary of state waited until Barlow closed the door. She signaled her driver to roll up the windows. An opaque divider rose behind the front seats, sealing off the rear of the vehicle. Hart wanted complete privacy.

"There appears to be a chink in the armor," Hart said. "I've just learned that someone on your National Security Council has been suppressing critical intel."

"I already spoke with Nathan. He'd only just verified the reporting on Chang. I know he doesn't always come across as a team player, but he would never—"

"Sullivan's a dick. A real custard shooter," Hart interjected. "But I'm not talking about him."

"What is it, then?"

"Take a look at this." The secretary pulled a photograph from her handbag.

Barlow unfolded the glossy paper, revealing an image of a man and a woman he didn't recognize. The lighting wasn't spectacular, but it had probably been taken in some sort of park. There were tall metal fences in the background. A zoo, maybe.

"What am I looking at?" the president asked.

"This photo was taken by an MI6 spook yesterday morning, our time, in Singapore."

"Who's the man?"

Darlene Hart looked Barlow square in the eye. "Marc Chen." The secretary spat the name with contempt.

"The missing VECTOR officer? So, he's alive. That's good."

"Not exactly. Chen hasn't filed a report in weeks. As far as the Community was concerned, the man was dead as disco."

"How long have we known otherwise?" Barlow asked.

"Well, *I* just found out forty-five minutes ago. I was wrapping up a meeting at Foggy Bottom with our British counterparts. We were casually debating the relative prestige of Cowes Week versus the America's Cup—as if it's not obvious—when an aide to the foreign secretary asked about our guy in Singapore, wondering if he's learned anything from their Security and Intelligence Division. I just about shit my britches, Jim. That's when he showed me this." Hart pointed to the photograph. "MI6 snapped it, and their analysts flagged our man, Chen."

"Why didn't the British aide mention it sooner?"

"That's just it. He was shocked that I didn't already know. He said someone from the British embassy passed the photograph to U.S. intelligence last night."

"You're kidding. We've known about this for a full day?"

"Well, at least one of us did," Hart said flatly.

President Barlow didn't want to ask the obvious question. He could tell where the conversation was headed. After the Brits bumped into Chen, they would've immediately contacted Director Cameron. They knew she ran VECTOR and that Marc Chen was her officer. It would've made sense to go to her directly.

"The bitch just sat there, Jim." Secretary Hart growled with a quiet rage. "Allyson sat there, in the White House Situation Room, and said nothing."

Barlow frowned. Why would Cam withhold such valuable information? What reason could she have to make everyone think her officer in China was still missing? For Allyson's sake, the president hoped she had a damn good one.

45

McLean, Virginia, USA

CHAIN BRIDGE ROAD was a straight shot, six miles east to CIA headquarters. Allyson knew the route well. Years ago the drive had taken less than twenty minutes, even in heavy traffic. Now the same commute took twice as long due to major road renovations. Construction crews moved in every night around nine PM. A caravan of diesel-powered dump trucks squeezed the road down to a single lane, and bulky cement barriers blocked all turnoffs to intersecting side streets. Once drivers entered the mile-long work zone, their only option was to drive straight through in a long, single-file line.

The work zone was a perfect choke point, and if Allyson could lure her pursuer into it, she'd have no problem identifying his car. The Beirut Bottleneck—a simple yet effective trap.

The director's pulse accelerated. God, she missed the rush of fieldwork.

* * *

Snyder maintained a careful distance, watching the monitor as the dot traveled east. Was she heading to Langley? A former CIA operations officer—one under suspicion—taking a midnight jaunt to her old office would make for a juicy report.

Director Cameron would have no trouble getting past the guard gate. Her security clearance still gave her access to CIA headquarters. It was getting late, so most employees would've left already. Cameron would have the run of the place. What better time to poke around where she didn't belong?

The former FBI agent was surprised to see the bright flood-lights washing over the road ahead. He heard the low growl of diesel engines. Road construction. He'd driven this same route just hours before, and it had been completely clear. An orange sign flashed: LANE CLOSURES NEXT TWO MILES. MERGE RIGHT.

Snyder grimaced. The narrowing roadway was a problem. He risked exposure by driving into the bottleneck. The greatest concern of any surveillance specialist was being spotted—getting burned by the white rabbit. And bottlenecks burned like bonfires.

The red dot moved smoothly into the work zone. Snyder considered his options. Most people would abort. It was too risky. Should he turn around, leave, let Cameron go?

No. Surveilling a high-value target took guts. That's why they'd selected him for this ultrasensitive assignment. He wasn't *most people.*

Snyder popped a handful of sunflower seeds for good luck, held his breath, and merged into the right lane. He was heading into the choke point.

*　*　*

Allyson smiled when she saw the two glowing orbs drift into her rearview mirror. Her shadow had taken the bait. The director's sense of satisfaction faded as the unfortunate reality of her situation sunk in. She was being watched, followed, *spied on*, in her own country.

Careful not to spook her tail, Allyson kept her speed slow and steady. She was almost there. It was time to turn the tables.

*　*　*

Snyder worked the digital display and felt a hot panic churning in his gut. The red dot had stopped. Director Cameron had driven to the end of the work zone and pulled over.

She knew. She'd lured him into a choke point so she could burn him on the way out. Snyder's Audi was the only car in sight traveling through the one-lane stretch of road. The frozen red dot was still about a half mile downstream. Waist-high concrete blocks flanked the street. There was no escape. Cameron would spot his car as soon as he emerged from the work zone. Snyder felt like an idiot. She'd set him up, and he'd fallen for it like a Quantico rookie.

Eyes darting side to side, Snyder surveyed the roadway ahead, searching for a detour. He tried not to think about what he'd write in his log. Director Cameron had trapped him with a rudimentary countersurveillance maneuver.

Then another orange sign flashed overhead: I-495 INNER LOOP NEXT RIGHT.

The Beltway! The on-ramp was open.

Interstate 495, the Capital Beltway, was a sixty-four-mile loop that circumnavigated the District of Columbia—a godsend for surveillance work. Snyder often relied on it to slip in and out of Washington's prolific suburbs without attracting attention.

He felt a rush of relief. He wouldn't need to drive to the end of the work zone, where Director Cameron had parked, waiting for him. He could still abort the surveillance operation and take the Beltway back to Maryland. The director had set a clever trap, but she'd overlooked the obvious egress. A critical error. Instead of exposing himself at the end of the choke point, Snyder would simply divert onto the freeway unnoticed. Director Cameron would never know he'd been following her. She'd assume the driver of the black Audi was just another well-paid workaholic, heading home after a marathon day at the office.

Snyder flipped on his right turn signal and glided up the ramp. His eyes danced back and forth from the road to his GPS monitor. The red dot remained motionless. He accelerated to fifty-five miles per hour. He'd return to Fort Meade and report the incident. Snyder had less than an hour to figure out how to break the news to the higher-ups.

*   *   *

Allyson kept about four or five cars between her and the black Audi as she cruised the interstate. Her plan had worked flawlessly. Just as expected, her shadow had panicked when her Ford Focus stopped at the end of the work zone. Left with no alternative, the driver of the Audi was forced onto the Beltway to avoid exposure.

Shortly after emerging from the single-lane work zone, Allyson had turned into the parking lot of Capital One's headquarters, where the company had stationed a row of Zipcars. The general public could rent the vehicles by the hour, and Allyson had reserved an electric blue Toyota Prius before leaving her condo. It took less than thirty seconds to locate the car, which she unlocked with her membership card. A square key fob dangled from the Prius's steering column. Allyson silently rolled out of the parking lot just in time to see the black Audi flick on its right turn signal.

From her location, initiating pursuit was easy. The northbound Beltway on-ramp arced right up to the mouth of the parking lot. In moments, the subject became the shadow. Who the hell had been tracking her anyway? Now was her chance to get some answers. She'd follow the Audi until sunrise if necessary.

46

Fort Meade, Maryland, USA

S NYDER HUNCHED OVER his keyboard, sipping burnt coffee.
The drive to NSA headquarters had been a slog, thanks to an
unexpected cloudburst. The pelting rain and crashing thunder
foreshadowed the fury he'd face when his superiors learned he'd
aborted the surveillance op.

Snyder stood by his decision to fall back. He laid out his justification in an artfully constructed memorandum. When working
as a team, he explained, you had the option to break pursuit and
radio a partner to pick up the target downstream. It was like passing the baton in a relay race. But solo observation was more limit-
ing. If things got hairy and you were alone, the only options were
to terminate or get scorched.

His gut told him Cameron had maneuvered through the construction zone to check for shadows. Revealing himself would have
validated the director's suspicions. A mole was hard enough to catch. A
paranoid mole, nearly impossible. Once spooked, they dug deeper
underground. Snyder had had no choice but to abort, he told himself.

On the other hand, Cameron's evasiveness might have indi-
cated that she was operational. Basic surveillance detection tactics
were standard procedure for a trained spy. They didn't necessarily

prove Cameron had spotted Snyder's Audi. What if the director had merely paused to look over her shoulder?

Whatever the outcome, praise or admonishment, Snyder would take it like a professional. Winning the war was more important than winning a single battle. Ferreting out traitors took patience. In the last two decades, he'd exposed four. The last one had taken three years to pin down. And Cameron was a powerful target, with allies and officers all over the world. Officers like Olen Grave, the man who'd used the TRIDENT system to request a code six—immediate exfiltration from denied enemy territory.

The intelligence community took code sixes very seriously. CIA extraction teams stood by twenty-four hours a day, seven days a week. Nevertheless, given the outbreak and military coup, an exfiltration from the Tibetan Autonomous Region would be nearly impossible. Officer Grave would know that, so he must've been desperate.

To leave a man in-theater, twisting in the wind, was truly callous, if not treasonous. The thought of abandoning a fellow intelligence officer in distress had been eating away at Snyder ever since he'd intercepted the signal. Espionage was hazardous work, and operatives relied on each other for backup when things went south. Even if Allyson Cameron had chosen to neglect her officer in Tibet, Grave's blood would be on Snyder's hands. *He* had deleted the TRIDENT alert. He had no one else to blame.

To hell with his orders. He had to make it right. Snyder dialed a number for a personal contact at Langley. A familiar female voice picked up.

"We have a code six," Snyder explained. "Tibet. It's—"

The woman cut him off. "Don't say any more. Can you meet me at the usual spot?"

"Of course, but we've got to do it now."

"Twenty-five minutes."

The line went dead. The request to meet in person didn't surprise Snyder. Agency folk despised speaking over open phone lines. Especially government phone lines.

Finally, Snyder flicked off his desk lamp and powered down his computer. He pulled his jacket off the back of his swivel chair, shaking free the raindrops still clinging to the leather.

Just as he turned away from his workstation, the portable GPS monitor, now sitting on the corner of his desk, made a faint, high-pitched beep. A message on the screen read LOW BATTERY.

Something still bothered Snyder about the night's failed surveillance operation. The red dot indicating the location of Director Cameron's Ford Focus hadn't moved an inch since Snyder broke pursuit. It hovered over the same parking lot at the end of the work zone on Chain Bridge Road. Snyder knew Cameron hadn't removed the tracker. Any attempt to tamper with the mechanism would have alerted him. Had Cameron's destination been the parking lot all along? Maybe she hadn't stopped there just to burn her tail.

Zipping his jacket, Snyder considered another possibility. Director Cameron had dumped her car and switched vehicles. She was nowhere near that frozen red dot. The woman could be anywhere.

*　*　*

Allyson gripped the steering wheel of the rented Prius. She'd followed the black Audi for forty-one miles, all the way to Fort Meade. It wasn't shock burning inside her sternum. It was red-hot anger. The NSA was keeping tabs on her. An order like that had to come from someone high up the chain.

The armed soldiers protecting the fort's main gate had ushered the director through uncontested. She noticed one of the guards eyeing the green Zipcar logo on the side of her vehicle.

"Mine's in the shop. Shoddy alternator," Allyson explained. She leaned in. "Don't tell anyone I'm driving an import."

The young buck grinned, returned Allyson's VECTOR credentials, and waved her through the checkpoint with a stiff salute.

Fort Meade was a fortified city. Government offices and military training facilities sprawled over eight densely wooded square miles. There was even a residential neighborhood, complete with picket fences and cul-de-sacs—home to a population of nearly ten thousand. Newcomers could get lost navigating the vast compound, but Allyson knew where to find the black Audi. The employee parking lot.

CHAPTER

47

Beijing, People's Republic of China

OLEN SNAKED THROUGH the narrow streets on a cherry-red
Linhai. The scooter's ultralightweight body maneuvered
effortlessly through the gauntlet of curbside vendors selling coun-
terfeit handbags out of dirty carts. A few reckless tourists—those
daring enough to remain in Beijing during the pandemic—sifted
through the merchandise, hunting for plastic treasure. There was
something unsettling about women in surgical face masks clawing
through piles of imitation Louis Vuitton.

Olen twisted the scooter's handle as far it would go, but the
Linhai wasn't built for speed. Jo's Italian-made Vespa GTS 300
packed a heftier punch, and Olen struggled to keep pace. The doctor's black hair whipped as she sped away, always just out of reach.

Without warning, Jo braked in front of a three-hundred-year-
old quadrangle home. A long white sheet hung loosely in its entry-
way, twisting and snapping in the breeze, swatting away unwelcome
guests. An older woman sat on the stoop, puffing on a thin Baisha
cigarette. She didn't react to the motorcycle's growling engine.
Her shock of silver hair—cropped short along the sides and spiked
on top—gave her a decidedly modern edge against the traditional

architecture. She sat with impeccable posture, back arched, head tilted back, smoke spilling from her nostrils.

"How many times have I told you, Zhinü, my sweetheart? Those wretched things aren't safe," the silver-haired woman chided in English as Jo dismounted from her scooter.

Jo smoothed the tangles from her windblown hair. "This coming from a woman who's two packs deep before breakfast."

"Take a deep breath, love. This is Beijing. Living here, we're all two packs deep. Might as well enjoy it."

Jo smiled broadly. "Aunt Jin, you look absolutely radiant."

"It's a new cream from Milan. You'd think they made it from crushed diamonds. The stuff's ferociously expensive, but you can't put a price on youth. You'll understand one day, my darling." Jin pulled back the loose skin around her left eye. She lifted her chin and angled her head to catch the most flattering light. A collection of gold bracelets jingled when she raised her arm.

"So, what's up?" In one graceful motion, the woman rose from the stoop and floated toward them. She kissed Jo on both cheeks as if they were European aristocracy. "I see you've brought me an American." The woman inspected Olen with a playfully suspicious gaze.

"What makes you think I'm American?" Olen asked.

Jin reached out and squeezed one of Olen's biceps. "You're American," she said confidently, her voice low and sultry. Olen shot a surprised look at Jo, who could barely conceal her amusement.

* * *

The moment Jo stepped into Jin Meihui's home, a rush of childhood memories flashed in her mind like a flickering filmstrip. A scraped knee, the smell of freshly steamed dumplings, tearing into little red envelopes, her first kiss.

Jo wasn't sentimental, as a general rule. Jin had taught her to remain emotionally detached from material treasure. *Nothing is permanent*, Jin had warned, careful to add, *Nothing except the trust and loyalty of family*. The aphorism was intended to comfort a child who'd learned the pain of loss far too early, but the inescapable irony only cut deeper. Jin—the woman who'd taken her in, raised her after her parents' death—wasn't really her aunt. Jo had no family.

But this modest residence, carved out of a centuries-old neighborhood, was the closest thing Jo had to a home. She'd always feel connected to it on some level. In this place, Jin Meihui had molded a miserable, dejected orphan girl into a confident, successful woman.

"I've done some renovating," Jin announced fleetingly as she led her visitors through a manicured courtyard and into the kitchen. She glided like a swan across a still pond. A milky wave of silk rippled in her wake.

The feudal architecture of the quadrangle's facade belied its ultramodern interior. The contrast was striking but not particularly unusual. For the past decade, wealthy real estate investors had been grabbing up historic *hutong* residences, only to gut their interiors and rebuild from scratch. Jo knew Beijing's new upper crust craved the nostalgia of the old city—as long as they didn't need to sacrifice the amenities of modern life.

"Everything looks so different," Jo said. She didn't recognize the place. "When did you do all of this?"

"You've been away for a while, my dear."

Jo felt a tinge of guilt. Over the past few years, her budding career had claimed whatever time her failing marriage hadn't. She'd neglected the one person who had never let her down.

"I've missed you," Jo said apologetically. The doctor lowered herself into an egg-shaped chair. It was even more uncomfortable than it looked.

Jin poured hot tea into three canary-yellow cups and placed one in front of each of her guests.

"All right. Let's cut the sentimental crapola," Jin said sharply. "I don't hear from you in three years, and then you pop in unannounced with an American puppy dog." She glared at Olen. This time she wasn't smiling. "You two screwing or something?"

Jo's cheeks flushed. "That's none of your business."

Jin looked the American over, assessing his statuesque physique like an art dealer, then winked at Jo. "Attagirl."

Aunt Jin had a particular way of getting to the heart of a matter. She'd passed on the skill to her adopted niece as a necessity in their shared trade. More than just a maternal figure, Jin was also Jo's mentor and colleague. On Jo's sixteenth birthday, her aunt had offered her a job with the Ministry of State Security. It was an unusual gift, but one Jo had eagerly accepted. Following in her dead parents' footsteps and joining the nation's prestigious spy service had always seemed like her destiny.

"The Q-Zone—" Jo began.

"Was bunk. I know," Jin blurted.

"What do you mean, you *know*?"

"Well, I *surmise*, at least. Blood River virus ravages the coast, and you're sent to poke around some village in Timbuktu."

"Epidemiological surveys always begin at the outbreak site. If we don't find the source—"

"Yet here you are," Jin interrupted. "The scientist sent to figure out the whole thing is drinking tea at my kitchen table." Jin blew into her cup to cool the piping liquid. "Don't get yourself down, honey. No one expected you to find anything out there."

"I see that now." Jo's thoughts flashed to the assassin writhing on the monastery floor seconds before the fireball consumed the building. "But that's just it. I did."

"Did what, my dear?" Jin's eyelids fluttered.

"I found something," Jo replied. She described the dead drop, the hypodermic needle, and even her ex-husband's likely involvement in the engineering of the virus. Jo spoke with detached precision, as if delivering an intelligence briefing to a superior.

"BRV45 is a weapon, and Ru built it," Jo concluded.

Jin set her empty cup on the table with a hollow tap. Throughout Jo's revelation, her aunt had sipped calmly. Jo could sense her skepticism. Jin never took anything at face value. The old spy would need more compelling evidence to believe such a convoluted conspiracy.

"There's more," Jo said. "Patient zero was NSB."

Jin snorted. "Oh, honey. You really have been living in quarantine." Jin reached back and pulled a newspaper from the kitchen counter. She slapped it in front of her niece. The corners had curled from the lingering humidity. "That's old news, Zhinü."

Written across the front page in bold Chinese characters was the headline **Taiwanese Spy Source of Blood River Virus Outbreak**. A grainy head shot took up most of the page above the fold. Even with the photograph's slight blur, Jo recognized the man as Chang Yingjie, patient zero. The doctor's forehead furrowed.

"What's the matter?" Jin asked. "Sounds like you've known about this for a week."

"That's not it." Jo slid the paper toward Jin. "The date." She pointed to the article's byline. "This story broke *yesterday*."

"Uh-huh," Jin mumbled knowingly.

"But we were attacked in the Q-Zone less than six hours ago."

"And the lab was destroyed, I presume. So you don't have a sample of the original virus—the Taiwanese superweapon. Correct?" Jin asked.

"The lab was *bombed*," Jo snapped defensively. "We were lucky to have escaped at all."

"Uh-huh." Jin blinked slowly, allowing Jo to compile the pieces herself. A good teacher never simply handed her student the answer.

The doctor's expression grew grim. "The PLA wouldn't have destroyed the only evidence of Taiwan's involvement," Jo reasoned. "Especially not after the NSB connection went public." The corners of Jin's mouth formed a weak, sad smile.

"And BRV45 spread beyond Dzongsar more than a week ago. Level three quarantine of the outbreak site was completely unnecessary," Jo said. "There was nothing to contain. I tried to tell them that. I thought it was just a foolhardy overreaction. That the army was . . ." Jo shook her head, not wanting to believe it. "The army wasn't trying to keep the virus *inside* Dzongsar Village. They were trying to keep me *out*, to stifle my investigation."

"Now, why on earth would the PLA want to do that?" Jin asked sarcastically. She poured herself another cup of tea.

"It can only mean . . ." Jo started. "Taiwan wasn't actually behind the attack, and the PLA knows it."

Jin tapped her spoon against the side of her porcelain teacup. The chime sounded like a game show bell.

"But that doesn't explain Chang," Jo said. "Patient zero was unequivocally NSB. We identified him from his post in Sudan."

*   *   *

Jin's face turned stone-cold. She was reluctant to give any more hints with a foreigner in the room.

The American boy spoke for the first time. "You know something, don't you?"

Jin smirked. "Muscles *and* brains."

Jo reached out and touched her aunt's arm, imploring her to share more.

"Chang Yingjie was NSB, you're right about that," Jin confirmed. "But he wasn't spying for the Taiwanese."

"I don't understand," Jo replied. "You just acknowledged he was Taiwanese intelligence."

"Chang was spying for me, Zhinü."

Jo pulled her hand back, as if she'd touched a hot stove.

"Oh, don't look so shocked. You know what I do." Jin twisted one of the silver spikes on her head, pinching the tip with a crunch.

The reporter leaned forward. "You're a mirror."

"That's one way to put it," Jin said.

Officially, her title was senior recruiter, but the designation wasn't completely accurate. Jin didn't pluck wide-eyed college students from the halls of Beijing University. That was child's play. For more than thirty years, Officer Jin Meihui had specialized in something far more dangerous. She recruited double agents.

Convincing an enemy spy to commit treason was a sophisticated procedure. It didn't happen over small talk and sushi. Jin picked her targets with painstaking precision and only after conducting meticulous research. Sometimes she'd spend years cultivating a susceptible target. It wasn't always obvious what the person really wanted. Money was a common motivator, but it was too ephemeral. When the cash dried up, so did the loyalty. Revenge worked better.

Jin would single out a foreign intelligence officer whose talents had gone wholly underappreciated by his home country. All men had egos, and all egos could be manipulated. The best mirrors reflected not what was actually there but what someone *wished* was there, staring back at them. And Jin was a flawless mirror. She lured men with visions of power, respect, and stature. If she'd done her job correctly, her targets actually felt good about their seditious acts. One grateful man had bought Jin flowers. Another proposed marriage.

"Chang hated the Sudan," Jin explained. "New recruits always get lousy assignments. Heck, we all did. But Chang thought he deserved better. And so did I. Eight months ago, I convinced him to come over to our side. I instructed him to stay put at the NSB, for a time, and feed us information on demand. He leapt at the chance to screw the people who'd screwed him. Our resentful little mole."

"Then you must know why Chang went to Tibet," the American asserted.

"In fact, I don't. I haven't communicated with Chang since August."

"Did he get cold feet?"

"On the contrary. Officer Chang loved being a double for Chinese intelligence. For once, he felt important and valuable. Unfortunately, he wasn't either. At least not to the MSS." Jin rose and moved to the kitchen sink to rinse her teacup. "Chang was too impatient. He wanted to be Jackie Chan. I needed him to sit tight and get a promotion or two. After a few months, his impetuousness worried me too much to continue. I was about to cut him loose."

"So, what happened?" the American pressed.

"The PLA got news of my asset and started firing off RFIs."

"Requests for information," Jo clarified.

Jin eyed the American carefully. "Yes, they wanted intel from Chang, and as his handler, they had to go through me. It was a waste of time. I told them to come back in ten years. But one handsome lieutenant in particular just wouldn't give up. I had already decided to dump Chang, so it made sense to hand him off and get the PLA off my back."

"Wait a second," Jo said. "Chang was working for the Chinese army when he traveled to Tibet?"

"Zhinü, there is more going on here than you or I will ever know. Look outside. See the foot soldiers marching in our streets? The People's Liberation Army is in charge now. We don't know who our friends are. It's a dangerous time to be asking questions. I want to make sure you understand that."

Jin dried her hands on a threadbare dish towel—one she'd had since Jo was a child. She should've replaced it, but sometimes it made sense to hang on to things. Especially if they reminded her of simpler times, before she'd made so many mistakes, when she could still protect what mattered most.

* * *

Jo ran her palm across the newspaper, smoothing the crinkled page on the kitchen table. Everyone in China believed the Taiwanese government had unleashed a vicious biological weapon in Tibet. As soon as the story broke and Chang's face appeared across every state-run media outlet, Jin would have recognized him and instantly known the truth. She knew patient zero was working for the PLA, and that meant the Taiwanese hadn't attacked the mainland. The Blood River virus outbreak was an inside job, orchestrated in Beijing.

"The PLA is responsible," Jo stated bluntly. "Our own government did this."

Jin's story was the final piece of evidence that revealed a sinister plot that had been months, maybe years, in the making. The 2PLA had wanted Jin to hand over Chang, but not for information. That was why his impulsiveness hadn't deterred their interest. The army was simply looking for a body—someone who could turn up dead from an unknown disease and trigger a firestorm. Jin's double agent, a Taiwanese intelligence officer, was the perfect pawn.

Jo had unwittingly played her part in the conspiracy. Her epidemiological team had identified patient zero and reported his NSB affiliation up the chain, and then all eyes had turned toward Taipei. President Tang of Taiwan had been beating the drum for independence, so everyone had assumed the bioattack was simply Tang making good on his campaign promises. He'd declare independence from China while the virus mired the mainland. Beijing would be too politically unstable to respond. None of that was true, of course, but when the media reported that patient zero was a Taiwanese spy, no one had believed President Tang's denial.

The plot had played out on the front pages of every global newspaper and even on the floor of the UN General Assembly. In China, people were watching the death toll rise every day, wondering how long they could hide from the Blood River virus. They were suffering, and they wanted revenge. The people had turned sharply against the floundering government in Beijing in favor of the army's hawkish pledge of retaliation. Within a week, the nation had become ripe for political change.

Jo had never imagined that the truth behind BRV45 would be so elaborate, so nefarious. The PLA hadn't just exploited the crisis;

it had *manufactured* the crisis in the first place. Within a week of the outbreak, the public was practically begging the army to step in. The PLA had overthrown the government without firing a single shot, and the people cheered.

Jo's logical mind worked to create order from the chaos—patient zero, the haphazard field lab in Dzongsar, the buried syringe, the bombing of the monastery. The PLA brimmed with megalomaniacs. Irrepressible ambition, boundless resources, dubious ethics—these were not unusual qualities in China's leaders, but few possessed all three simultaneously. One man immediately came to Jo's mind.

General Huang Yipeng.

"We have to tell President Li," Jo said. "There must be something he can do. He can go to the United Nations, and—"

Jin cut her off. "No one has seen the president for two days. The MSS believes he's been assassinated. General Huang has turned Zhongnanhai into his personal palace. It's over, my love."

Jo looked at Kipton. "That explains why Li wanted me to have a CIA shadow."

The American's eyes grew wide. "Jo, you're mistaken, I—"

"Oh, cut the bullpucky," Jin interjected. "Just look at you, young man. You may as well have CIA stamped on your ass cheek."

"After I briefed the Standing Committee last week, President Li took me aside and instructed me to give an American journalist unrestricted access to the investigation," Jo explained. "It seemed so strange—letting a foreign reporter see everything firsthand. But Li knew the Americans would send an undercover intelligence officer. It was his insurance policy. He must have suspected General Huang was somehow involved, but he couldn't prove it. With a spy on my team, whatever we uncovered in Dzongsar would flow directly to Langley. Li was counting on it."

"Well, no offense to President Li's intuition, but—"

"Kip, give me a little credit. Even if I believed a scrappy freelance writer could wrestle an assassin and brush off a bullet wound like it was a beesting, and—"

"And maintain the buttocks of a Mykonos pool boy," Jin added, making a thumbs-up sign.

A smile flickered over Jo's face. "Even if I accepted all of those ridiculously implausible things about you, Kip," she went on, "I would be a fool to assume the Americans would pass up the chance to embed an operative in my field investigation. Plus, the Ministry of State Security flagged you as a known intelligence officer before the ink had even dried on your visa. They emailed me your file three days ago. I read it on our flight to Lhasa."

"So, Kip," Jin added. "It appears we've got a unique opportunity before us."

Both women turned to the fake American reporter, staring at him with identical, insistent expressions.

*   *   *

Olen sat motionless, his yellow teacup suspended halfway to his lips. Jo continued to surprise him. There was no point in maintaining his cover. Evidently, he'd never had one to begin with.

"Looks like I've got a report to file," he said, fighting back a smile.

"Good boy," Jin returned.

"There's still something that doesn't add up," Olen added. "The woman who attacked us in the monastery. Why would the PLA send in an assassin and then level the place with firebombs minutes later?"

"They must have been two independent operations," Jo reasoned.

"So, if the bombers were PLA, who sent the assassin?"

Olen pictured the lithe woman in the slick neoprene suit clutching her shoulder where Jo's bullet had pierced her flesh. He'd seen her before, but where? One thing was for certain; he'd never see her again. If the bullet hadn't killer her, the fire would have. In either case, there was no way that woman had gotten out of Dzongsar Village alive.

48

Arundel Hills, Maryland, USA

CIA OPERATIONS OFFICER Julia Rhodes drizzled a sinful amount of maple syrup onto a stack of blueberry pancakes. She'd just returned from an unbearably long overseas assignment, and she was famished. The weeks away from home made her crave a hot American breakfast from a greasy-spoon diner. She'd earned it. Her entire body ached from the last op, which only reminded her that she was getting too old for this job.

But tonight, no regrets, no shame. Just pancakes.

The flight back to Baltimore had been long and crowded, but Julia had still managed to grab a few hours of sleep. She felt rested and alert, despite the late hour. It was a familiar sensation. Her body clock almost never synchronized with the appropriate time zone—an unavoidable drawback of life in the CIA's National Clandestine Service. She'd probably crash around sunrise.

Julia picked a corner booth so she could monitor the diner's front door. When a short, middle-aged man with salt-and-pepper hair entered, Julia didn't bother waving. The man knew where to find her. He practically sprinted over and slid into her booth. The vinyl cushion squeaked under his weight.

"I know this is a little unconventional, but you're the only person I can trust with this," the man blurted, skipping the customary pleasantries. He looked totally freaked out.

"Hey, Gabe," she replied with a mouthful of pancakes. "You want a menu? This is fabulous. Totally worth the early-onset diabetes."

"*Julia!* Did you hear what I said on the phone? We've got a code six from Tibet. One of our guys is in some serious shit."

Julia sighed and clinked her fork against her plate. She'd known Gabriel Snyder for long enough to see that he was genuinely unsettled. An operative in the field would have to be pretty desperate to request an exfiltration through TRIDENT. NSA monitored the system, but then it had to notify the appropriate agency of any incoming signals. Dissemination of intel to anyone outside Fort Meade required about fifteen signatures. TRIDENT was probably the least efficient way to cut through the intelligence community's administrative red tape.

"Which agency?" Julia asked.

"VECTOR," Snyder replied.

"Just write it up and release the intel to Director Cameron. She'll handle it, and I'll finish my breakfast in peace."

"It's more complicated than that."

Julia cocked her head. "Now you've got me interested. What's the scoop on Cameron?"

Snyder paused. He lowered his voice. "Look, here's what I know. A VECTOR operations officer named Olen Grave has run into some trouble. It could be you or me out there, Julia. I won't say much more, just that I can't disseminate the TRIDENT signal. Not officially. That's why I called you. This needs to be totally back-channel."

Julia scooted a syrup-soaked blueberry around her plate, digesting Snyder's request. He'd placed her in an awkward situation. "You realize a Tibetan exfil right now is about as probable as discovering intelligent life on Mars, right? You'd need Wonder Woman to get him out."

Snyder grinned. "So, I came to the right place."

Julia groaned. "I suppose he has to be breathing when I bring him back?" She chugged her last swig of OJ.

Snyder seemed satisfied with her acquiescence and started to get up to leave. "How'd you hurt your shoulder?" he asked, sliding out of the booth. He must've seen her wince when she lifted her glass.

"Fly-fishing accident." Julia winked. "Snagged an eighteen-pounder. Worst part is, he got away."

Snyder snorted. He should've known better than to ask.

*   *   *

From an empty parking lot across the street, Allyson watched the doughy man in the leather jacket lumber out of the diner. He moved slowly, not like when he'd rushed inside moments before. *He met someone inside*, she thought. But who?

The answer came seconds after Snyder's black Audi turned the corner and drove away. A slender woman with tan skin emerged from the diner, holding a cell phone to her ear. She'd slicked her sable hair into a tight bun, but Allyson recognized her immediately. She was the woman from the MI6 surveillance pic taken at the Singapore Zoo. In the photo, she was standing next to a man Allyson knew quite well—Marc Chen, Allyson's missing officer.

The director had known Chen wasn't dead when the Ngari blueprints showed up on her doorstep. The air base plans were top-secret PLA documents, and only Chen had that kind of access in China. His deep-cover placement as General Huang's aide-de-camp was so sensitive that not even Barlow knew the details. The president would understand Allyson's need for secrecy. The White House had too many leaks.

Officer Chen still hadn't formally reported in since the outbreak, though. Was he working with this woman? Was she a source? Or maybe a handler? If Chen had turned—and he wouldn't be the first American spy to switch sides—that could mean the Ngari air base plans were fake. Or maybe the PLA had discovered Chen was a double agent and fed him phony intel, hoping it would find its way into the president's daily brief. Whatever the case, Officer Marc Chen was hiding something.

*   *   *

A horrid day was quickly becoming a horrid week, Julia thought to herself as she slipped around the back of the diner. Working under the alias Kalina, she'd failed her last mission in Tibet and nearly died in the process.

The assassin had underestimated Grave and that female doctor. If not for the impenetrable tungsten plates sewn into the lining of Julia's polyurethane bodysuit, the bullet would've sliced through her liver. She rubbed her shoulder. Her wrestling match with Grave had left her a little tender. Why hadn't he finished her off? Was it possible he'd recognized her?

And what was Grave thinking, using TRIDENT to request an exfiltration from the TAR? Julia had found it fairly easy to slip out. She'd stolen a Roketa dirt bike from the abandoned PLA installation and ridden north on a mountain road to Changdu Bangda Airport. From there, a Spanish CASA CN-235 transport aircraft with a Pakistani crew had delivered her safely to Islamabad. A CIA jet bound for Washington was already on the tarmac, awaiting her arrival.

Julia had no intention of returning to that hellscape in Tibet, despite what she'd promised Snyder. By tomorrow morning, she'd be stretched out on a beach in San Pedro, enjoying her hard-earned vacation. *Let Olen Grave burn*, she thought. *Let him burn like that pile of dead monks.*

49

Beijing, People's Republic of China

"HANG ON, LADIES," Olen said. "My boss is going to want more concrete evidence." He planned to report everything he'd learned to Allyson as soon as they left Jin's home. It wouldn't be an easy task—he couldn't exactly ring Fort Detrick from his hotel room—but he could pass a short written message to a cutout working with the U.S. embassy.

Still, though Jin's story was juicy intel, it would only leave Allyson hungry for more. "Unless we can prove that Blood River virus was genetically engineered and released by the Chinese military, she'll say all I've got is the word of a paranoid spy-doctor and her batty old aunt." Olen turned to Jin. "No offense."

Jin snorted. "You don't know the half of it, honey."

"He's right," Jo said. "We've got to have solid proof or Langley will just blow it off."

Olen waited for Jo to speak the words. It was her call.

The doctor stood up. "We're going to the Black Egg. That's where Ru made BRV45. We'll find the evidence we need there."

"We're just going to mosey into a heavily guarded military laboratory?" Olen challenged. "I don't exactly blend in."

"I'll handle that," Jo said dismissively. She locked eyes with her aunt. "Do you still have it?"

Jin was already floating into the great room.

Olen wasn't surprised to see Jin tug on a Ming-era wardrobe to reveal a hidden door. He'd noticed an abnormality in the house's floor plan when passing through the central courtyard. The walls didn't line up. He'd thought maybe the woman had installed a panic room during the renovation.

With a light swat of Jin's hand, the enormous antique swung weightlessly on a set of hinges, revealing a room the size of a freight elevator. Weapons of every deadly variety hung in neat rows from steel hooks. There must have been a hundred firearms, ranging from assault weapons to six-shooters.

"Add a few cans of low-sodium kidney beans and I'm ready for the end times," Jin said.

Olen bypassed the high-powered sniper rifles and snub-nosed shotguns for something easier to conceal. He examined the collection of knives. Over his shoulder, he saw Jo sorting through a box of passports. A stack of colorful currency sat on the ledge beside her.

Olen emerged from Jin's arsenal and found the woman sitting on the edge of a taut sofa. She pulled her shoulders back and stretched out her neck, like a royal posing for a portrait. A puff of white smoke lingered above her silver spikes.

"I thought you didn't smoke inside," Olen said. Jin shrugged and looked away. He moved closer. "You weren't planning to tell Jo that you recruited patient zero. Why not?"

"The world is a filthy place. My niece thinks it's her job to clean it up. Some diseases can't be cured." She took another drag of her Baisha.

"Where will you go?"

Jin sighed. "I'm a loose end. It doesn't matter where I go." The old spymaster mashed the end of her cigarette into an expensive-looking coffee table as Jo emerged from the secret room.

"I saw that," Jo scolded, pointing at the smoldering cigarette butt.

Jin tossed up her hands. "What can I say? You caught me."

"Are you sure you want to do this?" Olen asked Jo, eyeing the brown duffel bag slung over the doctor's shoulder.

"Are *you*?" Jo sounded defensive. She clearly had no choice in the matter. Whether she liked it or not, she was already involved. Her ex-husband had engineered the disease and her aunt had recruited patient zero. For Jo, this was now a family affair.

The virologist handed Olen a thick white envelope. "You're an environmental systems engineer working for a Swiss company under a government contract. Docs, cash—it's all there."

"So, a WHO spy, basically."

"Hey, it's better than CIA. It's enough to get you to Shanghai."

Olen worried about using such a thin cover, but he didn't let it show. "I've worked with less."

Jo leaned over to kiss her aunt's forehead. "Don't worry about us. We'll be fine."

The old woman smiled. "Do I look worried, Zhinü?"

"Shanghai's a pretty big town. Where exactly is the Black Egg?" Olen asked.

The doctor was already marching toward the front door. "It's this way," she replied.

* * *

Senior recruiter Jin Meihui sat alone, squeezing her box of cigarettes. The package felt light in her palm. There was only one left. She reached inside and pinched the smooth round cigarette, comforted by its familiar shape and texture.

After Jo and the American left, Jin reconsidered her options. She had the means to disappear, just not the energy. She allowed herself a quiet moment to admire her elegant home. She'd saved for decades to create her little haven from the world's ugliness. It had been foolish to think she could live out her sunset years in Beijing.

Jin slid the last remaining Baisha back into its crumpled box. She'd save it for later, she thought. One last lie.

The old woman never heard the man enter, but she knew he was there. Jin had been expecting him.

"You're right on time," she said to the seemingly empty room. A shadow flickered in the corner of her eye. "When we met three years ago—when I gave you Chang Yingjie—this wasn't what I had in mind."

Jin twisted in her chair to see a tall, handsome man in an olive-green military uniform standing in her doorway. He carried a pistol with a long-barrel silencer. As she looked into the man's stone eyes, Jin's disappointment overwhelmed her.

"You look so much older now, Lieutenant Wang."

CHAPTER

50

Washington, DC, USA

THE CORRIDOR, LIT with harsh overhead fluorescents, was almost fifty feet underground. Tasteful art decorated the walls every twenty paces, complemented by the occasional potted ficus. The subterranean passageway running the length of Pennsylvania Avenue was convenient but rarely necessary. There were certainly more civilized ways to shuttle between the White House and Capitol Hill. At such an early hour, however, the president's motorcade squealing through downtown Washington would have attracted too much attention. The Beltway media would've conjured hysterical explanations for Barlow's predawn congressional confab. Ironically, none of them would've been as sensational as the truth.

Barlow strode shoulder to shoulder with Nathan Sullivan, sandwiched by two pairs of Secret Service bodyguards. The president spoke to his national security adviser in a lowered tone, his words barely audible above the rapping of a dozen black wing tips.

"If we're even going to consider your plan, we've got to engage Congress," Barlow argued.

"Mr. President, with all due respect, those grandstanding cretins will turn this crisis into a political football. You want a real disaster, then take this to Congress, but just know that they're more interested in self-preservation than national security."

"You're right. The Senate could never bring this matter to the floor. That's why we're going through back channels. You may have noticed we've literally gone underground."

The men turned a sharp corner, breezing through the passage in lockstep.

"The Senate Foreign Relations Committee may not want to hear what you have to say," Sullivan said.

"Maybe not."

"And there's still that little problem."

"Darlene."

"Secretary Hart may no longer chair the committee, but she's got powerful allies in this town."

"I'm aware." The president smiled. "I'm one of them."

Sullivan paused, allowing Barlow to advance a few paces. "Do you remember Plebe Summer at the Naval Academy?"

"It's hard to forget, my friend. You looked terrible with a buzz cut," the president joked. The men had been assigned to the same squad on Induction Day.

The national security adviser grinned. "How about sailing lessons on those Lasers?"

"Sure, the one-man bottle caps. Those fuckers tipped over in a stiff breeze."

"Our company commander sprung a surprise muster midway through one of our lessons," Sullivan continued.

"Midshipman First Class Stephen Slaughter. Can you believe that was his real name?"

"He certainly did his best to live up to it."

"What's this all about, Nate?" Barlow began walking again, slowly, allowing Sullivan to catch up.

"Slaughter blew that goddamn whistle like it was the commandant's cock, and our whole squad sailed back to the dock."

"It was a scramble. He didn't appreciate tardiness, if memory serves."

"Right. Everyone lined up on the dock, necks braced, good to go," Sullivan said. "Except one of us was missing—still out in the bay, trying to right-size his overturned Laser, his lanky arms tugging at the keel."

"I thought Slaughter's eyeballs were going to pop out of his head." Barlow laughed hoarsely.

"You didn't hesitate. You catapulted your body into the water like a torpedo and swam out to help him. No one else moved an inch, but you mounted the hull to counterbalance the mast and helped him flip the Laser over."

"You'd never have been able to do it alone, Nate. No one really could," Barlow said.

"I know. Not to mention I was a pencil-thin teenager from Phoenix who didn't know piss about sailboats. Here's my point, Jim. You're hardwired to stick up for the little guy, to restore some sense of fairness to this messed-up world. It's part of what makes you a good person, and a damn great president."

Barlow rubbed his chin. "You think I have a moral obligation to stand up for Taiwan. Even if it means a preemptive strike? Even if it means war?"

"You read Allyson's report," Sullivan said. "Her VECTOR officer in the field finally sent some useful intel from Beijing. Grave claims that patient zero was actually working for the Chinese army. The biological attack was a false-flag operation, orchestrated by the PLA and designed to incriminate Taiwan. It makes sense. General Huang gained justification for his coup *and* for a hostile takeover of the island. If VECTOR's reports are true and Huang is to blame for the outbreak, then the Taiwanese are innocent, Jim. They don't deserve to be bullied by Beijing."

"You may have a point," Barlow agreed. "Huang has ratcheted up his rhetoric, threatening a full-scale invasion. And then there's the new Chinese missile site in Ngari. The evidence is certainly mounting."

"East Asia is about to erupt. Russia, North Korea—they'll all get pulled in. Forget the virus. This will be a bloodbath," Sullivan warned.

Barlow slapped a hand on his friend's shoulder and smiled warmly. The men had arrived at the door to a Senate conference room. "Let's see what the Committee thinks."

"She doesn't appreciate the role of military power in state-craft," Sullivan warned. "A preemptive strike will be totally out of the question. Not to mention, it's going to take one hell of a missile to penetrate those underground silos. The entire Ngari region is basically tungsten, which they tell me is almost as hard as diamond. A standard bunker-buster won't work. We'd need a nuclear-tipped Minuteman III. She'll never go for it."

Barlow twisted the handle and opened the door to reveal nine exhausted, dour faces.

"Won't go for what, dear?" An impeccably dressed Secretary Darlene Hart grinned from the head of the conference room table.

51

Shanghai, People's Republic of China

THE HOTEL INTERCONTINENTAL shimmered against the Shanghai cityscape. Jo had reserved rooms for her and Kipton, but the reservations weren't showing up in the hotel's computer. The front desk manager couldn't stop apologizing. He had only one vacant room, but it was a suite with a knockout view, he said consolingly. The Skyline Suite. Jo didn't care if the room had a gold-plated toilet; she only wanted a quiet place to think. Her mind was a swirling stew of emotions: confusion, sadness, *rage*. Her government had murdered thousands of people, and she was an unwitting accomplice. General Huang had used her, and she'd played the fool.

The suite had a midcentury vibe. Purple lounge chairs made from crushed velvet encircled an oval coffee table with flared legs. A massive TV sat inside a boxy, wooden media cabinet that swiveled to face either the living area or the kitchenette. The walls were floor-to-ceiling windows, offering a stunning panorama of the glittering city.

Kipton swaggered down a hallway, kicking his boots into a corner like he'd lived there for years. He oozed confidence. The man's mission was clear: uncover the truth, stop the bad guys. He hadn't just learned that he worked *for* the bad guys.

For decades, Jo had tirelessly served her country, the same country now behind the deadliest bioattack in history. Her identity, her life's purpose—it had all been torpedoed in the span of an afternoon. Now she was adrift, bobbing in a wide ocean while cold waves crashed over her. Jo needed to grasp something solid, something she could *feel* and know was real.

Kipton found the bedroom and called over his shoulder. "Looks like there's only one bed, so I guess I'll sleep on the—"

Jo grabbed Kipton's shoulder from behind and whipped him around. Impulsively, she lunged into him, kissing him roughly.

"We can't! I mean, it wouldn't be right for me to—" Kipton stammered.

Jo breathed heavily into his mouth. "And why not? Don't you trust me?"

"Of course I trust you. It's just . . . I'm a—"

"You're a spy," Jo finished. "We've covered that already. It doesn't matter."

It was a lie. Going to bed with an American intelligence officer would raise a great deal of suspicion with her MSS comrades. But she was going to take it even further, wasn't she? She was going to *help* him. Jo had never considered turning against her government before tonight. Partnering with a foreign spy was practically treasonous. *To hell with it,* she thought. Maybe the situation called for a little treason.

Jo clawed at Kipton's shirt. Buttons chattered on the floor as she stripped it from his body. She raked her nails down his biceps, over the ridges of his abs, following the thin trail of hair below his navel.

"Technically we're adversaries," Kipton protested, his confidence waning as Jo lit a fire of temptation. The man's breathing grew ragged, and he gasped when Jo slid a palm down the front of his pants.

"Do I look like an adversary, Kipton?" Jo bit her lip, and with a sudden, firm grip, she'd won.

Over the next hour, Jo felt her spirit returning. Waves of heat flowed between her and the American spy, throbbing inside her core, circulating through her like electric current. Kipton was a skilled lover, but Jo didn't lust for pleasure; she craved control.

Kipton's body was rough, masculine, powerful, and she had complete command of it.

She mounted Kipton and ground her hips in tight circles, harvesting his virility. For balance, Jo pressed both palms into the windowpane above the headboard. Fifty-six stories below, red taillights streaked the pavement. The glass pulsated, creaking ominously, threatening to crack open and send her plummeting to the ground. Below her, Kipton's eyes flashed a look of concern, but Jo only grinned and rocked faster.

Dr. Zhou Weilin would decide her own fate tonight, and every night thereafter. She was a doormat for no man. She'd bring them all down, one by one, even if it killed her. And she'd start with General Huang.

With a terrific shudder, Jo threw back her head and released a guttural scream of unrestrained, honest freedom.

DAY 13

CHAPTER

52

Shanghai, People's Republic of China

OLEN'S SKIN RADIATED heat. He swung his legs over the edge of the mattress, his feet landing in a jumble of discarded clothing. Jo stood at the hotel room's panoramic window, clutching a sheet loosely around her body.

Outside, Shanghai's skyline hummed like a neomodern opus—a neon kaleidoscope with the hypnotic allure of a fever dream. Nightmarish blades, slippery and smooth, slashed sheets of gray smog with serrated edges.

"I like how the tower lights up at night," Jo said.

Olen looked down at his exposed body and smirked.

Jo rolled her eyes and pointed to an ashen structure across the river. "There," she said. "That's the Black Egg."

Her gaze zeroed in on an unremarkable building among the forest of steel and glass. The structure was easy to overlook. Upstaged by its soaring, dazzling neighbors, the edifice was extraordinarily plain. It rose a modest fifty-five stories—a dwarf among giants. Its exterior was painted the same pallid gray as the viscid haze encircling its cap. Only a crown of red, blinking lights—necessary beacons to warn low-flying aircraft—drew attention to the otherwise lifeless tower. Its dull sides looked thick and impenetrable, and they were completely featureless. No windows, balconies, ridges, or ledges interrupted its rigidly geometric shape. In a city famous for hyperbolic architecture, the Black Egg's prosaic facade made it nearly invisible among the glittering skyscrapers—a colorless shadow, cloaked by its own banality.

"China built a biosafety level four facility in the middle of downtown Shanghai?" Olen asked.

"Look around, Kip. This city is blossoming. The last five scientific breakthroughs happened right here, in Shanghai. It's got more brainpower per square inch than Silicon Valley in the nineties. That's why the greatest minds of our time are flocking to this city. Shanghai is the epicenter of modern human advancement. Building the Black Egg here made perfect sense."

Olen turned back toward the austere building, shrouded in urban camouflage. It reminded him of the blocky cement citadels of the Soviet era. There was nothing outwardly modern about the Black Egg.

"Besides," Jo added, "we took precautions."

"What do you mean, 'precautions'?"

"The Ministry of Public Security maintains a perimeter around the base of the building. There are only two entrances—at the north and south ends—both lined with concrete barriers and guarded by men with assault rifles." Jo traced the outline of the building on the window. "And as you probably noticed, there are no windows or doors on the exterior."

"So, we go in through the rooftop ventilation," Olen suggested.

"Not a chance. The vents are completely inaccessible. Any air coming in or out of the facility travels through a network of filters designed to capture anything smaller than zero-point-three microns. They catch even the smallest airborne microbes. And the vents are monitored with extremely responsive sensors. If the air pressure inside the ductwork drops suddenly, the sensors trigger an alarm and the whole place goes into lock-down."

"Sounds like the Black Egg is unbreakable," Olen mused. "How are we supposed to infiltrate a facility designed to keep out microscopic particles? Last time I checked, I'm larger than zero-point-three microns."

"There's only one way I know of," Jo began. "Constructing a facility to study dangerous microbes in the heart of our most populated city was, admittedly, controversial. If a pathogen stored inside that building were to escape, it would have a near-unlimited supply of victims. The army's biggest concern was a bomb or missile attack. The PLA insisted on safeguards."

"Like what?"

"The Black Egg was erected on top of four narrow shafts that burrow deep into the ground. Each shaft is lined with lead, so they are capable of withstanding a nuclear explosion. In an Alpha Five emergency—if the facility's vital containment systems are somehow compromised—all microbial samples are to be loaded onto small elevators, like dumbwaiters, and lowered into the shafts. They're called incident chambers."

"The shafts are the way in," Olen said. "But if they're lead lined, how do we—"

"The engineers couldn't have bored into the ground this close to the coast without installing pumps and drainage pipes at the base of the shafts. Otherwise the chambers would fill with water."

"Where do the drainage pipes lead?" he asked.

"They dump into the Huangpu River," she answered. The river ran directly through downtown Shanghai. The Hotel Inter-Continental butted up to its eastern bank.

"We'll need diving gear," Olen said, beginning to think through the operation. "We can use the ropes and clamps we got from Jin to climb the elevator's steel cable. It'll be dark down there, so we'll need to pick up a few waterproof lights. Any idea where we can score a couple scuba tanks?"

"We only need one."

"What? Why?"

"Because I'm not going with you," Jo said. "Not through the incident chambers. They're sealed at the top. They have to be. It's the only way to prevent contamination of the laboratory. I'll have to open the access door from the inside."

"And how do you plan to get past the guards?" Olen asked.

"With this." Jo held up her Ministry of Health security badge. "I'm a high-ranking government scientist with level four access."

"Timing will be crucial," Olen said. "With all the security precautions, I won't be able to stay inside the shaft undetected for very long. You'll need to go straight to the incident chambers. Once you're inside, how will you find them?"

"My lab is in that building," Jo replied. "The Black Egg is my office."

Olen blinked.

Jo pointed to the gray block. "I have a team of a hundred scientists working for me behind those walls."

"So, Blood River virus was engineered in the same building where you went to work every day? You traveled three thousand miles to hunt for the virus's origin when you could've just taken the elevator?"

"Now you see why they wanted me out of the way. The bastards knew I'd figure it out." Jo turned away from the windows. "But forget it, Kip. The incident chambers won't work either. It's insane to go in that way. We'll have to think of something else."

Olen picked through the pile of tangled clothing and recovered his boxers, slipping them on. "It sounds like our best option, Jo."

"Maybe if you like the idea of being burned alive." Jo turned back to the window, causing the sheet to fall off her shoulders and reveal her smooth back. "In an emergency situation, the biological samples are placed into the shafts, and then they're incinerated. The air in the chamber must be kept as antiseptic as possible at all times. Incineration isn't only triggered in an emergency. A two-second burst of superheated gas sterilizes the shaft every twenty minutes, like clockwork."

"The whole freaking chamber is an oven?"

"If your oven reaches a thousand degrees Celsius, then yes."

"Fuck me," Olen mumbled, rubbing his face.

"So, like I said, Kip, the incident chambers are out. I'll go in alone and retrieve the data that we need to prove—"

Olen raised an open palm to cut her off. He knew his boss, Allyson, would never believe intelligence this hot coming from an MSS officer she'd never met. Hell, Olen didn't trust Jo either, not completely. She'd only recently come clean about her affiliation with the Chinese intelligence service. It was a good start, but there were procedures, vetting protocols, operational tests to conduct. It took months to establish a pattern of reliability with new double agents.

And he shouldn't have made love to her. But was that what he had done? No, not really. *She* had seduced *him*. The FBI counter-intelligence division would assume Jo was an MSS honey trap, assigned to bed an American spy, feed him misinformation, pump him for secrets. The fellas back home would scrutinize the hell out of everything she reported. They'd cross-check and triple-verify every detail, and it would take an eternity. By the time the techs authenticated Jo's data, God only knew what General Huang would have done.

Olen scratched the back of his head. Breaking into the Black Egg would be dangerous, possibly fatal. But if he succeeded—if he exposed the true origin of the virus—he could save millions.

"No. I've got to collect the evidence myself," he announced firmly. "There's no other option."

Jo paused, then nodded. They both knew he was right.

Olen finished dressing, pulling on a T-shirt. "You said the incident chambers only unseal in the event of an Alpha Five emergency, right? So, how do we plan to make 'em pop?"

"That part's simple," she said, pushing a loose strand of hair from her face. "I'll just have to initiate an Alpha Five emergency."

Jo let the bedsheet slip away fully from her body, revealing her taut silhouette, still glowing from the night's activities. She drifted sensuously toward the bathroom, her back to Olen.

"I'm going to detonate a bomb inside the laboratory," she added casually, pausing in the doorway, eyebrow arched invitingly. Looking over her shoulder, Jo mouthed the word *pop* and disappeared into the bathroom.

Olen coughed into his fist, waited a beat, drummed his fingers on his thighs. Then, cursing under his breath, he ripped his T-shirt over his head, scrambled out of his jeans, and followed Jo into the shower.

53

Beijing, People's Republic of China

G ENERAL HUANG'S HEART squeezed into a tight knot. He ignored the familiar sensation and concentrated on sucking in sharp breaths each time his mouth rose above the water's surface. He chopped and kicked to propel himself from one end of the pool to the other.

The general preferred to exercise before sunrise. He never needed much sleep, and now more than ever, his veins burned with red-hot energy. He felt as if every cell in his body was evolving as he physically transformed into the supreme leader he'd always aspired to be. The leader China cried out for.

With a smack, Huang's palm slapped the wall of the pool. He paused, fingers grasping the tiled edge, before submerging his entire body. He swished weightlessly in the lingering undercurrent. Even the ineluctable force of gravity had no domain over his formidable being.

Peering up through glassy ripples, Huang saw a dark figure materialize at the edge of the pool. The general thrust upward, shaking beads of water from his hair and onto Lieutenant Wang's trousers, making dark polka dots on the fabric.

"Sir, we have a problem," Wang said.

* * *

Lieutenant Wang handed his boss a towel as the general climbed out of the pool. For a man in his midsixties, Huang kept fit. A decade of lavish state dinners might have softened his waistline, but the general's torso was otherwise solid. Routine waxing stripped every follicle of hair from his chest, stomach, even his armpits. From a distance, Huang appeared much younger.

The general patted himself dry and tossed the towel onto a chair. "Report, Lieutenant," he barked, slicking back his hair with both hands.

"Dr. Zhou Weilin and the American journalist are no longer in the Quarantine Zone."

"And I suppose you are not here to tell me they're roasting in some merciless netherworld, along with our dear President Li," Huang said.

"They're in Shanghai."

The general appeared genuinely surprised. "Source?" he asked tersely.

"Project TALON," Wang reported.

Huang turned. "Really?" he said curiously.

When China hosted the Olympics in 2008, the Ministry of Public Security had taken extreme measures to ensure public safety. With the entire world watching, China couldn't afford any embarrassing incidents. As part of an initiative named Project TALON, the domestic spy agency had installed pinhole cameras and ultrasensitive microphones in the suites of hundreds of luxury hotels throughout the city—especially the foreign-operated ones.

After the Games' closing ceremonies, the MPS hadn't seen any reason to dismantle the valuable network of electronic surveillance. Instead, they'd expanded the program to include more major cities. Through Project TALON, the Chinese government had learned which of the world's political and business leaders engaged in drugs, prostitution, and a whole host of other odious acts. Beijing exploited the intelligence mostly for blackmail and coercion. A growing collection of trade accords and corporate mergers owed their just-under-the-wire agreements to Project TALON's strategically positioned cameras.

Wang knew the most salacious videos went viral among the PRC's top-secret personnel. A recent clip from the Skyline Suite at the Shanghai InterContinental Hotel had generated quite a buzz for its particularly pornographic content. Over the last few hours, it had bounced around China's intelligence community. Wang had gotten the video file from his contact in the Ministry of Foreign Affairs, who had gleefully noted the "chick's hot rack."

The sex tape was indeed graphic, but Wang wasn't at all surprised by Grave's libertine recklessness. The doctor, however, was another matter. Wang hadn't pegged her as so injudicious. Moreover, Wang was stunned that the pair had evacuated Dzongsar alive. And there was only one reason Grave would suddenly surface in Shanghai.

"Project TALON picked them up in the Pudong district, at the InterContinental," Wang added.

"I see." General Huang paced along the edge of the pool.

"We assume they're headed to Institute 414." Wang used the official military designation for the Black Egg. He knew the general found its nickname trivializing.

General Huang shot Lieutenant Wang an intense glare. "Well?" he asked, hands on hips.

"Yes, sir," Wang responded, spinning on a heel, heading for the exit. Huang's unspoken orders were clear.

"And Lieutenant," Huang called after him. "I want a copy of that video in my in-box within the hour."

CHAPTER

54

Shanghai, People's Republic of China

Forget Anbar Province. A biosafety level four laboratory was a far more inhospitable place to spend an afternoon. BSL-4 was reserved for the study of exotic diseases with no known vaccine or effective treatment. A crucible for some of the nastiest plagues, the Black Egg was home to Ebola, Lassa, and Crimean-Congo hemorrhagic fever—Jo had said—but those bugs didn't really concern Olen. Like Blood River virus, they were transmitted only through direct contact. The airborne viruses—H1N1, SARS, anthrax—scared the snot out of him. The atmosphere inside the building could be swarming with invisible killers.

For protection, the scientists working inside the Black Egg wore tangerine biosafety suits. The suits were clumsy, but more importantly, they were airtight and offered a supply of clean, pathogen-free oxygen.

Not until zipping into a paper-thin wetsuit did Olen fully register how exposed he'd be when entering the laboratory. Jo had continued to try to talk him out of it, but Olen saw no other way. Through the embassy cutout, he'd already reported everything he'd learned from Jin to Allyson—that patient zero was a double agent working for the PLA—and just as expected, the boss wanted something more concrete. Olen could only imagine how the situation had escalated in Washington, especially after General Huang's coup. Undoubtedly, decisions were being made. Irrevocable decisions. President Barlow would demand more than the word of a semiretired Chinese spy with zero history of reporting. And time was running out. Allyson couldn't order Olen to infiltrate the laboratory, but she didn't have to. Olen knew the woman would deep fry his balls if he backed out.

Now, gliding silently twenty feet below the surface of the Huangpu River, Olen had passed the point of no return. Jo was already inside the Black Egg.

The mouth of the drainage pipe looked like a perfect circle floating in the murky water—a portal to another world. Suddenly, it glowed bright teal. Olen heard a faint rumble. It was low, like an engine turning over. The brilliant color lasted a few seconds before dying out, returning the cloudy water to near darkness.

Olen tapped his waterproof Suunto watch, and big digital numbers began counting down. It would take two full minutes for the chambers to cool off. Olen hovered at the mouth of the pipe while high-powered jets sprayed liquid nitrogen onto the walls of the shaft, dropping the interior temperature to a safe level. Once inside the portal, he'd have precisely eighteen minutes before the incinerators flamed up again. In that short amount of time, he'd need to swim through the pipe to the pumping station and then make the hundred-foot vertical climb up the shaft. Then it was up to Jo to open the hatch at the top. Otherwise, he'd be a cooked goose.

* * *

For six years, the Black Egg had been Jo's home away from home. Plucked from China's roster of top virologists, she'd always felt honored to oversee her own lab within the nation's most advanced research facility.

A decade ago, her country had lagged behind the industrialized world when it came to preventing the spread of infectious diseases. The SARS epidemic had caught everyone off guard. The Chinese government was wholly unprepared for the threat posed by microbial outbreaks. The Politburo naïvely thought it could keep secret the most serious epidemic of the twenty-first century. But it wasn't so easy to convince a billion people to just look the other way. News of the government cover-up had spread faster than the disease itself. Rumors flew that Zhongnanhai had intentionally released SARS as a draconian form of population control. At the time, Jo had thought the idea utterly delusional—the result of mass paranoia. She hadn't believed anyone could be so blackhearted. Now, after learning the truth behind BRV45, she felt differently.

The Black Egg was Beijing's insurance policy against another microbial threat. For eighteen months, construction crews had worked around the clock to erect a state-of-the-art laboratory to rival America's Centers for Disease Control.

Jo had been thrilled when the MSS selected her to lead an elite team of research scientists. Her mission was one of national security, and she was proud of her work. When she wasn't in the field, she spent most of her waking hours inside the lab's sealed walls, fighting to protect her country from another public health disaster. How could it be that the very threat she'd worked tirelessly to suppress had been spawned within the Black Egg itself?

She would find those responsible. She would hold them accountable for their crimes against her people.

Jo had never imagined she'd secretly collaborate with the CIA, but her mission to expose Huang was too much to take on alone. Did that make her a traitor against her government? Arguably, her government no longer existed, not after the coup. Huang was a bullheaded military junta. He would never represent China. Not legitimately. Jo would oppose him vehemently. She would reveal to the world the devil that he was. No, she wasn't a traitor, she kept reminding herself. She was a patriot.

Even though the Black Egg housed three fully equipped biosafety level four laboratories, it also doubled as an administrative office for the Ministry of Health. Wrinkled lab coats flapped behind waves of distressed scientists scuttling in all directions. Some of them looked completely lost—a familiar sight within the mazelike corridors. After the first cases of BRV45 appeared in Tibet, researchers from all over China had converged on the facility. Jo passed twenty people without recognizing a single face. She hoped to keep it that way as she swiftly made her way to the second-floor lab. That was where she'd find the incident chambers.

Jo didn't want to bump into a colleague on the elevator, so she took the stairs. As far as everyone knew, she was still in Dzongsar searching for the origins of BRV45. By now some people would've heard about the destruction of the Q-Zone. People would wonder if she'd evacuated in time. If they saw her at the Black Egg, they'd have a million questions—ones she didn't have time to answer.

Jo looked at her watch, which she'd synchronized to the incident chambers' incineration cycle.

Seventeen minutes.

* * *

The air inside the incident chamber was muggy but tolerable. The temperature gauge on Olen's tactical Suunto watch read ninety-six degrees, but a powerful heat still emanated from the walls. The incinerator's cooling process had lowered the temperature of the lead only to about five hundred degrees Fahrenheit—hot enough to dissolve skin on contact. If he touched the chamber's casing, Olen's wetsuit would probably ignite, charring his entire body in a matter of seconds. So, he'd have to climb the elevator cables straight up the middle of the narrow chamber.

Olen secured a heavy-duty cable ascender to the elevator's thick cord. A nylon rope wrapped around his waist and under his crotch hooked into the aluminum carabiner attached to the U-shaped ascender. The device would support his weight as he used both hands to inch up the cable. Rock climbers used similar gear to take short rests during challenging climbs. Olen wouldn't have that luxury. By the time he reached the top, his biceps would be Jell-O.

Olen cracked a couple Cyalume light sticks, and the chamber glowed lime green. He looked up. The top of the chamber was a speck. Now accessing the difficulty of the climb in person, he knew he'd never make it with fifty pounds of diving gear weighing him down. Olen stripped off the tank, respirator, gauges, and mask. He kept his tactical vest to carry a few supplies, and a small switchblade.

Olen's stomach sank. Jo had given him strict instructions to breathe through his scuba mouthpiece once inside the lab. It wouldn't fully protect him, but at least the oxygen in his tank would be untainted. Ditching the heavy equipment meant he'd have to enter the level four lab without clean air. He imagined those nasty pathogens floating invisibly, searching for new hosts to infect, flowing directly into his lungs.

Pushing the thought from his mind, Olen focused on the climb. He locked the ascender, gripped the cable, and tugged his hundred-ninety-five-pound body straight up.

* * *

Entering a level four laboratory the correct way took a lot of time and patience. The main entrance to the lab marked the beginning of a complex, multistep process to ensure the safety of the scientists and prevent cross-contamination from the outside. After waving a security badge over a sensor and staring into a retinal scanner, visitors with the proper clearance stepped into a reception area. From there, men went left and women went right into separate locker rooms. Every scrap of clothing, jewelry, even contact lenses had to be removed. Lab workers called that area the Dirty Room.

The walls of the Dirty Room were fire engine red—a not-so-subtle reminder to stop and remove anything from the outside world that could pollute the lab. Jo stripped and stuffed her clothes into an empty locker. She didn't bother spinning the combination dial. No one did. Her colleagues at the Black Egg held the nation's highest-level security clearance. Petty theft wasn't a problem.

Naked, Jo walked through a double-door air lock into a dressing room, where she donned a pair of powder-blue medical scrubs made of coated paper. Everyone hated the disposable underwear. They bunched and scratched after a few hours of work. Most just skipped the paper panties and went commando.

Jo pulled a set of surgical gloves from a cardboard box. She grabbed a roll of masking tape, peeled off two long strips, and wrapped them tightly around her wrists to seal the cuffs of her scrubs. Next, Jo passed through a second set of airtight doors— one of many intentional redundancies—into a bleak room with glacier-white walls and shiny tile. The Clean Room.

Bright-tangerine hazmat suits hung from steel hooks. Nick-named "space suits" for their airtight seals, bubble-domed hel-mets, and built-in life support systems, the cumbersome apparatuses were tough to put on without help. Nevertheless, Jo was relived to find the Clean Room unoccupied. Then, she noticed three empty hooks at the end of the row and frowned. A few of her colleagues were getting an early start to the day. With any luck, Jo could avoid them inside the sprawling facility.

A soft hissing sound, like a punctured tire deflating, came from the double doors to her left. A cool breeze rushed past her—the effects of the Clean Room's negative pressure, which sucked in air to prevent microorganisms from escaping. The air lock to the men's dressing room slid open. Jo spun to see the stunned face of a young microbiologist on her team. He looked at Jo, his bug eyes growing wide.

55

Shanghai, People's Republic of China

VECTOR OPERATIONS OFFICER Marc Chen—known to some as Lieutenant Wang, Hudson Reece, and a handful of other names—despised Shanghai more than any Chinese city. His deep-cover assignment rarely included trips to the coastal metropolis, but whenever his duties required it, he felt the same disgust.

Marc had good reason for such visceral antipathy. Three summers ago he'd arrived in Shanghai carrying an American passport. The document's photo was authentic, but it matched to the name Dr. Vincent Wu, a midlevel executive for a Seattle-based biotechnology start-up. The fictitious Dr. Wu was a real go-getter, and as such, he'd come to Shanghai to kick off three weeks of whirlwind meetings with prospective Chinese investors.

The op had almost gotten Marc killed. He'd studied his alias meticulously, as he did before any mission, but he'd underestimated one man's compulsive curiosity into the spurious life of Dr. Wu.

It began with the usual cable traffic. The analysts believed the Chinese military had established a private biotechnology company as a means of quietly acquiring sensitive technology. The CIA's East Asia desk even peddled a wild theory about experiments with human genetic enhancements—supersoldiers with sharper intelligence, greater resiliency, even certain forms of extrasensory perception. It was the typical Langley melodrama that spooked everyone in Washington.

Director Allyson Cameron sent Marc to Shanghai, where, as planned, he represented himself as a doctor of genetic engineering. He'd earned a PhD from the University of Washington in the late 2000s, so the story went. His reputation in America had helped him clinch a string of confabs with leading Chinese firms. It was a simple fishing expedition. Marc would strike up conversations about cutting-edge genetic research—the type that could be repurposed for military application—and see who took the bait.

Marc's op hit a snag when a particularly skeptical director of R&D at the Chinese-owned Heliogen Corp. had asked a barrage of very specific questions about the University of Washington. The man claimed that his nephew had studied electrical engineering around the same time Dr. Wu supposedly attended. Perhaps they knew one another, the Heliogen director suggested. But, of course, they did not. No one at the university had ever heard of Vincent Wu—a fact easily obtained with a few phone calls. Officer Chen was in handcuffs before lunch.

Facing some of the world's most stringent antiespionage laws (with punishments to match), Marc did the unthinkable. He demanded to speak with the Shanghai station chief of the Ministry of State Security. Marc's captors—two Heliogen security guards with cannonball biceps—brushed off the absurd request. Then he asked again, but the second time, he asked for the station chief by name.

Marc knew the guards would never contact anyone from the MSS. No chance in hell. Heliogen Corp. was most certainly the PLA shell company he'd been searching for. The entire security detail likely comprised active-duty soldiers. Heliogen wouldn't report Marc's capture. They had something else in mind. The guards stripped him of every scrap of clothing—as if spies still walked around with cyanide pills sewn into their collars. For three nights Marc slept naked on the concrete floor of a cell no bigger than a coat closet. He drank dirty water from a small bowl like an animal.

Heliogen's chief of security visited daily. He was a fat man with a thick neck covered in black moles. The obese misanthrope taunted his new prisoner with a bowl of steamed rice, only to eat it himself while Marc looked on ravenously. By the fourth day, Marc was convinced he would die in that room.

That's when another visitor arrived. She was the complete antithesis of the security chief—polite, well dressed, hair swooped into a silver flame. Her blouse, with its gleaming gold buttons and scarlet floral pattern, looked like something from the London *Times* style section. When two fire-engine lips spread across her perfect, gleaming teeth, Marc's belly filled with warmth.

The woman perched regally on the edge of an aluminum chair that she'd carried into the cell. She crinkled her nose at the smell but graciously concealed her repugnance at the sight of the nude, half-dead prisoner curled up in the corner. She offered Marc a cup of black coffee and a generous drag on her lipstick-stained Baisha cigarette.

The encounter lasted three hours, after which the woman departed, dragging the chair behind her. Another day or two passed—tracking time was impossible inside the windowless cell—before she returned with a tray of hot food, a robe, and an irresistible offer.

Marc was no fool. After the vile, dehumanizing treatment he'd received, he knew the elegant woman hadn't materialized spontaneously. But she'd made him feel important, worthy, even courageous. His fairy godmother. In truth, she was an intelligence officer specializing in the fine art of developing turncoats. The Chinese knew they had captured an American spy, and they intended to flip Marc's loyalty. The bastard Heliogen security chief had gotten nowhere, so they'd brought in a professional. She had one task: convince the prisoner to spy for China, and then disappear. Marc doubted he would ever see the woman again. She probably had a long list of other men to inveigle. Fortunately, she'd bought Marc's well-rehearsed story. She believed he wanted to betray the United States.

Within an hour, Marc was barreling down the runway at Pudong International Airport, showered, clean-shaven, and fully clothed. The Chinese army was taking him to Beijing. After eighteen months of fastidious planning, Officer Marc Chen was finally going to meet General Huang, chairman of the People's Liberation Army.

*   *   *

Now, three years later, Marc found himself once again at the doorstep of Heliogen Corp.'s headquarters, but the company had a new address. Its sensitive mission—exploiting stolen intellectual property—required a more advanced laboratory and military-grade security. Only one building in Shanghai fit the bill: Institute 414, the Black Egg.

Wang presented his PLA credentials to a sentry posted outside the Black Egg's main entrance. The sentry scanned the document carefully, taking note of the embossed gold seal that identified Lieutenant Wang as a member of General Huang's staff. The guard nodded sharply and stepped aside.

"Take me to Heliogen's chief of security," Marc ordered. "Immediately."

CHAPTER

56

Shanghai, People's Republic of China

"Dr. Zhou!" the young microbiologist shouted.
Jo stopped dead.

"The Q-Zone. We thought you . . . We were told everyone . . ."

"I left Dzongsar *before* the sanitization," Jo responded bluntly. "It doesn't matter. I'm here now, and I'll need a full report on your progress. We'll wait until the entire team arrives to regroup, but since you're already here, I suggest you begin pulling together the data from the past week."

The man tensed up. He'd have to work fast. Synthesizing a week's worth of data before sunrise would keep him thoroughly occupied. And completely out of Jo's way.

"Well, don't just stand there, Doctor," Jo barked. "Help me into this space suit, and let's get moving."

* * *

It was difficult to hear much of anything inside the airtight protective suit—the built-in breathing system generated persistent white noise. Pure, HEPA-filtered air flowed through a thick gray tube, like a vacuum hose, connected to the back of her bubble helmet, feeding in from a heavy pack strapped around Jo's waist. People complained about the fan's constant whooshing. Like most peculiarities of working within a level four laboratory, Jo had acclimated to the minor annoyance long ago.

The lab's interior looked exactly as Jo had left it a little more than a week ago. Rows of workstations positioned under ventilated hoods striped the cavernous space. The counters, tables, and chairs all had rounded edges to prevent accidental tears in the space suits. There were no knickknacks, family photos, house plants, or personal items of any kind. To an outsider, the facility probably felt cold and impersonal. To Jo, the level four environment offered more comfort than any other place on earth. She knew every square inch of that lab, including where to find the incident chambers. However, Jo had to make a quick detour first, to the chemical storage cabinet.

She had a bomb to build.

The Black Egg wasn't only home to some of the planet's deadliest pathogens. It also housed a collection of some uniquely hazardous chemicals. Corrosive acids, highly reactive metals, combustible gases—these were everyday tools of the modern biochemist.

Jo didn't have time to prepare anything elaborate, and she couldn't risk mishandling unstable substances and blowing off her fingers. Instead, she turned to a simpler solution—triacetone triperoxide, known in Al-Qaeda shorthand as TATP.

The bomb's key ingredients could be found in nearly every sorority girl's medicine cabinet. TATP was nothing more than a careful mixture of nail polish remover and hair bleach. To be fair, most bottle blondes couldn't get their hands on hydrogen peroxide potent enough to make a decent explosive—the drugstore version was only 3 percent concentrated—but in the Black Egg, Jo had a range of options. A 30 percent concentration would give her a pop just big enough to trigger the lab's emergency protocols without punching a hole in the side of the building. That bit was important.

Working quickly, Jo filled an Erlenmeyer flask halfway with acetone. Then she dropped in a corked test tube containing twenty milliliters of the concentrated hydrogen peroxide. She capped the conical flask, careful not to slosh its contents.

Jo examined her homemade bomb, lifting it to eye level. The sealed test tube clanked against the inside of the glass flask. The makeshift bomb was safe to carry, as long as the test tube didn't have any cracks or leaks. Separately, the two liquids were harmless, but when combined, they would spark a violent chemical reaction. The simple concoction was the reason travelers could no longer bring liquids over three ounces on board commercial flights.

She checked her watch. Jo had six minutes to get to the incident chamber and open the hatch before the next incineration cycle. She just hoped Kipton had made it to the top of the shaft.

* * *

Inside the wetsuit, Olen dripped with sweat. His forearms burned with each hoist up the cable. Even through his rubber grip climbing gloves, he could feel the skin on his palms starting to blister. At least the ascender was holding firm. Olen sank into the harness and momentarily relaxed his arms to let the blood recirculate through his hands. He'd climbed about seventy feet up the elevator cable. The green glow from the light stick at the bottom of the chamber looked like a faint speck. Olen tapped his Suunto and used its light to scan the space. The underside of the elevator was less than thirty feet up. With six minutes remaining, he could easily finish the climb, but something else on his watch's digital display worried him. Just under the large digits indicating the time were smaller ones that read 110°.

The temperature inside the chamber was rising.

* * *

Marc Chen recognized Heliogen's chief of security from the man's grotesque neck moles. At first, the chief didn't react upon seeing his former captive. He couldn't see past Marc's uniform. He likely assumed the olive-clad visitor was just another army prick trespassing on his turf. Marc got within ten feet before the torpid creature's jaw went slack.

"How did you—" The words spilled from the security chief's grease-covered lips just before the butt of Marc's QSZ-92 pistol cut them off with a thwack across his mouth. The chief toppled from his chair and fell face first to the floor. A tooth rattled underneath his chair. The man was out cold, his paunchy abdomen bulging. He looked like a beached whale.

Marc holstered his weapon and smoothed the front of his shirt. The other security personnel in the room sat frozen at their posts.

"Gentlemen," Marc said politely. "There's been an intrusion. A foreign spy has penetrated this facility. He's working with someone on the inside, I'm afraid. One of our own. A female doctor. We believe they're both somewhere in this building."

A fresh-faced technician wearing a headset microphone spoke up. "It should be easy to find them, sir. If she's an employee, we can look up her access badge and see where she last coded in."

Marc gave the doctor's name, and Fresh Face turned to his computer screen, his fingers flying across the keyboard. Heliogen's central command post was the nerve center of the Black Egg. A building housing such sophisticated laboratories required 24/7 systems monitoring. Careful management of the negative pressure inside the air locks, temperature controls, ventilation procedures, and a complex network of surveillance cameras all happened from this room. Now that the chief of security lay unconscious in a smear of blood, Marc Chen—as Lieutenant Wang—had swiftly asserted dominance.

"Dr. Zhou entered the main security checkpoint twelve minutes ago," Fresh Face reported. "She's currently in the BSL-4 on the second floor."

"Give me your badge," Marc ordered.

"Sure, but you can't just walk into level four. There are protocols. Besides, that lab is gigantic. She could be anywhere. Let me check the cameras."

A red warning box blinked on the terminal monitor. A moment later, the command center erupted in beeps and flashing lights.

"What did you do?" Marc hissed.

"It wasn't me! It's the alarm. The systems on the second floor are shutting down." The security tech typed frantically. "Oh God. It's an Alpha Five. There's been an explosion in the BSL-4."

"Initiate lock-down. Secure all floors. No one leaves this building," Marc commanded.

"Sir, we need to evacuate! The situation has become extremely dangerous. You don't mess with level four. There's some seriously bad stuff in there."

"The explosion is a diversion. Send a security team to investigate, and keep searching for the doctor on the surveillance feeds."

"It's pointless. The feed's crap." Fresh Face swiveled his monitor for Marc to see. The screen had filled with smoke. Marc couldn't make out a thing.

* * *

"Dammit," Jo cursed, ducking around a corner. Had she miscalculated the volume of hydrogen peroxide? Had someone mislabeled its concentration? Whatever the case, the explosion had been bigger than she'd anticipated. It had rocked the floor and torn the door off a utility closet.

The homemade bomb had worked like a glass grenade. She'd thrown it down the hallway, and upon impact with the tile, the Erlenmeyer flask and the test tube floating inside it had both shattered, mixing the two volatile chemicals.

Luckily, Jo had flung the grenade far enough to avoid the brunt of the blast. The air turned gray, but no one was hurt. She checked her space suit for tears. Even one small breach in the material could lead to fatal exposure.

An alarm squealed. Strobing red lights reflected off thick swirls of smoke. Jo heard shouting and footsteps pounding down the corridor. Within seconds, the pristine laboratory had transformed into a war zone.

* * *

Olen heard a low-pitched boom echo through the chamber.

Jo's bomb.

The explosion had sounded big. A little too big. The taut cable running down the center of the incident chamber vibrated violently, threatening to snap. The two-ton elevator car, hanging just a few feet above Olen's head, groaned as metal scraped against metal.

Olen squeezed his hands tighter around the cable, pushing into raw blisters, but the thick wire shook too much to maintain a solid grip. His hands slipped. He lost his balance and felt his body falling backward, into the black abyss.

C H A P T E R

57

Washington, DC, USA

GABRIEL SNYDER ENTERED his pitch-black apartment. He couldn't remember the last time he'd been home in the daytime, and that was probably for the best. In the dark, he couldn't see the water stains on the ceiling or the chipped Formica counter tops. There was nothing he could do about the odor, though. The whole place smelled like cigarette smoke and sweat.

Coming home to this repulsive unit only reminded Snyder of the spacious two-story colonial on the tree-lined street in Alexandria now enjoyed by his ex-wife and her spiffy new husband. Snyder imagined his old walk-in closet now stuffed with the man's fitted polo shirts and freshly creased size-thirty-two chinos.

Snyder ambled down the hallway to his bedroom, unbuttoning his shirt. His soft belly sagged over his waistband. Against his better judgment, he flipped on the light.

"Hello, Gabriel," said a woman's voice. She stood in the corner, her hands concealed inside a camel overcoat.

Snyder jumped. He reached into his closet for the 9mm he kept hidden in a shoe box.

"That won't be necessary." The woman revealed her empty palms. "I'm only here to talk."

The retired FBI agent felt his heart pounding. His lungs tightened briefly, but luckily the sensation dissipated.

"You know who I am," Director Allyson Cameron said. It wasn't a question.

Snyder just nodded.

"Don't be embarrassed. Your surveillance technique was exemplary, for the most part. You could teach my guys a thing or two." She lit a cigarette.

"You can't smoke in here."

"Are you going to turn me in?" Cameron took a long drag. "Listen, Gabriel. We've both been in this business long enough to know our friends can be just as dangerous as our enemies. In the end, we're all driven by self-preservation."

"Director Cameron, I don't know what you're talking about," Snyder said.

"Cut the bullshit," Cameron barked. "It's Nathan Sullivan. He ordered you to follow me." She approached Snyder slowly. "He's bad news, Gabriel."

"Worse than you?"

Cameron frowned.

"What do you want?" Snyder asked.

"Information," the director said.

"That, I don't have. My job is to follow orders, not to go on some self-righteous quest for truth," Snyder said.

"Who said anything about the truth? I'd rather know what *lies* Sullivan has told you to make you suspect me, a career intelligence officer, of treason." Director Cameron was now inches from Snyder's face. "So, Gabriel. Friend or enemy?"

58

Shanghai, People's Republic of China

OLEN TWISTED AND kicked, trying to regain control of his swinging body. The ascender remained locked in place, so he'd fallen only a few feet after losing his grip on the elevator cable. He hung upside down, still tethered by the harness, swaying side to side like an animal ensnared in a hunter's trap.

His elbow grazed the scalding interior casing of the chamber, singeing his wetsuit and searing the skin underneath. He slapped the charred material to keep the suit from igniting. The burn hurt like hell, but the pain wasn't the worst part. He'd now have to enter a level four laboratory with no protective suit and an open wound.

The chamber stopped vibrating, and Olen paused to catch his breath. Blood rushed to his head. His heartbeat pounded in his eardrums.

The glowing light sticks at the bottom of the shaft began to fade. Olen couldn't see beyond a few feet. He slipped a fresh stick from his tactical vest. With a sharp snap, the chamber illuminated in electric lime. He watched the stick fall to the bottom of the shaft. It bounced off something hard.

The scuba tank.

Olen cursed under his breath. He'd forgotten about the tank. The container of highly combustible, compressed oxygen sat inside an oven that was heating up. If it exploded, the force would thrust straight up the narrow chamber—a scorching fireball rushing directly into his ass.

The temperature gauge on Olen's Suunto now read 117 degrees. Heat alone wouldn't detonate the oxygen, but a single spark from the incinerators could be catastrophic. Olen probably had less time to get out of the chamber than he'd originally thought. Maybe two minutes max.

Squeezing his abdominal muscles, he pulled himself up and grabbed the cable. With an outstretched arm, he could touch the underside of the elevator car. It was warm, but not blisteringly hot like the chamber's walls. A thin seam traced the perimeter of a rectangular panel. Olen pushed firmly, and the panel lifted with a squeal. He pulled himself through the cutout and into the tiny car. He had to crouch on his hands and knees to fit inside the confined space, but he was relieved to have made it to the top of the shaft. His back burned from the strenuous climb.

As expected, the elevator door was sealed. Jo had explained that it could be opened only from inside the lab. Olen settled into a low squat, peering through the opening in the bottom of the car, down into the deep chamber. Heading back the way he'd come wasn't an option. He had no choice but to wait. His life was in Jo's hands. She was committed and capable. Olen trusted her. Then again, he'd only known the woman since Friday.

*   *   *

A tinny voice instructed all personnel to evacuate the building. Jo knew the security detail would be slow to respond. The guards would require biohazard suits to enter level four, and many of them wouldn't know how to put them on. They'd take their time figuring out the zippers and the breathing apparatuses. No one would want to take chances with what lived behind the air lock. The delay would buy Jo some time to open the incident chamber and let Kipton crawl out. She had less than two minutes before the incinerators fired again. Everything had to go perfectly as planned, or Kip would be roasted alive.

Jo reached the incident chamber. The Alpha Five emergency would allow her to open the elevator door, but she still needed a code to unlock it. She began to punch it into the keypad with her thickly gloved hand.

"What are you doing?" a voice shouted over the wailing alarm.

Jo whirled around to see the young microbiologist waving wildly. Through his fogged-up bubble helmet, his faced looked panicked.

"Dr. Zhou, we've got to evacuate. There's been a terrorist attack!" the man yelled, his voice muffled by the airtight space suit.

"Not yet," Jo responded. "I need to secure the Four Pests."

The term "Four Pests" was a euphemism for the nastiest of level four's microbial inhabitants—Marburg, Ebola, Lassa, and Crimean-Congo fever—and an homage to Mao Zedong's bizarre effort to rid China of all rats, flies, mosquitoes, and sparrows. The chairman had thought he could control nature. One hour in a level four laboratory would've changed his mind.

"You know the procedure. We must destroy the samples," Jo said.

"I'll help."

"No. It will only take a minute. You should go."

The doctor hesitated, as if struggling with the ethics of leaving a colleague behind in a burning laboratory.

The clock was ticking. Jo grew impatient. "Godammit! I said go. That's an order."

Without another word, the young man raced down the corridor. He didn't look back.

Jo began to sweat. How many seconds had that boy-doctor wasted?

She punched in the remaining digits of her code, her hand trembling. A light above the keypad flashed red. Nothing happened. The elevator doors remained sealed shut. Someone had locked her out. Someone in the Black Egg had known she was coming.

*　*　*

Through the steel elevator doors, Olen could hear faint electronic beeps. Someone was trying to open the incident chamber.

Jo. She made it.

Ten seconds. Twenty seconds. Nothing. The door didn't budge.

The shaft radiated. The incinerator was charging up. Beads of sweat rolled down the bridge of Olen's nose, evaporating almost as soon as they dripped off the tip. His skin felt like it was peeling away. The first sparks from the incinerator would ignite the compressed oxygen inside the scuba tank. He'd never survive.

Olen pounded on the elevator door. The time for stealth had passed. His pulse raced, and it became impossible to breathe. He gulped the hot air, but it seared his dry throat. His shouts were hoarse. They echoed in the hollow shaft like ashen voices bellowing from the depths of hell.

He knew it was over.

*   *   *

Jo wanted to smash her fist into the keypad. She jabbed at the numbers, trying her code again and again. Each time, a red light flashed and buzzed. *No entry.*

A series of dull thuds came from inside the chamber. Kip had made it to the top. Jo only had a few seconds to open the doors before white-hot flames engulfed him. She shouldn't have let him come to the Black Egg. She could've retrieved the evidence alone. Why hadn't he listened? If Kipton didn't trust her, the CIA wouldn't either. So he had to climb into an oven to save the world. And now, if she couldn't open the doors, she'd be responsible for his death.

Closing her eyes, Jo tried to focus. Her code had been deactivated. Fine. What else could she try?

A string of numbers flashed in her mind, beaming neon orange. *Of course!* She entered them quickly, making sure not to mistype. She had one shot to get it right.

The light above the keypad flashed green. The elevator doors slid open. A man in a black wetsuit stared back at her with two bloodshot eyes. His cracked lips formed a weak smile. Jo felt a powerful flush of relief. "Kipton! I was worried that you—"

An invisible force hurled Kipton toward her, and Jo tumbled backward. The back of her helmet smacked the ceramic floor.

Kipton collapsed on top of her. A fireball rushed out of the elevator doors. The lab's negative pressure sucked in the flames like a vacuum, igniting the ceiling and walls.

Jo shouted through her bubble helmet. "We must get to decontamination. *Now!*"

She rolled Kipton off her body and helped him to his feet. He was weak, but he needed to move fast if they hoped to escape the roaring fire. The pair sprinted through the lab as smoldering ash rained down around them.

* * *

The water in the decontamination shower stabbed Olen's flesh like poisoned needles. It felt scalding, but he knew it was lukewarm at most. He needed to cool his body down. Jo had helped him strip off the wetsuit and pulled him under the stream. The procedure would clean his skin, but it would do nothing to neutralize the pathogens that Olen might have inhaled inside level four. He had been exposed for less than a minute, but if even a single virus particle had entered his nostrils, it would eventually lodge itself in his lungs. It would burrow into the soft, pink tissue and replicate millions of deadly copies. Once the disease entered his bloodstream, he was as good as dead. What were the odds he'd been infected in such a blink of time? Olen shuddered at the thought.

"Put these on. We've got to keep moving," Jo ordered. She pushed a vintage Rolling Stones T-shirt and rust-colored corduroys into Olen's dripping chest. The doctor had already changed into a pair of Listerine-green scrubs and a white lab coat. The muscles in her neck looked tense.

"Where did you get this?" Olen asked, pulling the shirt over his torso. His shoulders stretched the fabric.

"I grabbed it from one of the lockers. You'll just have to make it fit."

"We're in the men's locker room?"

"Yes, but this floor has already evacuated. We're alone. That said, security teams will arrive any minute."

"We have to go back in . . . to find BRV45," Olen argued.

"You won't find it in there. Level three is two floors up."

"Wait a minute. The virus that's already wiped out thousands of people isn't designated biosafety level four?"

"That's correct," Jo said. "BRV45 is bad, but it's no match for what's in there." Jo pointed to the air lock from which they'd just come.

Olen felt a tickle in his throat. Probably just ash from the fire.

Jo touched his arm. "If you start showing symptoms, any at all, you'll never leave this building. You must accept that, Kip."

Olen nodded. He'd considered the risks. "Hey, I'm just glad you got that elevator door open. Took you long enough."

"My code had been deactivated."

"Someone was expecting us."

"Looks that way," Jo agreed.

"Then we've got to find the evidence we need and get the hell out of here." Olen hopped on one foot, pulling on the corduroys. He slipped his switchblade into the back pocket. "If your code didn't work, how did you open the doors?"

"Ru . . ." Jo started. "If my ex-husband worked on Blood River virus here, at the Black Egg, he also would've had access to all safety protocols, including his own code to the incident chambers. I made a lucky guess." The words seemed to get caught in Jo's throat. "Ru's code was a date. Our wedding anniversary."

59

Shanghai, People's Republic of China

"OKAY, THERE SHE is." The fresh-faced security technician tapped the monitor.

"What am I looking at?" Marc asked, leaning in.

"Dr. Zhou. She just used her badge to call an elevator on the second floor."

"The elevators are running? Why didn't the fire alarm deactivate them?"

"She's a department head. Her badge can override the elevator's automatic safety protocols."

"Well, deactivate her badge!" Marc barked. "Like you did with her code to the incident chambers."

"I can't do that, sir. Security badges run on a separate system. Her clearance outranks mine. You have to enter a command code to supersede Dr. Zhou's authority." Fresh Face's eyes wandered to the chief of security's limp body, crumpled in a mountain of cellulite on the floor. The silent implication was clear. Only the chief could override Dr. Zhou's badge and halt the elevator. Marc wouldn't revive the man for that. He'd find another way.

"At least tell me if she's going up or down," Marc ordered.

"Up. The elevator is stopping on the fourth floor. I can pull up the cameras."

"No, you won't be able to do that."

Fresh Face tapped a few keys. "You're right," he said, stunned. "It looks like all the cameras on the fourth floor have been switched off. That's a complete breach of protocol. Someone really high up the chain would've had to give that order. Why would they do that? And how did you know—"

"It doesn't matter," Marc blurted. He knew why the cameras had been deactivated. He'd given the order six months ago, under the authority of General Huang's office. He didn't want anyone snooping around on the fourth floor. If Dr. Zhou and Grave were headed there now, Marc was already too late.

Another message flashed on the screen.

"She just entered the fourth-floor viewing room," Fresh Face reported.

"What's a viewing room?"

"It's where we keep the electron microscopes and data servers."

Marc was puzzled. "She didn't enter the level three air lock?"

"No, sir." The technician plinked a few keys. "Definitely not. The air lock is still sealed."

Electron microscopes? It made no sense. Marc turned and shouted to the room. "Someone get me a map of the fourth floor."

"Sir, you won't be able to access the viewing room. That's classified as a top-secret data storage facility. It requires a retinal scan," Fresh Face explained.

Marc Chen looked at the mole-speckled walrus on the floor.

* * *

"What are we looking for?" Olen asked. "We need proof BRV45 was a PLA bioweapon, but we can't exactly walk out of here with a test tube of the stuff."

"We don't need to find the actual virus," Jo said. "BRV45 was manmade, but it's not completely artificial. The DNA of other viruses—natural viruses—was split apart, resequenced, and recombined to create BRV45. Designing a pathogen is extremely complicated. Most synthetic viruses degrade after the first few transmissions. The pieces of DNA become unglued, and they reduce to a harmless jumble of proteins. Creating a virus deadly enough to spark a pandemic would have taken months, if not years, to establish a stable genetic structure. If Ru engineered BRV45 in this building, there would be a mountain of data documenting his experiments."

"So, we won't need to extract live virus?" Olen asked, relieved.

"Nope." Jo held up a hot-pink memory drive the size of a quarter. "Just data."

* * *

Marc Chen's pistol bounced against his hip as he ran. The fourth-floor viewing room was at the end of the hall. The door would be locked, but Chen had stolen the security chief's badge. As for the retinal scan . . .

Marc gently squeezed a slippery orb in his fist. It oozed between his fingers. He'd make a point to smash the thing under his heel afterward.

* * *

Jo located Ru's research file on the main server. Olen watched the progress bar inch across the screen as BRV45's secrets spilled into her memory drive. Eleven percent to go.

The viewing room door buzzed, and the latch clicked.

"Time's up, Doc," Olen said.

"Almost there." Six percent to go.

The door flew open. A man in a military uniform burst through, arm outstretched, brandishing a pistol. He said nothing and moved swiftly across the room.

The man shot Jo first, and she collapsed instantly. He then aimed at Olen, and the men locked eyes. Fiery anger flared inside Olen's chest at the sight of Marc Chen, his missing colleague. He pivoted on his back foot, preparing to charge, but Marc dropped him with a direct shot to Olen's neck.

* * *

The fresh-faced security guard rushed into the viewing room, panting, his baby-soft skin flushed from exertion. He saw the bodies on the floor. "You *killed* them." The guard doubled over at the waist, hands pressed into his gangly thighs.

"Compose yourself, comrade," Marc ordered. "They're not dead." He wedged the tip of his boot under Olen's rib cage and flipped over the man's flaccid body. Olen's abdomen expanded with each weak breath. A trickle of blood seeped from his neck, where the dart had struck flesh.

"Should I have them transferred to confinement?" Fresh Face asked.

"The doctor, yes."

"What about the man?"

"General Huang wants to meet with him. He lands in an hour. Deliver him to Jiangwan Airfield, but keep him sedated," Marc warned. "*Heavily* sedated."

"Who is he?" Fresh Faced asked.

"Is it not obvious, comrade?" Marc turned to leave. "He's a journalist."

60

New York, New York, USA

T HE ELEVATOR NUMBERS lit up one by one, ticking off as the car inched higher. For President James Barlow, the doors couldn't open fast enough. He'd spent the evening grinning and backslapping with puffed-up campaign donors, and it made his stomach churn more than a North Korean disarmament negotiation. Unfortunately, begging America's corporate class for money was all part of the Washington game.

The elevator stopped, and a Secret Service agent with thick eyebrows escorted Barlow to his suite—a palatial residence encompassing the entire penthouse floor of New York's Waldorf Astoria. The president had no intention of staying overnight, but the lavish space easily converted to a command post during his short trip. Stepping inside, he heard a familiar voice coming from the living room.

"Is that Jim Barlow or George Clooney?" The jab might have been viewed as disrespectful coming from anyone else, but Secretary Darlene Hart's soft drawl somehow made the remark acceptable, even charming. If only Barlow felt as smooth as Clooney in the tuxedo strangling his body. He promptly ripped the silk bow tie from his starched collar and shrugged off his jacket, eliciting a disapproving groan from the secretary.

"East Asia's on the brink of collapse, and I'm sucking stuffed olives off tiny toothpicks," Barlow said.

"The midterms are in two weeks, Jim. You'd consider sucking more than olives if it'd help us pick up four congressional seats in the battlegrounds."

The president cracked a smile. "Did you just suggest the president of the United States perform fellatio to pad the DNC's coffers?"

Hart raised both palms in mock defense. "I'm just saying we're working with a thin margin in Virginia's sixth. Pucker up, pretty boy."

Barlow grabbed a bottle of Evian, wishing it were a bottle of Scotch. "Where are Nate and Bruce?"

"In the bedroom. It's not what you think. They're on the horn with—"

Before the secretary could finish, the suite's bedroom door flew open and the two men lunged into the living room.

"Jesus Christ, Nate!" Bruce exclaimed, his face flushed. "Tang has been stirring up the separatists on the mainland for months now, poking China in the eyeball. If Beijing wants to smack him down, it's not our problem. We're really going to get drawn into a war over a little island?" The director of national intelligence rolled up his sleeves to cool off.

"We're talking about military invasion by a hostile foreign power," Sullivan countered. "If we let China take Taiwan, it won't stop there. They will pursue a path of aggressive territorial expansion, especially if unchecked by the United States. President Li was rational—he wouldn't have taken such a risk—but he's gone now. No one could have predicted the goddamn PLA would take over Zhongnanhai."

"But that's exactly what Langley has been telling us for years! We knew about the fracturing of the Politburo Standing Committee, the rival factions within the Party. The China desk has had a file on Huang since . . . since . . ." Bruce gestured at Barlow. "Since Jim was chasing CIA tail at the Farm."

"General Huang is preparing to use nuclear weapons, Bruce. Activity around the Ngari launch site is heating up. Huang will obliterate every living soul in Taipei. To let it happen would be criminal."

Bruce shook his head and turned to the secretary of state. "You believe this horseshit, Darlene?"

"Here's what I know," Hart started. "East Asia's at a tipping point. An egomaniacal madman now runs Beijing, and an irrational nutjob runs Taipei. These men are on a collision course, and it's not a fair fight. Nukes, missiles, land invasion, drones—any way you crack it, Taiwan loses. Big-time. America has always been the stabilizing force in Asia. Now is no different. We're needed more than ever to diffuse the situation."

"A preemptive strike on a Chinese air base isn't very diffusive," President Barlow challenged.

"How long do we wait, Jim?" Sullivan asked. "Until red flags are flying over Tokyo and Seoul too?"

Barlow pressed both fists into his forehead. It felt like someone was squeezing his gray matter like a sponge. He flumped into a chair.

"Get him a pill. Nate, where is the president's medication?" Hart asked.

"My jacket pocket," Barlow said, his voice strained.

Hart fumbled with the president's tuxedo jacket, which he'd flung over the back of a chair. "I'm not finding anything in here."

"I know I have a few left. Look again."

Hart pulled an empty Ziploc baggie from the breast pocket. "It's empty, Jim. Maybe there are more in—"

"Forget it," Barlow snapped. "It's fading. It's nothing. Probably too much champagne."

The room fell silent, wide eyes fixated on Barlow.

"I said it's *nothing*, godammit!" the president shouted. He sat up and fought through the pain, like he always did. Now wasn't the time to show weakness. "Nate, where does Russia stand?"

"Firmly with Beijing," Sullivan answered.

"Words I never wanted to live to hear," Barlow mused. "NATO allies?"

"It's wait-and-see. No surprise there," Hart said.

"There's no going back from this," the president warned. "If we do this—if we challenge Huang with a preemptive strike—we've got to be one hundred percent committed."

Barlow steadied his gaze on Hart. His old friend's eyes were hopeful, prescient. "You'll make the right call, Jim," she said. "You always do."

The president rubbed the heels of his palms against the sides of his head, making circles above his ears. Then he simply nodded, and it was done.

CHAPTER

61

Shanghai, People's Republic of China

JO OPENED HER eyes to see that the world had tilted on its side. Her cheek pressed into cold concrete. Saliva dripped from her parted lips. A dull heaviness pinned her to the floor, every joint, every muscle smashed under the weight.

The paralytic began to wear off. Although her body was a frozen cast, she wasn't completely numb. Everything ached. Jo attempted to blink. Her eyelids slid across her corneas in slow motion. Then, a breakthrough; she wiggled her right hand. No, someone else had moved it. Jo tried to call out, but her brittle vocal cords managed only a whimper.

"You're awake. That means you're almost out of it," a voice said. It was a man's voice. A voice she knew well. "It takes a few hours to metabolize the vecuronium bromide, depending on how much the bastards used."

Jo's vision cleared a bit, and she slowly regained control of her eyes, but not her head. Still, it was enough to determine where she was.

The Slammer.

Officially, it was named the Patient Isolation Suite, but that made it sound like a comfortable place—some kind of spa with feather beds and Netflix. In reality, it was an airtight detention cell. Anyone who might have come into contact with a hot agent checked into quarantine until they either manifested symptoms—and most likely died—or waited out the incubation period physically unharmed. Psychological harm was another matter. Two weeks sealed inside a five-by-five-foot Plexiglas cube with nothing but a cot and a toilet would drive anyone mad. No one reemerged from the Slammer quite the same.

Reflected in the glass wall, Jo saw a figure hunched over her lifeless form. Gaunt and unshaven, he looked like a prisoner of war—nothing like how she remembered.

"My God, Weilin. I never thought it would come to this. You must believe me."

The man's words quivered. Over the two years of their marriage, Jo couldn't recall if she'd ever seen Ru cry.

62

Shanghai, People's Republic of China

OLEN AWOKE WITH a jolt and coughed violently. He rolled onto his stomach to let a trail of mucus drain from his throat. He attempted to wipe his lips, but his half-frozen muscles refused. It wouldn't have mattered; his wrists were bound behind his back.

Disoriented and freezing, Olen scanned the dark space. There was just enough light for him to see clouds of fog puffing from his mouth—his breath crystallizing on contact with the frigid air. His mouth felt dry and sweet, like he'd taken a bite of cotton candy. They'd probably injected him with some sort of psychoactive sedative, and it was screwing with his senses. (At least that would explain the naked mountain troll he saw salivating in the shadows.) At that moment, Olen was sure of just one thing: he was moving.

The steel floor shook. His ears filled with a familiar pressure. The droning hum of jet engines was unmistakable. Either he was still shuddering from a drug-induced, hallucinogenic mind fuck, or he was in the cargo hold of an aircraft.

Olen struggled to remember what had happened before he lost consciousness.

Marc. That son of a bitch was alive.

The memory materialized like a thunderhead. The anger returned too. Shot by Marc Chen? His old roomie. Chen wasn't a friend by any stretch, but Olen had never expected the man to be on the other side of a bullet. Though it hadn't been a bullet. A bullet would have killed him, and Olen was too effing freezing to be in hell.

A thin, bright line of amber light drew Olen's eyes up. Its two-foot length disappeared and reappeared as the plane bounced. The light emanated from the main cabin. A section of the ceiling had come loose. An access panel.

Blood rushed to Olen's extremities, and the feeling in his arms and legs returned. He rolled over and stretched his neck toward the light—the way out.

63

Shanghai, People's Republic of China

RU TRIED TO help Jo sit up, but his emaciated frame lacked the strength. The man had withered into a graying waif. His expression looked completely despondent, tortured. That was the worst part, Jo thought.

"Ru." Jo's numb tongue began to form words that dribbled from her mouth, one by one. "You . . . look . . . like . . . shit."

"Why they've kept me alive, I have no idea," he replied. "Maybe they worried it wouldn't work."

"The bioweapon, you mean?"

Jo's ex-husband rested on one knee. His head hung behind a curtain of salt-and-pepper bangs. His breath smelled like liquor. Jo spotted two bottles of *baijiu* in the corner of the cell.

"Only the great Dr. Sun Ru could invent such an impossibly perfect virus," Jo said, speaking slowly through tingling lips. "A bioweapon that shows no compassion, mutates at will. Few creatures on this earth can morph into something else entirely when it suits their narcissistic ambition. Yet the ones who can seem to be drawn to one another."

"Viruses have no ego, Weilin. Only men. I suppose you know that better than I'd like to admit." Ru leaned against the Plexiglas wall for balance. His breathing became shallow and labored.

"Why did you do it?" Jo's eyes welled, but her face was a mask, still immobilized by the vecuronium bromide. The disgust in her voice said enough.

"I developed the virus here, at the Black Egg, with a small grant from the Ministry of Health's Oncology Research Center."

"Oncology?"

"Blood River virus, as you call it, was originally designed to kill cancer cells, not people," Ru explained. "I programmed the virus to ignore healthy cells and target tumors. It was decontamination on a microscopic level. The virus infected a damaged cell and recoded its DNA. It inhibited the cancer cell's ability to divide. In the past, a specific virus had to be developed for each type of cancer. That level of customization was nearly impossible to sustain.

"So, I gave my virus mutative properties that allowed it to adapt to a whole range of cancers. Pancreatic, breast, lung, liver cancer—my little bug adapted intelligently to each patient's unique circumstance."

"Ru, that's incredible!"

"You're not the only one who had that reaction," he said grimly. "The Ministry of Health took notice of my work. The money poured in. My research had the potential to rid the earth of mankind's deadliest and least understood disease. Finally, a cure for cancer. I remember celebrating with a bottle of Henri Jayer Vosne-Romanee. Remember, like the one your aunt gave us?"

"I had no idea what you were working on."

"No one did. Not at first, but eventually word spread. The next knock on my door wasn't the Ministry of Health. It was the People's Liberation Army."

"I'm guessing they weren't interested in the public health benefits."

Ru looked away and nodded silently. "Evidently, the technology was too valuable to be used for something as trivial as saving lives. The PLA had other plans."

"The army made you alter the virus," Jo said, mortified.

"They didn't coerce me, if that's what you mean. A couple uniforms visited my lab once a month. They weren't the uptight soldiers you'd expect. They were different guys every time, but the night always went the same way. We'd head to a bar, meet a few women. At some point, we'd all sit down for a lavish dinner and someone would pass me an envelope underneath the table. Occasionally it was one of the women."

"You took the army's money and kept working. I would have too. No one can predict where scientific research will lead," Jo said.

"And that's all it was. Research. I soon determined the virus could target nearly any type of cell, not just cancer cells. That's what made it so novel. I could program it to target skin cells, muscle cells, even brain cells. When I discovered how to target blood cells, the PLA pulled the plug. The next visit was from a junior officer named Lieutenant Wang. *He* didn't take me to dinner."

"When was that?" Jo asked.

"About six months ago. I'm not entirely sure. I've lost track." Ru sighed, looking around the barren cell. "So, what have I missed?"

64

Shanghai, People's Republic of China

IT TOOK OLEN a bit of time to cut through the plastic zip ties that bound his wrists, even once he got a grip on the switchblade hidden in his back pocket. He was surprised to find it still there. Wouldn't the guards have searched him for weapons? Why hadn't they confiscated the knife?

Olen searched through a stack of aluminum storage boxes for anything useful. One container buried at the bottom looked promising. He couldn't read the Chinese writing on its lid, but the cartoon image of a man suspended from a dome-shaped canopy offered a clue to the box's contents. Parachutes. And not just parachutes either. The box contained flares and portable oxygen too. A midflight escapee's survival kit. Hot damn.

Olen lifted the access panel in the ceiling and peered into the cabin. He recognized the plane. Plush carpeting, ornate mahogany chair legs. It was a VIP jet—the same one that had transported him to the TAR. The plane where he'd first met Jo.

A dull ache pounded behind Olen's eye sockets. Flashes of those last moments in the Black Egg exploded across his synapses like firecrackers—the impassive look in Marc's eyes, the way he'd stepped through the door with his arm outstretched. Olen's brain struggled to reboot, to process the last images his eyes had collected.

Marc had looked different. Bigger. Sharper, somehow. Scaly, like a dragon. Wings and snout. *Wrong*. The drugs had mixed up his memories. Olen shook his head, swishing the watery images around like tie-dye. It didn't make sense. Marc was green. Olive. *Olive green*. He was wearing a PLA uniform. A disguise? No, they'd gotten to him. Turned him. Could it be possible?

Marc was an arrogant dick, but the man was no traitor. He must have infiltrated the Black Egg for the same reason Olen had: to find the source of Blood River virus. Marc had posed as a Chinese military officer and talked his way past security—a smarter strategy than scaling a hundred-foot incinerator shaft but no less dangerous. If Marc had been caught, they'd have dragged him by his nose hairs to a PLA black site for "questioning." Marc must've seen Olen and freaked. Two clandestine operatives working independently, without knowledge of one another, could get messy, even if they shared the same objective. So, Marc had shot him to save himself. What a champ. Now Olen would get to visit that black site instead. He'd remember to send Marc a postcard.

Or . . . Olen could just jump out of this effing plane.

The cartoon parachute man beckoned to him, then flipped up two chubby middle fingers. *Cock tease.* Olen knew his gizzards would blow out of his nostrils if he tried to bail at thirty-three thousand feet. He needed to get the plane to drop to a lower altitude. Maybe he could sweet-talk the pilots into helping him out. First, he'd need to slip past that drooling mountain troll, who'd fallen asleep (and fortunately turned out to be just a PLA guard with wicked jet lag).

Through the access panel, now slightly ajar, Olen spotted a barrel-chested man with stars on his shoulders and flecks of white dusting his sideburns. He was sitting behind the desk near the rear bulkhead, peering down a bird-beak nose, reading a book. A pair of barbed horns sprouted from the man's forehead. Then the demon looked up, and the plane trembled.

65

Shanghai, People's Republic of China

"HOW BAD IS it? Will Taipei recover?" Ru asked.

"Taipei?" Jo pulled herself up on an elbow. "Taipei is unaffected, as far as I know."

"But the invasion—"

"Hasn't even begun yet," Jo interjected. "The PLA used your virus to overthrow the Politburo, here, on the mainland. General Huang has his finger on the trigger, no doubt, but so far he hasn't touched Taiwan. The Americans probably have something to do with that."

"B-but the virus," Ru sputtered. "You said it had been weaponized."

At that moment, Jo realized that her ex-husband had no idea of the extent of his crime. The architect of this weapon of mass destruction was completely unaware of the devastation he'd caused.

Jo watched Ru's face melt in horror as she explained what had happened in Dzongsar Village. The smoldering pit of dead monks. The riots in Beijing and Shanghai and Guangzhou. The bombing of the Great Hall of the People. The coup and the curfew. The imposition of martial law and the imminent PLA invasion of

Taiwan. She spared no detail, no matter how disgustingly grue-some, and she paused only when there was nothing left to say.

Ru collapsed into a pile of bones. He buried his face and mut-tered through deep sobs, "Oh God! *Oh God!*"

Jo slid closer, dragging herself as the paralytic faded. She resisted the human urge to place a hand on Ru's back, to comfort the tortured scientist. He didn't deserve comfort. "Why did you think the army had attacked Taipei?" she asked. "You sounded so sure."

"Aiguo," Ru mumbled into the floor. He squeezed his eyes shut, trying to disappear into his own body.

"I know your brother is involved. He helped deploy the weapon."

"No," Ru said. "He warned me not to trust the military. He begged me to refuse their money. Aiguo knew something like this would happen, but I didn't want to hear it. I just wanted to keep going."

"Your brother was in Dzongsar Village," Jo said coolly. She watched her ex-husband's face carefully. "He went there to destroy the evidence of what you did. I spoke with him. I have proof."

"What proof do you have, Weilin? A man in a distant hot zone inexplicably impersonates his own brother. And for what reason? He was probably just investigating the outbreak, same as you."

Jo perked up. The hairs on the back of her neck bristled. "How did you know Aiguo had impersonated you?" she asked flatly. She hadn't mentioned that detail. Ru wasn't telling her everything.

Ru glared like a cornered animal. His sobbing ceased.

"It was you," Jo hissed, her mouth curling in disgust. "*You* weaponized Blood River virus!" She wanted to hit him, strangle his thin neck, but her body still refused to respond.

"Everything I've told you is true. I invented the virus to fight cancer," Ru insisted.

"Maybe that's how it started, but you couldn't stop, not when you'd discovered its true power." Jo's face flushed with fury. "You contacted the army yourself, didn't you? You knew about Dzongsar. Hell, you probably pitched them the idea."

"It was supposed to be a controlled experiment. The village was remote and the terrain made it nearly inaccessible, not to mention the heavy restrictions isolating the entire region. Dzong-sar was the perfect testing ground. Quarantine should've been a breeze. Lieutenant Wang assured me the PLA would take what-ever measures necessary to lock down the village, keep the disease contained."

Jo spat in Ru's face. The man just looked away, not bothering to wipe the saliva from his cheek.

"You murdered all of those people," she said. "That's why Aiguo went to Dzongsar. To *stop* what you'd done. But he was too late."

"Don't be so naïve, Weilin." Ru's voice sharpened. "They used me, the same way they used you. The PLA never intended to quar-antine the village, and it never intended for you to conduct a legit-imate epidemiological investigation. Don't you see? That lieutenant *wanted* the virus to get out. By the time my brother and I figured it out, that we'd been deceived, it was probably too late, but we had to try anyway. The army got to me first, and I ended up in this plastic box, but Aiguo got away. I'm glad he made it to Tibet, but obviously he couldn't stop it."

"Aiguo's dead," Jo blurted. She wanted the words to hurt, to stab at her ex-husband like poison-tipped daggers. Ru adored his brother. She remembered the two men at her wedding, the bear hugs and back slaps.

Ru sat, statue-still, eyes wide. Maybe he already knew. Maybe he'd already come to terms with his role in Aiguo's agonizing death. But then her ex-husband began jerking, thrashing, as if try-ing to physically expel the information the way a body rejected a transplanted organ. He crawled toward the corner of the cell, toward the bottles of *baijiu*. One was empty. Ru grabbed its long neck and slammed it into the cement floor, sending shards of green glass exploding in all directions. Jo shielded her face in the crook of her elbow. When she looked up, Ru was pouring the remains of the other bottle over his head. His eyes reddened with irritation from contact with the potent spirit. Suddenly, he had a lighter in his hand. Where had he even gotten one? *From Huang's men*, she reasoned. *They have no more use for him. They want him to . . .*

"Ru, don't!" Jo shouted. The man probably deserved to be executed for what he'd done, but at that moment a remnant of the love she'd once felt wormed to the surface. "Please, Ru. *Think*. What are you going to do?"

"You must see," he said. "They've been waiting for me to do it. They've *all* been waiting."

"Then don't give them the satisfaction," Jo whispered hoarsely.

Ru kneeled in a puddle, his hair and clothes sopping with alcohol. He held the lighter in one hand high above his head. A small orange flame danced in his white-knuckled fist. Jo had never seen that expression on Ru's face: pure anguish, guilt, regret.

"This isn't for them," he said.

With a flick, Ru's palm opened, releasing his grip on the lighter. Then came the heat, gnashing and snapping its jaws, mauling the man's body like a beast, savage and bloodthirsty. Seconds later, water poured down from fire sprinklers overhead, but it was too late. The fire had consumed Ru's frail form.

Wiping her eyes, Jo watched the door to the Slammer slide open—an automatic safety precaution. She raced out of the cell, down the stairs, through the deserted lobby, into the street. Bent over on the sidewalk, Jo fought for breath, her throat still choking on the smell of Ru's burning flesh.

CHAPTER

66

Shanghai, People's Republic of China

TWO BLACK MARBLES fixed inside the horned beast's eye sockets zeroed in on Olen and then alerted a military sentry with inky flares. A pair of tree-trunk arms wrenched Olen from his burrow.

"Thank God you fellas pulled me outa there," Olen said, his words slurring from the effects of the drugs. "It was so cold my balls were beginning to tunnel into my abdomen."

Within moments, olive-clad guards had splayed him facedown on the cabin floor. A thick rubber sole crushed his cheekbone. The staccato of angry Mandarin pelted his body like a hailstorm. The demon-man behind the desk raised a palm to silence the icy deluge.

"You're the American, yes?" The man spoke English with a Cambridge accent that lacked the slightest hint of trepidation. The shoulder stars, the European education, the plane—it had to be him. General Huang Yipeng, in the flesh.

With the boot grinding into Olen's jaw, he couldn't have responded if he'd tried. The best he could manage was a red-faced snort.

"The benzodiazepine should've kept you sedated. You have impressive metabolism," the general went on. "It explains your exceptional stamina, I suppose. As demonstrated by your recent recreations in the InterContinental's Skyline Suite."

Olen ground his teeth. He should've swept the suite for bugs right away. He would've found the microphones. Had there been cameras too? Olen thought of Jo, smashing her lips into his, clawing at his shirt, yanking on his belt, the moment they'd entered the hotel room. They'd both succumbed to the heat of passion and skipped right over standard operating procedures. That meant the PLA had known Olen and Jo planned to infiltrate the Black Egg. They'd heard everything in the suite. *Seen* everything.

"You sick fuck!" Olen barked. "Did you get off, watching us? I swear to God, I'll—"

The rubber sole pressed into his cheek flesh, smothering Olen's words.

"What? *Murder* me? I shouldn't be surprised. Even the self-righteous CIA hasn't dispensed with old-fashioned political assassination." Huang waved a finger, signaling his soldier to release some pressure. "It's something I can relate to." Huang's timbre vibrated with intensity, his words like heavy velvet. At least five men stood over Olen's pinned body in menacing poses. "Of course, the strategy often backfires. People underestimate the potency of martyrdom. The influence of the living never quite outshines the imperium of the dead. Don't you think?"

The soldier sitting on Olen's spine pulled his arms back against their sockets. His shoulders screamed.

"I wonder, would you have made it look accidental? Or maybe mutinous?" Huang paused, breathing slowly, eyes locked on his captive. "What a tempest that would have unleashed. The gates of Hades unbolted." The general hissed like a serpent.

Jo was right, Olen thought. He read a hint of delight in Huang's expression—the satisfaction of a plan unfolding with irreversible momentum. Was anyone in Washington even aware of what Huang had done, that he had released BRV45 on his own people?

Olen stared into the hollow eyes of China's newest junta. Searing pain shot through his body, muddling his thoughts. Huang barked in Mandarin, and the two soldiers released their maddening grip. They hoisted Olen into a chair bolted to the floor. A black hood flew over his head. Olen heard the high-pitched zip of plastic ties binding his wrists to the armrests.

Enveloped in darkness, Olen could feel the general looming. He pictured Huang glowering from behind his enormous desk. *A mahogany desk.* With a slick polished top and deep spirals carved into the legs. And an American surveillance device implanted on its smooth surface—the one Olen had installed while on the flight to Lhasa with Jo.

The bug!

"You're not my first," Huang continued. The hood's thick fabric dampened the general's baritone. "Power attracts men of your trade like fruit flies to the goji berry. Emperor Qing faced down more than a dozen assassins. One even made it into his private chamber."

"What happened to him?" Olen asked, thinking of the bug and trying to keep the conversation moving. He wanted to agitate the general, get him to talk about the virus.

"He went on to unify the Middle Kingdom. Emperor Qing pulverized his enemies and snuffed out the centuries-old wars tearing us apart. We began our journey as a great power."

"I meant the assassin," Olen said. "What happened to *him*?"

"History remembers only his failure. That, and the shame he brought upon his country."

"And what will history say about you?"

Silence. Perhaps Huang had more composure than Olen thought. He heard a soft rustling—sheets of loose-leaf paper being pushed into alignment on the desktop, objects being reordered. Olen prayed the general hadn't covered the bug. Without direct light, its battery would shut off and it would stop transmitting to Maryland.

Then Huang spoke again. "These are difficult times, as I'm sure you are aware. How much money has your country spent over the past decade to fight ideology? How many lives were lost to such foolhardy policy? One cannot repress an idea with fire from the sky. It will only get stronger. Burn hotter. No, an *old* idea can only be supplanted by a *new* one, a better one. That's how to change the course of history."

"Ruling by fear? Is that how you win hearts and minds?"

"Not really. There will always be brave men who disagree with me and have nothing to lose."

"Then what makes them toe the Party line, if not fear?"

Huang leaned closer, his voice scraping like sandpaper on cement. "Suffering."

A chill.

"Let me explain something to you," Huang said. "Long before you were born, Chairman Mao told us we were powerful, capable people. And we believed every word. We were agrarian then—a nation of simple farmers—but Mao convinced us we could produce glorious amounts of steel. More than Russia! Can you believe that? Every man, woman, and child scoured their homes for anything metal. The activity was compulsory, to be sure, but I remember the look on my father's face. Pride. He wanted to do his part.

"Cooking pots, pans, knives, bicycles—everything was carried into the center of the village and burned, smelted into an impossibly impure, completely unusable raw material, packed up, and sent to the city. Never mind this left us no tools to plant or harvest our crops. Mao called it the Great Leap Forward. That's what everyone called it, in fact. Even after sixty million of our countrymen starved to death.

"We eventually fled our home, desperate to find food, traveling on the dirt roads spider-webbing the countryside. I always knew when we were approaching another village. The trees lining the road would suddenly be bare, not a single leaf remaining on their branches, even in summertime. They'd been eaten, you see. Plucked by spindly fingers and digested in the distended bellies of the most miserably loyal peasants you could imagine."

Olen was mortified. "What could all that possibly accomplish?"

"Mao had to break them," Huang rasped with delight. "Just like that worthless metal, he needed the people to burn and warp and struggle until their individuality—their very identity—dissolved and melted into a single, solid mass." Olen pictured the general squeezing his hands into a tight fist. "Then, that mass cooled. Unified. Unbreakable."

Huang spoke in metaphors, making his point but admitting nothing. Olen needed to force him into the open, get him to confess.

"Is that what you're doing with Blood River virus? You'll make the people suffer so you can control them? Like Mao did?" Olen asked bluntly. He could almost hear the smile breaking across the madman's face.

"The virus is a tragedy, but one China can overcome. The disease may weaken our bodies, but never our spirit."

Enough pussyfooting. "I know your military engineered BRV45 as a bioweapon," Olen pressed. "I know you used it against your own people. You used the outbreak to seize control of the government."

"Condemn me as an opportunist, then," Huang replied.

"Thousands will die when you invade Taiwan."

"Ah, Taiwan. How one little block of rock has hamstrung our progress for seventy years, I'll never understand."

"Isn't Taiwan the ultimate prize?" Olen asked.

"Prize? If you call war with the United States a prize. You must think I'm truly foolish."

"Then what is it you want?"

"It's simple. I want to restore China's greatness, to compel nations to prostrate themselves and pay tribute to her rightful eminence. I don't care about Taiwan. I want to rule the Middle Kingdom."

"You want to be emperor."

"It's a start."

"Then why use a biological weapon?" Olen asked. "Why the elaborate scheme to frame Taiwan for the outbreak if invasion isn't your end game?"

"American." Huang sounded eerily placid. "This virus has ravaged our cities, destabilized our countryside, threatened the vitality of our economy. And yet, even Mao once advised, 'Viruses are bad things, but they sometimes perform a useful function.' Hmm," he growled. "Useful indeed."

After a beat, the general gave another order in Mandarin. Olen could hear the soldiers moving around him. One of them yanked on the drawstring of Olen's hood. The cord cut into his neck. Seconds later, a hot pinch electrified his thigh. A needle's prick.

Olen thrashed his head side to side. Was that another sedative? Or the virus? "What did you do? *Godammit!* What was that?" Olen's body shook. Fire coursed through his veins.

General Huang ripped off the hood, his face almost touching Olen's, nose to nose, with a look of demonic intensity. His eyelashes, a hundred venomous snakes, writhed and bared their fangs. At any moment they'd strike, inject their poison, stop Olen's heart midbeat. Time was running out.

67

Washington, DC, USA

"CERBERUS IS ONLINE, Mr. President," General Goodyear reported, indicating the activation of four U.S. nuclear warheads. "We're go-for-launch on your command."

James Barlow looked to Sullivan, whose reassuring nod only raised more doubt in the president. Was Nate right about the ethics? Would bombing the PLA's Ngari launch site save millions of innocent lives? Or would it begin a chain reaction of death and destruction? Secretary Hart seemed to side with Nate. She'd always had impeccable instincts in situations like this. It probably should have been her sitting at the head of this table, giving the command. God knew a woman like Darlene would make a hell of a president, Barlow thought. Tough as Teflon.

Director Cameron, on the other hand, looked ragged, defeated. She'd opposed military intervention from the start. Yet it was *her* operations officer who had suggested the Chinese military might have been responsible for the Blood River virus outbreak. That meant General Huang had murdered countless people with a bioweapon. Barlow had never known Allyson Cameron to cower before a monster like Huang. What was her agenda?

His decision made, President Barlow stiffened his spine. "Execute," he ordered, sending the room into a flurry.

Moments later, the big screen in the Situation Room displayed a map of the Pacific. He watched as four blinking green orbs, somewhere above the Montana badlands, inched westerly toward Ngari Prefecture, and toward the Chinese nukes hidden in underground missile silos, encased in tungsten fifty feet thick. America's ICBMs were in flight.

"Forty-three minutes to impact," Goodyear reported.

In less than one hour, the world would change forever because Barlow had single-handedly decided to change it. What gave him the right? The president felt a pang deep in his brain, like an ice pick piercing his eyeball.

Fort Meade, Maryland, USA

GABRIEL SNYDER WALKED to the break room closest to his NSA workstation. He relished the little trips to the coffee-maker, even enjoyed the trivial chitchat with a linguist or systems analyst that often accompanied them, but most everyone had left for the day. He trudged through the darkened office, returned to his computer terminal, loosened his tie, and prepared to settle in for a few more hours of signals monitoring—a less-than-oblique euphemism for sitting on one's ass.

Snyder's arm jerked when he saw the flashing alert on his computer screen. Piping coffee sloshed over the rim of his mug, nearly scalding his hand. His heart thumped as he read the message.

Intake posted. HVT. Source JX-0056.

One of the NSA's bugs had picked something up. On its face, this wasn't abnormal, since most of the agency's listening devices were switched on permanently. They absorbed everything, most of it useless white noise. That's why the folks in R&D had developed ultrasensitive voice recognition software to weed out background chatter from the words spoken by known intelligence targets. The system could even distinguish twins with near perfect accuracy. Snyder's computer screen had lit up because it had detected someone important—an HVT. *High-value target.*

Snyder wiped his hand on the side of his pants and clicked the blinking alert to get the details. General Huang of the People's Republic of China had just been heard on his plane for the first time since VECTOR officer Olen Grave planted the NSA bug there four days earlier. And, according to the system, Grave was with Huang. Snyder fumbled with his headphones and clicked the play button.

The computer offered rudimentary translations of most foreign languages—some of them embarrassingly crude, if you asked the linguists—but this latest posting required no such conversion. Huang's confession was crystal clear, in English, and unequivocally explicit.

Snyder replayed the audio recording three times. He listened for hints of duress in the general's wispy growl. Nothing. And the system's polygraph software detected none of the typical vocal indicators of deception.

Snyder felt acidic bile creep up his esophagus and thought he might be sick. He'd never imagined the truth behind the Blood River virus outbreak in Asia could be so wrought with malice. He reached for his desk phone and pushed a button to activate a secure line. A blue light flashed on the cradle, and he punched in a number. He'd memorized it in case of an emergency like this one. Not until the trill of the first ring did Snyder begin to question his decision. He could be making an irreversible mistake, but he didn't know who to trust anymore.

Washington, DC, USA

ALLYSON STEPPED INTO the vestibule outside the Situation Room to catch her breath. A preemptive nuclear strike—the very idea of it seemed unimaginable. Yet she'd just witnessed the president make a decision equivalent to Truman's Hiroshima. Sure, bombing the rocky Tibetan badlands wasn't the same as hitting a dense metropolis, but the ramifications would reverberate just as violently. Barlow had just attacked a nuclear power.

Allyson had known James Barlow since he'd served as the CIA's Paris station chief. His instincts were generally solid. But this time the man's calculus was way off, and it made her insides reel. It had to be the migraines. The president was seriously ill. Maybe it was a brain tumor. The pain had clouded his judgment. Or had Sullivan gotten to him? Barlow's Achilles heel was his bleeding heart. Nate knew the president couldn't stomach the thought of a million innocent Taiwanese burning in the streets of Taipei. So by all means, declare war on an unstable superpower. Let's see how that turns out.

A faint buzzing came from the wooden cubbies lining the vestibule. Electronic devices were prohibited inside the Situation

Room, so everyone had to leave their phone outside. Allyson pushed her hair away from her face and saw it was her own phone humming.

"Director Cameron," she answered. Allyson listened carefully to the man on the other end of the line. His message magnified her dread.

"Listen, I'm twenty feet from the president. I need to know you're one hundred percent confident in what you're telling me."

* * *

Moments later, Allyson burst into the Situation Room, gripping her cell phone.

"You can't bring that in here," someone yelled.

"Mr. President," Allyson shouted with pinched urgency. The room fell silent. "We have red-hot ELSUR. It's Grave, our guy in China. He's with General Huang *right now*."

Barlow turned. "Well, let's have it," he said.

Allyson tapped the speakerphone button and held her phone over her head. "Go ahead, Snyder."

The recording crackled through the phone's speakers. The members of the National Security Council listened silently to General Huang's confession. President Barlow felt the blood drain from his face when the general's voice said, "I don't care about Taiwan. I want to rule the Middle Kingdom."

The recording ended with a spit of static.

"What happened?" General Goodyear asked.

"The intake ends there. We don't know why it cut off. Could be the bug's battery," Allyson explained.

"Jesus Christ," Barlow said under his breath.

"Mr. President," Bruce Kinsey, director of national intelligence, called out from the back of the room. "This just came in from our clandestine source within China State Construction Engineering, the contractor hired to build the Ngari air base."

"Since when did we acquire a source in CSCE?" Secretary Hart asked, her voice strained.

Kinsey tapped on his laptop, and an image filled the big screen on the wall. He rotated through a series of photographs.

"What am I looking at, Bruce?" Barlow asked.

"It's the southeastern corner of the base, the section hidden from our satellite's view. The NSA confirmed the geolocation through the photographs' metadata. These were taken about an hour ago."

The images showed a large open area blanketed with bright-green Astroturf. A taut triangular tarp hung overhead.

"It's just a goddamn soccer field," Barlow said. "Where are the missile silos?"

"There don't appear to be any missile silos at the Ngari site, Mr. President," Kinsey reported.

"Then why the tarps?" Barlow asked, his voice modulating to a higher pitch.

Kinsey exhaled with an exasperated huff. "Shade, sir."

"*Shade!*"

"The intel about the launch site was false. There are no ICBMs in Ngari," Kinsey explained.

Silence.

The green orbs flashed on the map, pinging softly as they floated over the Oregon coast. Sullivan, Cameron, and the entire National Security Council had been wrong. Or worse, *deceived*. General Huang had no intention of invading Taiwan. He had no plans to bomb the island. He didn't need to. The general already had everything he wanted—supreme control of the government and the military. And of China's future.

"General Goodyear." President Barlow turned to the chairman of the Joint Chiefs. "Abort CERBERUS. *Now!*"

"Yes, sir," Goodyear replied, and the Situation Room erupted in a mad scramble. The United States had come within twenty minutes of making a disastrous mistake. Barlow's team had screwed him. First, Nathan Sullivan had insisted that patient zero was a rogue former NSB officer. Then, Allyson Cameron's man in China had reported that the outbreak was orchestrated by the PLA—an inside job. Cam had produced those engineering plans for missile silos in Ngari. She'd believed the Chinese were hiding nuclear weapons, but she'd been wrong. They were never there.

How had it happened? What in God's name was going on?

C H A P T E R

70

Shanghai, People's Republic of China

"YOU'RE A SOCIOPATH," Olen said to General Huang. His thigh burned from the injection.

"That's another matter altogether. But tell me, American, if the PLA had developed the virus, wouldn't I have wanted a way to control it?"

"I don't understand."

"That's clear. You've been playing catch-up for days. If you really want to know the truth about the disease, I urge you to seek answers closer to home, but quite frankly, there's no time left for that."

Olen's muscles seized up. He pictured microscopic BRV45 particles attaching themselves to his healthy cells, tearing them apart. The onslaught had begun.

"You think you're immune. You think you're some kind of god. How many more must suffer, General?"

"Hopefully none." Huang rolled up his left sleeve, and a latex-gloved soldier carefully pushed a needle into the general's tricep.

"The shot . . ." Olen's heartbeat pulsed in his ears. "It's a vaccine. So I'll live?"

"If that's what you prefer to call it," Huang hissed.

* * *

A violent boom rocked the fuselage, like a train jumping the rails. The aircraft's nose tilted downward and the plane banked sharply. General Huang whipped his head toward the window, perhaps looking for lightning. Olen knew a thunderbolt hadn't caused the sound. It was a throat-scraping, guttural eruption from inside the belly of the jet. From a bomb.

More like an improvised incendiary device, hastily assembled by Olen himself, using a flare from the emergency kit in the luggage compartment. He was pleased to know that even in a drug-induced stupor, he could still blow shit up. Olen had rigged the device with a long fuse, giving him ample time to climb out of the cargo hold. He'd only wanted to make a little smoke—just enough to trigger the aircraft's sensors and force the pilots to descend to ten thousand feet, low enough for him to bail out safely. Judging by the tangle of yellow oxygen masks dangling overhead, his homemade explosive must have torn a hole in the fuselage. *Whoops.*

A few of the soldiers were flung across the cabin. Olen remained stationary, his wrists still tied to the chair bolted to the floor. The spiraling jet pulled several g-forces, making him lightheaded. The plane was going down, and Olen with it.

The aircraft rolled and the chair tugged at its bolts. Olen leaned into the turn with his full body weight, straining the chair's unreinforced aluminum joints. The armrests broke off with a pop, freeing his hands. The overhead lights flickered, then died out completely. Smoke seeped into the cabin. Coughing, Olen felt around in the dark for the general's desk. Huang was gone.

One of the teen soldiers appeared from within the thickening haze, leaping like a spooked gazelle, nearly colliding with Olen. The man wore a black backpack with straps that crisscrossed his torso—a parachute. He darted for the emergency exit and yanked on the door's metal lever.

"No!" Olen yelled, as the boy released the lock. The hatch disappeared, sucked into the atmosphere, along with the soldier. Loose papers fluttered toward the door like a flock of sparrows. Olen's body ripped away from the desk and followed the little white birds out of the plane into wide-open sky.

Olen's lungs tightened as he plummeted. The air was thin but breathable, meaning the plane had already descended thousands of feet. The rushing wind forced his eyes shut, but even through thin slits he could see the soldier boy spinning just below him, still wearing the parachute.

Olen stiffened his body so that it sliced through the air like an arrow. His freefall accelerated, and he closed in on the black back-pack, now just an arm's reach away. Within seconds, Olen crashed into Soldier Boy. The young man freaked and flailed, sending them both into a tumble. Olen wrapped his arms and legs around the soldier, bringing them face-to-face. Mouth agape in terror, Soldier Boy fought against Olen's grip, making it difficult to main-tain a solid hold on his gangly frame. Olen slammed his forehead into the boy's face, and the soldier's head fell back, limp, blood spiraling from his nose.

A moment later, the chute deployed with a rough yank. A bil-lowing canopy fanned out above them, slowing their fall to a graceful glide. Just above the horizon, Olen watched the general's 747 dip behind a rocky hilltop, black contrails swirling in its wake.

DAY 16

71

Beijing, People's Republic of China

IT TOOK OFFICER Olen Grave three days to get out of China. Most major airports had reopened, and he was lucky enough to grab a seat on a flight to Bangkok. Regrettably, Olen still had to connect through Beijing. The People's Republic refused to let him go.

A weathered rucksack slung over his shoulder, Olen crossed the jet bridge into the terminal. He recognized the man waiting just past the doorway, and for a moment Olen considered turning around and reboarding the plane.

Maverick—Beijing International Airport's handsy ambassador—stood stiff legged and scowl faced, the mirrored aviators still perched above his puffy cheeks. "Mr. Stone," he said, squeezing the words out with an irritating whine. "How nice of you to visit us again so soon."

Two large men stood behind the Chinese host—a comically dramatic attempt at intimidation.

"Are we going back to the champagne room, or should I just strip right here?" Olen fumbled with his belt.

Maverick's eyes flared. "Right this way, Mr. Stone."

The beefy bodyguards escorted Olen down the same white hallway he'd walked through a week prior. They arrived at the small interrogation room, but this time it wasn't empty.

"Our colleagues in public affairs at the Associated Press already wrote your obituary. Really moving stuff," said Director Cameron, seated at the table. "I brought a handsome cedar box to retrieve you. Guess we'll save it for next time." She took a long drag on a cigarette—some cheap Chinese brand by the smell of it—and blew a stream of smoke out the corner of her mouth.

"This is a nonsmoking facility," Maverick scolded. "Where did you get that, madam?"

Allyson nodded to a scrawny security guard standing at attention in the corner. "Ask my new friend," she replied, flicking away loose ash.

*   *   *

Olen followed Allyson up a metal staircase into a private Learjet. Once inside, she turned to Olen. "Try to keep your cool, Officer Grave. It's been a long two weeks."

"My cool?" Olen asked. Then he spotted the man in the rear of the aircraft, sipping a ginger ale, with ice.

Motherfucking Marc Chen.

Olen bounded down the center aisle, bloodshot eyes bulging, and ripped Marc from his seat, splashing Canada Dry on the man's leather jacket.

"Hey! I just bought this, asshole," Marc complained. Olen slammed his colleague against the lavatory door, which bowed from the force.

"Is your PLA uniform at the cleaners, Lieutenant?" Olen's throat pulsed.

"It took us nearly three years to get that uniform," Allyson cut in.

"What?" Olen cocked his head but didn't loosen his grip.

"Deep cover's a bitch, Olen. You should cut the man some slack." Allyson settled into a window seat a few rows up, pulled down the shade, and closed her eyes. "We'll formally debrief you at Fort Detrick. In the meantime, you boys will be spending about thirteen hours together in this aluminum tube. So, make the most of it."

Marc shoved Olen back, breaking his hold.

"What did she mean by 'three years'?" Olen asked.

"Piece it together, Grave. She meant I pulled off the highest-level infiltration of the Chinese military in history."

"You've been working for General Huang for three *years*?" Olen said. "You and Cam planned it from the beginning? Holy shit, Chen. That's why she picked you for VECTOR."

"What can I say? She needed the best." Marc laid out across an entire row and draped an open magazine over his face.

Olen stood dumb struck. "Dude, you fuckin' shot me."

"Yet you're still breathing. It's a Christmas miracle," Marc mumbled.

"You must've known the PLA would string me up by my nutsack."

"As satisfying as that would've been—for everyone involved—I was more interested in getting you onto Huang's plane. Didn't you wonder why your knife was still in your pocket? I knew you would take that dickhead down. If there's one thing you're actually good at, it's crashing things." Marc lifted a corner of the magazine. "Thanks, bud."

Olen stomped up the aisle, hands on his head, muttering under his breath. "*Thanks, bud?* Un-freaking-believable."

CHAPTER

72

Beijing, People's Republic of China

OLEN SLEPT FOR the first ninety minutes of the flight to Washington, but even in the cozy leather chair, his subconscious churned. His dreams mixed with memories of his mission in Iraq with Allyson. They'd spent weeks together, squeezed between a pair of steel-jawed marines, crisscrossing the Arabian Desert in search of Saddam's weapons of death. A snatch of uncorroborated intel from a grocer in Fallujah had led their convoy into a field of roadside IEDs. If they'd kept going, it might have earned them both stars on Langley's Memorial Wall. But Allyson had sniffed out the problems with the reporting, the subtle inconsistencies in the grocer's story, and she'd turned the team around. The woman had the instincts of a panther. Olen had learned a crucial lesson in Anbar: Allyson was always right.

* * *

Allyson was dead wrong. Her gut had told her to dismiss the Ngari blueprints. She'd had no way to verify the intelligence, and the stakes had been extraordinarily high. Why had she gone against her better judgment and shared the blueprints with President Barlow?

Ego. Sullivan had humiliated her in the Situation Room, and the Ngari plans had made her a hero.

But they were fake. The Chinese had fed them to Marc Chen to misdirect and deceive the United States. General Huang must have known that Chen was working for the enemy. Huang had used Allyson's own infiltration against her.

There was another possibility. Allyson thought of the MI6 photo, of Chen's unexplained trip to Singapore, of his rendezvous with the mystery woman in the turquoise dress. Where did Chen's true loyalty lie? Allyson would do everything in her power to find out. If she discovered Chen had intentionally deceived her—if he had known the Ngari blueprints were fake but passed them along anyway—Allyson would skin him alive.

* * *

The jet angled north and then leveled out. Olen turned to Allyson, seated next to him. The soft glow of her laptop screen illuminated a subtle scar across her cheek.

"How bad is it stateside?" Olen asked his boss.

Allyson shut her computer and rubbed her eyes. "Micro outbreaks popped up in New York and San Francisco—both in hospitals—but we were ready. Containment was swift," Allyson answered.

"It's not spreading?" Olen asked.

"The Chinese government released the PLA's vaccine to the WHO and the CDC. We've already inoculated a few hundred thousand, but deploying the vaccine to millions more won't be simple. The majority of the population won't be fully protected for months."

"So, more will die?"

"Yes, they will. Most people who have come into contact with Blood River virus won't survive. It's a miracle you weren't infected, Olen."

"So, it was luck," he said.

"No," Allyson responded. "It's never luck. You were spared so you could fight the people who created this thing." Her voice was strong, assured. "You sent Blood River virus back to hell."

"Along with General Huang," Olen added.

"Amen." Allyson popped a piece of Nicorette into her mouth, leaned back, and closed her eyes.

73

Annapolis, Maryland, USA

T HE SEVERN UNDULATED restlessly, its moss-green water slosh-
ing against the sea wall, then retreating, leaving a foamy film
on the concrete. A half dozen sailboats bobbed along its surface,
unfazed by the river's agita. The day's light had begun to dim, so
Marc Chen knew the sailors would return to the harbor soon. A
pair of Naval Academy midshipmen had already finished securing
their boat to the dock and were folding their blue-and-gold spin-
naker. They headed in the direction of campus, clapping each
other on the back, laughing. The young military men had no idea
that their country had come within minutes of nuclear conflict
with a rival superpower. And that the United States would have
fired the first shot.

Marc imagined the fifty-million-dollar warheads splashing
into the cold waters of the Pacific Ocean. The president's command to abort the strike had disarmed the missiles and safely redi-
rected them into the open waters. International waters. Down
they sank, where they would stay until retrieved by a U.S. Navy
deepwater submarine. Thanks to Allyson Cameron's well-timed
intelligence, the United States had stepped back from the brink of
an unimaginable war.

A war Marc Chen had worked so hard to induce. He'd risked everything to penetrate the Chinese military and achieve the position of General Huang's aide-de-camp. Access and placement that good were nearly impossible.

Marc's three-year op was VECTOR's crown jewel. Director Cameron had believed she'd opened a window into China's secretive ruling body—the elusive Politburo Standing Committee. Her fledgling organization would collect the most sensitive intelligence on China's political and military leadership, and Barlow would shower her with presidential accolades.

In reality, the woman was clueless. Marc had fed Cameron worthless chicken feed for the last year, including the erroneous engineering plans for PLA missile silos at the Ngari air base. The document wasn't exactly a forgery. Huang's initial plans for Ngari actually had included ICBM launch facilities, but they had been scrapped months ago. Too provocative, the general ultimately reasoned. The man planned to overthrow the government; he wasn't interested in drawing the ire of the United States. So, Marc had simply altered the date on an old blueprint and fired it off to Cameron via SwissPax. To be perfectly frank, he hadn't expected the director to buy it. But hell, the woman didn't have the best judgment. After all, she'd trusted *him*.

Marc knew that Cameron had dismissed the Chinese threat from the beginning, so coming from her, the discovery of hidden PLA nukes carried more credibility. Plus, Barlow had a raging boner for Cameron. The president would believe Mount Rushmore was packed with pirate gold if Director Cameron told him so. Sure, the Ngari missile site was farfetched, but it was also impossible to verify with the lack of coverage in the region. The president required clear evidence of an imminent Chinese attack on Taiwan to authorize a preemptive strike. Secret nukes pointed right up Taipei's nostrils were about as imminent as it got.

Marc had played Director Cameron, but that didn't make her an idiot. She'd be furious about the false Ngari intelligence. She'd demand to know how it happened, and she'd strap Marc to a waterboard if that was what it took to learn the truth. And Cameron wouldn't be the only problem. There would be congressional investigations, grand juries, scapegoats. The thought made

Marc's veins surge with currents of heat. He refused to take the fall. He hadn't masterminded the outbreak, or the Chinese coup, or the nuclear crisis. That responsibility rested with someone far more powerful.

The twilight turned the river glassy black, like liquefied onyx. A flash of blood red caught Marc's eye when a billowing mainsail puffed up with air after executing an expert tack. The lone mariner trimmed the sail and the boat picked up speed, propelled by a stiff wind back to shore. Marc locked eyes with the approaching sailor, who glowered but didn't steer away. *Good*, Marc thought, reaching for the loaded Browning holstered at his side.

CHAPTER

74

Sanya, Hainan Island, People's Republic of China

Dr. Zhou Weilin removed her shoes so the powder-white sand could squeeze between her toes. A predawn mist wafted across the South China Sea, fleeing from the rising sun's first light. The air was warm but not yet heavy with humidity. She could stay on Hainan Island for all eternity if the universe were more accommodating. For now, two blissful weeks would have to suffice. Extending her vacation any longer would raise too many questions. Soon enough she'd return to the real world and all the inquiries and investigations that would entail. Of course, they'd all conclude that the events at the Black Egg had resulted from "inadvertent mishandling of volatile materials." A blameless accident. General Huang was gone and Zhongnanhai had returned to civilian control. No one wanted to dwell on the last sixteen days. The state-run media had already pivoted to stories about the Mid-Autumn Festival and moon cake recipes.

For Jo, a return to the banal beat of normal life wouldn't be so simple. Not after all she'd seen.

A soft clinking, like wind chimes, accompanied the hush of the waves. Jo turned to see an older woman in a sapphire one-piece gliding across the beach in her direction. The woman carried a brightly colored drink in each hand, both embellished with festive pink umbrellas. Jo gave a toothy smile.

"The bar wasn't open, but a delightful young man was gracious enough to make an exception. You've seen him, the one with the glorious backside. Well, in any case, I'll introduce you after brunch." Aunt Jin handed Jo a glass and leaned in for a double-cheek kiss.

"A bit early for a cocktail, don't you think?" Jo asked.

"Honey, when you're my age, it's never too early," Jin answered. "Certainly not for a mai tai," she added, taking a quick sip. Plum lipstick stained her straw.

"How did you know I'd be here?"

Jin ignored the question and stared out to sea. "An admiral once told me this island guarded a deep secret. It's hollowed out, he said. Underneath those hills behind us is a gargantuan, hidden shipyard. The Chinese navy has spent years building the world's most advanced blue-water fleet. Any day now, the side of that mountain will open up and the ships will sail right out, one by one."

"Don't tell me you believed him," Jo said.

"I stopped believing men with stars on their shoulders decades ago."

The two women shared a laugh, but the moment quickly passed.

"I'm officially out, you know. I tendered my resignation yesterday," Jo said. "I'm through with the MSS."

"Out. In. You make it sound so binary. Have I taught you nothing, Zhinü?"

"I mean it," Jo insisted.

"I'm sure you do." Jin linked arms with her niece. "The ocean is calm now. Let's take a walk."

Aunt Jin and Jo followed the shoreline, letting the frothy tide lick their ankles. The old woman gleefully drained her mai tai (and then Jo's), and after a mile or two, she broke the peaceful quietude.

"Your parents' death—"

"Aunt Jin, please, you don't have to explain anything," Jo interrupted.

"Hear me out. An old woman has something to say—something that ought to have been said long before today." Jin paused, took both of Jo's hands, and looked deeply into her adopted niece's eyes. "Your parents died that tragic afternoon in Tiananmen Square, in June of 1989. This you know."

"They were working undercover. They infiltrated the dissidents camped out in the square. Some trigger-happy soldier mistook them for students trying to foment rebellion."

"No, the PLA soldier who shot your parents made no mistake," Jin said.

"What do you mean? My parents worked for the Chinese government. They were MSS. You should know; you recruited them."

"Zhinü, your mother and father were magnificent human beings. They fought for what they believed in."

"Where is this going, Aunt Jin?" Jo grew impatient.

"I didn't recruit your parents. In fact, they recruited *me*." Jin squeezed Jo's hands harder, before she could rip them away. "They didn't work for the MSS. They worked for the NSB. For Taiwan."

Jo crossed her arms and hugged herself, facing the water.

"We all wanted the same thing," Jin continued. "One China. One free, democratic China. The Communists in Beijing should've fallen that day in eighty-nine, just as the entire Soviet bloc did that summer. No one expected Zhongnanhai to send in the army. It was a bloodbath. Your mother and father paid the ultimate sacrifice."

"All these years, I've tried to follow in my parents' footsteps to honor their memory—and instead I've spent a career serving their killers?"

"You don't have to anymore."

"You came here to pitch me." Jo felt sick, wounded, betrayed. "There's always some hidden agenda with you. I'm supposed to join the NSB now, become a double agent like you, is that it?"

"God, no. Taipei is just as corrupt as Beijing. Here we are, thirty years after Tiananmen, and nothing has really changed." Jin picked a bloom from a wild hibiscus bush growing in the sand. "As long as the Chinese Communist Party rules the mainland, reunification is impossible."

"What are you planning?" Jo asked.

"Zhongnanhai makes a great effort to project strength, but we know—now more than ever—there are cracks. There are a handful of us who still see a path to complete regime change."

"You're talking about sedition. *Treason.*"

"Yep," Jin replied, popping her lips.

"Who do you work for, Aunt Jin?"

"No more flags, no more corrupt bureaucrats, no more lying men with starry shoulder pads. Our future requires new leadership."

"Whose leadership?"

"We follow HELMSMAN," Jin answered.

"HELMSMAN. Sounds awfully cryptic."

"Three years ago, I met an American spy," Jin explained. "We were holding him in a prison cell, actually. He was a tough cookie, so they sent me in to flip him. One and done. It would have been a piece of cake—the man was in rough shape—but then he made a fascinating counterproposal. I considered it for two days and then thought, what the hell. For three decades, I'd tried everything to make things better, but the Communist regime had only grown more powerful, more corrupt. I had nothing left to lose. This half-dead, naked, smelly American spy fell into my lap and changed my life. He offered a new vision for the future HELMSMAN's vision."

"HELMSMAN is American? How do you know he can be trusted?" Jo asked.

Jin tucked the hibiscus behind Jo's ear with motherly affection. "Zhinü, my sweet girl, who said anything about *he*?"

Annapolis, Maryland, USA

"YOU SHOULDN'T BE here," Secretary Darlene Hart said, maneuvering her sailboat into a slip. The breeze whipped up silver strands of hair that slithered around her head like Medusa's snakes. "But since you are, you might as well make yourself useful." She tossed Marc a bow line to loop around the cleat.

"What if I'm done helping you?" Marc shoved his hands into his pockets, and his right palm brushed past the handgun, still concealed underneath the tail of his jacket. Hart noticed the weapon and shot him a surly look. Fine creases webbed the corners of her downturned lips. They weren't laugh lines. HELMSMAN didn't laugh.

"If you think you're the first man to come at me with a suspicious bulge in his britches, you're sadly mistaken." Hart completed the cleat hitch herself and began to lower the jibe.

Marc bristled at the secretary's casual nature. This shit storm wouldn't pass over so quickly. How many people knew about his involvement? How many knew about the outbreak's true origin? Marc couldn't be sure, and neither could Secretary Hart.

"You ordered me to leak the Ngari missile site plans. You assured me no one would find out they were fake. Now I'm exposed. It's time to tell the president—" Marc began.

"Jim would never understand," Hart spat. "I honestly thought he had the right head for this job, if not the balls, but he's fighting the last war. He's no different than all the other Langley eggheads, swinging their doctoral degrees around like ten-inch dicks. Jim's still obsessed with Al-Qaeda—nothing but desert cockroaches. Meanwhile, the People's Republic of China grows more powerful every day. America is still on top, but that only means we've got a massive bull's-eye on our back. The PRC is undermining our authority at every turn, chipping away. The United States must defend its right to greatness, or someone will wrench it away. As long as I draw breath, Officer Chen, I won't let that happen. President Barlow doesn't appreciate the stakes. There's no getting through to him."

"Then how did you convince him to order the nuclear strike?" Marc asked.

"Men are simple creatures, for the most part, especially when they are suffering."

Hart produced two yellow pills from her pea coat—President Barlow's missing medication. She flung the pills into the water.

"James Barlow is no use to us now," Hart went on, her voice barely audible over the waves slapping the hull of her sailboat. "He wouldn't understand the importance of our work. But you, Chen, have always understood. The world may see China's booming economy, how it lifted a billion people out of poverty within a generation. But you know the People's Republic is no exemplar of human progress. For seventy years, the communists running Beijing have terrorized their own people. Dissidents murdered in the streets, journalists tossed in prison, Christians, Jews, and Muslims persecuted simply for praying to their Almighty. Your grandfather learned this the hard way, didn't he?"

Marc's neck tensed.

"There is only one path, Chen," Hart continued. "Complete and total regime change. We've tried for decades to spur political dissent, to instigate a domestic movement to overthrow the Chinese government from within. Everything has failed. The Party is far too entrenched. Military confrontation is the only option we have left."

Chen didn't disagree. He wanted nothing more than to destroy the Chinese government, especially after what they had done to his family. Thousands of innocent people would die in a war with the PRC, but if the conflict ultimately liberated one-fifth of humanity—the people living within China's borders—wouldn't it be worth the cost? They'd come so close with Blood River virus, but in the end the scheme had failed. Marc wouldn't give up. There had to be a way to bring down the Communist regime. Of course, he couldn't do anything from a prison cell, and that was precisely where he'd end up if Director Cameron and the president discovered he'd deceived them.

"Barlow is a powerful man," Marc argued. "He won't just let this go. He'll launch an investigation. None of us will be safe. Not me or Kalina or any of the others."

Hart flicked her hand. "Real power is the ability to manipulate the powerful. I'll handle Jim. Just as I always have."

The blood drained from Marc's face. "You'll throw me to the wolves to save yourself."

The secretary raised an eyebrow. "What would you do in my position?"

"You *bitch*." Marc gripped the Browning still holstered to his hip.

Hart snorted. "Do you think that will help you, Officer Chen? Murder me, and this all goes away? More than one body has been dumped into this river, I assure you, but the thing about cadavers is you can't hold them under long enough to escape the stink."

Marc flew across the dock and leveled the Browning at Hart. His arm swayed slightly, but he wasn't afraid. He was through taking orders from her.

The silver-haired woman smoothed the sides of her coif, taming the wriggling serpents. "Relax, Officer Chen." Secretary Hart, HELMSMAN, leaned forward, eyes ablaze. "I've got much bigger plans for you."

*   *   *

Darlene Hart refused to let the aborted missile launch defeat her. Defeat meant she'd lost, and Hart never lost. She just took the long view.

Ages ago, rumors had zipped around the Beltway that Hart would make a run for the presidency herself. The idea of a fiery southern woman whipping a dysfunctional Washington into shape appealed to disillusioned voters, according to a few snake-oil pollsters, anyway. Hart couldn't imagine such a ridiculous idea. She'd never let the carnivorous Washington media tear into every carefully guarded detail of her private life only to win an office gunked up with swamp water. The president of the United States couldn't take a shit without the *Washington Post* logging the length and weight of the excrement. And there was the small matter of Hart lacking a penis. Regrettably, the American people still preferred residents of the Oval Office to wear their reproductive organs on the outside. Why stall under the bright lights of public scrutiny when she could manipulate the course of history more effectively from the shadows?

For nearly twenty years, one alliance at a time, Hart had built a network of devoted officers embedded within the darkest corners of the intelligence community. These men and women recognized what Hart knew to be true—the system was simply too rigid to adapt to a changing world. Protecting American supremacy required bending the rules. The man now pointing the pistol at her knew this too, which was why Officer Marc Chen had dutifully followed Hart's leadership from the beginning. His loyalty would continue, and she'd forget about his injudicious indiscretion. People made stupid decisions when stressed. Besides, Officer Chen was truly gifted, Hart thought. He'd infiltrated General Huang's inner circle, stolen Blood River virus from the Chinese military, and recruited a Taiwanese intelligence officer to deliver the disease. What glorious talent! A man like Marc Chen could reach incredible heights if properly cultivated. Hart shouldn't be wasting her energy on a cockwaffle like James Barlow.

"Who else knows that patient zero was working for me?" Hart asked, ignoring the elevated Browning.

"Except us?" Chen said, lowering the gun. "That's all. No one else knows we sent Chang to Tibet. No one knows the truth behind Blood River virus."

* * *

For the next hour, Marc walked along Prince George Street in downtown Annapolis, ambling past antique shops and mom-and-pop bakeries selling pistachio macarons. He'd wandered haphazardly, following the disorderly network of sidewalks linking the Maryland State House to the water's edge. He eventually circled back to the harbor. Hart was long gone, and the docks were quiet.

Marc removed a small object from his pocket. The Red Guard badge. He rubbed his thumb over the embossed flame. It had belonged to his grandfather, but the old man had never worn it himself. He'd kept it only as a reminder of the dangers surging at the time. Overheated populism. Anti-intellectualism. Mao worship.

It was 1966, and Chairman Mao Zedong had just declared war on China's traditional past. Old culture, old customs, old ideas—these were to be destroyed to make room for modern, Communist dogma. A Cultural Revolution. It was a horrifically dangerous time for a young professor of dynastic history. Marc's grandfather, his research, and his academic courses at Beijing Normal University became the symbols of everything holding China back. Students he'd lectured for years—the studious young men and women who'd sat in the front row of the hall, diligently capturing notes on the Qing dynasty and the Silk Road—transformed overnight into fiendish foot soldiers of Mao's deranged vision. The student Red Guards defaced historic landmarks on campus, burned priceless scholarly texts, desecrated ancient mausoleums.

Then they came for the professors. The students, donning olive jackets and red armbands, yanked Marc's grandfather from his office and hauled him into the university's central courtyard. They hung a sign around his neck that read BOURGEOIS SWINE, stripped him, and flogged him until his lungs filled with fluid. And then they hung his naked corpse from a tree.

Terrified, Marc's grandmother swaddled their baby girl and fled to Japan on a fishing boat. She affixed the pin to the infant's blanket—a display of loyalty, in case the Red Guards accused them of defecting. The pair eventually made it to San Diego by the time Marc's mother turned three.

Mao was dead and the Red Guards were history, but the Communist regime had lived on, thriving for decades on a foundation built by evil. Marc wanted to burn it down. He'd never known his grandfather, but Marc carried his name, and with it a responsibility to uphold his family's honor. He wouldn't rest until the Party of Mao Zedong crumbled to ash.

The Severn River looked still now—smooth, like a mirror reflecting the night sky. Marc stood tall on the edge of the sea wall, gripping the Red Guard badge so tight that the flaming torch indented the skin of his palm. Just as his family had worn the pin, Marc had worn a false identity and feigned loyalty to a corrupt, savage government. He'd operated covertly, protected by a veil of secrecy and deception.

Never again, Marc swore to himself. He wasn't going to hide anymore. He'd take the fight to the Communists' doorstep. He'd confront them head on, as himself, Marc Chen.

With a flick of his wrist, the Red Guard badge sailed over the slick mirror and made two images, one above, one below, until they converged on the river's surface, sending out deep ripples in all directions.

DAY 28

CHAPTER

76

Mumbai, India

OVERSTUFFED PICKUP TRUCKS muscled through vehicular clots clogging up Khara Tank Road. Daredevil cyclists threaded the cracks. Allyson had suggested a cheap restaurant near the medical college on the south side of the city, primarily so she could monitor the street from the adjacent Chor Bazaar— Mumbai's largest flea market. She wanted to observe her contact approaching the designated meeting spot from a safe distance.

The director stopped to examine an array of clay pots, each filled with brightly colored spices. She leaned over a vessel of dried cardamom to take in its sweet, woody fragrance.

"If you dust the pods with cinnamon and grind them into a fine powder, it makes delicious coffee," a woman standing behind Allyson explained.

Allyson grinned. It seemed her contact took similar premeet precautions. The director had completely missed the woman's emergence from the market's crowded maze.

"Dr. Zhou, it's a pleasure to finally meet you," Allyson said.

The two women crossed MS Ali Road and ducked into a smoky café selling spiced shawarma and mutton *xacuti*. Allyson had read enough about the phenom virologist in Officer Grave's reports to know the doctor would speak incisively. Dr. Zhou would skip over small talk, get right to the meat, and probably try to end the conversation as quickly as possible. Allyson didn't mind. She'd learned to shut up and let new sources speak their piece.

"Well?" Dr. Zhou asked, eyebrows perched. "Wouldn't you like to know why I contacted you?"

"I would," Allyson responded. "If you feel comfortable talking. If not, that's fine too. I'm perfectly content to share a hot meal with a new friend."

Dr. Zhou tapped her fork against the side of her plate. "You've known Kipton for a long time."

"Yes, I have," Allyson said, rolling with Olen's cover identity for the Tibet op. The director offered Dr. Zhou a cigarette. She politely refused.

"He's a good man."

"That's generally my take," Allyson agreed.

Dr. Zhou leaned in. "I'm going to trust you, Director Cameron. Not because you seem like a nice person or because Kip vouches for you. I'm going to trust you because I believe our interests have aligned."

Allyson smoothed her linen napkin over her lap. "Well, that's a fantastic place to start, isn't it? I'm all ears, Doctor."

The director took a long drag, relishing the freedom to enjoy a little nicotine in a public restaurant, as God had intended.

Dr. Zhou Weilin told Allyson about her aunt, about their walk on the beach on Hainan Island, about the malevolent, netherworldly figure HELMSMAN. The story was sensational. A shadowy cabal, operated by a Machiavellian mastermind, had infiltrated America's most elite power centers and threatened to dismantle East Asia. Dr. Zhou didn't know HELMSMAN's identity, just that she'd built a secret network of loyal foot soldiers devoted to her radical vision. In fact, HELMSMAN had been the one to orchestrate the devastating Blood River virus outbreak, not General Huang, making her responsible for the deaths of thousands.

When Allyson pressed Dr. Zhou about what the elusive madwoman planned next, the virologist could only speculate. God only knew what destruction HELMSMAN would bring in pursuit of her bloodthirsty quest for power.

Riveting stuff, but hardly viable intelligence. Allyson had flown eight thousand miles for conspiracy theories over curry.

"But we know General Huang planned the whole thing. Kipton told me that patient zero worked for the PLA," Allyson said, punctuating her *p*s with small puffs of smoke.

"That's what we thought. But consider the evidence for a moment. Did Huang actually confess to planning the outbreak, or did he merely take advantage of a tragic circumstance?" Dr. Zhou argued. "A megalomaniac tried to hijack our government, and he nearly succeeded. I refuse to stand aside and allow it to happen again. I care about my aunt, and I'm confident I can secure her cooperation. In return, I trust you will protect her. I don't believe she knew what HELMSMAN had planned. And I don't believe she understands how much damage this woman could cause."

Allyson had heard enough. She snuffed out her cigarette. "I'm thankful you contacted me—you're a venerated scientist and Kipton simply gushes over you—but you're claiming everything we know about General Huang is wrong. That he didn't premeditate the bioattack. You say someone else did, yet you have no idea who. Just that she's a senior U.S. government official. You don't know her name, age, position—anything meaningful about her, really." Allyson leaned back in her chair, exasperated. "Unfortunately, Doctor, I have absolutely no way to verify the—frankly, rather melodramatic—plot you've described."

Dr. Zhou removed a hot-pink, quarter-sized object from her purse and placed it on the table next to Director Cameron's water glass. "You do now."

Allyson pinched the memory drive, squeezing it gingerly between two fingers. She studied the object like a rare gemstone. When the director looked up, she saw nothing but an empty chair across the table and the swish of a black ponytail flashing in the doorway.

EPILOGUE

Montreal, Canada

"I'M STILL NOT entirely clear on the problem, Mr. Root." The junior account manager was visibly nervous, evidenced by the yellow sweat ring forming around his starched collar. Even if the man was aware of his company's egregious bookkeeping errors, he probably wasn't complicit in any crime. Either way, the manager was a minnow, and forensic accountant Spencer Root was hunting marlins.

Mr. Root adjusted his Coke-bottle glasses and blinked rapidly with agitation. He tilted his head at odd angles, attempting to get a clearer view through the heavy lenses. "Well, let me explain it more precisely. You've got a stack of purchase orders for raw aluminum, but upon review of your inventory records and sales sheets, you're coming in about a mile short. According to this paperwork, Magento Aviation should have a warehouse bursting with product." The forensic accountant smoothed his bushy moustache, releasing a few rogue Cheetos crumbs that had burrowed into the thick fur.

"The aluminum comes from Liberia. Sometimes shipping containers fall overboard at sea. I read that somewhere," the manager offered.

Mr. Root smacked his dry, chapped lips. His face flushed, the ruddy discoloration spreading from his blemished cheeks all the way up his wide forehead and blending into a faint sunburn on his balding scalp. "Sir, if you'd examined my pivot tables, you'd surely see the discrepancy is quite staggering. Either there are three metric tons of jet engine turbines littering the seabed of the Atlantic, or someone's been skimming off the top."

"How much are we talking about?" the manager asked. Avoiding direct eye contact, the man kept staring at the coffee stain on Root's too-short necktie.

"Five-hundred forty-seven million, three-hundred twenty-nine thousand, six-hundred and sixteen dollars," the forensic accountant reported. "And thirty-three cents. More or less." Root adjusted his glasses again.

The manager rubbed his temples, eyes shut tight. "I'm sorry. Mr. Root, is it? Who did you say you worked for again?"

* * *

Spencer Root padded down the front steps of the Magento Aviation office tower and into a cobblestone plaza. He moved slowly, and his knees turned out slightly, resulting in a bowlegged toddle. A light breeze parted the thin strands of hair he'd carefully combed over his peeling bald spot. The forensic accountant guarded an unruly stack of loose papers under his arm, which made it difficult to answer his cell phone when it chirped in his belt clip.

"Root," he finally announced into the mouthpiece.

A woman's voice responded. "Any progress?"

"Yes, well. Inch by inch, I believe."

"We need to make a minor detour," the woman said. "Meet me at Hotel Le St-James. Now. There's a rooftop bar."

Root pushed back. "They're laundering millions—I can prove it—and the overseas connections are worrisome. We shouldn't walk away from this unless it's for something of grave consequence."

The woman fell silent.

"It's something of grave consequence, isn't it?" Root asked.

"Magento can wait. I have new intel from India, from a new source. Something you need to see right away. Head to the hotel.

I'll be there shortly. Based on what I've reviewed so far, we've got a truckload of work ahead of us, and things are probably going to get messy."

"Very well. Anything else?"

"My contact," Director Allyson Cameron continued. "She asked me to deliver a message to you."

"To me?"

"Something about wanting to see the tower light up again, whatever the hell that means."

Olen's eyes grew wide. Jo was Allyson's new source. The two had met in India. But why? Olen didn't care; he was just relieved to know that Jo was alive.

He ended the call. A double-decker grin spread wide across his face.

ACKNOWLEDGMENTS

In 2012, when I began writing about a fictional virus that emerges mysteriously from China, I never imagined the world would soon face a very real pandemic like COVID-19. Terms such as *epidemic curve, superspreader,* and *T cells* are now part of our vernacular, but to study these concepts in the Time Before, I relied on the meticulous writings of journalists, scientists, and academics—the intrepid professionals who hunted deadly viruses in far-flung rain forests, developed vital therapeutics and vaccines in state-of-the-art laboratories, and formulated life-saving public health policies in the halls of our great universities. These trailblazers helped me to conjure a fictitious geopolitical crisis resulting from an outbreak, and for their tireless work, I am grateful.

Writing these words in 2020, I recognize that the *real* pandemic we face has touched every nation on earth and tested the strength and stability of our world order. COVID-19 has strained the U.S.-China relationship, but thus far it has not pushed the two nations to the brink of war, thankfully. Still, it's not difficult to imagine a nightmare scenario, where flashpoints like Taiwan and Tibet ignite under the pressure and spark a dangerous conflict between America and the People's Republic of China. Any modest understanding that I have of such consequential matters, I owe to my former professors at Columbia University, including Andrew Nathan, Madeleine Zelin, and Eugenia Lean. During my graduate studies, those many years ago, they challenged me to consider the enduring threads of history and culture that are woven into the tapestry of modern China and create the intricate patterns that define our relationship with this complex nation. I am grateful for their wisdom and generosity. Any errors I have made in writing this book are purely my own.

Finally, traversing the winding, often treacherous path from Page One to a published novel requires a skilled and dedicated team. I must recognize my literary agent, Elizabeth Winick Rubinstein, for her unwavering enthusiasm for this project. Also, I want to thank the teams at McIntosh & Otis and Crooked Lane, including Zoë Bodzas, Matt Martz, Jessica Renheim, Katie McGuire, Rachel Keith, Melissa Rechter, Madeline Rathle, and Michael Rehder. I'm grateful to my early readers, Steve Smith and Cynthia Houchin, who gave me superb advice. I appreciate my former colleagues at the FBI for their efficient prepublication review of the manuscript. And lastly, this story may have never made it off of the airplane napkin without the encouragement (and patience) of my wife, Kelly. Thank you for the long walks, unconditional love, and for our two incredible daughters, Naya and Ameya.